Praise for Kat...
from *RT Book Reviews*

The Charmer

"Hoffmann's deeply felt, emotional story is riveting.
It's impossible to put down."

Your Bed or Mine?

"Fully developed characters and perfect pacing
make this story feel completely right."

Doing Ireland!

"Sexy and wildly romantic."

The Mighty Quinns: Ian

"A very hot story mixes with great characters to
make every page a delight."

Who Needs Mistletoe?

"Romantic, sexy and heartwarming."

The Mighty Quinns: Teague

"Sexy, heartwarming and romantic...a story to
settle down with and enjoy—and then reread."

Blaze

Dear Reader,

I can't believe another Quinn saga is coming to an end. *The Mighty Quinns: Ronan* is the fourth and final book about the Seattle branch of the Quinn family and marks my twenty-second Quinn book.

Will I be writing more? Of course! I've already begun planning for the next set of Quinns. I'm going to switch things up a bit and there will definitely be some surprises along the way. But you'll recognize those sexy Irish boys you've all come to love. Watch for them in April and May 2013, then again in November and December 2013. (Like many Irish families, sometimes you have to split people up to keep some sort of control.) :)

Happy reading!

Kate Hoffmann

Kate Hoffmann

THE MIGHTY QUINNS: RONAN
&
THE MIGHTY QUINNS: MARCUS

HARLEQUIN®

entertain, enrich, inspire™

ISBN-13: 978-0-373-79723-3

THE MIGHTY QUINNS: RONAN

Copyright © 2012 by Harlequin Books S.A.

The publisher acknowledges the copyright holder of the individual works as follows:

THE MIGHTY QUINNS: RONAN
Copyright © 2012 by Peggy A. Hoffmann

THE MIGHTY QUINNS: MARCUS
Copyright © 2006 by Peggy A. Hoffmann

Recycling programs for this product may not exist in your area.

CONTENTS

ABOUT THE AUTHOR

Kate Hoffmann has written more than seventy novels for Harlequin Books, most of them for the Harlequin Temptation and Blaze lines. She spent time as a music teacher, a retail assistant buyer and an advertising exec before she settled into a career as a full-time writer. She continues to pursue her interests in music, theater and musical theater, working with local schools in various productions. She lives in southeastern Wisconsin with her cat, Chloe.

Books by Kate Hoffmann

THE MIGHTY QUINNS: RONAN

To Brenda, my friend and my editor
and my own best critic.

These Quinns are for you!

Prologue

THE CLOSET WAS dark and quiet. Ronan Quinn clutched the flashlight in his hand, the failing batteries providing a weak shaft of light. Closing his eyes, he tried to banish the disturbing images from his thoughts.

The dreams had started just a few months ago, right after his eighth birthday party. It had been the first party his family had attempted since his parents had disappeared the previous year.

Of course, it hadn't been the same. Birthday parties were what his mother did best. She could turn an ordinary day into the most wonderful, magical event of a person's life. For his seventh birthday, she'd taken him and his whole Cub Scout troop to the aquarium. They'd seen the most amazing thing. There'd been octopus cupcakes with long, licorice tentacles. And games like "Pin The Fin" on the shark. There had even been a fish shaped piñata filled with gum and jawbreakers and all his favorite candy.

At the end of the day, after the party was over and he was exhausted from the excitement, he'd received his gift, a beautiful aquarium, placed on a stand right next to his bed. He remembered how he'd stayed up all night, just watching the fish swimming back and forth in the blue light.

The aquarium was empty now, all the fish dead and the water drained. It was one of those things that had been forgotten once their world had been turned upside down. There was never any time to shop for fish. No one wanted to bother keeping the aquarium clean.

This year, his grandfather and older brothers had planned a party on the family sailboat, gathering ten of Ronan's classmates for a sail on the sound. But when they'd gotten to the dock, Ronan had refused to get on the boat.

Fear had welled up inside of him as he stared at the dark water slapping against the hull. His stomach had begun to roil and his hands had grown ice cold. Ronan knew that if he got on the boat, the sea would swallow him up and pull him down to the very bottom where he would drown.

Dermot had stayed with him on the dock while the rest of the party left. And though his older brother tried to reassure him that everything would be fine, Ronan had seen the looks on his friends' faces. He'd already been marked as being different since his parents' disappearance. Now, he'd be completely alone, the subject of whispers and pity.

Ronan looked down at the book clutched in his arms. The huge picture book of ocean fish had been another gift from his mother. But this one had appeared next to his breakfast one morning. It hadn't been his birthday or Christmas or any type of holiday at all. She'd just decided that he needed the book.

He turned the flashlight onto the pages and stared at the pretty pictures. But when he flipped the page to the chapter on sharks, Ronan slammed the book closed and hugged his knees to his chest.

There were always sharks in his nightmares. Sharks circling in the dark water. He tried not to think about what might have happened to his parents, but the nightmares brought it up again and again.

He'd asked questions that his grandfather and brothers refused to answer. How long could they live in the water? How far could they swim? If they were in the life raft, wouldn't they drift to land? But there were never any explanations. He'd just been told to accept the fact that his mother and father were gone.

But he didn't want to accept it. There was always a chance that they'd be found. Maybe on an island. Or maybe the boat was just floating around in the ocean, the sails torn or lost. Why couldn't anyone see that?

"Ronan?"

His breath caught in his throat and he watched the door, shadows playing with the shaft of light. A few seconds later, the door swung open. His oldest brother, Cameron, stood in front of him.

"What are you doing in here?"

"Nothing," Ronan said.

"You got a book. Are you reading?"

Ronan shook his head.

"Come on," Cameron said. "You need to get back to bed."

"I can't," Ronan said. "I'll have bad dreams again."

Cameron squatted down and rubbed Ronan's knee. "You're having nightmares?"

Ronan nodded. "Bad ones. With sharks. And Mom and Dad are swimming and trying to get away. But the water is dark and they can't see anything." Cameron held out his hands and Ronan crawled into his embrace. "I don't want to go to sleep."

"How about you sleep in my bed tonight," Cameron said.

"Okay," Ronan said, a flood of relief washing over him. Cameron would be able to protect him from the bad dreams. His older brother could do anything.

"You want to bring your book?" Cam asked. He handed it to Ronan. "Your fish book. You really like this book, don't you?"

"Mom gave it to me," Ronan said.

"You like fish? Maybe we could go fishing sometime."

Ronan frowned. He never wanted to go near the ocean again. "I don't like fish that way," he said. "I don't want to go near the black water. It might suck me up and pull me down to the bottom."

"You don't have to be scared of that," Cam said.

But that was one point that Ronan refused to give to his older brother. He was never, ever going to go on the ocean again. "I like my aquarium fish," Ronan ventured.

"You don't have any aquarium fish," Cameron said.

"I know. But I used to like them. They helped me sleep."

"Well, maybe we could ask Grandda if we could go get you some new fish. Would that make you feel better?"

In truth, the only thing that could make Ronan feel better was if his mother was there to tuck him in and his father was there to kiss him goodnight.

Maybe his older brothers could do without that. Cameron was twelve and the twins, Kieran and Dermot were nine, almost ten. Maybe when you got older, hugs and kisses weren't important. But it wasn't a baby thing, was it, to want hugs and kisses?

Ronan reached out and grabbed his brother's hand as they walked out of Ronan's room and into the hall. He needed to be braver. That's what older boys were expected to do. It was time to grow up.

1

THE SUN ROSE as the bus rolled across the state line from New Hampshire into Maine. After four days on the road, crossing the country accompanied by complete strangers, eating at roadside diners and truck stops and sleeping in fits and starts, Ronan was ready to reach his destination.

The sunrise had become an important event for him, something he looked forward to when there was little else to mark the passing time. But now that they'd reached the Atlantic coast, he saw a completely different sunrise, a blaze of color over the blue ocean.

Like Seattle, the passing landscape was dominated by the sea and Ronan felt a hint of familiarity in such a strange, new place. The villages along the route were populated with white clapboard buildings and red brick churches, towering hardwood trees and tidy town squares, and harbors filled with bobbing sailboats.

"Thanks, Grandda," he murmured to himself. He couldn't imagine that his brothers' destinations in New

Mexico, Kentucky and Wisconsin came close to the natural beauty he was seeing here.

The bus ride really hadn't been that bad. As a kid, he'd spent a lot of time alone, riding his bike around the neighborhood or mastering tricks on his skateboard. As he grew older, he'd hiked and climbed and camped, he'd taught himself to ski and snowboard, but always alone, finding comfort in the quiet of a silent mountaintop or a lush forest.

His fondness for solitude had made him a bit of a black sheep in a family of brothers who were impossibly close. Ronan had just never found a proper place for himself. His oldest brother, Cameron, was the responsible one, charged with holding their fractured family together. Dermot was the charmer and Kieran the quiet one. Ronan was the outsider.

It didn't help that Ronan was the only one of the four Quinn boys who harbored an unshakable fear of the water. It had been difficult when every Quinn family activity revolved around boats and sailing. Cam, Dermot and Kieran spent their free time on the water, while Ronan had been forced to find solitary activities on land.

Ronan knew his fear of water had everything to do with what had happened to his parents. He didn't remember many details about that time when the world went black and everyone was sad. Yet, to this day, he remembered the nightmares of cold water and high waves, endless depths and interminable storms, and a deep and utter feeling of loss.

The mother who had comforted him, the father he'd

adored, were suddenly gone, and no one had ever really explained to him how that could have happened. He was the one who held hope the longest, certain that one day, his parents would walk in the door and life would get back to normal.

Ronan didn't mind that he was labeled the odd little brother. It was his place in the family hierarchy and it was comfortable amidst brothers who seemed to thrive on competition. He didn't mind that making friends didn't come easily to him. Or that he was twenty-six and drifted between women the same way he drifted between jobs at the yachtworks.

He didn't want to make plans, he avoided commitment. No one could know what the future held so he didn't think about the future. He lived his days, and his nights, one at a time.

But last week, his grandfather had asked them all to imagine a different life, to put aside the responsibilities they'd taken on as kids and to follow their dreams. To his surprise, the further he got from Seattle and his life there, the more his past began to fade in his mind.

The only dream he'd ever had as a child was more of a fantasy, one where his parents magically reappeared in their lives. Maybe it was time to start making a plan for himself, to focus on a goal and make it come true. Without his family around, he was no longer the black sheep. He was simply Ronan Quinn, a clean slate, a fresh start.

When the bus driver finally called "Sibleyville," Ronan jumped to his feet. He was about to walk into a different life for the next six weeks. A month and a half was what his grandfather had required for this challenge and starting now, Ronan would have to find a job and a place to sleep.

The bus pulled up in front of a drug store and the driver opened the door. "Sibleyville. Anyone for Sibleyville?"

Ronan walked down the aisle, his duffel slung over his shoulder. "Thanks," he said to the driver as he stepped onto the sidewalk.

If there was a picture next to the definition of quaint in the dictionary, this was it, Ronan thought to himself. A neon Rexall Drug sign hung over his head and a variety of merchandise was displayed behind the gleaming plate glass windows on either side of the entrance. The bus pulled away behind him and Ronan turned and watched it disappear down the street.

He drew a deep breath and the salt-tinged sea air filled Ronan's lungs. It was a different smell from home, he mused. Familiar, but different. Small town life was bound to be a change for him. He enjoyed having all the conveniences that a big city provided. But then, people were supposed to be friendlier in places like this. And for a guy who usually depended on himself, Ronan might need the kindness of a few strangers right now.

He walked inside the drug store and immediately noticed the lunch counter along one wall. He still had a little cash left in his pocket so he decided to take a seat and have something to drink while he got his bearings.

An elderly man stepped behind the counter. "What can I get for you?"

"Chocolate malt," he said.

"Made with vanilla ice cream or chocolate?"

The man's New England accent was thick, the words flattened out until Ronan could barely understand. "Vanilla," Ronan said.

He grabbed a menu from the rack in front of him and perused the prices. They served soda fountain treats and sandwiches for lunch, but he'd have to find another spot for breakfast and dinner. "I'm looking for a place to stay," Ronan said. "Something cheap. Can you suggest anything?"

"Well, it's still high season around here, but there are a few boarding houses in town that you could try. Mrs. Morey has a place over on Second Street and Miss Harrington has a few rooms in her house on Whitney. They're pretty fussy about who they rent to. No funny business, if you get my drift."

"Do you know how much they charge?" Ronan asked.

The old man considered the question for a long moment as he prepared the malt. "Can't say that I do."

"I'm also looking for a job," Ronan said.

"There's a board over at the visitors center," he said. "There's always someone looking for help. They'll help you find a room, too, if you ask Maxine. She's usually behind the desk."

He placed the malt in front of Ronan. The old fountain glass was filled to the brim, then topped with whipped cream and a cherry. "That'll be three-ninety-five," he said.

Ronan pulled out his wallet and laid a five on the counter. "Keep the change," he said.

Ronan lingered over the malt, watching as customers came and went, getting a feel for the locals. Everyone in town seemed pretty friendly. There was a certain civility in their manner that he'd never seen in big city residents. Maybe it was because they all knew each other that they went out of their way to greet each other with a friendly hello or a short conversation.

When he finished his malt, Ronan grabbed his duffel and headed out to the visitor's center. The converted railroad station was home to the local merchant's association as well as the tourist office. He went to the job board and scanned the opportunities. There were jobs in restaurants and motels, a job at the local library and one at the marina.

A job at a local oyster farm caught his eye. He glanced around, then pulled the card from the board and tucked it in his pocket. He loved oysters and farming meant that he'd be spending his time outdoors. He couldn't think of a better combination.

Ronan walked over to the hospitality counter and gave the elderly woman sitting behind it a quick smile. "Are you Maxine?"

She nodded. "I am."

"I'm looking for a room. I'm going to be in town for six weeks. It needs to be cheap. I don't have a lot of money."

"We have a couple of boarding houses in town," she said. "And Isiah Crawford rents out a few of his motel rooms on a monthly basis. Let me try Mrs. Morey first."

The woman dialed a number. "Hello, Elvira. It's Maxine down at the Visitor's Center. I have a young man down here looking for a room. Do you have anything available?" She paused. "Wonderful. How much?" She scribbled something on her pad, then glanced up at Ronan. "What's your name?"

"Ronan Quinn?"

Maxine's eyes went wide for a moment, then she cleared her throat. "Yes, Elvira, you heard that right. Well, I'm sure he'll understand. If you forgot, you forgot."

Maxine hung up the phone and smiled apologetically. "It seems that she doesn't have a room after all. Some big group coming in."

"Could you try the other boarding house?" he asked.

"I—I don't think Tillie has anything available either. I just saw her at church this morning and she—she would have mentioned it. Maybe you could try across the river in Newcastle?"

Ronan had the distinct impression that he was getting the runaround. Why were these people suddenly unwilling to rent to him? "Maybe you could try the motel?"

With a reluctant smile, she dialed the phone. "Hi there, Josiah. It's Maxine over at the Visitor's Center. I have a young man here named Ronan Quinn and he's looking for a—yes, that's what I said. He's looking for a room. Well, that's a shame. All right. You, too, Josiah."

She hung up the phone again and shrugged. "He doesn't have any vacancies either. Newcastle really is your best option. It's just over the bridge."

"I need to stay here, in Sibleyville," he said. Ronan picked up his duffel bag. "Never mind, I'll find a place on my own."

Maxine forced a smile. "Can I offer you a bit of advice? Don't give them your name. In fact, use a different name entirely. But don't dare tell anyone I gave you this advice. Run along now."

With a soft curse, Ronan walked outside, keeping his temper in check. What the hell was going on here? Did the town have something against the Irish? Or was it just because he was a single guy? From what he could tell, the town thrived on tourism so it didn't make sense they'd turn anyone away. If he'd thought Sibleyville looked like a friendly place at first glance, he'd been sadly mistaken.

He looked down at the card he held. Mistry Bay Oyster Farm. Contact Charlie Sibley. Would a potential employer feel the same? Especially one named after this very village? For now, he'd keep his name to himself until he knew for sure.

"Maybe living a different life is going to be more difficult than I thought it would be," he muttered.

"You NEED TO scrape harder than that," Charlotte Sibley said, running her hand over the rough hull of the skiff. "All this old paint has to come off. If you paint on top of it, it won't stick."

Her fourteen-year-old brother, Garrett, looked up from the task she'd given him and rolled his eyes. "I know what I'm doing."

"Of course you do. You're just not doing a very good job of it. You've been bugging Dad to let you work the boats on your own but you're not willing to put in the effort that comes with it." She ruffled his hair. "Come on, princess, put some muscle into it. We're going to need that skiff this season."

"Who made you the boss of me? You're not the boss of me, Charlie. Dad is."

"And if you haven't noticed, Einstein, Dad is laid up with a bad back. His doctor says he can't work for at least a month or two. He made me the boss of things, so that makes me the boss of you, too."

Garrett muttered something beneath his breath and went back to work. Charlotte smiled to herself. Now that she'd been put in charge of the Mistry Bay oyster farm, it had been a bit of a rocky ascension from worker to boss. Charlie knew the business from top to bottom, after working it for years with her family. And six years away hadn't been long enough to forget the ropes. But being in charge meant that she'd had to rein in the members of the Sibley clan who preferred malingering to hard work.

A knock sounded on the door of the boathouse and Charlotte strode over to the door. She'd been expecting a visit from an up and coming chef from Boston who was visiting the area. Chef Joel Bellingham had already made a name for himself in Boston with one highly rated restaurant and would soon be opening a second—a seafood place that might feature Mistry Bay oysters.

She yanked the door open, but her greeting died in her throat as she came face-to-face with an impossibly handsome man, not much older than she was. He watched her with pale blue eyes, as she tried to regain her breath, his gaze holding hers. Charlie swallowed hard, then cleared her throat. "Hello! Come on in. I hope you didn't have any trouble finding the place." She'd met Bellingham over the phone earlier that morning and had somehow gotten the impression he was much older. This guy could be thirty, tops.

"There was a sign above the door," he said, glancing around.

They stood there for an uncomfortable moment before Charlie could shake herself into action. "How was your trip?" she asked. "The traffic on Highway 1 can be really bad on the weekends."

"It was fine."

He was a man of few words. Charlie felt a stab of disappointment. He obviously wasn't interested in chatting with her. And usually she was so good with customers. But this guy, though stunningly handsome, didn't have much of a personality. "Let me show you around."

The waterfront building served multiple purposes for the family business. Charlie pointed out the shop area where they repaired equipment and boat engines. Housed in the other half of the lower floor was the shipping area, where workers cleaned and sorted oysters before they were boxed to be sent all over the east coast and beyond. As Charlie rattled off her talking points, she realized she wasn't even listening to herself. He stood beside her, nodding politely.

The second floor housed the business offices and a small apartment Charlotte sometimes used when she needed to get away from the craziness at her parents' house. It also included a finely appointed tasting room, modeled after a gourmet kitchen, where they often entertained visitors interested in featuring Mistry Bay oysters at their restaurants or seafood counters. The room overlooked the river and was the perfect setting to talk oysters.

"Mistry Bay is a family business," she said as they walked up the stairs. "We've had the oyster farm for nearly twenty years and we think we have some of the best oysters on the east coast. But I'm a bit prejudiced." She drew a ragged breath. "Why don't we taste some oysters."

He walked beside her into the tasting room and she couldn't help but notice how tall and well built he was, dressed in cargo shorts and a T-shirt that hugged his muscular chest. He hadn't shaved in a few days, but the stubble made him look slightly dangerous. He was like the kind of guy who wore his sex appeal with a casual indifference, as if he didn't care if women noticed him.

Since she'd left Danny in New York over a year ago, Charlotte hadn't found herself attracted to any man. In truth, she'd written off men completely. As long as she was living in Sibleyville, romance was an exercise in futility anyway. But she wasn't averse to indulging in a little fantasy every now and then and Chef Joel Bellingham provided plenty of raw material.

She pointed to a stool at the granite-topped counter then moved to the other side of it to retrieve a bowl of freshly harvested oysters from the refrigerator. As she stood across from him, she laid a folded towel on the counter and grabbed an oyster. Charlotte felt him watching her. She was almost worried to look up, afraid that he'd be able to read her thoughts.

She held the oyster with another towel and popped

the shell open at the hinge. After carefully slicing the meat from the shell, she placed the fresh oyster on a Mistry Bay oyster plate, preserving the liquid in the shell. "Lemon?" she asked.

"No," he said. "I like them plain."

"Can I offer you a pairing? We have champagne, muscadet and ice-cold vodka. All three really enhance the taste of our oysters. Not all together, of course. Each one separately."

"It's eleven in the morning," he said.

"Right."

He regarded her warily. "Champagne would be good. If you're going to join me."

She found a split of bubbly in the fridge, popped it open and poured it into two flutes. Drawing a deep breath, she went into her business pitch as she continued to open oysters. "We ship from September through June and use overnight delivery. That means you can have fresh oysters Tuesday through Saturday mornings. We harvest early in the morning and ship that afternoon."

Charlotte continued to shuck oysters and place them on the plate, describing the attributes of the Mistry Bay oyster in sensual terms. They were plump and juicy, briny and sweet. Usually a half dozen on the half-shell satisfied most customers, but Chef Joel seemed to be particularly hungry.

When she wasn't talking, she was nervously sipping champagne, trying to keep herself from spinning right out of the room. He finally held up his hand at a dozen, then drew a deep breath. "They were really good. Thanks."

Really good? Usually her oysters received more than a "good." Exquisite, delicate, satisfying, better than sex. Really good wasn't that good at all. "Do you have any questions?" she asked.

"Just one. Does this mean I have the job?"

She sent him a quizzical look. "Job? I—I don't understand."

He reached into his pocket and pulled out an index card, then held it out to her. "I found this over at the visitor's center. It said you were looking for help?"

A gasp slipped from her throat. "Wait a second. You're not Chef Joel from Boston?"

"Nope. I'm Ronan. Ronan Smith from Seattle. I don't mind working hard. I'll be here early and stay late. You tell me to do something and it'll be done." He gazed at her silently.

Charlie felt a shiver skitter down her spine and she had to force herself to look away. She cleared her throat. "You ate a dozen oysters," she said. "Did you think that was part of the interview?"

"I just thought you were showing me the product. And I was hungry."

She really couldn't blame him for the mix-up. She'd been caught off guard from the moment she set eyes on him. The fluttery feeling in her stomach and the buzzing in her head had made it impossible to think clearly. Maybe if she'd had her wits about her, she might have seen his confusion sooner.

"So, do I have the job?" he asked again.

"Come with me," Charlotte said. She had just posted the job yesterday. Considering the other employment opportunities available, she hadn't expected such a quick response. Nor such an interesting prospect. But here was guy who set her heart racing and she had a perfectly good reason to keep him around a little longer.

"The job is hard, with long hours. The pay isn't great, but with the hours you work, you should make a decent living. Are you going to have a problem with that?"

"Nope," he said as he followed her downstairs.

She led him over to the inverted skiff. "This is my brother, Garrett. Garrett, this is Ronan Smith. He's interviewing for the job. Give him your scraper."

"No problem," Garrett said, handing Ronan the paint scraper. "I'm going home, Charlie."

Charlotte didn't argue this time. She was glad to be rid of her little brother. She certainly didn't need him watching her fall all over herself around the gorgeous new employee. "Cut the lawn when you get home. You know Dad can't do it and Mom is too busy."

"Yeah, yeah," Garrett said.

"Teenagers," she murmured as they watched Garrett walk out the door. When she turned back to Ronan, she caught him staring, his blue eyes direct and intense.

"You're Charlie?" he asked. "You're the boss?"

"Yes. Charlotte. Charlie. Sibley."

"I was expecting a man."

"And I was expecting a chef," she countered.

"What do you want me to call you?"

She caught a look in his eyes that appeared to be amusement. Was he just toying with her? Or had she completely lost control of this interview. "You don't have the job yet." She picked up the paint scraper and safety glasses and handed them to him. "If you want the job, show me what you can do with this scraper first."

He nodded. And for the first time since they met, he smiled. To Charlie, it was as if the morning mist had suddenly parted and the sunshine shone down. He was even more attractive, if that was possible.

Men who looked like Ronan Smith usually learned to wield their charm early on. By the time they reached their teens, they knew the effect they had on the opposite sex and used it to their advantage. But Ronan seemed reluctant to use his God-given advantages.

He set to work on the skiff, a shower of paint chips flying off with each stroke. Charlie watched him for a moment, her gaze falling on the finely cut muscles in his arms. A shiver skittered down her spine and she turned and hurried back upstairs to clean up the tasting room. A bit of privacy gave her a chance to take a deep breath and focus her runaway thoughts—on Ronan Smith. It was an odd name, Ronan.

She grabbed the bottle and guzzled the remainder of the champagne, then opened another split. He'd mentioned he was from Seattle. She really ought to ask for references. Or a resume. For all she knew, he could be a criminal or a con artist—or a competitor, out to get an inside look at their operation.

Sliding onto one of the stools, she opened up another oyster and slurped it down. Ronan was a complete enigma. But then, when it came to men, she really didn't know what she was doing. She'd only had one romantic relationship in her life and that had lasted six years.

She and Danny had started dating when they were

juniors in high school, playing opposite each other in the school musical. When they graduated, they were both determined to chase their dreams on Broadway.

But New York was a rude awakening. Danny was easily discouraged and took a full time job selling cell phones. After some minor parts in a criminal drama, a series of commercials for generic laundry detergent, and an appearance in an off-off-Broadway play, Charlie was beginning to break through.

But as she got more work, Danny became more and more distant—and jealous. Their relationship began to fracture and Charlie realized that New York wasn't where she wanted to be. So, she moved out and came home to Sibleyville, older and a little wiser.

She glanced up at the chef's mirror above the granite counter. A groan slipped from her throat. Her chestnut hair looked liked a tangle of seaweed. Charlie grabbed a clean oyster brush from the drawer next to the fridge and ran it though the shoulder-length strands, then pinched her cheeks to give herself some color.

She rarely wore make-up when she was working and usually didn't care to dress in anything that showed off her figure. Yet she couldn't help but regret that it wasn't the New York City actress Charlotte Sibley that opened the door to Ronan Smith rather than the oyster farmer Charlie Sibley.

She looked at herself in the mirror once more. Though she could pretend to be a myriad of interesting and exotic characters, Charlie knew that the woman she was would have to be enough.

Shaking her head, she walked to the door, but found

herself off balance from the champagne she'd guzzled. If she was going to hire Ronan, than she'd have to keep her feelings to herself and her wits about her. A man like Ronan probably had women drooling over him everyday. And Charlie had never aspired to be one of the crowd.

RONAN SMOOTHED HIS hand over the hull of the twenty-foot skiff. The boat was old, maybe sixty or seventy years old from the clues he'd found in the construction. Nowadays, most commercial outfits chose fiberglass boats for their easy upkeep and long life.

"How's it going?"

He glanced up to see Charlie watching him. Jaysus, she was pretty. Her wavy dark hair framed a beautiful face, each of her features a perfect complement to the others. She had the kind of beauty that made him want to sit her down in front of him so he might study her in greater detail, like a fine painting or a famous sculpture.

"Good. This is a beautiful boat," he said. "I love the lines."

"It's old," she said.

"They don't make them like this anymore. I think the best boats are made of wood."

"My dad would totally agree with you." Charlie came closer to examine his work. "You're very thorough," she murmured.

The compliment pleased him, more so because it came from her. "This scraper is kind of dull. If you've got a way for me to sharpen it, I'd get more done. And you might want to use a better grade of marine paint next time," he said. "If you apply it properly and maintain it, you shouldn't have to repaint as often." He stopped himself. Now he was sounding like the boss.

"You know something about boats?" she asked, raising an eyebrow.

"Yeah," Ronan said. "Just a little."

"You said you were from Seattle. What are you doing in Maine?"

"Just traveling," Ronan said. "Seeing America."

"Well, if you're willing to work hard, I'll pay you a fair wage," she said. "We have the office and shop here in town. And our nursery and hatchery is out at Kepley Pond. Then we grow out the oysters at Mistry Bay."

Kepley Pond. Mistry Bay. That sounded like a lot of water. Since he'd been eight years old, Ronan made a point to stay off the water, at least the ocean. But he wanted this job and he'd need to put his fears aside. Maybe it was time to face the past. Besides, no one ever got lost at pond or at bay like they got lost at sea.

"You've done good work on the boat," she said. "The job is yours, if you'd like it."

"There is one thing," he said. "I need to find somewhere to stay. I was hoping you might be able to help me."

"We've got a small apartment upstairs next to the office. I could rent that to you," she said. "As long as you're quiet and tidy, I don't see any problems."

"Great," he said. Ronan knew he ought to tell her his real name. She didn't seem like the type to discriminate, although he still hadn't figured out what the problem was with the rest of the town. "I tried to find a place in town, but no one wanted to rent to me."

"Why not?"

He shrugged. "I don't know. As soon as I told them my name, they suddenly didn't have a room to rent."

"Ronan?" she asked. "Or Smith?"

"Quinn," he said. "My name is Ronan Quinn, not Smith." He paused and watched as surprise came over her pretty features. "See. That's the look right there. So it is the name."

She laughed softly and then a sudden hiccup stopped her. Pressing her fingers to her lips, she sent him an apologetic smile. "Yeah. People around here have a pretty big grudge against anyone named Quinn."

"How could they have a grudge against me? They don't even know me."

Charlotte shrugged. "Well, I don't really believe in all the silliness. Spells and curses and witches. I'm willing to give you a job, Ronan Quinn. And a place to stay, if you want."

"What did this Quinn do to make everyone mad?"

"It's a complicated story," Charlie said, waving him off.

"Don't you think I ought to hear it, so I know what I'm up against?"

She shook her head. "If I tell you the story, you'll think we're all so crazy that you'll want to leave town. And I need an oysterman." She pointed to his duffel. "Grab your bag and I'll show you the apartment."

Ronan breathed a silent sigh of relief. "I didn't mean

to lie about my name. I was just trying to figure things out."

"No matter," she said, walking him back upstairs.

When they got to the second floor, a doorway opened into a lobby for a spacious office opposite the tasting room. "Things usually get busy in here in the afternoon when we're preparing packing lists and labels for our shipments but all that starts next week."

She showed him a comfortable one-bedroom apartment with a galley kitchen and a comfortable bed. A bay window overlooked the water and he could hear the metallic clank of the boat riggings through the glass. "This is nice," he said.

"If you need an advance to buy groceries, I can help you out there."

"I could use that," he said. "And I can finish the skiff today. I'll work on it all night if I have to."

"Great," she murmured. Charlie stood in front of him, her gaze flitting nervously around the room. Though Ronan had tried to hide his attraction to his new boss, he hadn't really considered that she might be attracted to him. As she shifted nervously, her fingers twisted together, he decided to test a theory.

He leaned a bit closer, just a few inches, waiting for her response. Would she lean in as well, and close her eyes, expecting a kiss?

"Bathroom," she said, turning away.

He followed her into the tiny bathroom. It looked like the room had once been a small closet and they had to struggle to move around. When they finally maneuvered themselves into a comfortable position, they were so close Ronan could feel the heat from her body.

"You—you have to jiggle the handle on the toilet to get it to stop running. And the—the tub drains real slow," she said, glancing over her shoulder. "So it's probably best to use the shower stall instead. Unless you're a bath guy." She paused. "Most guys aren't."

He leaned a bit closer and when she turned back to him, she sucked in a sharp breath, startled by the move. Charlie retreated a step, but didn't realize how close she was to the edge of the tub. She began to lose her balance, flailing her arms.

Ronan had to think quick and decided to save her the pain and humiliation of falling into the bathtub. He slipped his arm around her waist and pulled her against his body. But this didn't have the intended effect at all. She shifted to evade slamming up against his chest and ran face first into the edge of the door.

"Ow!" she cried, covering her eye with her palm.

"Are you all right?" Ronan asked.

Charlie pulled her hand away and shook her head. "I think I'm bleeding." She struggled to get to the medicine chest above the sink and Ronan wrapped his hands around her waist.

"Out. I'll get them." Ronan found a box of band-aids and then grabbed a washcloth from the towel rack and soaked it with cold water. He found Charlie leaning against the kitchen counter, her fingers doing little to staunch the flow of blood.

"Let me look," Ronan said.

Wincing, she pulled her hand away. "It's bleeding a lot. Does it look like it needs stitches?"

Ronan dabbed at the small cut. "No. It's tiny. There's a lot of blood. Here, hold this."

She pressed the cold cloth to her head as he fumbled to open the bandage. "Sorry," she murmured.

"What are you apologizing for? It's not your fault." Ronan wanted to reach out and touch her cheek, to see if it was as soft as it looked. His gaze drifted down to her mouth. If they were going to spend time together, it was going to be hard to resist kissing her.

Though Ronan didn't work hard at romance, he had enjoyed the regular company of a number of beautiful women. But he usually liked to spend his free time in solitary pursuits, which left little for long-term, serious relationships. Still, he was curious about this particular woman. What was it about Charlie Sibley that he found so intriguing?

"Hello! Anyone home?"

She forced a smile. "That would be the real Joel Bellingham," Charlie murmured.

Ronan drew her wash cloth away and then neatly covered the cut with a small band-aid. "There. All better."

"Thanks," she said.

"No problem."

She stared at him for a long moment and Ronan's gaze fell to her lips, so lush and slightly parted. He wanted to lean forward and take just a quick taste, but she seemed to sense what was on his mind and quickly stepped back.

He watched as she hurried out of the apartment, her footsteps fading on the stairs. They'd have plenty of time to figure this all out, Ronan mused. A lot could happen in six weeks.

2

CHARLIE WALKED CHEF Joel to the door, then shook his hand. "We'll be looking forward to your first order. Please, don't hesitate to call me if you have any questions or concerns."

He patted the folder she'd given him. "I've got everything I need right here," he said. "It was a pleasure to meet you, Charlotte. We'll talk soon."

She closed the door behind him and smiled. Mistry Bay oysters in one of the best new restaurants in Boston would be a huge account for the farm.

The effects of the champagne had worn off and she counted herself lucky that she'd been able to complete her sale pitch without an embarrassing incident. What had she been thinking? Ronan Quinn had thrown her into a complete tizzy.

"A tizzy," she murmured to herself. It was the perfect word for how she felt when she thought about Ronan. In fact, the word applied to her everyday life lately.

Since she'd been back from New York, she'd been waiting for some sign, some new direction for her life.

Charlie had always had a laser-like focus on a goal. At first, it had been the move after high school, and then auditioning and attending acting classes and finding an agent. After that came the jobs, each one bigger and better than the last.

But here in Sibleyville, there was no goal anymore, besides getting up in the morning and going to sleep at night. She was drifting aimlessly through life and she couldn't seem to stop herself. It really was time to make a few hard decisions about what she really wanted to do. Cursing softly, she climbed the stairs to the second floor.

When she got to the tasting room, she quickly tidied up the mess from Chef Joel's visit. She'd heard the shower through the door of the apartment, but the water was off now. Drawing a deep breath, she crossed to the door and rapped on it softly.

The door swung open and Ronan stood on the other side, shirtless, his cargo shorts riding low on his hips. His hair was damp and droplets clung to the smooth expanse of his chest.

Charlie drew a deep breath and the scent of soap and shampoo filled her head. Her fingers twitched and she fought the urge to reach out and smooth the water from his skin. "I thought it might be good to show you the nursery and the farm," she said. "You're going to be working at both."

"All right," Ronan said. "Just let me grab a shirt."

She swallowed hard. "I'll just wait outside in the truck."

The image of Ronan Quinn half-naked was now

burned into her brain and it was a memory she didn't really want to forget. His body was beautiful, lean yet muscular, every limb in perfect proportion. It had taken every last ounce of her resolve to walk away.

She could have reached out and touched him, knowing that he might take the action as an invitation. But what then? Would he have kissed her? She wanted to believe that she saw desire in his eyes, but she'd only ever been with one man and that gave her little to use as a reference.

The only option left to her was to wait until he made the first move. At least then she wouldn't be humiliated by misreading his signals. Charlie hurried down the stairs, stumbling on the last step and grabbing the rail for balance. But maintaining her composure was going to be the difficult part. Whenever she looked at him, her knees got wobbly and her brain refused to function.

Charlie grabbed a brochure from the rack near the front door, then walked outside to her SUV. She hopped behind the wheel, the started it up, a love song blaring from the radio. With a soft curse, she reached out and turned it off. The last thing she needed was to start thinking about romance. Besides, if the curse was to be believed, then falling in love within the village limits of Sibleyville was impossible.

A few minutes later, Ronan stepped outside, squinting his eyes against the noonday sun. He slipped his sunglasses on. She honked the horn and Ronan started toward her. When he was settled in the passenger seat, she handed him the brochure. "There's a map inside. You'll need to learn how to get to the pond and the bay by road as well as by water. I'll show you by water tomorrow, but today, we'll go by land."

"I don't have a car," he said.

"How did you get here?" she asked as she pulled out of the parking lot onto the street.

"Bus?"

Charlie frowned. Why would a guy like Ronan be traveling by bus? He might as well have told her that he'd rode up on a camel. "Bus?"

"Yeah. It was part of the deal," he said.

"What kind of deal was that?" A sudden sting of doubt pricked at her thoughts. "You didn't just get out of prison, did you?"

This time he laughed, a deep, resonant sound that caused her heart to flutter. She glanced over at him and took in his smile. God, he was really handsome when he smiled. "Did you?"

"No," he said. "My grandfather sent me on this trip. He picked the place, bought me the bus ticket and sent me on my way."

"Why?"

He paused for a long moment, as if he was deciding exactly how much to reveal to her. "When me and my three brothers were just kids, our folks died in an accident."

"I'm sorry to hear that," Charlie murmured.

"We all worked together on the family business," he said. "We build custom sailing yachts. Quinn Yachtworks in Seattle."

"So that's why you knew so much about the skiff." She risked another glance over at him and caught him staring at her from behind his dark glasses. "Why would he send you away?"

"He wanted us all to live a different life for a while. To figure out if we wanted to continue on with the family business or strike out on our own."

"So you decided to try oyster farming," she said. "I'm not sure that was a very sensible choice. It's not nearly as glamorous as building yachts. It's a lot of dirty, sweaty work. And some days, the mosquitoes are so thick they'll carry you away."

"I don't mind working hard," he said. "And I like being outside."

"All right," she said. "Now, watch that map because this next turn is kind of tricky. It's easy to miss."

Charlie pointed out the sign for the hatchery right before she turned down the narrow, winding road to Kepley Pond. "My dad's brother, Uncle Jake, runs the hatchery and nursery."

She stopped the SUV in front of the hatchery building, then jumped out and waited for Ronan to join her. "This is where we start," she said. "Kepley Pond. It's really not a pond, but an estuary. We bring adult stock into the nursery from the bay. Usually, oysters spawn in mid-summer, when the water reaches a certain temperature, but we gradually bring the temperature up, forcing them to lay their eggs in the spring. We also grow phytoplankton here to feed the larvae. When they're ready, we move the seed oysters into an upweller system beneath those six docks. We also sell seed oysters to other farmers in the area."

Charlie led him down to the pond. Long wooden

docks jutted out into the brackish water. "As they grow, we put them in containers that sit on the bottom of the pond, giving them space so that they grow evenly. And when they're big enough, we plant them out in the bay."

"How do you do that?"

"We toss them overboard with a snow shovel. Very high tech. Maine oysters grow slower in the colder water so they'll stay in the bay for about three or four years before we harvest them. We do that a lot of different ways, mostly dredging. In some areas we culture them in lantern nets. A few times a year at low tide, we can harvest them by hand." She smiled. "So, that's oyster farming in a…an oyster shell."

They walked to the end of one of the docks and Charlie showed him the upwell system. When she'd replaced the cover, she watched as he sat down at the end of the dock, as if his thoughts were elsewhere.

She sat down beside him, glancing over to study his expression. "Is there something wrong?"

He shook his head, his gaze still fixed on a point on the pond. "So, I'm going to have to go out on the water with a boat?"

"Yeah. That's how we plant and harvest. Can't you swim?"

"Oh, yeah, I can swim. I'm just not a real big fan of boats. And deep…dark water."

"That's going to be a problem," she said. Why would he have come to an oyster farm for work if he didn't like the water? Oysters didn't grow in a cornfield.

"No, it won't," he said, his voice on edge. "I need the job. I'm just going to have to suck it up and do it."

"We wear life vests," she said. "If you fall overboard, we'll pull you out. My brothers and sisters fall in all the time." She paused. "Why are you afraid of the water?"

"It's just something from my childhood. It really doesn't make a lot of sense."

"You can tell me," Charlie said.

"My parents—they were lost at sea," he said, turned to her. "They were sailing a yacht across the Pacific and it disappeared. Probably sank during a storm. Or maybe it got hit by a cargo ship. Nobody knows."

"Oh, my God," Charlie said. "That must have been horrible."

"After that, I couldn't bring myself to get onboard a boat and whenever I tried I'd get kind of freaked out."

Charlie reached out and took his hand, covering it with hers. "I guess we could work on that," she said.

"You don't have to pay me until I can do the work," he said. "It's my problem. I'll work it out."

"Sure. Why don't we take a little boat ride tonight," she said. "A test ride, and see how you feel. These estuaries are a lot different than the open ocean."

He stared down at their hands, then wove his fingers through hers. When he looked back up, their gazes met for a long moment. Ronan leaned closer and in a heartbeat, his lips met hers in a soft, lingering kiss. He drew back, then decided it wasn't enough, cupping her face in his hands and deepening the kiss.

It was so unexpected, but not at all unwanted. Charlie was afraid to breathe, afraid to make a sound for fear that the spell that had fallen over them would suddenly burst. It had been so long since a man had touched her this way, but all the old familiar feelings came back in a rush.

When he finally pulled back, a long sigh slipped from his body. He pressed his forehead to hers, still holding her face in his hands. "Was that all right?" he murmured.

Charlie wasn't sure if he wanted permission or if he was asking for a review of his technique. "It was very all right," she said. "I—I mean, good. Very good. And all right, too."

He smiled. "So I can do it again?"

"Sure," she said. "Right now?"

"Later," he said. Ronan pushed to his feet, then held out his hand. When she stood beside him, he drew her hand to his mouth and pressed his lips to her wrist. "What's next, boss?"

In truth, Charlie would have been happy to continue what they were doing. But maybe later would be better. "I think I'm going to take you home to meet the folks," she said.

He gasped. "What?"

"You kissed me. You know what that means. My mama and daddy are going to want to look you over."

"You're kidding, right?"

She laughed. "Yeah. But my dad will want to meet you. He has to meet everyone we hire. He's the president of the company."

"All right."

"I won't tell him about your fear of boats. I think I'll keep that to myself a little bit longer," she promised.

"GARRETT SIBLEY, CLOSE that door! You're letting flies in!"

Charlie's brother ran down the front steps of the porch, then turned back to grin at Ronan. "It's Indian food tonight," he said. "If I were you, I'd turn around and get out of here before she forces you to eat it."

Ronan turned to Charlie and she gave him a reassuring smile. "My mother likes to try cooking new cuisines. Don't worry, if it's really bad, we'll get something else to eat later. Just tell her it's good and eat really slowly."

"I like Indian food," he said.

"Me, too. But this won't taste like any Indian food you've ever had. Last month, she was mastering German food and everything tasted like vinegar."

The Sibley family lived in a sprawling white clapboard Victorian, set on a beautiful tree-lined street in the heart of Sibleyville. It was the biggest house in town by far, a testament to the family's position in a town that bore their name.

They climbed the steps to the wide porch, lined with old wicker furniture and decorated with hanging baskets of colorful flowers. Ronan heard another shout from inside the house and a moment later, a young girl came running out the door. "Garrett, come back here. You have to help me finish folding the laundry." She froze when she saw Charlie and Ronan, sending Ronan a suspicious look.

"This is my sister, Libby," Charlie said. "She's thirteen. Libby, this is Ronan. He's going to be working for us."

She rolled her eyes and continued her call for her brother, running down the steps and shouting his name.

"Is your whole family going to be here?"

She nodded. "Isaac is a senior in college and Abby is a sophomore. They're in college but they still live at home. Jane is eighteen and Ethan is sixteen and both are in high school. Don't try to remember them all."

"I'm not sure I could," Ronan said.

"When they're all around, things can get kind of crazy, but once you get used to them, they'll seem almost normal. Whatever you do, don't look the dog directly in the eyes and if my brother Ethan asks you to pull his finger, don't do it."

"If this is going to be a problem, I can always pick up some dinner at the grocery store," Ronan said.

"No, no, my dad is going to want to meet you before you start work. He has to approve my choices."

"Your dad hurt his back?"

"Last season. He was moving a crate of oysters off the boat and onto the dock. He just twisted the wrong way and herniated a disc." She reached for the door. "Ready?"

"I guess so."

How bad could it be, Ronan wondered. Charlie was nice enough. Actually, she was more than that. She was funny and sexy and smart. But there was something else about her he found attractive, a warmth that he rarely saw in the women he'd dated.

She pulled the door open and he stepped inside. The old Victorian was decorated in a style that Ronan could describe as early twenty-first century chaos mixed with beautiful antiques. The furniture was tattered but comfortable. Every available space was filled with some bizarre knickknack or strange painting. On one shelf alone, Ronan saw a stuffed raccoon, an old microscope, a doll with one eye, and a paint-by-numbers portrait of FDR.

"Look what the cat dragged in!" A young man walked through the room, giving Ronan the once over. He resembled Charlotte with her bronze eyes and wavy dark hair. "If I were you, I'd leave right now. It's Indian food."

"Isaac, this is Ronan Quinn."

Isaac's eyebrow shot up. "You brought a Quinn home? Maybe I will stay for dinner." He turned around. "Hey, Abs, come and see what Charlie brought home."

In less than a minute, Ronan realized that he probably should have opted for dinner alone. He could feel the energy in the house, as if the walls were vibrating and the roof was about the blow off.

An older woman appeared in the dining room, her graying hair twisted into a haphazard knot on top of her head. She held a fly swatter in her hand. "Hello, dear. You brought a friend. I'm cooking Indian tonight. Chicken tandoori. I was supposed to marinate the chicken in yogurt, but I had to use cottage cheese instead. And Delbert didn't have anything called garam masala down at the grocery, so I had to leave that out. You don't know what that is, do you?"

"Mama, this is Ronan Quinn. He's going to be helping us out for a few weeks."

She blinked in surprise. "Quinn? Really. Well, now,

that's very interesting. We'll have something good to talk about over dinner. I suppose you haven't had a very enthusiastic welcome in town. But our family really doesn't set much store in that curse. Charlotte, offer the man a drink."

"Curse?" Ronan asked.

"Is this the Quinn?" A young woman, about nineteen or twenty came running into the room. "I'm Abigail. Gosh, I almost expected you to have horns and a forked tail. You're totally hot." She turned to Charlie. "Good move, sissy."

"Charlie, if that's you, I need you in here right away."

"That's my dad," she said. She grabbed Ronan's hand and pulled him along through the spacious living room. "Come on. Let's introduce you to the big guy. Then I'll get you that drink."

When Charlie had called her father the "big guy", she'd used an apt description. The man sitting behind the desk in the library was tall and broad-shouldered. He struggled to his feet and held out his hand. "Peyton Sibley," he said.

"Daddy, this is Ronan Quinn. He answered the ad I put up at the visitor's center. He's from Seattle and he knows a lot about boats."

"Well, Charlotte, that was a lovely introduction," Peyton said as he sat down again, "but maybe we should let this young man speak for himself. You say your name is Quinn?"

Ronan nodded.

"I suppose you haven't had a very enthusiastic reception here in Sibleyville."

"Nobody has really explained that to me, sir. Maybe you could."

"No, no, no. We don't really believe in all that silliness. So, you think you can help us out here?"

"Yes, sir."

"You just listen to Charlotte. She'll teach you the ropes. If you get stuck working with my brother, Jake, do not let him goad you into talking about religion, politics or his three ex-wives. And if you're staying for dinner, please tell my wife that whatever she's been cooking all day—"

"Tandoori chicken," Charlie said.

"I have no idea what that is, but I'm sure I'll regret it in another four to six hours." He opened the drawer of his desk and pulled out a big bottle of antacid tablets. Peyton popped a few into his mouth and offered the bottle to Ronan. "Might want to get a jump on it."

"No, that's fine, sir. I have a pretty strong stomach."

He slammed his hand on the surface of his desk. "Charlotte, I approve! Put this man on the payroll. Anyone who calls me 'sir' can't be all bad. Even if he is named Quinn."

"Thanks, Daddy," Charlotte said. She grabbed Ronan's arm and pulled him along, back out into the foyer. "See, that wasn't so bad."

"For a Quinn," Ronan muttered.

"Why don't you go sit out on the porch and I'll get us something to drink," she said.

Ronan nodded and headed back outside. He walked to the end of the porch and sat down on a swing. As he pushed off with his toes, he felt the movement relax him. This entire day had been just a little strange. And the longer it lasted, the stranger it became. Except for one thing—that kiss he'd shared with Charlie.

He drew a deep breath. That had been the only thing that made perfect sense to him. And he didn't want to wait to do it again.

"I hope beer is all right," Charlie said as she walked out the front door. She glanced around, then saw him on the end of the porch and slowly approached. She handed him the bottle, then leaned up against the railing and watched him. "Are you all right?"

"Maybe you ought to tell me why everyone in Sibleyville has a problem with me. I think I need to know a little more about this curse."

She sat down beside him, her shoulder brushing against his. It was an innocent contact, but it sent his senses spinning. He could feel her warmth, smell her hair, listen to the soft sound of her voice. She excited him and relaxed him all at once. How was that possible?

"It's really kind of silly. And it's not you. Just your last name." She paused as if to gather her thoughts. "Her name was Bridget Quinn, but everyone called her Bridie. She lived in Sibleyville about a hundred and fifty years ago and worked as a maid in my great-great-great grandfather's home. She came from Ireland with her daughter to escape the potato famine. Her daughter, Moira, fell in love with Edward Sibley, my great-great-grandfather and they wanted to get married, but his father refused permission. When Edward wouldn't give up Moira, his father started a rumor that Bridie was a witch and the folks in Sibleyville ran her and her daughter out of town. But before she left, Bridie cursed the town."

"Good for her," Ronan said. "What was the curse?"

"That no one would ever find love within the village limits of Sibleyville. And no one ever has."

Ronan frowned. "The curse worked?"

"In one hundred and fifty years, no man and woman from Sibleyville have ever married each other. To find love, we have to go out of town. We even have a matchmaker who helps out with that."

"But Sibleyville is pretty small. That isn't unusual."

"For one-hundred and fifty years?" She shrugged. "There was one couple and every one thought the curse would be broken, but it didn't work out."

"Who was that?"

"Just a couple of infatuated kids." She turned and gave him a smile. "You want to see something really cool?"

"Sure," Ronan said.

They walked around the house to the backyard, a large expanse of grass surrounded by deep gardens and a white picket fence. A huge oak tree stood at the rear of the lot and Charlie led him over to it and pointed up.

Hidden amidst the leafy boughs was an intricate tree house with all the gingerbread detail of the main house. "Oh, man. Look at that. I always wanted a tree house when I was a kid."

"Pull on the rope and a ladder will drop down."

Ronan did as she told him and climbed the ladder. When he was halfway up, he turned to look down on her. "Are you coming up?"

"Right after you," she said.

He had to open a trap door to get inside, but once he was standing, he was amazed at the amount of room in the little house. Charlie joined him, then closed the trap door.

Hinged wood panels covered the top part of the walls and Charlie pulled each panel up and hooked it overhead, allowing the breeze to blow through the tree house. Ronan stood at one of the windows and looked down into the yard. "I can barely remember my childhood," he said. "I know I should be able to, but all of it was so…dark."

Charlie stood next to him, leaning in until her shoulder rubbed against his. "You can't remember one happy time?"

"No." He stared down at her, transfixed by the strange color of her eyes. "We didn't have the freedom most kids have. You know, what I'm talking about. The time to be completely carefree, without any responsibilities. From the time my parents disappeared, we all had a job to do. We had to work hard and help my grandfather because he was good enough to take us in." Ronan had never really opened up about his childhood, but now, he couldn't seem to stop talking.

"Was there any doubt that he would?"

Ronan shrugged. "Probably not. But when you're an orphan, you're always living on the edge of disaster. At least, that's what we thought. We just never laughed. It was almost as if having fun would have been disrespectful to the memory of my parents. Even though I know they would have wanted us to be happy." He glanced over at her, and shook his head. "I've never talked about this before. Not to anyone."

"I'm a good listener," Charlie said.

"You are." He smiled and she turned to him. And instant later, she wrapped her arms around his neck and kissed him. Her lips parted and she let the kiss play out, their tongues teasing and tasting. And when she was finished, she stepped back.

"Please tell me that's part of the job."

"If it was, we probably wouldn't get much else done," Charlie said. "I just thought it was important that we got that out of the way."

He chuckled softly. "You've been thinking about it?"

"No," she said. "I mean, yes, I was. It just seemed to be hanging between us, so I thought I'd get it out there so we wouldn't have to keep wondering."

"I'm not sure that worked," Ronan said. "Because now I can't stop thinking about it."

RONAN STOOD ON the pier, staring down into the skiff. Charlie held out her hand, sending him an encouraging smile. "We're not going anywhere. You're just going to step into the skiff and sit for a while. I promise, we won't untie the lines from the dock. Come on. Baby steps."

After a rollicking dinner with her family, Charlie was grateful for the relative peace and quiet of the waterfront. Gulls circled above and every now and then, the strains of a rock song drifted out the door of a nearby pub. It was a perfect summer night, a cool breeze blowing off the ocean, the water calm. And now that she was alone with Ronan, all she could think about was kissing him again.

Her mind wandered back to their encounter in the tree house. Charlie had never been a patient person. When there was something to be done, she just got it done. Apparently, that now applied to men. She'd felt the attraction between them, knew what he was thinking about and couldn't help herself.

Thankfully, Ronan didn't seem to mind a more aggressive approach. It was obvious that he enjoyed the kiss. But this next time, she was going to let him take the lead. She didn't want to seem like some love-starved fool—even though that's exactly what she felt like.

"You said you swim. What's different about that water?" Charlie asked.

"It has sides," he said. "The pool has sides. And a bottom. And no sharks or killer whales."

"All right," she said. "This river has sides. We're on one side and you can see the other right over there," she said, pointing toward Newcastle. "And I can assure you, it has a bottom. About twenty feet down in the center. Does that make you feel better?" She wiggled her fingers. "Baby steps."

Taking a deep breath, Ronan stepped off the dock into the skiff. "There you go," she said, reaching out to give his hands a squeeze. "See, that wasn't so bad. How do you feel?"

"Good," Ronan murmured. He quickly stepped out of th skiff and back onto the dock. "Surprisingly good." He rubbed his hands on the front of his shorts. "I'm really not feeling bad at all."

"All right. I'm going to let you decide what we do next. When you're ready." She sat down in the seat behind the controls and waited.

He stepped down into the boat again. "I don't feel so bad."

"You could sit here next to me. See how that feels."

He did as he was told, his fingers clutching onto the back of the seat.

Charlie leaned toward him. "You could kiss me again," she suggested.

"I think that might just confuse my issues."

"Maybe that's exactly what you need."

He grinned and shook his head. "Why don't you start the engine?"

Charlie sat behind the wheel and turned the key. An instant later, the outboard rumbled. She watched Ronan, but nothing in his expression changed. "We could just take a little ride across the river. That might be a good start."

He nodded, fixing his gaze across the river at the destination. "All right. Let's go. Just do it before I can say no."

She tossed off the lines, then lowered the engine into the water and pushed the throttle into reverse. The skiff was easy to maneuver, low in the water and wide enough to offer a stable ride. Charlie kept a close eye on Ronan, but he seemed remarkably calm.

"Are you all right?"

"No," he said. "Do I look all right?"

"You look good. I—I mean, you look calm."

"I don't feel calm. I feel like I'm ready to jump out of my skin." He drew a ragged breath. "Go faster."

"Not around here," she said. "No wake. But if we go further down the river we can."

He nodded. "All right, let's go." Charlie turned the boat down the river. Like most of the waterways on the seacoast of Maine, it was really more of a narrow point in an estuary. The water in Sibleyville was brackish and still affected by the tides.

Charlie smiled against the cool evening air as it blew through her hair. She couldn't think of a more perfect end to the day. There was every chance that Ronan would kiss her again and maybe, after that, something more intimate might happen.

She couldn't deny that she'd considered the possibility. She was a young, healthy woman, with normal sexual desires. It was easy to forget those desires when there was no possibility of satisfying them. But this man had suddenly dropped into her life. It was only natural to take advantage, right?

The river widened significantly south of Sibleyville, pushing the shores out into the distance. She slowed the boat, wondering at Ronan's reaction. "We can turn back if you like."

Ronan shook his head. "No, not yet."

"Battle Cove is right over there," she said. She brought the skiff around and headed toward the entrance to the cove. It was a pretty little spot that she used to come to with her siblings when they wanted to swim in the summer.

Stone cliffs surrounded the shallow water, the cliffs

lined with tall pines. She dropped the anchor in the middle of the cove and turned off the engine. It was so quiet, they could hear the birds singing on shore.

"This is better," he said. "It's like a swimming pool."

"It is." She shifted in her seat to face him. "I think you're doing pretty well."

"I want to puke."

"Don't do that," she said.

"I'm fine." He ran his fingers through his hair. "Although who knows what kind of nightmares this is going to bring tonight."

"You haven't tried going out on a boat since you were a kid?"

"There wasn't a reason. I didn't need to be on the water. Man, that fear was so huge in my mind." He met her gaze. "Maybe it would be different out on the ocean. Just the thought of that makes me a little queasy."

"Well, we stick pretty close to shore," she said. "And the bay is much wider where we harvest, but it's not deep. I think you'll be all right."

He reached out and took her hand. "I've had a pretty unusual day. When my grandfather sent me here, I didn't expect this."

"What?"

"You," he said.

Her breath caught in her throat and Charlie had to remind herself to take another. She reached out and brushed a windblown strand of hair from his eyes. "I never expected you either," she said, her voice soft.

"What are we going to do with ourselves?"

"I have no idea. Maybe you could kiss me again and we could figure it out?"

Ronan reached out and grabbed her waist, pulling her toward him. She straddled his legs, her arms wrapped around his neck. His hands skimmed over her shoulders and down her back. And then he pulled her into a kiss, his mouth plundering hers.

It wasn't a kiss meant to tease but one that told her exactly what he wanted from her. There was no reason to question his attraction anymore. And though it may be purely physical, Charlie didn't see anything wrong with that. They were both consenting adults and it had been far too long since she'd been to bed with a man.

His lips traced a path from her mouth to her collarbone and she tipped her head back, her fingers tangled in his hair. Though she'd just met him that morning, they didn't feel like strangers.

His hands slipped beneath her T-shirt, finding naked skin and the sensation of his touch sent a flood of heat racing through her body. If they'd been somewhere more private, Charlie knew that her clothes would have been discarded without a second thought.

She wanted to see his body, to touch the places that were still hidden beneath clothes, to know him in a more intimate way. He was almost too perfect and yet, his desires had overwhelmed him in the same way hers had crushed her inhibitions.

When his palm cupped her breast, a moan slipped from her throat and Charlie knew that resisting him would be impossible. She reached for the hem of his

T-shirt and pulled it over his head, breaking their contact for just an instant.

Her mouth found his again and Charlie let her fingers drift over his shoulders and his back. Though she'd seen him earlier, after his shower, this was different. Touch was much a much more powerful sense than sight. The act of touching his skin was almost more than she could handle.

She'd only been with one man in her life. From the first time he'd kissed her when she was sixteen until the day she'd walked out on him eight years later. They'd learned about sex together and over the years, it hadn't grown more passionate—only more ordinary.

But Ronan Quinn was not an ordinary man. And any intimacy with him would probably be something extraordinary. Would she know how to please him? Were there things that she didn't know?

She'd always been a good actress, always been able to fake her way through almost anything. But sex with a man like Ronan was something that couldn't be faked. He'd know if her need was real.

"Do you think we might be able to find somewhere a bit more comfortable?" he murmured. "Maybe someplace that doesn't rock back and forth?"

She drew back and smiled. "You don't think a smelly oyster boat is comfortable?"

He growled, gently biting at her lower lip. "No."

"Maybe we should go back, then." She crawled off his lap and pulled him to his feet. "You can drive. You have to learn sometime."

Charlie watched as he walked to the bow and pulled

up the anchor. When he sat down next to her, she showed him how to start the boat. A few seconds later, they were back out on the bay, traveling north toward town.

It had been a strange and wonderful day, Charlie thought to herself. That morning, when she crawled out of bed, all she'd had to look forward to was a long day at work. But now, with Ronan around, there were so many more possibilities to consider.

"So how do you feel?" she shouted.

He laughed. "Not good. But I think I'm getting better at hiding it."

3

"I'M SORRY ABOUT dinner," Charlie said. "That chicken was pretty bad."

She set the oyster plate down on the table and sat down next to him, tucking her feet beneath her. Ronan's arm was draped across the back of the wicker sofa and he felt her hair against his skin, a tumble of silken strands.

Every time they made contact he found himself wanting more. He wasn't satisfied to just enjoy a short interlude. Ronan craved endless hours to explore and to touch, to discover everything about her that was sweet and sexy and perfect.

And it wasn't just the touching and the kissing that he craved. He loved to talk to her. It was like she held some secret key to his tongue. He wanted to tell her more about himself, as if she was the only one in the world that might understand him.

How was it possible that a woman like Charlotte Sibley was still single? Did men in this part of the country not find her attractive? Sure, she was strong and resilient and clever. And she walked around in torn jeans and yellow rubber boots. But those were all qualities he found undeniably attractive. And she was also just about the prettiest woman he'd ever met.

After tying up the boat, they'd found a spot on the small terrace outside the tasting room, a spot that overlooked the river. The sun had gone down and the lights from Newcastle twinkled from across the water.

"Hot cottage cheese, curry and chicken was a pretty strange combination. I'm used to lots of different ethnic food, but I've never tasted anything quite like that."

"My mother believes in developing an adventuresome palate in all of her children."

He reached out and picked up an oyster from the plate she'd prepared. "I think I could survive quite nicely on oysters."

"You'll get tired of them sooner or later," she said. "It's like anything you get too much of."

"I can't imagine getting too much of kissing you," he said. Ronan's fingers tangled in her hair and he gently pulled her closer. He was ready to take her to bed, to find out how good they could be together. But he wasn't sure they ought to move so fast. He had six weeks with her. Taking such a big step on their first night together didn't seem like a sensible course of action. Still, if she offered, he wasn't going to refuse.

"I enjoyed meeting your family," he said, taking her hand. "They're so different from mine."

She watched him toy with her fingers as she spoke. "They're different from everyone's family. My mother has always let us go our own way. She wanted us to express our individuality. I think that's really good in theory, but it doesn't always work out in practice. We were known around town as a houseful of hooligans." She shook her head. "That's why I ran away to New York."

"At dinner, your mother mentioned that you lived there."

"I left Sibleyville the day I graduated from high school. With my boyfriend, Danny. We were going to take Broadway by storm. We did all the shows in high school and did a few years of summer stock up in Bar Harbor. Lots of people said we'd be big stars."

"It didn't work out?"

"Not at first. But after three years, things started to click for me. I got a few decent acting jobs. I found an agent. Got my SAG card. But then I had this long dry spell and I decided, if I was going to be miserable, I'd rather be miserable at home, with my family around me."

"Did you like being an actress?"

"I did. I really liked it when I actually got work. But I spent six years going nowhere. And Danny and I weren't getting along, so when I moved out, I came back home for a while. I was just going to stay for a month or two, but then I never went back. When my dad got hurt, I started to run the farm for him." She glanced up at him. "So, that was my big dream. Over by the time I turned twenty-four."

"I'm just impressed that you can sing and dance as well as shuck oysters and drive a boat."

"Yes. And I'm an excellent tap dancer. I actually

got a callback for the revival of Anything Goes. But I didn't get the part."

"But you followed your dream, right?"

"Yeah, but where did it leave me? I didn't go to college. What I should have been doing was getting a business degree."

"Were you in love with him?"

"Danny?" She shook her head. "We were so young. Everyone thought we'd be the ones to break the curse. The first couple from Sibleyville to fall in love and get married. But I'm not sure we ever were in love. We thought we were. We pretended to be in love, but we were just kids with big dreams."

"I'm glad you came back. If you hadn't, I'd still be looking for a job right now. And I'd be sleeping on a park bench."

"Oh, I'm sure some pretty girl would have picked you up and taken you home with her."

A long silence grew between them as that idea hung in the air. Ronan waited, wondering if she'd change her mind and spend the night. He could see the indecision in her expression and decided to help her along. "What time does work start in the morning?"

"Sunrise," she said. Charlie glanced at her watch. "It's almost nine-thirty. I should probably let you get to bed."

She started to rise, but Ronan grabbed her hand and pulled her back down. He gave her one last kiss, his palm smoothing over her cheek as his lips captured hers. "I'd ask you to stay, but I'm not going to do that."

"You shouldn't," she said, breathless, watching him

with wide eyes. "I—I think that would probably be best. I might just agree to stay."

He ran his thumb along her lower lip. "We wouldn't want to move too fast," he said.

"No. Fast is bad," she said. She slowly got to her feet, her fingers still tangled with his. "I'm going to go now. I'll see you in the morning."

"In the morning," Ronan said, standing up beside her. He leaned close and kissed her cheek. "Sleep well."

A tiny laugh bubbled up in her throat. "Right. I'm not sure I'll be doing a lot of sleeping tonight." Charlie drew a deep breath. "I'm going to lock up downstairs. If you decide to leave, you can just use this door and go down the steps from the porch. There's a key on the hook by the door."

"I'll be fine," he said. "I don't think I'll be going anywhere."

"Good," she said. "I'd hate to think we scared you away after only one day."

He didn't want to her leave, which was an odd feeling for Ronan. He was usually the kind of guy who used the "early meeting" excuse to avoid waking up with a woman in his bed. But he'd had such a nice day with Charlotte that he wanted it to go on a little longer.

He stood up and grabbed her hands. "You don't scare me, Charlie."

She shifted nervously, her gaze fixed on his chest. "You kinda scare me, a little bit."

He hooked his thumb beneath her chin and tipped her gaze up to meet his. "We'll have to work on that," he said. "Baby steps."

"I'll see you in the morning," she said.

"All right." He kissed her again, softly, his tongue teasing at the crease of her lips. And when he drew back, he pressed his damp lips to her forehead. "You better go while I'm still willing to let you."

Charlie turned and walked back inside. He watched her in the dim light from the living room lamps and when he heard the door shut behind her, he let out a long breath.

"Charlotte Sibley," he murmured to himself. He leaned against the railing and stared out at the water. What where his brothers doing right now, he wondered. Were they staring out into the night sky and wondering what changes would come over the next six weeks. Had they found an interesting woman to occupy their thoughts?

If he couldn't imagine a different life, here in Sibleyville, with Charlotte Sibley, then he had no imagination at all. This place was perfect, Charlie was beautiful, and there was every chance that they'd be sharing a bed before long.

He'd been drifting for so long, trying to find his place in life. Now, suddenly, he felt the gentle tug of an anchor. The wind might blow and the current might catch him, but he was here to stay, at least for a while. And whatever happened between them, Ronan suspected it might just change his life. And yet he didn't care. His life needed changing, the more, the better. And he'd start with his fear of water.

"Bring it on," he said, taking a sip of his beer. "I'm ready."

THE STREETS WERE silent as Charlie walked home from the boathouse. She'd decided to leave her truck behind, knowing that the exercise and the time to think would give her at least a shot at sleeping.

A soft breeze rustled the trees above her head, the old streetlamps creating strange shadows on the sidewalk in front of her. Though it was late August, she could feel autumn in the air. It was waiting, just a few weeks away, ready to begin turning the trees and chilling the air and making her favorite season of the year come alive again. It would be nice to share it all with someone new.

Since walking out on Danny, she hadn't seriously considered getting involved with a man again. There had been a couple possibilities, but neither of them seemed worth the effort it would take. And there just hadn't been any chemistry.

But Ronan was different. There was something about him that promised excitement and passion and time together that was new and real and special. She felt a tremor course through her body and Charlie rubbed her arms against the goose bumps that prickled her skin.

"Charlotte? Charlotte Sibley, is that you?"

Charlie squinted into the dark and saw a shadowy figure approach with a familiar little dog trotting at her side. Leticia Trowbridge was Sibleyville's chief matchmaker. Ever since the spell was cast, extra help was needed to introduce eligible bachelors to the potential brides and vice versa. The Trowbridge family always provided a spinster relative to take care of the task.

Leticia visited the surrounding towns, looking for

interested mates for the residents. Charlie's mother was introduced to her father by Leticia's great-aunt, the previous matchmaker. Charlie considered turning around and walking in the opposite direction. But Lettie was as tenacious as her little terrier and ignoring her now would make her only more determined,

"Evening, Lettie."

Her little Westie pranced along at her side and Charlie bent down to pet the dog. "Hello, Poppy. How are you tonight?"

"She has a sore paw," Lettie said. "I think she might have stepped on a piece of glass on our morning walk. I'm glad I ran into you, Charlotte."

Charlie had her doubts that their meeting had happened by chance. In truth, she'd been expecting Lettie to show up all evening, ready to evaluate the new man in town, especially since he was a Quinn and sleeping at the Sibley boathouse.

No doubt she knew of Ronan Quinn's arrival just minutes after it happened. Maxine at the visitor's center had Lettie on speed dial. She'd probably already done a background check, a credit check and a Google search, preparing a file that would rival those of the Secret Service.

"I'm just on my way home, Lettie. I've had a really long day."

"I know! And that's exactly what I wanted to talk to you about. I hear we have a new man in town. And he's single and handsome and will be working for you."

"All of that is correct," she said. "And he's a Quinn."

"You know what this means, don't you?"

Charlie sighed and ran her fingers through her wind-blown hair. "I really don't think he's going to want to be set up on any dates, Lettie. He's only here for six weeks and then he's heading back to Seattle. So he won't have time to date. You can ask him, but I think he'll agree."

"I'm not thinking of him for my other clients. I'm thinking of him for you, Charlotte."

"Me?" Charlie shook her head. "No, no, no. He's my employee. You are not going to bother him with any of your manipulations. Especially if they're on my behalf. I'm not interested in getting married."

"Don't you understand, Charlotte? If you fall in love with this man and marry him, the curse will be broken. He's a Quinn, you're a Sibley. It's meant to be. After all these years, the marriage that Bridie wanted can happen."

"Shhh! Lettie, please. Don't start with this. I'm not interested in marrying Ronan. We don't even know each other. Besides, he lives in Seattle."

Lettie wagged her finger at Charlie. "Let me be very clear here, Charlotte. The entire town is depending on you. We've lived with this curse for far too long. And I've been thinking about retiring to Florida for the last three years only I've been stuck here trying to fix people up so that at least a few of our citizens can find a happily-ever-after. I'm tired. I want to spend my days playing shuffleboard and my nights playing canasta with my sister, Prudy."

What was she supposed to say? If Ronan got wind of Lettie's plans, he'd be on the next bus out of town. "How many people have you told about this?" Charlie asked.

"No one. I wanted to talk to you first."

"All right. I want to keep it that way. There's no use getting the whole town all excited about something that might never happen."

Charlie knew she'd need to buy herself some time. If she could convince Lettie to keep her plans to herself, maybe she might manage to save herself some embarrassment. After all, she had no intention of marrying Ronan Quinn! Maybe she'd fool around a little with him, but in six weeks, he'd return to Seattle and she'd go on with her life in Sibleyville.

"I'm going to need all the advice you can give me. But you cannot tell my mother about this. We're going to have to meet secretly. I'll let you know how things are going, you can tell me what I need to do to close the deal."

Lettie took a moment to mull over this request before she nodded. "All right. But first, tell me everything you know about him. I need to know exactly what we're up against."

"This is going to have to wait until tomorrow. Maybe I could stop by your house and we could talk?"

"Fine," Lettie said. She drew Charlie into a fierce hug. "We're going to do this together. We're going to make him fall madly in love with you and then we're going to break this horrid curse. I'm going to be the Trowbridge that brings love back to Sibleyville." She giggled softly and started off down the street, Poppy beside her. "I may just write a book about it."

As if she wasn't having enough trouble maintaining her composure around Ronan, now she'd have Lettie looking over her shoulder, questioning her every move. Charlie always knew that when it came time to find a man, she'd find one on her own, without outside help. After all, she really didn't believe in the curse.

She drew a deep breath of the night air, the scent of salt drifting up from the river. As she approached her parents' house, she noticed that it was ablaze with light. It looked like everyone was still up.

She slowly climbed the front steps, then noticed her mother, sitting on the porch swing, a cool drink in her hand. Charlie wandered over and sat down beside her. They rocked back and forth for a long time, neither one of them saying anything.

"Dinner was good," Charlie said.

Her mother took her hand and gave it a pat. "You're a sweet daughter," she said. "But I don't need you to lie to me. It was pretty awful. I'm just sorry that your new friend had to suffer through it."

Charlie wrapped her arm around her mother's and rested her head on her shoulder. "He didn't mind. We had oysters later."

"He seems like a nice young man."

"Yes, mother, he is a very nice young man." Her mind flashed back to the kisses they'd shared, to the feel of his hands on her body, to the wild sensations that raced through her at his touch. He was also a very bad boy.

"Handsome, too."

"Ummmm-hmmmm."

"How long before you think Lettie will come calling?"

"She met me on the street on my way home. She thinks we should get married and that will break the curse." Charlie drew back. "You and daddy met through the matchmaker, didn't you?"

"Well, not really. We knew each other before that. She just suggested that we give it a go. And we did. I liked him as much the second time I met him as I did the first. What girl wouldn't love him?"

"I'm not sure I want to fall in love," Charlie said.

"Why not?"

"I can't imagine wanting to spend my whole entire life with the same person."

"That's your problem, Charlotte. You can't imagine it. When the right man comes along, it doesn't require any thought or imagination. You'll just know and it will be right."

"You're very smart," Charlie teased.

"Did I ever tell you how glad we are to have you home? I don't know what we'd do without you now that your dad is laid up."

"I'm happy to help, Mom. I like working the farm."

"But if I ever get the sense that you're just hiding out here, to avoid making the difficult choices, I'm going to have to kick you right back out of the nest. You need to go out into the world and make your dreams come true. And if it doesn't happen the first time, then you keep trying until it does happen."

Charlie kissed her mother's cheek. "Yes, Mom." She stood up. "I need a long, hot shower and then I'm going to bed."

"You're going to have a hard day at work tomorrow," he mother said.

"Yes, I am."

"Spending all that time and energy trying not to fall for Ronan Quinn. I suspect it will be exhausting."

It already was, Charlie thought to herself.

FOR THE FIRST time in four days, Ronan had gotten a full night's sleep. No more uncomfortable bus seats or noisy children or bumpy highways. He now had the luxury of a lovely queen size bed in an apartment overlooking the water.

He'd turned off the air-conditioning, thrown open the window and drifted off to the sounds of the river. But his internal clock, reset during his bus drive, woke him in time to see the sun just peeking over the horizon.

Ronan crawled out of bed, wearing only his boxers, and rubbed his arms against the damp chill in the air. The kitchen had basic supplies and after a quick search, he found coffee, filters and the coffee maker. By the time the coffee was filling the pot, he was waiting with a mug.

Wisps of steam drifted up from the mug as he stepped out onto the terrace. The commercial boats that tied up along the docks in Sibleyville were already up and running. Though he was about to start his first day of work at the Mistry Bay Oyster Farm, Ronan wasn't thinking about the job. His mind was firmly fixed on his boss.

He'd never had close friends. When he needed someone's advice or company, he always relied on his brothers. And when it came to women, he'd always held them at a careful distance. But with Charlotte Sibley, Ronan felt like he could have both—a friend and a lover. That had never happened before and he wasn't sure how to handle it.

Should they solidify their friendship first and then indulge in physical pleasures? Or would the physical intimacies make for a deeper friendship. Ronan was at a loss when it came to his next step. All he knew was that he needed to spend more time with Charlie. A lot more time.

He heard a knock at the front door of the apartment and Ronan strode back inside and grabbed a pair of jeans, tugging them on before he continued to the door. When he opened it, the object of his early morning fantasies was standing in the hallway, her hair still damp from her shower. She clutched a bag in her hand and had tucked a thermos under her arm.

"Morning," she said, stepping inside. "Did you sleep well?"

"Like a baby," Ronan said, grinning at her. "How about you?"

"Not a wink," she muttered. She quickly turned to face him. "Listen, we need to set some ground rules. I was up all last night just thinking about kissing you and—"

"You were?" Ronan slipped his arms around her waist. "What were you thinking about?"

She backed away from him and walked to the table. "If we're going to…you know…mess around, then we need to do it outside of work. I can't focus on the job if all I'm thinking about is you." She paused and glanced up at him. "Can we do that?"

"Sure," he said.

She released a tightly held breath and nodded. "All right. Then grab a shirt. We'll get you a pair of waders and some boots. Do you have a sweater or a jacket?"

"Nothing I can wear on a boat," he said.

"Come on, then," Charlie said. "I'll get you what you need."

Five minutes later, they were downstairs, rummaging through his wardrobe choices. When he'd been outfitted in a fleece jacket, gloves, rubber waders and boots, they headed out to the dock. Charlie jumped into the skiff and pointed to the stern line. "Grab that one," she said as she crawled to the bow.

He did as he was told, but when it came time to jump into the boat, Ronan hesitated. She looked up at him. "Take your time," she said.

"Right." He nodded, then began to slowly pace back and forth on the pier. "I don't know why this is giving me a problem. I think the water just looks…darker."

She reached into the bag she'd carried and pulled out a donut. "Bearclaw?" she asked.

Ronan shook his head. Right now, anything he ate was guaranteed to come right back up again. "Baby steps," he murmured.

She nodded and took a bite, slowly chewing as she watched him from the boat. Cursing softly, he drew a deep breath and jumped into the skiff. His head slammed in his chest and he felt a familiar rush of panic.

But he wasn't going to let it overwhelm him. "All right," he murmured. "Let's go."

True to their arrangement, she was keeping everything very professional, including her attitude toward him. He needed a kiss, a touch, anything to distract his thoughts. He knew if he pulled her into his arms, she'd relent and respond. But he could certainly control his impulses—at least for the next eight to ten hours.

His thoughts, however, were an entirely different matter. She couldn't keep him from enjoying a vivid fantasy during the workday. And though baggy waders and faded fleece jacket weren't the height of sexy attire, Ronan didn't care. He liked the way she looked, all tough and ready to meet the elements.

As she maneuvered away from the dock and into the river, he felt a sliver of fear, but focused his mind on a careful study of her features, outlined by the soft light of the sunrise.

"Here," she said, stepping away. "Take the wheel. Just stay to the center of the channel."

He did as ordered, sliding into the seat behind the controls. Charlie opened the thermos, then grabbed a pair of mugs from a locker beneath her seat. She handed him a mug, the poured one for herself.

"Thanks," he said. "Maybe I should try one of those donuts. It might settle my stomach."

She opened the bag and held it out to him. "Bearclaw. Breakfast of champions."

Ronan chuckled. He set the mug on a nearby ledge and grabbed the pastry, taking a huge bite. "Oh, God, it's still warm."

She nodded as she bit into her breakfast. "Yeah. You can't go wrong. There's a bakery just down the street from the boathouse. They open at five a.m. Sunrise is at six these days, so there's always something coming out of the oven."

He stared at her for a long moment, then turned to look out over the water. "This is going to be pretty tricky," he said.

"Just follow the buoys," she said. "Keep the red on your left and the green on your right as we're going out to sea. And then, the opposite as we're coming in. Red on the left, going on the right, returning. Just remember that."

"That's not what I was talking about," Ronan said.

"What were you talking about?"

"I was thinking about how difficult it would be to keep from kissing you. You look beautiful this morning," he said.

Charlie laughed, the sound echoing over the water and through the early morning mist. "Oh, please."

"You do. I really like the outfit. I know it sounds crazy, but it's taking all my strength not to grab you and have my way with you."

"Eat your bearclaw," she said with a coy smile. "And you are full of it, by the way. Any man who thinks this is sexy is sick, sick, sick."

Maybe that was it, Ronan mused. Maybe this was some kind of physical malady that would disappear with a few days rest. Whenever he was close to her, he did feel a little feverish.

"So, boss, what are we doing today?"

"We're going to stop by the nursery and pick up some crates of seed oysters and then we're going to plant them in the bay."

"How do we do that?"

"It's a very complicated technique," she said. "We put on our snorkel gear and jump in the water and take each little oyster and plant it in a perfect row on the bottom of the bay."

"Really?"

"No. Weren't you listening last night? I think I explained it."

Ronan groaned. "I had other things on my mind. Maybe you should go over it again."

She laughed at him and the sound was sweet and musical. He'd never known any woman who could make him smile as much as Charlie could. Nothing ever seemed to bother her. Maybe he'd just dated the wrong women, Ronan thought to himself, somber, depressing women who never smiled or laughed. Was this what a relationship was supposed to be like—light and teasing and fun?

"Wait, let me see if I can find my notes," Ronan said. "I was taking notes, wasn't I?"

"All right, I'll explain once more, but pay attention."

His gaze skimmed her pretty features and he nodded.

"You're going to carefully take a shovel full of oysters and you're going to toss them over the side as I'm driving the boat very slowly over the beds. They're going to sink to the bottom and stay there for a few years, until we're ready to harvest them. We have two more days of planting, then we have to start harvesting some of the mature beds."

"How do you make sure you get the oysters that are ready?"

"We plant the bay in sections. This season we'll harvest the section that we planted a few years ago."

He poked at his forehead with his gloved finger. "Got it. I won't forget that."

She reached over and ruffled his hair. It was such an innocent gesture, but it said everything about the two of them. After only a day, they were completely comfortable with each other. He didn't have to think about what he said before he said it. She was so open and honest, not the kind of girl who played games.

She looked out over the water, then pointed to one of the red buoys. "Watch out," she warned.

He changed direction, then took another bite of his bearclaw. Right now, Ronan couldn't imagine wanting to be any other place in the world. For a guy who never felt like he belonged, this was exactly where he needed to be for the moment. And maybe for longer than that.

4

THE AFTERNOON SUN beat down on the skiff and Charlie slowly maneuvered the boat along a line running parallel to the shore. Ronan stood in the open bow, his jacket and shirt discarded, his tanned body gleaming with perspiration.

He'd started the day uneasy about being on the water. Charlie had seen the look of panic in his eyes whenever she caught him looking down into the dark water. But she'd advised him to keep his eyes on the horizon and that seemed to calm his fears.

Though she'd barely known him a day, she couldn't help but wonder about the complex man who stood before her. He seemed invincible, yet flawed. Strong, yet sensitive. Engaged yet indifferent in many ways. Though he admitted that he felt most comfortable when he was alone, she'd found him to be a clever conversationalist, when he felt like talking.

Ronan gently scooped up a shovel full of seed oysters and then, in a wide sweeping motion, tossed them into the water. Charlie had showed him the technique earlier and it had taken him only a few tries before he understood what she needed.

She watched the play of muscle across his back and a tiny shiver of desire skittered through her. If this was what she'd have to put up with every day, then keeping her hands off of Ronan was going to be nearly impossible. She couldn't keep her eyes off him, either. He was standing there, right in front of her, like some beautiful statue made of flesh and bone instead of cold marble.

"What do you have left up there?" she called as she brought the boat around. Her voice wavered slightly and she cleared her throat.

An image flashed in her mind and she brushed it aside. If her mind insisted on removing the rest of his clothes, then she had no choice but to think about other things. "Oysters," she muttered to herself. "Oysters."

"Maybe five or six more tosses," he called.

"Let me go down to the south end. We can push that a little further out, I think." She watched her depth finder as she navigated to the spot.

Buoys marked off the different areas of the bay and the oysters were scattered in carefully drawn areas, chosen for optimum growing conditions. Charlie knew the bay like the back of her hand, the shoreline, the depths, the muddy flats and the spots where the current ran strong.

"How much of this water is yours?" Ronan asked, bracing his arm on the shovel handle.

"None of it is ours. We lease it from the state. We own the land on Kepley Pond where the hatchery is, but none of this."

Charlie found the spot she wanted and called to him and Ronan finished the last of the seed oysters. After setting the shovel down, he made his way back to Charlie, flopping down on the seat next to her. "Do we have another load to do?"

They'd gone back to the hatchery twice already that day. "Nope. We're finished."

He raised his hands above his head and shouted. "All right! I survived." Ronan turned to her and slipped his arm around her shoulder, pulling her into a long, deep kiss. When he drew back, he had a devilish smile on his face. "Wait. Did I jump the gun? Do I have to wait until we dock at the boathouse?"

"No," she said. "Work is officially over. You did well. How do you feel?"

"Exhausted. There were times when I just wanted off this boat, but I tried to focus on the job and that helped." He kissed her again, tossing off his gloves so he could cup her face in his hands. "Thanks for being so patient with me. Can we drive home closer to the shore?"

"It'll take us longer," she said.

"I'm good with that."

He kissed her again, so sweet and so gentle, yet there was a raw power to his kiss that promised so much more. Charlie found it impossible to resist him. She was, after just a day, completely infatuated with the man.

She'd always considered herself a fairly sensible person when it came to romance. With Danny, everything had been simple and straight-forward. But this romance was completely the opposite, a maelstrom of intense and uncontrollable feelings.

The urge to toss aside her inhibitions and totally surrender to Ronan was becoming more and more difficult to ignore. She wanted to laugh out loud and leap through fields of daisies and sing love songs at the top of her voice. The old Charlotte Sibley would have been mortified to caught doing anything so ridiculous. But Charlie didn't care what other people thought. The only thing she cared about was the man sitting next to her.

"What are we going to do tonight?" he murmured, his breath soft against her ear.

She smoothed her hands across his chest and drew back. "Do you want to do anything? I thought you might want to relax. You're going to be sore tomorrow."

"I'm in good shape," he said. "I won't be sore."

"You will be. Believe me, unless you make a living shoveling snow, you're going to feel it. The first time I did that job, I couldn't move for three days."

He chuckled. "That's because you're a girl," he said with a shrug.

Charlie gasped. "You did not just say that."

He winced. "Backsies," Ronan said. An odd look suddenly came over his face and he turned away.

"Backsies? What is that?"

He laughed softly. "I don't know where that came from. It was buried really deep. Twenty years deep."

"What is it?"

He turned back to her and forced a smile. "My mom used to say that. Whenever one of us would say something nasty, she'd ask if we wanted a backsie, which meant we could take it back before anyone heard it. It was her way of making us think before we spoke."

"You don't have to take it back. I knew you were teasing." She turned her gaze to meet his. "Are you all right?"

"Yeah," he said. "It was a nice memory." Ronan drew a deep breath. "Are we having dinner with your folks again?"

Charlie shook her head. "No, we don't have to."

"What cuisine is it tonight?"

"Most of the time we have normal food," she explained. "Maybe meatloaf or roasted chicken or pork chops. Mona's really a pretty decent cook. And once a month we have Thanksgiving."

"Thanksgiving?"

Charlie nodded. "My mother thinks that a meal so wonderful should be enjoyed more than once a year. So she makes a turkey and dressing and mashed potatoes and all the fixings. We eat off my great-grandmother's china and use the Sibley silver. And everyone has to be there. I think we're having Thanksgiving next week."

"That sounds pretty wonderful," he said. "We never really celebrated Thanksgiving, at least not after my folks died. My grandfather is from Ireland and he didn't quite understand the tradition."

"What are you in the mood for tonight?" she asked.

"Can we eat raw oysters and drink beer again?"

"You can. I'll order Thai food. But before we do anything, you're going to need to take a shower. You smell like oysters."

"You don't smell like a rose garden yourself," he said, hugging her close. He drew a deep breath, his face buried in her windswept hair. "Nope, no roses there."

Charlie's cellphone rang and she reached into her waders and pulled it from her jacket pocket. The caller I.D. said "Isaac." "Hey, what's up? Where are you?"

"I got a call from Uncle Jake," Isaac said. "They lost a dredging basket when the line broke so we came over to see if we could snag it. Abs and I are diving for it, but we're getting a little cold. Should we leave it and come back with scuba gear tomorrow?"

"No, let me give it a try. You're across from Palmer Cove?"

"Yep," Isaac said.

"Be there in about ten minutes." Charlie put her phone back in her pocket. "We have to give Isaac a hand. It'll only take a few minutes. Then we'll head back to the boathouse."

She turned the skiff toward the mouth of the bay and hit the throttle. From end to end, Mistry Bay was nearly forty miles long. Work crews from the farm were often on the bay at the same time, yet rarely saw each other. She found her siblings across from the cove they'd been seeding, their skiff bobbing on the water. Abby and Isaac were huddled in the boat.

Charlie maneuvered the skiff next to theirs and tied it up at the bow and stern. "How deep is it?"

"About fifteen feet," Isaac said. "I had it once, but my knot slipped. Without a mask, I couldn't really see. It's full of oysters." He looked over at Ronan. "Charlie is the best diver in the family."

Ronan stared at her, his mouth agape. "You're going to jump in the water?"

Charlie nodded. "Don't worry. I've done this lots of times."

"She sometimes harvests oysters by diving," Abby said. "She can hold her breath longer than anyone in the family. Almost two minutes."

Kicking off her rubber boots, Charlie slipped the straps of her waders over her shoulders and stepped out of them. Her jacket came next and then her jeans. When she was down to her panties and her T-shirt, she stepped to the stern of the boat.

"Wait a minute," Ronan said. "Is this really necessary? I'll buy you a new basket."

"We don't want to lose equipment." She motioned to Isaac. "Hand me the line." She wrapped the rope around her waist and knotted it, then dove over the side.

The bottom of the bay was mud and unlike sand, it didn't reflect the light. But Charlie saw the dredge right away and swam over to it. She unwrapped the line from her waist and then, taking her time, tied it through the bracket, making sure the knot was tight. She grabbed an oyster from the bottom, then kicked for the surface.

Ronan was waiting, staring over the stern with a worried expression. He held out his hand and helped her into the skiff, then wrapped his jacket around her shoulders and rubbed her back. "Are you all right?"

"Yeah." She held out the oyster to him. "I brought you a present."

"An oyster?"

"The freshest oyster you've ever eaten," she said. "Come on, I'll open it for you."

Isaac and Abby had managed to drag the basket into the boat. "What do you want to do with these?"

"Take half home to Mom. She can make oyster stew. And leave about half of them at the boathouse. Ronan needs dinner."

Isaac untied his boat from Charlie's skiff and a few seconds later, he and Abby were skimming across the water toward the main channel. Ronan stared down at her, wiping the water from her face.

"That scared the crap out of me," he said. "Don't ever do that again."

"It's not that deep. And there's nothing down there to hurt me. I'll show you. Next time we have a low tide, we'll walk out here and harvest by hand."

He frowned. "You can do that?"

She pushed up on her toes and kissed him. "You have a lot to learn about oyster farming, rookie."

Ronan growled softly and pulled her into a fierce embrace. "I think I have a lot to learn about you, Charlotte Sibley," he said, before his mouth found hers again.

A LONG HOT shower was the perfect end to a hard day at work. Ronan had never felt this pleasant kind of exhaustion after a day of working at the yachtworks. Maybe it was all the fresh air or the intense labor, but every muscle in his body had been taxed.

He'd slipped into a pair of cargo shorts and then wandered out into the kitchen. To his surprise, the refrigerator had been stocked with food and drink sometime during the day. The cupboard above the sink also held a variety of snacks. Had Charlie done this?

He found the answer on a note in a basket of fresh fruit. Penny Sibley. Charlie's mother. He grabbed a beer from the fridge and twisted it open.

His stomach growled. They'd had a quick lunch of ham sandwiches at the hatchery, but nothing since then. "Oysters," he murmured.

Somewhere in this building were the oysters Isaac and Abby had pulled out of the bay. He grabbed the front door, but as he pulled it open, he found Charlie standing on the other side.

She held a paper bag, a plastic bucket of oysters and a six-pack of beer. "Help," she said. "Grab the bag."

The scent of Thai spices drifted through the air. "I was just going to search out those oysters."

"I brought these from home," she said. "My mom had cleaned them and set them aside for you."

"She stocked my refrigerator, too," Ronan said, stepping aside so Charlie could enter.

Charlie turned to face him, her surprise etched across her beautiful face. "She did? Well, that was very nice of her. She's taken a liking to you." She set the beer on the counter, then began to unpack the Thai food from the bag. But since she'd walked in, Ronan had suddenly forgotten all about food. He was hungry for Charlie instead.

He'd spent the entire day observing her, reveling in each new detail he discovered. Unlike other women he'd known, Charlie wasn't afraid to get her hands dirty. She worked a job that took strength and patience and insight. Her body wasn't toned by a trainer, but by hard, physical work. Her day began at dawn and ended when the work was done. She was a remarkable woman.

Ronan stood behind her and wrapped his arms around her waist. She smelled like citrus. He drew a deep breath and closed his eyes. "Leave the food," he said.

"You're not hungry?"

Ronan grabbed the bucket of oysters and put them in the fridge, then turned her around to face him. He grabbed her waist and set her on the edge of the counter. "God, you smell good. And you're so damn pretty."

"This is going to get out of hand," she warned, smoothing his hair away from his forehead. "You can't keep telling me I'm pretty. And you have to stop smelling my hair."

"Is that so bad? We managed to keep our hands off each other all day today."

With a groan, Charlie pulled him into a kiss. But this time, Ronan felt that the kiss was just a prelude to something more.

She ran her hands over his naked chest, her palms warm against his skin, her fingernails raking across his shoulders. It had been awhile since he'd been touched like this and Ronan felt an instant response. He stepped between her legs, wrapping them around his waist.

Ronan lost himself in the taste of her mouth, in the feel of her caress on his body. In one way, they were still strangers, unaware of the pleasures they could bring each other. But in just one day, he felt as if he knew her better than he'd ever known any another woman.

Ronan reached for the front of her shirt and slowly

brushed it over her shoulders, revealing the pretty camisole beneath. His lips traced a path from her mouth to her neck, the intoxicating scent of her skin making his body pulse with need.

He wanted to rush, to tear off their clothes and bury himself in her warmth. He needed to know how far she'd go. This wasn't some one-night stand, fueled by too many drinks and a need for release.

He'd found a woman who was more than just a beautiful face and a willing and warm body. He liked Charlie. He felt the need to protect her from anything that might hurt her. Ronan knew it the moment she'd jumped off the boat to retrieve that dredging basket. She was clever and resourceful—and fearless.

Ronan slipped his hands beneath her backside and picked her up, carrying her into the bedroom. He laid her on the bed and stretched out above her, their mouths still lost in a passionate kiss. Charlie pulled him down on top of her, wriggling until his hips fit perfectly against hers.

"I thought you were hungry," she murmured.

"There are some things more important than food," Ronan replied. He rolled to his side and drew back, taking in the perfect details of her face.

When he smoothed her hair out of her eyes, she looked up at him. "Don't stop," she murmured.

Ronan shrugged. "I won't. It feels too good."

Her lips curled into a smile and she nodded. "I've only ever been with one man," she said. "And we started dating when we were in high school. I'm not sure I know how to do this. Like a grown-up."

He ran his hand along her hip and slid it beneath her camisole. "There's no instruction book, Charlie," he said. "And they don't teach this in school. We just have to figure it out as we go along."

"Then tell me how to start," she said.

"We've already started," he said. Ronan pulled hcr into another kiss, his hand slipping beneath her shirt. He found the silky fabric of her bra and gently pulled it aside, cupping the soft flesh of her breast in his hand.

Charlie moaned softly as his thumb grazed her nipple. Her lips were parted slightly and her eyes were closed. Pleasure suffused her expression and she shifted beside him, arching into his touch.

In the end, it was enough to just touch her and kiss her. Though Ronan would have been happy to strip off their clothes and make love to her, he was willing to leave that for another time. He knew what he wanted and it was pretty clear that Charlie wanted the same.

The day had been long and busy for both of them and as they continued to kiss and touch each other, Ronan felt exhaustion suffusing his body. He yawned, then quickly covered his mouth. "That wasn't you," he murmured.

"Close your eyes," she said. "Let's just lie here for a few minutes and wait for our second wind."

"Are you tired, too?"

"Hmmm. I had to do my work and admire you at the same time. That takes a lot out of a girl." She nuzzled her face into his chest. "You looked really nice in those waders. Especially when you took your shirt off."

"And here I thought you were concentrating on your navigation."

"I could do that job in my sleep."

"I like it," Ronan said. "The work. I really do."

She pushed up on her elbow. "Yeah?"

"It's exhausting, but there's something about it that makes it satisfying. You're growing something that people can eat. Something really good to eat. I build yachts for rich people. People who really don't need yachts."

"But they're really beautiful yachts," she said.

"How do you know?"

"Lettie Trowbridge checked you out on Google and she left me a file with all sorts of pictures. I really liked the one you built for that senator from Oregon."

"Really? That was one of my favorites, too." He paused. "Who is Lettie Trowbridge?"

"The town busybody," Charlie said. "Everyone is talking about you. Because you're a Quinn."

"Maybe she was just watching out for you and your family. That's what's nice about a small town. Everyone takes care of everyone else."

"No," Charlie said, shaking her head. "Everyone is in everyone else's business. Do you want to know the truth about Lettie's motives? And the reason that my mother filled your refrigerator? They want you to stay. They want you to marry me so the curse will be broken. They're going to do everything they can to make me and Sibleyville look like paradise on earth. My mother even cleaned those oysters for you. She never cleans oysters."

The words had just tumbled out. He smoothed his

fingers along her jaw line. "I'm thinking you might want a backsie on that whole last rant."

Charlie grew silent, her brow furrowed, her lips pursed. "Okay. Pretend you didn't hear that."

Ronan leaned over her, teasing at the crease between her lips with his tongue. "They really want me to marry you?"

"If a Sibley marries a Quinn, it will break the curse. Lettie wants to retire to Florida. Did I tell you that she's the town matchmaker? If she can't make a match between the two of us, she's going to hook you up with some other girl in town. She has a whole list of Sibley descendants just waiting."

Ronan pressed his finger to her lips. "Shh. Don't let it bother you. I'm sure I can fight them off. I'll just tell them there's only one Sibley I'm interested in."

She sighed softly as she curled into his body. Maybe this was paradise on earth, Ronan thought, drawing her closer.

If it wasn't, it sure came close.

CHARLIE OPENED HER eyes. The room was dark and for a moment, she didn't know where she was. When the body beside her moved, she drew in a sharp breath. But then she remembered she was with Ronan. They'd fallen asleep in his bed.

What time was it? She glanced over her shoulder and squinted at the bedside table. It was just past two in the morning. They'd been asleep for six hours. Charlie sat up and ran her fingers through her hair. She ought to get up and go home, but she had to be up again in about four hours for work.

She bent over and touched her lips to his shoulder. He was lying on his stomach, sprawled across the bed, his breathing deep and even. "Ronan. Ronan, wake up." She gave him a shake and he groaned.

Ronan rolled to his side, then sat up. "We fell asleep. What time is it?"

"Past two. I have to go."

He reached out and rested his hand on her shoulder, his fingers tangling in her hair. "No," he said.

Charlie leaned into him and dropped a kiss on his lips. But he pulled her close again and drew her into a deeper, more desperate kiss. A groan slipped from her throat and she felt her resolve waver.

She'd lost her ability to resist. She'd known this man for two days and she was already in full surrender mode. Even though her instincts told her to be careful, the feelings racing through her body told her otherwise.

They'd found each other in this crazy, loveless town and he was sweet and sexy and everything she might want in a lover. She didn't care that he'd be gone in six weeks. She didn't care that they barely knew each other. Who knew when she'd have another chance like this? She'd been living in Sibleyville for almost a year and handsome, eligible men had been nonexistent.

Charlie reached for the hem of her camisole and pulled it up, breaking their kiss only to draw it over her head. She'd made her intentions clear, but it was up to Ronan to make the next move. He grabbed her hand and helped her off the bed and when they stood beside it, he cupped her face in his hands and pressed his forehead to hers.

"I can wait," he murmured. "This doesn't have to happen tonight."

"No," Charlie said, her voice wavering. "I can't wait." She unzipped her jeans and slid them over her hips, then kicked them aside. She was twenty-five years old and she'd known the touch of just one man. There were passions inside of her, raw and unfamiliar, that she wanted to explore.

Charlie took his hand and placed it on her breast. He drew a deep breath, his gaze still fixed on hers. Slowly, his touch drifted over the swell of flesh. She closed her eyes as he worked at the clasp of her bra and when it fell away, she knew that they'd reached the point of no return.

She'd always known that another man would come into her life, but when she'd pictured the intimate moments, Charlie had always felt a bit of hesitation. Would she know what to do? Would she please him?

With Ronan, there was no fear or doubt. He liked her exactly the way she was. Emboldened to act, she reached for the waistband of his cargo shorts and unbuttoned them. Only after they fell to his feet did she realize that he wasn't wearing boxers.

"Sorry," he murmured.

She reached out and smoothed her hand along his stiff shaft. He was hard and ready and more beautiful than she'd ever imagined. Charlie felt like she was living in the middle of a fantasy, every sensation more overwhelming than the last, making it impossible to think.

But she didn't need to think. She just needed to act. Drawing a ragged breath, she wrapped her fingers around him. Ronan groaned as she began to stroke him. But he wasn't content to let her control the pace of the seduction.

He grabbed her waist and pulled her over to the bed and when she was stretched out in front of him, he drew her panties down her legs and tossed them aside.

Suddenly, his touch was everywhere, his lips exploring her body, his hands gently moving over her curves and angles. Wave after wave of exquisite sensation washed over her with every new spot that he found. The base of her neck, the small of her back, the soft skin behind each knee.

Charlie felt like some erotic goddess, not an inexperienced 25-year old oyster farmer. Every intimacy was a revelation, a beautiful discovery. She'd never felt such intense desire. And when Ronan gently parted her thighs and kissed the damp folds between her legs, the need in her exploded.

Her fingers clutched the sheets as his tongue flicked at her sex. She wanted to stop, to enjoy the foreplay, but her body was at the mercy of his tongue. Like a rogue wave, her orgasm built, growing more powerful with each moment that passed. Pleasure had become a giant wall of water—she felt it surround her, overwhelm her, steal her breath from her lungs.

And then, the wave broke, dissolving in a rush around her. Charlie's body shuddered uncontrollably and she cried out, twisting beneath his assault.

It seemed to last forever, the exquisite pleasure making her fingers and toes tingle. As her pulse slowed and her breath returned, she opened her eyes. He was lying on his back, a satisfied smile on his face.

"What?" she said, resting her hand on his head.

"Oops," he said.

She pushed up on her elbows. "What?"

"I don't think that's happened to me since the first time a girl touched me." He pointed to a wet spot on the bedspread. "I kind of lost control. You were just so…incredible"

Charlie laughed. "I was incredible?"

"Ummm."

"Oops," she said. "I'd offer you a backsie on that, but I don't think that would work."

He growled softly as he crawled up beside her. "There's plenty more where that came from," he said. "Just give me a few minutes."

Charlie swung her legs off the bed. "I know exactly what you need." She walked out into the kitchen and found her shirt, then pulled it on over her naked body. Ronan followed her, the sheet wrapped around his waist.

"What are you doing?"

"Getting us something to eat. I'm starving and you were starving before you dragged me off to bed." She grabbed the bucket of fresh oysters from the refrigerator, then found an oyster knife in the drawer. "Do you think you can handle that without cutting a major artery?"

"Show me how to do it again."

Charlie grabbed a kitchen towel and set it down on the granite peninsula. "Hold it like this, stick the knife into the joint and then just twist." They oyster popped open and she cut out the meat and handed him the shell.

Ronan slurped the oyster down and sighed. "Perfect."

She grabbed a couple of plates and opened the cartons of Thai food. The noodles were cold, but Charlie liked them that way. She dumped some shrimp pad thai onto a plate and sat down across the counter from Ronan.

"Good food and great sex," Ronan said. "What more do I need?"

"Sleep," she said. "We have to be up for work in about three and a half hours."

He groaned, then held out a shucked oyster. She tipped her head back as he fed it to her, the delicacy sliding down her throat. "Umm," she said. "That was a good one."

"I'm kind of looking forward to work," he said as he continued to shuck the oysters. "I had fun yesterday. It was hard work, but it was nice to be outside. And I never thought I'd like being on the water, but…I think I'm going to be all right. It's going to take some time, but I felt like I could breathe out there."

"There are oyster farms in the Pacific Northwest," Charlie said. "When you go home, maybe you could take a job there. Or start your own oyster farm."

He slurped another oyster, then shrugged. "Or maybe I won't go home at all," he said. "Maybe I'll stay here."

Her heart stopped for a moment and then Charlie realized she must have heard him wrong. What exactly was he saying? He couldn't know Sibleyville well enough to make that kind of decision. Was he thinking about staying because of her? "If you're really interested in oyster farming, I could teach you all I know," she said. "There might be some differences out west, but there shouldn't be many."

"I'd like to learn more," he said. "But only during work hours. The rest of my time, I want to spend learning everything I can about you."

She shook her head. "There's not that much to know," Charlie said.

"I'll tell you something about you that you don't know," he said.

She regarded him with a dubious look. "All right."

"You don't have any idea how amazing you are," he said. "I've known a lot of women and not one of them as been as honest and direct as you. Everything that you say is real and true and I don't have to try to figure out what you really mean. You don't play any silly games."

"What kind of women have you been dating?" she asked.

"The wrong kind," he said.

"I don't know how to be that kind of woman," Charlie said. "I never learned. I mean, I'm a decent actress, so I can pretend, but—"

"No, don't do that," Ronan said. "You'd be like every other woman I've known." She rose up and leaned over the counter and he gave her another oyster, then wiped her bottom lip with his thumb. "I never expected you."

"I didn't expect you, either."

"I have no idea where this is going to go."

She shrugged. "Neither do I. But it's going to be fun finding out, don't you think?"

Ronan nodded. "So, are we going to do this every night? Is this going to cause problems with your family?"

"I ran away to New York with my high school boyfriend when I was eighteen. I'm pretty much considered a sexual rebel around Sibleyville." She held out a forkful of noodles and he grabbed the bite. "Besides, everyone in town wants us to get married so we'll break the curse. Believe me, they'll be more than happy that we're sleeping together."

He sent her a wicked grin. "All right then. I think it's our civic duty to make the citizens of Sibleyville happy." Ronan slid off the stool and slowly circled the counter. "I think I'm ready to continue now."

"I'm still eating," she teased.

He took the carton from Charlie's hand and set it down, then drew her along to the bedroom. "We only have three hours until we have to be up for work. I think we need to get started right now."

Charlie slipped out of his grasp and ran to the bedroom, then jumped into the center of the bed. He followed her, throwing the sheet off at the last minute.

He retrieved a box of condoms from his bag, then pulled her along with him as they tumbled onto the mattress. Ronan settled himself between her legs and caught her in a long and passionate kiss, his tongue teasing at hers, his hands skimming over her body.

But Charlie didn't want to waste time on foreplay. She grabbed the box and pulled out a packet. Ronan moaned softly as she sheathed him, his shaft hard and ready again.

Charlie wasn't prepared for what happened next. As he slowly entered her, a rush of emotion overwhelmed her and she realized that what she was about to share with him would probably change her life.

She'd never forget this man or the pleasure that he'd brought into her world in such a short time. Before he'd arrived, she'd been marking the days, drifting in a routine that was safe but certainly not satisfying.

Ronan slowly buried himself inside her, his lips grazing hers as he bent closer. Charlie held her breath until he could go no further, then let a soft moan escape. As he began to move, she found it difficult to focus on anything but the swirl of sensations coursing through her body.

It had been years since she'd felt this way, like a woman—like a sexy, desirable woman. In truth, maybe she'd never felt this way. And she didn't care how long the affair lasted. A day or a month, it didn't matter. For as long as Ronan wanted her, she would find her way into his bed.

5

RONAN JUMPED OUT of the skiff as Charlie maneuvered it alongside the dock. She grabbed the stern line and quickly knotted it around the cleat, then hurried to the stern to pull that line tight.

They'd been working together for a week and a half and now operated as a finely tuned team. They'd moved from seeding the oyster beds to harvesting, along with three other teams. Their mornings were spent pulling the lantern baskets full of harvested oysters from a spot in the bay.

Those oysters had been sorted and put in the baskets a few days before, then left in free flowing water in order to purge them of grit. After the lantern baskets were delivered to the boathouse for cleaning, packaging and shipping, Charlie and Ronan headed back out to harvest oysters from the bottom, pulling up dredge baskets full of the lumpy shells and sorting them into the lantern baskets.

He hadn't grown tired of the work. In fact, Charlie had been teaching him all about the farm and he was beginning to fall into the easy rhythms and routines. He glanced down at his work partner and smiled.

She was dressed in the typical uniform, rubber boots, chest-high waders, a long-sleeved T-shirt and heavy gloves. Today, she wore a battered Red Sox cap on her head that shaded her eyes from the sun, and her hair, tangled by the salty wind, peeked out from beneath the cap.

She'd never looked more beautiful, he thought to himself. In the past, Ronan had always entered a relationship with a woman knowing full well that it would come to an end within a month. Women had become a commodity and his romantic life had been short on romance and high on turnover.

Was it any wonder that he'd missed out on something like this? Had there been a woman in his past like Charlotte Sibley had? She was bright light, sunshine pouring into the dark corners of his soul.

Ronan jumped back down into the boat and grabbed Charlie, pulling her into a long kiss. "What do you say we get ourselves all dressed up and go out this evening? It's Friday night."

Charlie's eyebrow shot up. "You want to take me on a date?"

"Yeah. There must be somewhere we could go. The movies? Maybe a nice restaurant. I got paid yesterday. And the money is burning a hole in my waders."

"So first, we jump into bed and then we start dating." She grinned. "It didn't work for me the other way around so I guess we could give it a shot."

"All right. I'll make the plans." But before he could

go on, Ronan heard a scream from the wharf above them.

"Charlotte Sibley! Charlotte Sibley, I need youuuuuuu!"

Charlie peeked over Ronan's shoulder and groaned. "Oh, no. Lettie Trowbridge. If you get the lines, I think we should be able to make our escape before she gets down here."

"What does she want?" Ronan asked. He turned around when he heard the clomp of footsteps on the wooden stairs.

"Who knows. She may want an update on our sex life. Or she may want to know whether I read the books she dropped off at my parents' house."

"What kind of books?"

"How To Please Your Man. Catch Your Perfect Guy In Thirty Days. Make Love Like A Porn Star."

"That last one sounds good."

"Charlotte! Hellooo! Charlotte!"

Pasting a smile on her face, Charlie stepped out from behind Ronan and jumped up onto the dock. Lettie was an elderly woman with a shock of white hair that looked like it had been combed with a rake. She wore a blouse with flowers bigger than her head and carried a huge purse that hung from her shoulder.

"Hello," she said, sending him a warm smile. "You must be the Quinn. I've seen you around town, but we haven't officially met." She held out her hand. "Leticia Trowbridge. Sibleyville's official matchmaker." She reached into her purse and pulled out a camera then snapped a quick picture of him.

"Oh, look at that. Rugged. Handsome. The scruffy beard will have all the women swooning." She snapped another picture. "I'd love to get one after you've had a chance to clean up a bit."

"Lettie, is there something I can help you with? You came here looking for me, didn't you?"

The older woman slapped her forehead. "Yes! I did. I am in dire need of your help, Charlotte. As you know, I'm the head of the entertainment and culture committee for the Sibleyville Bicentennial Celebration which will begin two weeks from today. And I'm sure you've heard that we're doing a wonderful theatrical production called 'The Curse of Bridie Quinn.' It's a Romeo and Juliet tale of Edward Sibley and Moira Quinn. Only in this version, they get married."

"You can't change history," Charlie said.

"Of course I can. The whole last part of the play takes place in a dream. At the end, Edward wakes up and stares longingly out to sea. It's very tragic." She paused for a moment as if she'd forgotten her train of thought, then drew another breath. "The reason I've come is that we've lost our Moira. Ruth Ann Robinson tripped over her cat and broke her ankle. There's no way she'll be able to go on. Anyway, everyone in town thought that you'd be an excellent replacement since you were a professional actress at one time."

Ronan grabbed the lunch pail from the skiff and the extra clothes, then jumped onto the dock. "I'm going to head up to the apartment," he said.

"No, no, don't leave," Lettie said. "I understand you know you're way around a hammer and a saw. We could use your help with sets. It would mean a lot to everyone here in town."

"I really don't think I'll have time," he said.

"And I won't either, Lettie."

"But you could memorize everything quickly. You wouldn't have to come to rehearsal until the week after next. I'm sure you'll be able to learn the staging quickly. Please say you'll consider it."

Charlie glanced over at Ronan, shaking her head. "If you don't find anyone else to take the part, then I might consider it. But you should keep looking."

"Lovely," Lettie said. She pulled a sheaf of papers from her bag. "This is the script. Just give it a look. I'd love your input." She turned to Ronan. "And as for you, Mr. Quinn, I'll be keeping my eye on you."

With that, Leticia Trowbridge hurried off the dock, her hair blowing in the late afternoon breeze. Charlie grabbed Ronan's arm and leaned against him.

"I'd love to see you on stage," he murmured.

She gave him a playful slap with the script. "No way."

"I could help you memorize your lines," he said.

"You're going to take me out tonight," she said. "But first, I'm going to go home and take a nice long bath."

"Come on, then." He held her hand as they walked back to the boathouse. The Fed Ex truck was parked outside and the girls from the shipping department were helping to load the boxes of oysters and dry ice. One of the women stopped Charlie to discuss a problem with the previous day's shipments, so Ronan continued on to the boathouse. He stripped out of his boots and waders, then walked up to the apartment in his stocking feet.

As he passed the office, he noticed Charlie's mother, sitting at a desk with a ledger in front of her, her reading glasses perched on the end of her nose. She looked up as he neared and smiled.

"Hello, there," she said.

They hadn't seen each other since his first night in town, over a week ago, and Ronan had to wonder how she felt about her daughter spending her nights in his bed. "Hi," Ronan said.

"You're in early," she said, glancing up at the clock.

"Yeah, we got an early start this morning. And the dredging went really well." He paused. "I wanted to thank you for stocking the kitchen. I really appreciated that."

"I just wanted to make sure you were comfortable. So how do you like oyster farming?"

Ronan smiled. "I like it a lot," he said. "It's so nice to be outdoors and on the water. And I like working with Charlotte." He paused. "I'm sorry that I've been monopolizing her time."

"I'm happy that she has someone to monopolize her time," Penny said. "She's been at loose ends since she came back from New York. And she was spending too much time alone. Of course, we appreciate her help with the farm, but she needs to think about her own happiness."

"You don't think she's happy working on the oyster farm?"

"I think she feels a responsibility to help out the

family. I want her to find her own passion, to chase her own dreams."

She'd been chasing some of her passions with him every night. Since their first night together, they'd found new ways of expressing their desire and each interlude had provided intimate revelations that made his feelings for her grow even deeper.

"We're having Thanksgiving tomorrow night," she said. "We'd like you to come."

"I'd love to," Ronan said.

"Oysters," she said. "I have to take some oysters home for the stuffing. I hope you like oyster stuffing. If you don't, I could—"

"No, no," Ronan said. "Believe me, I'll eat anything that has oysters in it. I think I've eaten them every day since I've been here."

"Hmmm," Penny said. "No wonder my daughter hasn't spent a night at home in all that time." She gave him a shrewd look. "Oh, don't be embarrassed. I happen to think that sex is one of the two things that make life worth living. Food would be the other. I have seven children, proof that Mr. Sibley and I enjoy ourselves in that area." She paused. "Oh, I am embarrassing you. Well, run along. I hope I haven't done too much damage."

Ronan nodded and hurried to the apartment. As he closed the door behind him, he chuckled softly. Talking about sex with Charlie's mother was just about the strangest thing he'd ever done. But then, strange seemed to be almost normal when it came to the Sibley family. Irish curses. Chicken tandoori. Thanksgiving in September. What was next?

CHARLIE CLOSED THE front door of the apartment behind her. As she walked through the living room, she pulled her clothes over her head and tossed them on the floor. "Ronan?"

"I'm in here," he said, his voice coming from the bathroom.

"Mom said she invited you for Thanksgiving tomorrow night?"

"Yeah, we had a nice talk," he said.

Charlie frowned. That very short statement could mean just about anything. "A nice talk?" She opened the bathroom door and froze.

Candles illuminated the interior. They were scattered around the room, the flames flickering in the draft from the air conditioning. Ronan, his hair still damp from a shower, had filled the bathtub and sat on the floor beside it, wearing only his boxers, a glass of wine in his hand.

"What did you do?" she asked.

"You said you wanted a long bath. I made one for you. Hop in before it gets cold."

She squatted down beside him and gave him a kiss. "You're awfully nice to me. You're not angling for a raise are you?"

"I wasn't," he said. "But if this will get me one, I'll crawl in with you."

Charlie stripped off the rest of her clothes, then stepped into the tub. "No, I prefer to take my bath alone. But you can watch." As she slowly sank down into the water, she let out a long breath. "Oh, that's nice."

He handed her the glass of wine, then stretched his

legs out in front of him. "Your mother is very...open-minded."

Charlie nodded. "I know! She's always been that way. We were the first kids in school to know the truth about Santa Claus and the Tooth Fairy. She claimed that she just couldn't perpetuate a lie and she felt guilty deceiving her children past the age of ten."

"We had a nice chat about sex," Ronan said.

"Oh, God, no. Did she tell you the cow story?"

"No," he said.

"Good. I'm not going to tell it to you now, because I'd prefer to save myself the embarrassment. But I'm sure you'll hear it at some point."

"I like your mother," Ronan said. "I'd kind of like to think that my mother might have been a lot like her." He paused. "Since I've been here, there have been some things that I think I remember about her."

"Like what?"

He thought for a long moment. "I remember how much she used to laugh. She and my father always seemed to be sharing a private joke."

"My parents do that all the time. Even at their age, they still can't keep their hands off each other. That was really embarrassing when I was younger. Now, I think it's sweet." Charlie reached out and ran her finger along his arm. "What else do you remember?"

"It's just this vague feeling. Mom always wanted me to make my own choices. I remember one time, I think I was in kindergarten. I had these Superhero pajamas and I wanted to wear them to school. My brothers made all kinds of fun of me, but she backed me up.

She said if I wanted to wear them to school, I could. So I did. And she took a photo of me and her, standing on the porch of our house, on our way to school. I still have that photo."

"She sounds like a wonderful person," Charlie said.

"I think she was. I hope my memories are true. After my parents died, my grandfather never wanted to talk about them. And the older I get, the more I want to know who they were."

"Maybe you should find out," Charlie said. "Have you ever asked your grandfather?"

"No," Ronan said. "Whenever we tried, he'd tear up and get emotional. And he was a really strong man. But he just couldn't talk about it."

Ronan slipped his hand around her nape and drew her into a kiss. His gaze met hers and Charlie saw something there that she'd never seen before. What was it? There were times that he seemed to drift to a distant place and then, suddenly, he'd be back again.

Ronan helped her wash her hair and when she was done, he wrapped a towel around the damp strands. Then he grabbed another towel and gently wiped the water out of her eyes. "I've never been able to talk about this stuff," he said. "I've kept it bottled up inside of me for years. And yet, when I'm with you, it just comes pouring out."

"That's good, isn't it?" she said, her gaze fixed on his.

"Yeah," he murmured. "It is good."

She leaned back and closed her eyes, her fingers still laced through his. "If you want to know more about them, maybe you could find some of their friends. They must have had people that they hung around with. People they talked to."

"I never thought of that," he said.

A long silence grew between them, but Charlie didn't feel compelled to speak. She knew he was thinking about his parents, something he hadn't done very often in the past. Whatever he was working though, she wanted to give him the space to do it.

They shared the glass of wine and when the water in the tub had cooled, she stepped out into a towel he held. He took her hand and walked into the bedroom with her. They curled up on the bed facing each other, talking about the events of the day, discussing the problems she'd encountered and the solutions she'd chosen.

Every day he was learning more about the business and with each day that passed, Charlie was left to wonder if he might just stay in Sibleyville a little longer than he originally planned.

She silently scolded herself. It wouldn't do to plan a future around Ronan. From the beginning they'd been careful to keep their expectations in check. It was enough to enjoy the physical relationship and the emotional attachment, but a real commitment was something entirely different.

"What else did you and my mom talk about?"

"She invited me for Thanksgiving in September tomorrow night."

"Oh, boy, more of my family. I'm not sure that's a good thing."

"I like your family," he said. "They're what I imagine a real family is like. Everyone fits. And you love each other, even though you're all a little crazy. I don't think you realize how lucky you are."

"I know," she said in a soft voice. After hearing Ronan's story, it did make her more appreciative. It was strange how he'd made her look at things so differently. He was making her a better person just by helping her to see her life through clear eyes.

"If you want to do that play, I'll come along and help," Ronan said. "It might be fun."

"I don't know," Charlie replied. "I've kind of left that part of my life behind."

"But if you're good at it, you should do it. And we have some time."

"You mean you want to take time out of our sex life for community theatre."

He chuckled. "Well, if you put it that way, maybe not."

"Let's see if Lettie finds someone else first. If she doesn't, maybe I'll help her out."

He smoothed his hand over her temple, pushing the towel away from her hair. There were moments when she felt so close to him, as if they were connected by a tether strung between their souls. It was a strange feeling because Charlie had always assumed that this was what love was.

But she and Ronan had known each other less than two weeks. Granted, since they'd met, they'd spent every waking, and sleeping, hour together. And they'd even managed to work happily together. Though Ronan had all the confidence in the world, he didn't seem to have an ego, something she'd never seen in the most men she'd known. He was happy to defer to her when it came to work, taking each task she directed in stride.

"Make love to me," she murmured.

Ronan smiled then touched his lips to hers in a gentle kiss. Pulling her against his body, they rolled over until she was on top of him, her legs straddling his hips. He grabbed the towel and pulled it open, revealing her naked body beneath.

As his mouth found her nipple, she wrapped her arms around him, her fingers tangling in his thick hair. Everything she'd ever needed was here in this room. She wanted it to last forever.

But maybe for her, forever would have to come one day at a time.

The Sibley house was filled with the scents of a Thanksgiving meal. Ronan stood in the foyer and drew a deep breath through his nose, searching for a sense memory of his childhood. But the memories that had bubbled up since he'd arrived in Sibleyville weren't always the kind he could summon at will. They usually snuck up on him, surprising him with their clarity and intensity.

Charlie turned back to him, motioning him forward. "Come on. You've already seen them at their worst."

"The last time I was here, I was just the guy that you'd hired to work the oyster farm. Now, I'm the guy you're sleeping with."

"Are you under the impression that I come from a straight-laced, conservative family? I think they've made it quite clear that Peyton and Penelope Sibley didn't follow the normal rules raising their children."

"Hey, there!" Peyton Sibley appeared from the back of the house, his movement aided by a cane. "It's turkey day. We all love turkey day."

Ronan held out his hand. "Hello, Mr. Sibley."

Peyton grabbed his hand and shook it enthusiastically. "Is my old man here? He's the only Mr. Sibley I've ever known. Now that we know each other, you can call me Peyton."

"Peyton."

"I hear you're doing a bang-up job on the boats. Jake's been telling me that you can haul oysters with the best of them."

"I like the work," Ronan said. "And I'm pretty fond of oysters, too."

Her father laughed. "Well, that will probably change. Most folks would probably enjoy an endless supply of fresh oysters. Me? I'd like a job at Dunkin' Donuts. I could eat donuts all day long."

"No you couldn't." Penny Sibley appeared from behind her husband, stepping up to give her daughter a hug. "Hello, Charlotte. And Ronan, I'm glad you decided to come."

"I wasn't about to miss Thanksgiving in September," he said.

"Well, I thought you might want to avoid me," Penny explained. "After our little sex talk the other day. I fear I might have put you on the spot and I want to—"

"Mother, stop. You don't need to apologize. Just try to remember the difference between your family members and everyone else in the world. You can say whatever you like to us, but the rest of the world doesn't really understand you."

"Mom? Do we have any sulfuric acid?" Garrett came running through the foyer wearing a football helmet and carrying a hatchet. "Hey, Ronan."

"Hey, Garrett."

"Do we, Mom?" he asked, looking up at Penny.

"I don't think so, dear. But you could probably get some down at the drug store. What do you need it for?"

"An experiment," he said. He continued through the foyer and out the front door. "Hey, Isaac, can you drive me to the drug store?"

"Are you sure he should have acid?" Charlie asked.

"I suppose if he knows that he wants sulfuric acid, he's aware of what it does, don't you think?" Penny asked. "Besides, I doubt that Clayton down at the drugstore will sell him acid anyway. But I'd rather let Clayton be the bad guy." She smiled. "I have to get back to my turkey. Find Ronan a drink, dear. He looks uncomfortable."

"Got it!" Abby walked through the foyer, a freshly opened bottle of beer in her hand. "Here you go." She handed the beer to Ronan, then ran up the stairs, singing the refrain from a Lady Gaga song.

Peyton clapped him on the back. "Glad you came back," he said. With that, he wandered into the library and closed the doors behind him.

"Show me your bedroom," Ronan said.

Charlie grabbed his hand and they walked up the stairs to the second floor. But they didn't stop there. She opened a door to another narrower stairway and when they reached the top, he realized they were in the attic. The space had been finished into two bedrooms with a bathroom in between.

"This is where the servants used to live," she said. "Two maids in one room and the cook in the other." Charlie pointed to the door with her name emblazoned on the front with glitter. "This one's mine as you can see."

She opened the door and stepped inside, then waited for him to enter. Ronan wasn't sure what he expected. He'd only ever known Charlie as a grown woman. And when he tried to imagine her as a child, or even as a teenager, the picture became vague and unfocussed.

She sat down on the edge of the bed and watched him as he circled the room, taking in his surroundings. "Are you looking for anything in particular?" she asked.

"No, just checking it all out."

"Why?"

He shrugged. "Curiosity," he said. "Am I the first guy you've ever brought up here?"

"God, no," she said with a laugh. But when he turned to look at her, he saw a blush rise in her cheeks. "Sorry. That came out wrong. No, Danny used to climb up here on occasion. He'd crawl up the trellis to the second floor porch, then climb the drainpipe."

"Tell me about him," Ronan said, searching the photos in her room for a guy who might fit her description.

"I don't have any pictures," she said. "I burned them all after we split up."

"Tell me."

He couldn't help but be curious. After all, she'd spent six years with Danny. She'd thought she was in love. And yet, he was here and Danny was in New York.

"He was handsome and funny and popular," she began. "And he had this confidence that just rubbed off on all the people around him. People just seemed to gravitate toward him. Whenever you saw him, he was always in the middle of a group and everyone was watching him."

"Sounds like the perfect guy," Ronan said, feeling a twinge of envy. In high school, he'd barely attracted the attention of any girls. And those that had been interested were slightly odd, girls who preferred their boyfriends tragic and broken. He was the exact opposite of the typical golden boy.

"He was. But he wasn't the perfect one for me. That's the thing. Most people think that guys like that are generically attractive to every girl. And he was, for a while. But the longer I knew him, the more I came to realize that most of the good stuff about him was on the surface. There wasn't much underneath."

"And that's what you want. A man with depth."

Charlie shrugged. "I guess so."

Ronan grabbed her high school yearbook from the bookshelf and crossed to the bed, flopping down on the mattress behind her. "Let's see. Charlotte Sibley." He flipped though the senior section and found her picture. "You were beautiful even then," he said. "Hell, if we'd gone to high school together, you wouldn't have given me a second look."

"Believe me, I would have looked. In case you haven't noticed, you're pretty hot yourself. You must have had girls following you everywhere."

"Not so much," he said. "Girls thought I was weird."

"No! How?"

"I never talked. I never smiled. I didn't have friends. I mean, I talked to some of the guys in class, but we didn't hang out. I listened to music a lot and usually walked home for lunch just so I wouldn't have to spend time in the cafeteria. And I didn't play any sports." He stopped suddenly, then shook his head. "I don't know how you do it."

"Do what?"

"It's like you flip a switch inside of me and I just start babbling. I can say anything to you. In fact, I can't seem to stop."

Charlie sighed, then rested back across his chest, pulling the yearbook out of his hands. She worked at the buttons of his shirt, then pressed a kiss to the center of his chest. "I think that's a very good thing."

"What are you starting," he said, rebuttoning his shirt.

"I'm just kissing you," she said.

"Not here. Not in your parents' house."

Charlie laughed at him. "My parents own the apartment at the boathouse, so technically, that's their place, too."

"What if someone walks in?"

She jumped off the bed and walked to the door, then pulled it closed and locked it. "Better?"

"No. Now if someone tries to open the door, they're going to know what we're doing in here."

"Don't be such a prude." She grabbed his hand and placed it on her breast and Ronan gave her an impatient glare. "There is something kind of exciting about doing it here."

He crawled off the bed, shaking his head. She was teasing him and he wasn't going to let her get away with it. "No way. Besides, I'd only be second best in that bed, after your friend, Danny."

"Oh, now I understand. You're jealous." She jumped off the bed and crossed the room, slipping her arms around his waist. "There's nothing to be jealous of."

"Yes, there is," Ronan murmured. He cupped her face in his palm and kissed her. "He had you for six years. He had a life with you. He saw you every day and every night for months on end."

"Maybe it's the quality instead of the quantity," she said.

"What does that mean?"

"I had all those days and nights with him. But all of them put together didn't even come close to those that we've had. Danny and I were kids. We had no idea what passion really was."

"And now you do?" he asked.

Charlie nodded. "I think maybe I finally have it figured out." She cocked her head toward the bed. "I can show you if you want."

"You can try. But you're going to have to do it with your clothes on. And with my clothes on. Using only your lips."

"Oh, a challenge." She grabbed his hand and dragged him over to the bed, then gave him a gentle shove. He fell backwards onto the mattress. Charlie laid down on top of him, pinning his hands over his head.

"Happy Thanksgiving," she murmured.

"You are crazy," he said just before she captured his mouth in a playful kiss.

"And you're starting to like crazy," she said. "Admit it."

He groaned as she kissed him again. In truth, he needed her, crazy or not. He'd come to appreciate her quirky personality and irresistible smile. And in the end, he'd do anything to keep her in his life.

6

"If you bend this just a little bit, it should be okay."

Charlie stood over the broken dredge basket and shook her head. "No, no, you can't bend that."

"Sure you can," Ronan replied.

"It will break and then the whole basket will be useless."

"No, it's not that kind of steel."

"I know what my dredge baskets are made of," she said.

"And I know the characteristics of metal. I do have an engineering degree."

She looked up, surprised by his admission. "You do?"

He nodded. "Yeah. And that little piece of metal right there will bend. Once it does, the basket will work."

"You never told me you went to college."

Ronan grabbed the basket out of the bottom of the skiff and hefted it up on the deck, then jumped out of the boat. "It never came up."

"Yes, it did. We talked about how I skipped college

for New York and how you went to work for your grand-father's business."

"Well, I went to college. Not away to college. I lived at home and took a lot of night classes." He braced his hand on his waist and stared down at her. "Is this a problem? Are we having a fight?"

"No," Charlie said. "I—I'm just trying to explain that I—" She cursed softly. "Never mind. Just take the basket up to the shop."

He held out his hand to her. "Come on."

She climbed out of the skiff and the moment both feet were on the dock, he pulled her into an embrace. "Kiss me," he said.

She dropped a quick kiss on his lips.

"You can do better than that," Ronan said.

Frustrated, Charlie decided to make her point in the only way she knew how. She slipped her hand around his neck and pulled him into the most passionate kiss she could manage. She seduced him with her tongue and her lips, refusing to retreat until she knew he couldn't take anymore. "Better?" she asked as she stepped back.

He laughed softly. "Ah, yeah." He hugged her again. "Good thing I'm wearing waders."

He took her hand and they walked up to the boat-house. Charlie was surprised to see her youngest brother, Garrett, sitting on the step for the front door. He glanced up as they approached, then jumped to his feet.

"Hey, Ronan. I brought my video games over. I thought maybe you might want to play a little."

Ronan glanced over at Charlie and she smiled. After dinner Saturday evening, Ronan and Garrett had teamed up against Isaac and Ethan in a video game battle. Isaac and Ethan had always been very close, with Garrett usually the odd brother out. But once he'd claimed Ronan for his side, Garrett seemed to think that the scales were back in balance.

"Is there a system in the apartment?"

"In my dad's office," Garrett said. "He put it there for when we were younger and we'd come to the boathouse after school. But we can hook it up in the apartment."

"Well, all right. I guess I'm up for some fun before dinner. If that's all right with Charlie."

Garrett turned to his older sister, a hopeful look on his face. "Is it all right?"

"Sure," she said. "Maybe you can stay and have pizza with us. How does that sound?"

Garrett grinned. "That would be cool."

Ronan opened the door to the boathouse and ushered Charlie and her brother inside. "Why don't you get the system set up," Ronan suggested, "while I get cleaned up. I'll meet you upstairs in a few minutes."

Garrett raced to the door for the stairway and they both listened as he ran up the stairs. "I guess our plans have been made for us," he murmured, grabbing her hand and weaving his fingers through hers.

Charlie couldn't help but feel a flood of affection for him. He'd been so sweet to Garrett at dinner and it was clear that he understood the way her brother was feeling—like an outsider. "Thank you," she said. "You didn't have to do that."

"No, I wanted to. Hey, if it's a choice between video

games and hot sex with the most beautiful girl in Sibleyville, I'm afraid I have to go with the video games."

Charlie gasped and gave him a playful slap. "So that's how it is?"

"No. Garrett's a good kid. And I like to play video games. It's no fun to play them alone. Believe me, I did that enough as a kid."

Charlie gave him a hug. "You're a nice guy, Ronan Quinn."

He gave her a quick kiss. "Come on. Let's go get cleaned up and then maybe Garrett will let you play with us."

"No, I think I'll leave you two to have your fun."

They both stripped out of their waders and boots and put them on the rack near the door, then walked upstairs. Ronan took a quick shower, then joined Garrett in setting up the X-box on the apartment television.

Charlie called for the pizza and left enough cash on the counter to pay for it, then retired to the bathroom. She'd grabbed the script for Lettie's play, then filled the tub with warm water, adding a measure of her favorite lavender bath salts at the end.

She tossed her work clothes on a pile and stepped into the tub, then sank down beneath the surface until the water covered her body completely. A tiny moan slipped from her lips and she closed her eyes.

Over the past few weeks, she and Ronan had fallen into an easy daily routine, their days spent on the water working and their nights in his bed, discovering the pleasure between them. The more time she spent with

Ronan, the more she realized that a life with him could be something very good.

The notion had snuck up on her. She didn't want to think of Ronan as a potential husband. Thoughts like that frightened her. But she could imagine him staying with her, for another month or another year, or even longer.

She grabbed a washcloth from the rack next to the tub and dampened it, then put it over her face, the scent of lavender filling her head. Her thoughts drifted to the man in her life and she couldn't help but smile at herself. He was her man, at least temporarily. He made it clear to her every day in a million ways that they were a couple.

Charlie had always been so clear about the direction of her life. She'd seen her dreams and gone after them. The move to New York when she was eighteen had been bold and determined. But for some reason, she couldn't do the same with Ronan. Even though her feelings for him had grown deeper with each day, even though she couldn't imagine the moment that he'd walk out of her life, she wasn't prepared to make him her dream.

With a soft sigh, she reached out for the script that she'd dropped on the floor beside the tub. She held it out in front of her and began to read, but it only took a few pages to know that Lettie's theatrical talents lay somewhere other than play writing.

"The Curse of Bridie Quinn" was an overwrought melodrama that had no resemblance to Romeo and Juliet at all. Bridie was a mix of the Wicked Witch of the West and Cruella DeVille. Edward was a typical brooding anti-hero in the mold of Heathcliff. And Moira was a reasonable copy of Blanche DuBois from "Streetcar."

Some of the dialogue was laughable and the rest made her cringe. But for an amateur show, it would do what it was supposed to do, entertain. She made a mental note to call Lettie and tell her that she was going to be out of town on the night of the play so she'd be unable to step in, no matter what the circumstances.

She dropped the play on the floor. Her life as an actress seemed a long way away right now. Though she'd loved every minute of it, she could barely remember the woman she had been a year ago. So much had changed over that time. So much had changed since Ronan had arrived.

Charlie closed her eyes and let her body relax into the scented water. Her thoughts continued to drift, touching on images of Ronan, in her bed, his naked body stretched out beside her. A delicious warmth seeped through her body and for a moment, she felt herself caught up in the dream.

A soft knock sounded on the door and Charlie opened her eyes. A few seconds later, Ronan peeked in. "Pizza's here," he said.

"I'll be out in a few seconds," she said.

"You do know that I'd rather be in here with you, don't you?"

She smiled. "Yes. But we can pick up on that later."

He closed the door behind him and Charlie sighed. There were moments that she didn't want to believe how wonderful her life had become for fear that it would all change tomorrow. How much longer could she deny her feelings for him? No matter how she tried to rationalize their relationship, she knew one thing for certain. She was falling in love with Ronan Quinn.

RONAN RUBBED THE sleep out of his eyes. The early morning light had turned the eastern sky a dusky blue and the area around the wharf was beginning to come alive with everyday activity. He'd left Charlie in bed to get a few more minutes of sleep while he went out to fetch bearclaws for their breakfast.

In Seattle, he'd always eaten a healthy breakfast. But he worked so hard out on the oyster beds that a bearclaw or two was burned off by nine in the morning. He pushed open the front door to the bakery and nodded at the patrons who had become familiar to him over the past three weeks.

The older woman behind the counter smiled at him as he grabbed a numbered ticket from the roll. Ronan walked over to one of the small tables and picked up a discarded copy of the Boston Globe, distractedly scanning the front page.

"I thought I might see you here."

Ronan slowly lowered the paper to find the smiling face of Leticia Trowbridge standing on the other side. Though he'd only had a couple of encounters with her, he knew that she'd come looking for him for a reason. Was she about to enlist him in convincing Charlie to appear in her play? Or was there something else on her mind?

"Hello," Ronan said. "How are you?"

"I'm wonderful. Well, not exactly wonderful. My

play is a disaster of monumental proportions. I can't seem to find the talent I need to really make the roles sing with authenticity. Have you ever aspired to the stage, Mr. Quinn?"

"No, no, no," Ronan said. "I'm not one who enjoys the spotlight."

"Well, the spotlight would certainly enjoy you," she said. "Come and sit down. I have a very serious matter to discuss with you."

"I—I really have to go. Time to get to work."

Lettie pointed to the ticket. "But you haven't been called yet. I only need a few minutes. I promise."

"All right," Ronan said. He nodded toward one of the tables and they sat down across from each other. "What can I do for you?"

"You can marry Charlotte Sibley."

Her words caught him by surprise and his first reaction was to laugh uneasily. But when he did, everyone in the shop turned around to look. "Are you kidding?" he whispered.

"Oh, no. Let me be as direct as possible. The village of Sibleyville pays me a yearly salary to act as matchmaker for the single residents who desire my help. But with your arrival in town, I have the ability to make the very last match this town will ever need. I'm here to ask you how much it would take for you to marry Charlotte."

"Take?" He frowned. "Are you talking about money?"

"Yes. Or some other type of compensation if you

prefer. A car? Property? I'm not sure what you might want."

Ronan shook his head. "You're going to pay me to marry Charlotte?"

"Is there any other way we might convince you to marry her?"

"No," Ronan said. "I—I mean, I'm not going to marry her for money. Not that I don't want to marry her, but—but—" He cursed beneath his breath. "This is really a ridiculous conversation."

"If you marry her, the Sibley and Quinn families will finally be united. The curse will be broken and perhaps more of our young people will choose to fall in love and stay in Sibleyville."

Ronan glanced around at the patrons in the shop. They'd all gone back to their business and no one seemed interested in the conversation going on at Ronan's table. But he had no doubt every ear was trained on their conversation. "Have you talked to Charlie about this?"

"Of course I have."

"What did she say?"

"That she would consider it."

The answer shocked Ronan. Though Charlie wasn't afraid to show her affection for him, they'd never really discussed the future. Actually, she seemed to purposely avoid any mention of what might come of their relationship at the end of six weeks. Had she really considered marriage a possibility for them?

As Lettie chattered on, Ronan couldn't help but wonder what was really going on in Charlie's head. There were moments during their workdays when he'd watch her and know, deep inside his soul, that he'd never be able to let her go. But those thoughts hadn't yet transformed into a real plan for his life. It seemed that all the planning was being done by Lettie.

The woman behind the counter called Ronan's number and he jumped up from the table, grateful for the excuse to end the conversation. "It was really a pleasure," he said. "Have a nice day."

He hurried to the counter and ordered three bearclaws, laying the money out in front of him. The moment the clerk handed him the bag, he hurried out of the bakery.

As he walked back to the apartment, he decided that maybe it was time to talk about the future. He'd been in Sibleyville for exactly three weeks now. He knew the last three weeks would fly by faster than the first three. Nothing he could do would slow them down. So why not just stay? Why not forget the six-week deadline and stay until *he* wanted to leave?

He had a job that he could keep. He was learning more and more every day about the operation of the oyster farm. He'd already found a way to make himself indispensable—at least to Charlie. But he would have to work out this living situation.

Charlie had refused to take rent out of his paycheck and he couldn't continue living in the apartment for free. If he was going to set up a life in Sibleyville, then he'd have to close out his life in Seattle.

When he got back to the apartment, he found Charlie still sleeping soundly. They'd had a lot of late nights, spent in the pursuit of pleasure, and maybe the lack of sleep was beginning to catch up with her. He walked out to the kitchen and poured a cup of coffee into a mug, then carried it into the bedroom.

"Are you trying to wake me up?" she murmured, her eyes still closed.

"I thought you were still sleeping."

"No, I heard you come in." She sat up and brushed the hair from her eyes, then took the mug of coffee from his hand. "Thanks." She took a careful sip and then sighed. "I could use another three or four hours of sleep."

"Why don't you stay in bed? I can find my way to work on my own. And I'll just work on Jake's skiff today. You can have the whole day to yourself."

"No," she said. "I'll be fine once I have a few cups of coffee. We've got a lot to do today. And the bicentennial celebration starts next week. I want to harvest more this week and then give everyone Friday off since they have to work our food booth for a shift over the weekend."

He tucked an errant strand of hair behind her ear. "All right. But instead of engaging in other activities tonight we're going to go to bed and sleep."

She stretched out across his lap, her head resting on his thigh. "We keep saying we should do that, but we never do. Why is that?"

Ronan smoothed his hand over her hair. "Because I can't keep my hands off you. Maybe I should seek out professional help."

"What? Go to a hooker? We don't have any of those in Sibleyville."

"No! Go to a shrink. Someone who can help me stifle my desires."

"We don't have any shrinks in Sibleyville either. We're New Englanders. When we have a problem we just suck it up and get on with our lives. Besides, I don't want you to get rid of your desires. I've grown rather fond of them." She sat up and kissed him, nuzzling at his lips until he returned the favor. And when he was lost in the kiss, she gently pulled him back into bed.

Ronan groaned softly as his hands ran freely over her naked body. He'd grown so accustomed to touching her whenever it pleased him. "If you start this now, we're really going to be late for work."

"I'm the boss," she said.

He chuckled. "Yes, you are."

"And as the boss, I order you to remove your clothes and come back to bed."

It wasn't a difficult decision to make. Ronan followed his boss's request and stripped out of his clothes, then seduced her slowly and deliberately, taking the time to tease her until she begged for release.

And when she did, Ronan buried himself deep inside her, her body convulsing around his until he could no longer maintain his control. They were more together than either one of them could hope to be alone. And with every moment of exquisite pleasure that they shared, Ronan came closer to the conclusion that he couldn't live without her.

"Tonight, we'll crawl into bed early and just sleep," he whispered. "I promise. No messing around."

She kissed him again. "All right." Charlie drew a

deep breath and sat up, then retrieved the coffee mug from the bedside table.

"And there are some things I want to talk to you about," Ronan added.

She frowned. "That sounds serious."

"It is."

"Maybe we should talk now," she suggested.

"It'll wait." He hadn't quite decided how to begin the conversation about their future. But with everyone in town hellbent on putting them together, it was time for the two of them to decide what it was that *they* wanted.

THEY WALKED TOGETHER up to the boathouse, Ronan's arm thrown around her shoulder. It was a perfect relationship, she mused as she laughed at a silly joke Ronan had told. They got along as if they'd known each other for three decades rather than three weeks. And though they spent almost twenty-four hours a day together, it hadn't caused any problems in their relationship. They seemed perfectly suited to each other, a match that seemed almost too good to be true.

"Charlie!"

She looked up to find Michelle, her cousin, standing on the wharf above them. Michelle handled the shipping for Mistry Bay Oyster Farm. She worked afternoons, from one to five, packing oysters into dry ice and boxing them up to ship overnight.

"Hey!" Charlie called. "What's up?"

"We've got a huge problem."

"Hang on," she said. "I'll be up in a second."

She and Ronan climbed the stairs and found Michelle

waiting for them, a clipboard clutched in her hands, a worried look on her face.

"I'm gonna go clean up," Ronan said. "I'll see you upstairs."

Charlie and Michelle watched him walk the short distance to the boathouse and when he disappeared inside, Michelle sighed dramatically. "What a hunk," she muttered. She turned back to Charlie. "Are you going to marry him?"

"No!" Charlie said. "Have you been listening to Lettie?"

"Your mother," she said. "My mother. My aunt. Three of my cousins. The whole town is talking." She leaned close to Charlie. "I heard that Lettie approached your Ronan this morning at the bakery and offered him money!"

"For what?" Charlie asked.

"To marry you. I guess the village board authorized an emergency expenditure. And some of the folks have started a fund at the bank. They want to find a way to keep him here in town."

"Oh, God," Charlie murmured. "This has gotten completely out of hand." She reached out and patted Michelle's arm. "Thanks for telling me. If there's anything else, just—"

"That's not the problem," Michelle said.

"It's not?"

"No. We screwed up the Bellingham order," she said, wincing. "I don't know how it happened, but we put the wrong address on the package and it's going to one of our restaurants in New York instead of Boston. We tried to catch it, but once it's in the system, we can't." She sighed. "And this is his first order so we have a lot riding on it. His soft opening is tomorrow night."

"All right," she said. "Pack up another order. In fact, double the number and I'll take them down this evening. It's only a three-hour drive. I'll drop them at the restaurant and come right back."

"I can do that, Charlotte," Michelle said. "It's my fault. I didn't double check the address after we put it in the system."

Charlie shook her head. "No, I really need to get out of town for awhile." Her thoughts wandered back to earlier that morning. Ronan had come back from the bakery and mentioned he had some things he wanted to discuss that evening. After Michelle's revelation, Charlie knew exactly what would be on the agenda.

This kind of pressure wasn't fair to him. He'd come to town hoping to find a job and a place to live for six weeks. He hadn't bargained for an Irish curse, a misguided marriage proposal and two-thousand anxious citizens watching his every move.

"Leave the oysters on the work table and I'll grab them," Charlie said.

"Thanks," Michelle replied. "And it won't happen again, I promise."

"Hey, it's no big deal. At least we have a chance to fix it."

When she got inside the boathouse, she tossed off her waders and boots and ran up the stairs. As she walked inside, she stripped off her work clothes and tossed them into an empty laundry basket, then walked naked to the bathroom.

The room was filled with steam and she opened the door to the shower stall and stepped inside, smoothing her hand over Ronan's back.

"Hey, there," he said, glancing over his shoulder in surprise.

"Switch."

He grabbed her waist and turned them both, putting her beneath the warm spray. Charlie let the water sluice through her hair, then grabbed the shampoo.

"Let me do that," he said, taking the bottle from her.

She turned and tipped her head back. Ronan poured a bit of shampoo onto her head and slowly worked it through her wet hair. She closed her eyes and let his massaging fingers do their work. He always knew exactly how to touch her, how to make her feel excited or relaxed, desperate or determined. He read her moods like he owned the manual.

"You know, taking a shower together is not going to help us avoid sex tonight."

"Oh, right," Charlie said. "Well, forget that."

"I thought you wanted to get some sleep."

"We can't. We're driving to Boston as soon as we get out of the shower."

"Boston?"

Charlie finished rinsing her hair and opened her eyes, looking up into this handsome face. "There was a mistake in the delivery address for the Bellingham order. Remember Chef Joel? His restaurant opens tomorrow and he needs oysters. Right now his oysters are on their way to some restaurant in New York City. So we're taking him his order."

"Yeah? How far is it?"

"Three hours. I was thinking maybe we could have dinner there. Spend the night. Get a hotel. I need a day away from this town."

"You need a day to relax."

"We'll make it up day after tomorrow."

He cupped her face in his hands and gave her a long, deep kiss. "I'm going to get out of this shower before I take advantage of you."

"Wear something nice," she said. "We may go to an expensive restaurant."

"I'll do that," Ronan said.

He stepped out of the shower, leaving Charlie to finish on her own. She felt a surge of excitement at the thought of getting out of town. Though she enjoyed the routine that she and Ronan had fallen into, it was time to shake things up. If he thought he knew her, then this was a good opportunity for her to prove that there were still some surprises between them.

She finished her shower, then stepped out, wrapping a towel around her body. She wiped the steam off the mirror and looked at her reflection. A summer spent in the sun had given her a golden tan along with a light dusting of freckles across her nose. Charlie raked her fingers through her damp hair, pulling it away from her face, then reached for her make-up case.

She hadn't worn make-up in months. She'd left all the girly beauty routines behind in New York. But it was time to show Ronan that she wasn't just the plain old tomboy he thought she was. She could be glamorous and exotic and seductive if she wanted to.

After she finished with her make-up, she dried and curled her hair, fashioning it into a rumpled finger-curled style that had been her customary look as an actress. She looked…sexy.

She peeked out of the bathroom door. The bedroom was empty and Ronan's duffel was sitting on the end of the bed, packed. Charlie kept a few nice dresses at the apartment for business meetings. She found her favorite flowered sundress and slipped into it, the low cut back making it impossible to wear a bra. After pulling on a pair of lacy panties, she slipped her feet into her favorite sandals, then looked at herself in the mirror.

"All right," she murmured. "Time to shake things up."

"Hey, should I load the oysters into—" Ronan stopped dead the moment he saw her standing in the middle of the bedroom. He frowned and then a slow smile broke over his face. "Wow. Holy…wow. You look incredible."

His reaction was exactly what she needed. She felt beautiful and sexy and to have him react the way he did made her spirits soar. Everyone in town might have a vested interest in their relationship, but it really was all about this—the current of attraction that crackled between them.

"I just thought I'd dress up a little."

"You look so beautiful. Not that you don't look beautiful every other day. Because you do. You always look beautiful. But this is…different."

She smiled. "Thank you. Let me just put a few things in a bag and we'll be ready to go. We'll take the SUV. If you want, you can grab the boxes of oysters from the table downstairs and put them in the truck. I'll be down in a few minutes."

Ronan grabbed his duffel and slipped the strap over his shoulder. Then he crossed the room and pulled her into a lingering kiss. "I'm really looking forward to this," he said.

"You should be," Charlie said. "You might just get lucky tonight."

"With you?"

"Who else?"

"Are you wearing underwear?"

"Bottoms. No top."

He groaned. "All right. Well, I really didn't need to know that. Maybe you should put underwear on. It's going to be really distracting for me."

"I can't," she said. "Not with this dress. Do you want me to change?"

"Nope. I'm just gonna go put the oysters in the car. I'll meet you downstairs."

Charlie giggled softly as he hurried out of the room. No matter how she was dressed or how raggedy she looked, Ronan always made her feel like the most beautiful woman on the planet.

After she'd returned from New York, she hadn't really known what her life would be. She'd been waiting, wondering if anything—or anyone—might come along to change the course of her existence. And now that Ronan had, she felt as if her future might just lie with him. She had no idea where that might be or what they'd do, but since the moment she'd met him, she hadn't been able to picture her life without Ronan Quinn in it.

"Maybe it's time to talk about the future," she murmured as she grabbed a bag from the floor of the closet. A shiver of indecision skittered through her and she wondered if it might be too soon. But she wanted to call the terms, not leave it to Lettie and her town council. She needed to know how Ronan felt before all the busybodies started to weigh in on their prospects.

It would be tempting to stay in Boston a little longer. But one night would have to be enough. When they returned tomorrow, she'd have a better idea of where she stood with Ronan. And that was all she needed for now.

7

IT WAS A beautiful September night in Boston and after Ronan and Charlie had delivered the oysters to Chef Joel's new restaurant, he'd invited them to stay for dinner. At a small table in a quiet corner of the upscale bistro, they dined on diver scallops, red prawns and tiramisu for dessert.

Stuffed and sleepy, they decided to take a walk before looking for a hotel for the night. They hadn't had a lot of time to just relax and enjoy each other's company in public back in Sibeyville, spending most of their time alone at the apartment. For some odd reason, Ronan suddenly felt a little bit nervous away from his comfort zone.

Their respective roles in Sibleyville had been carefully outlined from the moment they met, but now, without the structure of a workday or the passion of a night in bed, he wasn't quite sure what was expected of him.

He wanted to talk to her about his encounter with Lettie in the bakery shop. He wanted to know how she felt about the plans they were making for her. But if he and Charlie had done one thing in their short time together, and done it well, they'd avoided talking about their relationship. He'd never been one to enjoy dissecting the dynamics between himself and a woman, but then, he'd never been particularly interested in what women had to say about him.

But with Charlie he felt differently. He wanted to know exactly where he stood with her. Was she falling for him as hard as he'd fallen for her? Did she think about a future together? Or was she simply enjoying herself until he got back on the bus and drove out of her life?

"You've been quiet," Charlie said. "Are you all right?"

Ronan nodded. He drew her hand up to his lips and kissed the soft skin on the inside of her wrist. "I'm great. It's nice to get away. I've always wanted to visit Boston. I think I have some distant cousins here. At least that's what my grandfather tells us."

"Maybe you *are* related to Bridie Quinn," she said. "Bridie came from Boston, too."

Another long silence grew between them. They usually had so much to talk about. Ronan searched for a subject but all that came to mind were the questions he had about the future. "I—I suppose Sibleyville must seem really small to you after living in New York."

She nodded, then stopped dead and turned to him, her gaze intent. "I know about what happened this morning at the bakery and I'm really sorry."

"How did you—"

"It's a small town, Ronan. Everyone knows everything about everybody. You certainly didn't deserve that. And I want you to know that what's going on with Lettie and the rest of the town has nothing to do with me."

"Of course I know that." He slipped his arms around her waist and pulled her against his body. "So you think I should refuse all that money? I was kind of thinking that I could use a little extra cash."

Her serious expression faded and she laughed. "Believe me, I'm the last person any man would want to marry."

He frowned. Did she actually believe what she was saying? In his mind, she was quickly becoming his first pick for a happily-ever-after. "And why is that?"

"I'm kind of bossy."

"Yes, you are."

"And I like to do what I like to do."

"Yes, I've noticed that, too. But those aren't really deal breakers. I kind of like you just the way you are."

"Kind of?"

He nodded.

Charlie hugged him tight. "You are the only man who has ever said that to me."

"Correct me if I'm wrong, but there's only been one other man in your life. And he was an idiot who let you go."

She took his hand and they continued their walk. "Yes, that is true."

Ronan reached out and brushed a strand of wind-blown hair from her eyes, then tucked it behind her ear. "So, do you think you need to go out there and try out a few more guys, just to be sure that you have the right one? Or is two enough?"

The moment he said the words, he knew they hadn't come out right. He'd meant to tease her, but his question sounded more like an upside down proposal. Hell, maybe it was. Maybe, deep down, he wanted to be the last man she ever kissed…or touched…or crawled into bed with.

"I'm not sure," she murmured.

Her answer took him by surprise. Yes, the question was clumsily worded. But her reply was quite clear. "So you do have plans to move on to someone else?"

"I don't have any plans," she snapped. "I haven't made plans since I came back from New York."

He shook his head. "Go ahead, say it, Charlie. I'm just the guy you're sleeping with for six weeks."

"No!" she cried. "That's not it."

"Then how is it? Tell me. Because I'd kinda like to know where I stand with you."

She hurried on ahead. "I really don't want to talk about this right now. Can we just find the SUV and go?"

"I thought we were going to stay for the night?"

"No. No, I just want to get home. Everything feels so different here. I don't like it."

She looked so upset that Ronan wasn't sure what to do. He'd always known Charlie to be cool and in control, but she seemed like she was dancing on the edge of a meltdown. Hell, he never knew what to do in situations like this. He could barely identify his own emotions, much less read those of the feminine variety.

Should he kiss her? Should he ask her what's wrong?

Or should he just find her a tissue and let her cry it out? She wanted to go home, so he'd work on that first. Hopefully, the rest would solve itself along the way.

After a short search for the SUV, they found it parked near Joel Bellingham's new restaurant. Charlie opened the locks with her keyfob, but then Ronan took the keys from her fingers and helped her into the passenger side. "I'll drive," he murmured.

"Fine," she said.

He settled himself behind the wheel and started the engine, then pulled out into traffic. He didn't really know where he was going, but Ronan wasn't about to ask for help. The atmosphere was so tense he was afraid that whatever was keeping her silent would suddenly snap.

It took a bit of driving around before he found a sign for the interstate, but a few minutes later they were pulling onto I-93 heading out of the city.

"I thought I'd have everything figured out by now," she said. "I thought I knew what my life was supposed to be and when that didn't work out, there wasn't anything else I really wanted. I guess I've just been waiting around for something to drop out of the sky at my feet." She turned to face him. "And then you did. And I wanted you."

Ronan reached out and slid his fingers through the hair at her nape. "There's nothing wrong with that, is there?"

"Not on the surface. But I can't figure out if I want you because I have nothing else or if I want you because you're supposed to be in my life." She cursed softly.

"And it doesn't help that the sex is so good, because that really confuses things."

"You'd rather we had bad sex?"

"No. But it would certainly make sorting out my feelings a lot easier."

"What do you want, Charlie?"

"I don't have a clue. I'm twenty-five years old. People are supposed to have it all figured out by now."

"I'm twenty-six and I'm still trying to figure it out," Ronan said. "But I think I'm getting closer."

Charlie studied him for a long moment. "What does that mean?"

Ronan wasn't sure how much he ought to say. He and Charlie had always been pretty honest with each other. And maybe it was time to admit his feelings for her. "I like Sibleyville. I like working on the farm with you. And I really like you. A lot."

"I—I really like you, too." She let out a long sigh. "And that's enough, right? We don't need to say anymore than that."

She seemed to be so happy with the decision that Ronan didn't have the heart to push Charlie any further. "What are we going to do about Lettie?"

"Ignore her?" Charlie suggested. "I know, that won't work. But she honestly believes that marrying the two of us off will break the curse. She's not going to let up until we're walking down the aisle or we both leave town."

Ronan ran his hand down her arm and tangled his fingers in hers. "Do you think she's right? Do you think the curse could be broken if we got married?"

"My family has always said that the curse was utter

nonsense. When Danny and I ran off to New York, everyone thought that it was finally broken. Two people from Sibleyville were in love and would finally end up together. Only when it didn't work out, everyone was disappointed. I feel badly because it's my ancestors' fault that there was a curse in the first place. No one in Sibleyville falls in love with each other because they believe in the curse. And they believe in the curse because no one in Sibleyville falls in love with each other."

"What do they call that?"

"Crazy," she muttered.

"No, a self-fulfilling prophecy."

"Exactly," Charlie said. "It happens because they believe it's going to happen. So why do I have to be a part of it all?"

"I think you should stop worrying about everyone else," Ronan said.

"That's easier said than done."

He took her hand and pressed it to his lips. "I promise I'll do my best to help."

Ronan wasn't sure what he could do for her, especially against an entire town who wanted to marry her off to a guy she'd just met three weeks ago. Considering that guy was him, he ought to be a bit more concerned. But the thought of marrying Charlie, of spending the rest of their lives together, didn't frighten him at all. In fact, it intrigued him.

Was this how it was all supposed to happen? Was this how he'd realize he was in love? His mind told him that falling in love in three weeks was impossible. But there had been something between them from the very start, a powerful, undeniable attraction. At first, he'd thought it was just sexual. But now, he knew it was more.

Ronan looked at the next exit coming up and noticed the name of a nice hotel chain. He didn't want to spend another three hours waiting to touch her and kiss her. He wanted Charlie in his arms and in his bed right now.

He pulled over to the off ramp and she glanced at him. "Where are we going?"

"To get a room," he said.

"I thought we were going back home."

Ronan shook his head. "Nope. Home is three hours away and I need to take care of a few things right now."

Once they parked at the hotel, it took him exactly fourteen minutes to register and get their key. They rode up the elevator in silence. But when Ronan opened the door to the room, need took over. Desperate, over-whelming, undeniable need.

Ronan pulled her body against his and captured her mouth in a fierce, possessive kiss. She responded immediately, her fingers fumbling with the zipper of his khakis. When she freed him, she quickly smoothed the latex over his hard shaft.

Grabbing her backside, he picked her up and wrapped her legs around his waist. Everything had moved so fast and then, suddenly, slowed again. The delicious sensation of burying himself deep inside of her stole the breath from his body and Ronan paused, his lips pressed into the curve of her neck.

As he drew on his self-control, Ronan had only one thought in his mind. This woman had stolen his heart and his soul. And he really didn't care.

CHARLIE GOT THE phone call from Lettie at six p.m., while she and Ronan were getting ready to make some dinner for themselves. When she saw Lettie's name on her caller I.D., she put the phone down, refusing to answer. But then a minute later, it rang again. Lettie was nothing if not tenacious.

"Hello, Lettie."

"Charlotte? I'm sorry to be calling you at such a late date. I know you're not anxious about resuming your career as an actress, but I've run out of choices. I need you to fill in. Opening night is just four days away."

"I thought you were going to try to get someone else," Charlie said.

"I'd convinced Emma Woburn to do it. But once we got to the stage kiss, she just couldn't. She has a terrible fear of germs, and she simply refused."

"Cut the kiss, then," Charlie said. "That's easy enough to do."

"No, the kiss is the climax of the entire play. I couldn't possibly do it. Besides, Emma was just horrid. She couldn't act her way out of a paper bag, even if you gave her a roadmap and a pair of scissors."

Charlie glanced over the counter to find Ronan watching her closely. "Maybe you should make a deal with her," he whispered.

She covered the phone. "What kind of deal?"

"If you do her play, she lays off the marriage talk."

Charlie grinned at the suggestion. "Lettie, I'll do it. Under one condition. You forget all about your plans to marry me off to Ronan Quinn."

The demand was met with twenty seconds of silence. "Lettie, are you still there?"

"All right," she finally said. "Fine. What's the point anyway? If I want to live with my sister, she can move back to Sibleyville."

"It's a deal," she said. "When do you need me?"

"Now," Lettie replied. "And bring your tap shoes."

"There's tap dancing?"

"Not yet. But I may add some if the mood strikes me."

Charlie switched off the phone and looked up at Ronan. He was having a hard time holding back his laughter. "Stop," she warned. "If you laugh at me, I will find a way to get you up on the stage with me."

He held out his hands in mock surrender. "No, no. Not me."

She pointed at him, her eyes narrowed. "Then stop it."

"I'm just looking forward to seeing tap dancing in a play about a nineteenth century Irish witch. That could be very interesting."

She circled the counter and stood in front of Ronan who was sitting on a kitchen stool. "You're going to come with me."

"Is that really necessary?"

"Yes. You can help me with my lines. The only thing that will make this remotely tolerable is you. And I know exactly what's going to happen the minute I set foot in that theater. Everyone is going to be pushing Lettie's plan—except Lettie."

"All right," he said. He grabbed the car keys from the

counter, then pulled a bottle of water from the fridge. "What else do you need? Should I go out and get you an entourage? Maybe a few celebrity photographers? How about a red carpet?"

She walked over to him and grabbed the front of his shirt, twisting it in her fingers. "Listen, Ronan Quinn. If you don't stop teasing me about this I will never kiss you again. Ever."

"You couldn't stop kissing me if you tried." He pulled her into his arms and bent close, but Charlie pressed her lips tight and turned her head away.

With a low growl, he scooped her up into his arms and carried her into the bedroom, tossing her down on the bed. When he crawled on top of her and caught her hands above her head, Charlie was ready to admit that he was right. "Okay, okay, I give up." She gave him a quick kiss and then struggled to crawl out from underneath him. "We need to go now."

Ronan leapt up from the bed. "Let's do it."

They held hands as they hurried out to Charlotte's SUV. He helped her inside, then followed her directions as they drove through town. The theatre was housed in an old stone building that had once been the Sibleyville High School. Now it served as a community center and museum with the village offices located on the first floor.

Ronan parked the SUV and they walked inside together. The smell of the place brought back so many memories for Charlie. She'd appeared in every high school and community production from the time she'd been thirteen and knew the stage as well as she knew the oyster beds on Mistry Bay.

As she walked down the aisle, Lettie caught sight of her and clapped her hands. "Ladies and gentlemen, please welcome our new Moira Quinn, our very own Broadway star, Miss Charlotte Sibley."

The people in the theatre erupted in applause and Charlie felt a blush warm her cheeks. Ronan gave her hand a squeeze and then let go, taking a seat near the middle of the auditorium. Charlie continued down he stairs until she was standing next to Lettie.

"Remember your promise," she warned the older woman.

"You know most of the cast. Maxine Forman will be playing Bridie, your mother."

Charlie smiled at Maxine, who usually manned the front desk at the visitor's center.

"And we have a very special surprise for you. We have a new Edward, too."

Charlie watched as a familiar figure stepped out of the crowd. Her heart stopped and she sucked in a sharp breath.

"Hello, Charlie," he said.

"Danny. I'm surprised to see you back in town."

"Oh, I'm just visiting. Doing Lettie a favor. How are you?"

Charlie's heart was slamming so hard, she wasn't sure she could draw another breath to speak. What was Danny Merrick doing back in town? She hadn't seen him in more than a year, hadn't spoken to him in all that time. And suddenly, he just turns up? She glanced over at Lettie, wondering if this was all part of some master scheme.

"I'm doing really well," she said. "Great, in fact."

"You're working for your father?"

"Yes, I am." She heard the hint of defensiveness in her voice and she fought the urge to turn and run. She didn't need to explain any of her decisions to Danny. He wasn't a part of her life anymore.

"Well, I know that Sally has missed you. You remember Sally Franklin, our agent, don't you?"

"Of course I do," she muttered. What kind of game was he playing? Or more accurately, what kind of part was he playing, Charlie wondered.

"She told me that she's had a couple of calls for you but when she tried to contact you about the auditions, you never returned her call. One of them was for a nice spot on a primetime show."

"I'm not an actress anymore, Danny," she said.

"And yet, here you are. Back to doing what you do best."

Charlie wanted to turn around and walk out of the theatre. She suspected that Danny was all part of the push to get her back on the stage again, even if it was in some silly, homegrown melodrama. She glanced over her shoulder at Ronan and he smiled at her, unaware of the conversation taking place on stage.

"Let's just get started," Charlie said. "I have an early day tomorrow and I need to get out of here as fast as I can."

Danny stepped over to her and placed his hand on the small of her back. "Come with me. I'll go over the blocking with you and we can run through our lines real quick." He steered her up onto the stage and they walked over to a table with chairs around it. "You look good, Charlie. Better than good."

"Danny, I'm here as a favor to Lettie. Had I known you'd be playing opposite me, I would have refused the part. But it looks like it's a little late for that. So I'm sure you'll agree that we'll be as professional as possible and just do the job we were hired to do." She studied him shrewdly. "So how much are you getting paid for this?"

"Two thousand," he said. "I was stunned at first. I just got the call a few days ago. Lettie said something about her leading man getting arrested? I guess the mayor was going to play the role but then just dropped out. Very strange. How much did they offer you?"

"Same," she lied.

"I knew you couldn't stay away. It's in your blood, Charlie. You belong in New York, on the stage. It's your career."

Charlie cursed beneath her breath. "What career? I didn't have a career, Danny. I had a series of small jobs that didn't even come close to paying the bills."

"I just read for a big part in a soap," he said. "I should find out about that next week. If it happens, I'm going to be heading out to the west coast."

"That's wonderful."

They started with a scene between Edward and his father and Charlie sat down at the table and copied the stage directions out of the stage manager's script and into her own. As she watched her ex-boyfriend, she couldn't help but compare him to the current man in her life.

It was only now, with distance and time between them that she could see Danny's obvious flaws. What she used to take as confidence now seemed like arrogance. And his preoccupation with his looks, the constant messing with his hair or checking his image in any reflective surface now made him appear shallow and vapid instead of simply cool. And the silly acting affectations, the way he talked about "his craft" was enough to drive her right up a wall.

How had she missed all this? Had it simply gotten worse since she'd left New York or had he always been a jerk? She turned her attention back to the script, but it was impossible to study her lines. Instead, her thoughts kept jumping to the guy waiting for her in the audience.

Unlike Danny, Ronan was a real man, one who didn't pretend to be something that he wasn't. A man completely comfortable in his own skin. The thought that she'd given so much of her life to someone she could barely tolerate now was…embarrassing. And humiliating.

But Charlie still had to wonder whether there were other motives for bringing Danny back to Sibleyville. The more she thought about the possibility, the more confusing it became. Did they expect her to fall in love with him all over again, just like some silly schoolgirl? Or was the opposite supposed to happen? Was she supposed to find Ronan a much superior choice.

She turned her attention back to the script. She had three days to memorize her lines and a few more to figure the whole thing out. But the first thing she'd need to work out is how to tell Ronan that her old boyfriend was back in town. If Charlie knew anything, she knew that no one in Sibleyville was going to keep *that* a secret.

REHEARSAL LASTED LONGER than Ronan anticipated, but the time seemed to fly by. He'd never really thought about Charlie's career as an actress. Though they'd talked about her time in New York, it had never seemed real to him. But watching her move around the stage, inhabiting a completely different character than her own, was endlessly fascinating to him.

She spoke with a realistic Irish accent. Living with his grandfather for all those years, he knew what an Irish person was supposed to sound like. But more than anything, she managed to make Lettie's clumsy dialogue sound interesting.

The majority of the cast was dismissed after the first hour and Lettie worked with Charlie and the other lead for a hour longer. Ronan had been watching the male actor all evening, noticing how he reacted to Charlie, how he touched her, how he looked directly into her eyes when he spoke to her.

For an amateur actor, he wasn't bad. A little overblown in a few scenes, but he and Charlie seemed to make a good team, which was a relief considering all of Charlie's doubts about the play. Between the two of them, the story was almost believable.

When rehearsal ended, he watched as Charlie made her way up the aisle, smiling at him.

"Hey, Charlie, wait up!"

She glanced over her shoulder at her fellow actor, then quickened her pace. As she passed him, she reached out and grabbed his arm. "Come on, let's get out of here."

Ronan looked back and forth between Charlie and the guy standing on the stage, then followed Charlie out of the auditorium. "He was asking you to wait," Ronan said.

"I know. I didn't want to."

He'd never known Charlie to be impolite. "Okay," he said.

When they reached the parking lot, he slipped his arm around her waist and pulled her into a kiss. "You were really good."

"Thank you," she murmured.

"I'm not just saying that. You made the play better than it deserved to be. And your Irish accent was spot on. My grandfather would agree."

"I should quit," Charlie muttered. "I can't believe Lettie did this."

"Did what?"

She drew a deep breath and turned to him. "The guy playing opposite me is Danny Merrick. She convinced him to come back from New York to appear in her play. In fact, she paid him two thousand dollars to do it."

Ronan wasn't sure what to do with that revelation. She'd talked so little about her previous relationship that it never seemed like it would be an issue in theirs. Considering the ex was all the way in New York City, Ronan had simply put Danny Merrick out of his thoughts. But now, the guy was in town, spending time with Charlie, touching her—and at some point kissing her.

"Say something," Charlie prodded.

"Well, that's a surprise." He opened the door to the SUV for her and she hopped inside. When he got behind the wheel, she was staring at him, a perplexed expression on her face. "It is a surprise."

"That's all you have to say?" she asked.

"He's a pretty good actor, too," Ronan added. He started the vehicle and pulled out of the parking lot. "What do you want me to say?"

"I just thought you'd be more…upset. I'm furious. It's like Lettie tricked me. She knew I'd never agree to work with him. And she's even *paying* him. Like she honestly believes that I'd just let him breeze back into my life as though nothing had happened."

Ronan really was at a loss. He knew he ought to act jealous, but it was hard to work up any anger against a guy that Charlie so obviously detested. "Okay. I am angry."

"Good. Why?"

"Because you are," he said, knowing that he'd have to tread carefully. "Why are you angry?"

"I don't know," she said. "I just feel like something is going on here and I'm stuck in the middle of it." She cursed softly. "I really don't need him telling me that I ought to go back to New York and resurrect my pitiful career."

Ronan frowned. "He wants you to go back to New York? With him?"

"Yes. I would assume with him. He said that my

agent had a few job offers for me. She's left me a few voicemails, but I haven't returned her calls."

Suddenly, the anger that Ronan thought he ought to feel was beginning to bubble up inside him. "You're not going to go back, are you?"

"No!" she said. "Of course not. I'm curious as to what she found for me. I mean, it's kind of ironic that the moment I leave New York people want to hire me." She drew a deep breath. "If he sticks his tongue in my mouth when he kisses me, I'm going to kill him."

"I could probably take care of that for you," Ronan said.

Charlie laughed. "Will you help me with my lines? I have to get these memorized before tomorrow night. The play is only thirty minutes long, but I should at least give it my best effort. Not that Lettie deserves my best effort, but there probably will be a few people in the audience."

Charlie's cell phone buzzed and she pulled it out of her pocket. Ronan glanced over at her to see a look of unease cross her face. "Who is it?"

"Danny," she said. "He must have gotten my phone number from Lettie. He wants to have a drink. So that we can discuss the play." She groaned. "Oh, my God. I'm going to go crazy here."

"Do you want to talk to him?"

"I have plenty to say to him, but no, I don't want to talk to him. You know what I'd like to do. I'd like to go get a drink. You and me. I need something to relax me or I'll never get any sleep."

Ronan could think of a few things that would relax

her just fine, but obviously she wasn't looking in that direction. "Where do you want to go?"

"Windjammer," she said.

Ronan knew the place. It was just a few blocks from the boathouse. "Why don't we leave the SUV at the boathouse and walk over there. Then we can both have a drink if we want to."

By the time they reached the bar, Charlie's temper had faded and she seemed resigned to whatever Lettie had in store for her. But Ronan wasn't feeling as charitable. He knew how difficult the next few days were going to be for her, balancing work and play practice, all while seeing her ex-lover.

They found a booth in the corner and Ronan went to the bar and ordered them a couple of beers. He also placed an order for two cheeseburgers and a basket of fries.

"I ordered us something to eat," he said when he returned to the table.

"I think I know what Lettie is up to," Charlie said.

He took a sip of his beer. "What?"

"She's not trying to manipulate me. She's trying to manipulate you! She's trying to make you jealous. She thinks if she throws Danny back into my life that you'll get all possessive and declare your undying love for me."

Ronan couldn't help but wonder it Lettie's plan was already working. He didn't really like the fact that she'd be spending so much time with Danny Merrick. And the guy's appearance had managed to remind him that his feelings for Charlie were getting deeper by the day.

He stared across the table at her, at the two spots of color on her cheeks and the flicker of anger in her eyes. She was the most beautiful woman he'd ever known. And his main worry was the Danny Merrick would recognize that fact and want her back.

8

THE CENTENNIAL CELEBRATION began at noon on Friday with a parade featuring the high school band, all the fire trucks in town and the local scout troops. Charlie had given everyone Friday afternoon off so that they could enjoy the festivities, as long as they took a shift at the Mistry Bay booth at the park.

Everyone had closed up shop for the celebration, the local businesses setting up in small booths in the village park. All weekend long, Sibleyville was ready to show visitors what a great place it was to raise a family. Unfortunately, it wasn't such a great place to fall in love. But the town officials kept that minor problem to themselves.

Charlie and Ronan sat on the curb and watched as the parade marched by. Mistry Bay Oyster Farm had a small float and her younger brother and sister were seated in a huge fiberglass oyster shell, tossing candy to the children along the route.

When Charlie's youngest siblings, Garrett and Libby, saw them, they stood up and hurled candy in their direction, causing a frantic scramble around their feet. Ronan laughed, helping the children get every last piece before they scurried off, looking for more.

"This is really great," he said. "It's exactly what I imagined smalltown life to be."

"I love it, too," she said. "I remember things like this from my childhood. It was the perfect place to grow up."

When she thought about raising a family of her own, she'd always pictured it happening in Sibleyville. But as she watched the parade, she realized that other people might have had the same dream, only to leave Sibleyville to find love.

Maybe it was a self-fulfilling prophecy. Or maybe the curse was real. But the simple fact was that people didn't fall in love in Sibleyville. They were forced to look for love elsewhere all because of a tragic love story so many years ago.

She wrapped her hands around Ronan's arm and leaned against him. If the curse was true, then why was she falling in love with Ronan? He was living in Sibleyville. For now, he was a resident. She stifled a groan. Maybe it was true. Maybe they were meant to break the curse.

A horse-drawn carriage passed by with Sibleyville's mayor and his wife waving from the shiny leather seats. The Ladies' Aid Society from the local Episcopal church followed, dressed as the founding mothers, carrying brooms and butter churns and knitting needles. Charlie waved at her mother as she passed and Penny Sibley threw her a kiss.

Her father marched by as part of the local veteran's

drum core, handling the cymbals as they pounded out a cadence. Ethan was carrying the state flag in front of them, dressed in his Eagle Scout uniform.

A lone police car signaled the end of the parade. Ronan helped her up from the curb. "What's next?"

"We walk down to the park for lunch," she said. "We have a booth that sells my mom's oyster stew. She's been cooking all week over at the church kitchen."

"I love oyster stew," he said. "Let's go get some lunch."

As they walked through the crowd, Charlie was surprised at how many people greeted Ronan. Over the course of the past three and a half weeks, he'd managed to become a bit of a celebrity around town—a real Quinn in their midst.

He bought her a lemonade and they strolled through the long aisle of games—ring toss and bottle knockdown and balloon pop. Charlie introduced Ronan to a few of her friends from high school and while they were chatting, Garrett rushed up and lured Ronan away with a plan to win a new iPod at one of the ring toss games.

A few minutes later, she felt a hand on the small of her back and she turned, expecting to see Ronan. But Danny stood behind her, a charming smile on his face.

"Hey there," he said. "I was hoping I'd run into you."

Charlie groaned. "Oh, go away, Danny. Just leave me alone."

"Come on, Charlie. Don't be such a drag. We can at least be civil to each other. We were in love once, weren't we?"

"Were we?" she asked. "I'm not so sure anymore. I

think we thought we were in love, but we weren't old enough to know what that really was." She paused. "We were great friends, for awhile. And we were lovers. But we weren't in love. I know that now."

"I miss you, Charlie. It's been a year and I still think about you every day. New York isn't the same without you."

"I'm sure you've made new friends," she said.

"But I like my old friends better."

He reached out and grabbed her hand, but she snatched it away. "I need to go."

"Just wait. Give me a few minutes. I have a proposal for you."

Charlie sighed softly, running her hand through her hair. "What?"

"I want you to come back to New York. We'll be friends. You can stay at the apartment and get your career going again. I really think there are big things on the horizon for you, Charlie."

"Charlie?"

She looked to see Ronan approaching. He was carrying a plastic bag with a goldfish in it. She felt a wave of relief wash over her. He looked so sweet, his dark hair tousled by the breeze, his skin burnished brown by his days on the water. He'd never looked more handsome than at that moment.

"Hi," she said. "Who's your friend?"

He held the bag up. "Garrett won him. Or her." He chuckled. "He didn't want to carry the fish around, so I said I'd hang on to…it." He looked at Danny, then held out his hand. "Hi. We haven't met yet. I'm Ronan Quinn."

Danny blinked in surprise. "You're the Quinn?" His face turned a strange shade of grey. "You were at the theatre the other night."

"Yeah," Ronan said. "Hey, I think you're a great actor. I can really believe you're Edward Sibley."

"Thanks," Danny said. "It's not the greatest part in the world, but it's for a good cause. And I hadn't seen my folks for awhile, so I thought, what the hell."

"And you hadn't seen Charlie for a long time, either," Ronan said.

"No," Danny said. "I hadn't. So, I heard you're working for Charlie."

"Can we stop acting like I'm not even here?" Charlie said. "Yes, Ronan works for the oyster farm. He also lives with me. We're a couple. In a relationship. Together. Any other questions?"

"So, are we boyfriend and girlfriend?" Ronan asked.

"No!" Charlie said. "I mean, yes. You're not supposed to ask the questions. I was talking to Danny."

Ronan grinned. "Sorry."

"Danny, I'll see you later tonight. Ronan, I think we need to get some lunch."

She grabbed Ronan's hand and pulled him along until they'd put some distance between themselves and Danny. "Ugh, I can't believe I ever thought I was in love with him. He's just so full of himself."

"I thought he was okay," Ronan said.

She turned to him, her mouth agape, then saw the teasing glint in his eyes. "Funny." She slapped his shoulder playfully. "You are such a comedian. You're so funny, I forgot to laugh."

"Can we just clear something up here?" Ronan asked. "Are we boyfriend and girlfriend?"

"No," she said. "We're more than that. We're...together. 'Boyfriend and girlfriend' sounds so juvenile. I don't know how to express it any better."

"And you like me more than you like Danny, right?"

She laughed again. "Yes. A ton more. A bazillion times more."

"And when you kiss him tonight at the end of the play, you're going to be thinking of me?"

"Absolutely."

He bent close and brushed a kiss across her lips. "All right. I'm cool. But I want to let you know, if he picks a fight over you, I have no problem beating the shit out of him."

A laugh burst from her lips and she pushed up on her toes and kissed him again. "I'll keep that in mind. I didn't realize you were such a scrappy guy."

"There are lots of things I haven't revealed about myself yet. I'm a man of mystery."

"You are a man who makes me smile even when I feel like tearing my hair out. That's much more important."

He handed her the goldfish. "Here. You can carry this. We're going to get some of your mom's oyster stew and then we'll go home and practice your lines. I'm thinking I could offer you a few tips on that kissing scene."

"I think I could use the help," Charlie said.

As they walked toward the Mistry Bay booth, Charlie laced her fingers through his. There was no doubt about it now. She'd fallen in love with Ronan Quinn. Against all odds, he'd arrived in Sibleyville and found her.

Somehow, there had to be more at work here than just a strange coincidence. Whether it was fate or karma or destiny, some power greater than luck had put him in her path. But was she ready to ask him to stay?

THE AUDITORIUM WAS filled to the rafters for the world premiere of Leticia Trowbridge's new play, "The Curse of Bridie Quinn." Charlie had reserved a block of seats for her family, but Ronan had been too nervous to sit and instead, had found a place to pace near the back.

After a lunch of oyster stew, he and Charlie had gone back to the apartment and spent the afternoon running her lines and talking through the staging. She'd left at four for a dress rehearsal and Ronan had decided to stay behind, knowing that watching her with Danny would probably be an unnecessary annoyance.

As the lights came down and the curtain opened, he found a place to stand near the doorway. As Charlie performed, he found himself reciting her lines with her. In truth, he was probably more nervous for her than Charlie was for herself. He wasn't quite sure why that was and it seemed to defy logic. But Ronan decided that it must have something to do with his feelings about her.

Maybe when a person was in love, the connection was so deep that they could feel each other's emotions, they could sense each other's insecurities and fears. Like experiencing sympathetic stage fright.

As the play was coming to a close and Charlie was reciting her last lines, Ronan felt himself relax a bit. They still had the kiss, but he was well aware of Charlie's abilities in that area. A girl didn't forget how to kiss no matter how nervous she might be.

But when the kiss did come, Ronan wasn't prepared for the audience reaction. Though a few people clapped, the rest of the audience reacted with absolute silence followed by a low murmur of dissatisfaction.

When it came time for the curtain calls, the cast members stepped forward one by one. He noticed that they clapped the loudest for Charlie and when the mayor stepped out on stage, he gave her, Maxine and Lettie each a bouquet of roses. But the mayor had more on his mind that just congratulations. He motioned for the crowd to quiet and when they did, he cleared his throat.

"Ladies and gentlemen, I'm happy to see so many of our townsfolk come out to see this wonderful little play, written by our own Leticia Trowbridge. But we have some serious business to do here tonight. As mayor of Sibleyville, I have been authorized to sanction a marriage. A marriage that I hope will put an end, once and for all, to Bridie's curse."

Ronan felt his stomach twist. Where was this going? Were they going to make Charlie stand up on the stage while they put her through yet another plea?

"Ronan Quinn!" the mayor shouted. "Are you in the house tonight!"

Ronan raised his hand and walked halfway down the right aisle. "I am," he called.

"Good," the mayor said. "Then we have both parties here. Now, I know we've made several offers to you two over the past week, but we are prepared to sweeten the deal." He withdrew a paper from his pocket and opened his mouth to speak.

But Charlie grabbed his arm, then whispered something to him before he could continue. He frowned. "Well, just let me finish the proposal before you refuse, Charlotte. You owe us at least that much."

"We have a contract here that we're willing to offer to you and Ronan. We'd like you to consider marriage in the hopes that it might finally serve to put aside the differences between the Sibleys and the Quinns and make Sibleyville whole again. I've been authorized to offer you fifty thousand dollars, which you can split anyway you choose, for one year of marriage."

The audience erupted in wild applause and shouts of "do it, Charlie!" and "marry him!" The mayor motioned for everyone to be quiet, then peered out into the audience at Ronan. "Mr. Quinn, what do you think?"

Ronan looked at the stricken expression on Charlie's face. She looked like she wanted to find the nearest hole and crawl inside. He slowly walked down the aisle, his gaze fixed on her face. The time had come for him to make his intentions clear. He knew what he wanted and there was no use putting it off any longer.

"I would love to marry Charlotte Sibley," he said, "if she'll have me."

Charlie gasped, staring at him as if he'd just sprouted horns. "What?"

"I'm asking you to marry me, Charlie," Ronan said.

"Wait a second," Danny said. "Just wait one second. Who says we need a Quinn in order to break this curse? Both Charlotte and I are residents of Sibleyville. I want to marry her. I think we could break the curse."

This caused a major rumble in the crowd, but Ronan didn't take his eyes off of Charlie. He took a step closer. "What's it going to be?" he asked, speaking directly to her. "Are you going to marry me, Charlotte Sibley?"

"Marry me, Charlie," Danny said.

"Well now, this is an unexpected turn," the mayor said. "Perhaps we should put this to a vote. Let's have a show of hands. How many people think Charlotte should marry the Quinn?"

"Stop!" Charlie cried. "Stop this. I'm not going to let the citizens of Sibleyville determine my future. I'm the one who'll make those decisions."

"All right," the mayor said. "What is your decision? Is it going to be Danny Merrick or Ronan Quinn?"

She slowly shook her head, her eyes filling with tears. "Neither one," she said, her voice wavering with emotion. "If you want the curse to end, just stop believing it. It's as simple as that. There is no curse if you don't believe there is."

With that, she turned and ran off the stage. Ronan saw her mother, seated in the front row, get up and make her way to one of the side exits along with her brother Isaac and sister, Abby. Ronan strode up the aisle to the theatre lobby, avoiding the encouraging words from the crowd. He ran to the front doors and stepped out into the warm September night, searching the street for Charlie.

He caught sight of a figure running down the darkened sidewalk and took off after her. He was sure it was Charlie when he found the apron from her costume tossed over a hedge.

"Charlie!" he called, his voice echoing in the night air.

The streets were strangely quiet. Most of the population had been in attendance at the play. But the shadows between the streetlights made it easy for her to elude him. There was only one place she could be going. Ronan decided to head back to the boathouse.

Though he understood her reaction, Ronan wanted to make it very clear that his proposal had nothing to do with the mayor's offer. He didn't care about the money or the curse. All he cared about was having a future with Charlie. And though his proposal was somewhat unconventional, it had come from his heart.

He knew all the reasons against making a commitment like that. They'd only known each other little more than three weeks. He was supposed to return to Seattle at the beginning of next month. They hadn't even decided they were in love yet.

But nothing about their relationship had ever been normal. So maybe the proposal had come at an odd time. That didn't make it any less valid. Ronan wanted her in his life, permanently. He didn't care where they lived or what he had to do to make a living. Whatever it was, he'd make it work.

Now, he'd just have to convince her that the feelings he had for her were strong enough to withstand any doubts she had.

CHARLIE STRODE THROUGH the boathouse, tearing at the costume as she hurried up the stairs. When she got inside the apartment, she tossed it aside, piece by piece, desperate to rid herself of any reminder of the night.

She glanced around the bedroom, unable to decide what she ought to do next. She couldn't stay here. But after being humiliated in front of the entire town, where was she supposed to go?

How could he have done this to her? She'd trusted him, believed in him. And then, without a word, he'd taken their side. Did he actually think she'd believe in his marriage proposal? Sure, maybe he was trying to save her some embarrassment, but pretending to want to marry her only made things worse.

Now, when it didn't happen, everyone would feel sorry for her, the same way they did when she came home from New York. She needed to get away, just a few days, to figure out her next move. She didn't have to be back to work until Monday morning. That gave her enough time to put some distance between her and Sibleyville…and Ronan.

"Charlie?"

Ronan's voice echoed through the boathouse. Charlie quickly grabbed a pair of jeans and tugged them on, then slipped into a T-shirt she'd left draped over the end of a chair. She found her bag in the closet and tossed it onto the bed.

"Charlie?"

He was closer, in the apartment now. She pulled some clothes from her closet and tucked them into the bag. Underwear followed, along with a sweater in case it was cold wherever she was going.

"Hey."

She glanced over her shoulder to find Ronan standing in the doorway. "Hey," she said.

"What are you doing?"

"I'm getting out of town," she said. "I can't stay here."

He took a step toward her but she held out her hand. "Don't. Just don't say anything."

"Are you angry at me?"

She spun around. "Why would you do that to me? Why would you take their side? Things were so good between us and then you had to ruin it all."

"How did I ruin it?" Ronan asked.

"With that ridiculous proposal. I don't need you to ride in on your white horse and save this town. And I don't need you to rescue me from an angry mob of townsfolk. They created this problem themselves. And they keep on perpetuating it. Like tonight. If I don't marry you, then everyone there will be convinced that the curse will go on." She screamed, pressing her hands to her temples. "And there isn't even a curse!"

"I proposed because I thought it would be the best way to ensure that we'd spend the rest of our lives together."

She stared at him a long moment, then shook her head. "I have no idea what you just said."

"I want to be with you," Ronan said. "For a long time. Forever."

"You barely know me."

"I know enough. I don't think I'm going to change my mind if I take more time. I'm in love with you now. So, I think we need to move on to the next step."

"You're crazy," she said. "I'm not going to marry someone I've only known for three weeks."

"But you'd marry someone you loved?" Ronan asked.

"Yes. Of course I would."

He reached out and caught her arms, forcing her to face him. When she looked away, Ronan tipped her chin up until she met his gaze. "How do you feel about me, Charlie? Be honest. In the deepest part of your soul, how do you feel?"

She opened her mouth, then snapped it shut, shaking her head. "I don't know." She pulled away from him and returned to her packing.

"I don't believe that. I think you do know. And I think you've been trying to rationalize it in your head but you can't. It's strange and scary and real, so real that you can't bring yourself to admit it. You're in love with me the same way I'm in love with you."

"If the curse is real, then that's impossible. Two people can't fall in love in Sibleyville. And if the curse isn't real, then you don't need to marry me." She picked up the bag from the bed and carried it into the bathroom, then began to dump her toiletries into it. "Problem solved."

"Where are you going?" Ronan asked.

"I don't know. But I need you to stay here and help

out on the farm. You know how things run. Uncle Jake will help you."

He grabbed her wrist and drew her toward him. But she pulled out of his grasp. "Please, don't. We'll talk when I get back. I promise. I just have to get out of here for a little while." She pushed up on her toes and kissed his cheek. "Let my folks know that I'm all right. Tell them that I'll call them."

"All right," he said. "But I want you to call me when you get where you're going."

She nodded. "I will."

He pressed his forehead to hers and Charlie choked back another surge of tears. She wanted to stay, to crawl into bed with Ronan and make love to him until she couldn't remember anything that had happened that day.

"I'll be waiting, Charlie. I'm not going anywhere, I promise."

Drawing a deep breath, she turned and walked out of the bedroom, heading to the front door. She wanted to look back at him, just once, just to reassure herself that everything he said was true. "Thank you," she murmured, refusing to face him. "I appreciate what you tried to do."

"I know," Ronan said.

She walked out the door, then hurried down the steps to the ground floor of the boathouse. When she got inside, she hopped into the SUV and turned the key. The engine roared to life. She threw the vehicle into gear and pointed it north, away from the celebration, away from the place of her humiliation.

It was only after she'd left the town limits that she

allowed herself to think about what Ronan had said to her. He loved her. And he wanted to stay with her. She ought to be jumping for joy, shouting to the rooftops, that she'd finally found the perfect man.

But she'd always expected that when her perfect man came along, she'd be perfectly certain that she was in love too. And right now, she wasn't certain about anything.

9

RONAN HAD WORKED until his muscles ached, until sweat poured out of his body and until he was so exhausted he could barely stand. It was the only way he could sleep.

Charlie had been gone for five days and he hadn't heard a word from her. He didn't know where she was or who she was with, but he'd convinced himself that as long as he stayed in Sibleyville, she'd come back to him.

Still, lying alone in bed, he'd had his doubts. Maybe she'd gone back to New York, back to the man she'd once loved. He'd seen her mother at the office and she'd assured him that the moment Charlie called, he'd be the first to know. But Penny Sibley didn't seem nearly as concerned as Ronan was.

As for the rest of the folks in Sibleyville, the gossip had been running wild. They knew that Charlie had left town and many of them had made it a point to thank Ronan for his efforts in ending the curse, even though it didn't look like a marriage was in the cards.

Ronan carefully steered the skiff into its spot along the dock, then grabbed the lines and fastened them around the cleats. He and Jack had worked together that afternoon, harvesting oysters from the west shore of Mistry Bay. They'd worked quickly, but silently, neither one of them interested in idle conversation.

He tucked the thermos under his arm and picked up the small cooler that had held his lunch, then jumped onto the dock. But as he climbed the steps up to the street, he noticed a figure at the top. Danny Merrick had left town right after the play and now he was back.

"What do you want?" Ronan asked.

"I need to talk to Charlie. Do you know where she is?"

Ronan shook his head. Even if he did know, he wasn't about to tell this guy. "I thought she was in New York," he muttered.

"Is she?"

"I don't know. I haven't heard from her."

"She's not in New York," Danny said.

"Well, then, why don't you just give me a message and if I see her, I'll try to remember to give it to her." He yanked open the front door of the boathouse and walked inside, ignoring the man who hurried in behind him.

Ronan kicked off his boots, then slipped out of the waders. "Well?"

"She needs to come back to New York. Not for me, but for her career. I know I made things impossible for her there, but she has an amazing talent and I don't want to see her waste her life harvesting oysters and growing old in this pathetic little town."

"Is that all?" Ronan asked.

"No. Tell her that her agent has been trying to reach

her. She's got an audition for a new television series next week. It's an important job. She should at least give it a shot."

"All right. Great. I'll tell her all that."

Danny gave him a suspicious look. "You think you know what's best for her?"

Ronan shook his head. "Nope. I want her to be happy. That's all I care about."

"And what if she decides she wants to be happy with me?"

"I don't think that will happen. But, if it does, then I'll wish her the best. And I'll also probably put an Irish curse on your career. I'm a Quinn. I can do that, you know."

For a moment, he thought Danny just might challenge him. He clenched his fists at his sides and his face turned red. "It was nice meeting you," he muttered. "When you see Charlie, tell her I'm sorry."

Ronan reached for the front door and held it open. Danny walked through and he let it swing shut behind him. He strode through the boathouse, then took the stairs two at a time. When he reached the second story, he found Mrs. Sibley at her desk, piles of receipts scattered around her.

"Ronan, how are you?"

"I'm fine," he said. "How about you?"

She smiled. "You don't look fine. You look exhausted."

"I am. But the hard work helps me sleep at night."

"Well, Jake says you're doing a wonderful job. He's hoping you'll stay on with us. And don't think we don't appreciate what you're doing, covering for Charlie while she's gone."

Ronan shrugged. "I don't mind. I enjoy the work."

Penny glanced up from her receipts, then pulled her reading glasses off. "She's not going to like that I told you, but she came home late last night."

A sigh of relief came out in a rush. "She's all right?"

Penny nodded. "She's fine. A little confused, perhaps. A bit embarrassed for running away in the first place. But I'm sure she'll work everything out in time."

"Thanks for letting me know," he said.

"Well, I was thinking you might like to come for dinner tonight. Nothing fancy. Or foreign. Meat loaf and mashed potatoes. Charlie is cooking. Maybe you'll have a chance to talk."

Ronan had thought a lot about what he would say to Charlie when he saw her again. But now that he had the chance, he was riddled with indecision. "Do you think she'd be okay with that?"

"We won't know until you try," Penny replied. "Get yourself cleaned up and see how you feel. We eat at six."

Ronan considered his options for a long moment. He'd missed her. He'd missed having her with him all day long. And he'd missed sleeping beside her at night. When a guy loved a girl, they were supposed to be together. The sooner he made that happen again, the better.

"I think I will take you up on that invitation," Ronan said. "Maybe I can start to repair some of the damage I've done."

"Oh, sweetheart, you haven't done any damage at

all. All you've done is make Charlie happy. There's no fault in that. If you do love her like you say you do, then nothing needs to be fixed. You just keep telling her how you feel and one day, she'll look at you and she'll believe you."

"All right. Well, I'm going to get ready."

"Wear that blue shirt," she said. "It brings out the color of your eyes."

Ronan grinned. "Okay. Thanks for the advice."

He wandered back to the apartment and when he closed the door behind him, he leaned back against it. He might only get one chance to make things right with her.

He hadn't had much experience wooing women. Hell, he'd never had to work hard to get women interested in being with him. When it came to flowers and candy and dating, he was at a loss.

Did all women like flowers? He knew Charlie wasn't a big fan of chocolate, but she loved gummy worms. But a bag of gummy worms didn't seem like a proper peace offering. There was always jewelry, but jewelry could sometimes be misinterpreted. A necklace didn't mean as much as a ring. And where did earrings fall into the mix?

Ronan groaned. Though he'd never solicited advice from his brothers regarding women, right now, he could actually use some. Between Cameron, Dermot and Kieran, at least one of them would know how to handle his dinner with Charlie.

He was on his own. And at this point, he knew a box of chocolates or a blue shirt or a diamond ring wasn't going to convince Charlie to fall in love with him. He'd have to find a way to show her that there wasn't a man in the world who'd ever love her as much as he did.

He'd stay in Sibleyville until that happened. If it took a year or even two, he was willing to show her that he wasn't going to cut and run. "Be prepared, Charlotte Sibley," he murmured to himself. "I've found a new life and it's not going to officially start unless you're a part of it."

CHARLIE BRUSHED A strand of hair from her face as she kneaded the dough for biscuits. Grabbing a handful of flour, she sprinkled it on the counter, then worked the dough into a neat square.

"Why are you making biscuits when we're having potatos?" Abby asked. "Double starch. That's kind of redundant."

The truth was Charlie didn't know why she was making biscuits. It was one of the only things she did well when it came to baking. And right now, she was looking for anything to take her mind off of Ronan. If she knew how to knit, she'd be making mittens. "I want biscuits," she said.

Charlie had arrived back home late last night from a five-day trip to Bar Harbor. She'd hoped to take long walks around town to clear her head. But instead, she found herself wishing that Ronan had come with her and that they could enjoy the fall weather together.

Depressed and lonely, she shut herself in her motel room and watched movies all day long. After running up a hundred dollar pay-per-view bill, she checked out and decided she could watch movies at home for free.

It felt safe here in familiar surroundings. She hadn't ventured out yet, unwilling to face the concerns, unable to provide any answers to the questions. Was she in love with Ronan Quinn? Was he going to stay in Sibleyville and marry her? Or was she going to go on as she had been for the last year, another sad spinster caught by the curse.

Abby walked into the kitchen. "I'm glad you're home, Charlie."

She gave her sister a hesitant smile. "Thanks. Me, too."

"I'm sorry for what happened to you after the play. They shouldn't have done that to you. Not in front of the whole town."

"It was pretty embarrassing. I guess I always thought that when a man finally asked for my hand, it might be just a little romantic."

"But it was romantic," Abby said. "I mean, he just walked right down that aisle and told the whole town that he wanted you. He was like some modern day knight and you were his damsel in distress."

"I think what he wanted was to save me from the humiliation."

"But isn't that what a guy in love would do?" Abby asked.

"Abs, you don't fall in love in three weeks. No one does."

"Mom and Dad always taught us that we Sibleys do things in our own way, not like other people. If you fall in love in three weeks, then that's just the way it's going to be for you." She paused. "Do you love him?"

Charlie closed her eyes and drew a slow breath. "Yes. I think I do. But my practical side says that I need more time to be sure."

Abby grinned and clapped her hands. "I knew you loved him. I told Mom that night after the play. I could see it in the way you looked at him." She jumped off the counter and threw her arms around Charlie's shoulders. "I have to tell you, the man is not hard on the eyes. He is a grade A hottie. And you two will make perfectly beautiful babies together."

"Don't get ahead of yourself," Charlie said. "I don't even know if he's still in town."

"Oh, he is. He's been working with Uncle Jake. Danny left though. And came back. And then left again after Ronan threatened to put a curse on his career. I don't think we'll be seeing him in Sibleyville anytime soon."

"What's the gossip around town?"

"Everyone is really sorry. Some people are calling for the mayor and Lettie Trowbridge to make a public apology."

The front door squeaked and Charlie wiped her hands on a towel. "If that's Libby, tell her I need her to come in and unload the dishwasher. It's her turn. And if it's Garrett, have him take the garbage out to the curb."

"No prob," Abby said as she pushed open the swinging door into the dining room.

"And go find Mom," Charlie called after her. "I'm

not sure where Dad went and I need to know if she still wants to eat at six."

She didn't get an answer from Abby and figured that her sister had already raced upstairs. She found the biscuit cutter in a drawer and began to cut circles from the flattened dough, tossing the rounds onto a baking sheet.

Ronan was still in town, she mused. Maybe after dinner she'd wander down to the boathouse and check her mail. Or she could wait until later and sneak into the apartment and—

The kitchen door swung open and she looked up, prepared to give a task to one of her younger siblings. But the order stopped in her throat as she came face to face with Ronan.

Charlie stared at him for a long moment, her heart pounding in her chest, her breath coming in quick gasps. She fought the urge to run into his arms, to throw herself at him until he kissed her like he used to.

She wasn't sure how long he waited, his hands tucked in the back pockets of his jeans, his blue shirt making his sun-burnished skin look even more beautiful. But at some point, he took a step toward her. She felt a shiver skitter up her spine and her knees wobbled slightly.

"Hello," she said.

"Hi," Ronan replied. "I'm glad you're back."

"Me—me, too."

"Did you get enough of a break?"

Charlie nodded. "I think so. I didn't want to take too much time away. I drove up to Bar Harbor."

"I don't know where that is," he said. He pulled his hands out of his pockets and rubbed his palms together.

"I was going to bring you flowers, but I didn't know what kind you liked. And I've never seen you eat much candy so that was out."

"How are things at the oyster farm?" she asked, trying to change the subject.

"Good. We've hardly missed you." He paused. "Actually, we've all missed you. But we've managed without you. Not that we wanted to. Everyone will be glad that you're back."

"Thanks. I knew you'd be able to handle everything."

Another uncomfortable silence grew between them and she could see that Ronan was growing impatient with the pace of the conversation. "So I'm going to say what I came here to say," he said. "And then I'm going to leave."

He slowly walked toward her and when he was close enough to touch her, Ronan stopped. She'd been dreaming about this moment for the past five days and now that it was here, Charlie wasn't sure what she ought to do. Listening to him would be a good start.

"Before I met you, I lived in a pretty dark place. I was carrying around a lot of pretty heavy baggage and I didn't feel like I belonged anywhere. And then, you opened the door of the boathouse and it was like I walked into sunshine for the first time in my life. And it was warm and bright and I felt like I could be happy."

"Ronan, I—"

He pressed a finger to her lips. "I have to say this all at once or I'll never get it out, Charlie." He drew a deep breath. "You've changed my life. I want to stay here with you. And if you don't want to marry me, that's fine. Just working with you will be enough." He paused for a moment, then hurried on. "And if you don't want to work with me, I'll find another job."

"You would?" she asked. "You'd quit."

Ronan took her hand and stared down at her fingers as he carefully slipped them between his. "I need to be near you. You're like air and water to me. I can't live unless I have you. And I'm willing to do whatever it takes to make that happen."

"You're sure you want to stay in Sibleyville?"

"I want to be wherever you want to be. We can go live on an island somewhere, in a hut with fish and co-conuts to eat and hours to lay around in the sun."

"That sounds more like a honeymoon to me."

He looked up at her, his gaze meeting hers, his eyes searching for an answer. "It could be. But we'd have to get married first."

"We've never done things the usual way in my family."

"All right, honeymoon first. We'll figure out the wedding later."

She drew his hands up and clutched them to her chest. "I think I could do that, Ronan."

For the first time since he walked in, he smiled at her. And for Charlie, it was like a door had opened up and the sun had come pouring in too. "I do love you, Ronan. I know it sounds crazy, but I don't think I can live without you either."

He pulled her into his arms and kissed her. Charlie felt her knees go weak and her pulse begin to race. Everything that she'd ever wanted in life was here in his arms. She'd never realized that her dreams didn't have to be a career or an interesting place to live, fame and fortune. She'd found her dreams in this man, this stranger who'd walked into her life and stolen her heart.

As long as they were together, life would be perfect. "Are you going to be staying for dinner?" she asked.

"I was hoping we could go back to the apartment and eat some oysters."

"And?"

"I'm happy to start with the oysters," he said. "We'll see what happens after that."

She grabbed his hand and pulled him along through the house and toward the front door. "Abby, take care of dinner. Ronan and I are leaving."

"What?" her sister cried.

The screen door slammed and a minute later, she and Ronan were running across the lawn toward her SUV. "You know, I'm thinking we're going to have to fix one thing about this relationship of ours."

"And what's that?"

"I don't think I want to be your boss anymore. I think maybe we ought to try business partners."

"Will you still boss me around in bed?" Ronan asked.

She laughed. "I think you can count on that."

Epilogue

THE FOUR QUINN brothers gathered around the table in the conference room at Quinn Yachtworks. It was New Year's Eve and a celebration had been planned for later that evening at one of Seattle's best restaurants. But for now, Martin Quinn was in charge of the festivities.

He surveyed the room, studying each of his grandsons and the women they'd brought to the party. When he'd sent them off to find a new life for themselves, he'd expected some major revelations. But he'd never expected each of them to return with fiances and in one case, a wife.

Cameron had been living in Albuquerque for the past few months, the love of his life a pretty ex-cop named Sofia Reyes. He'd split the design business away from Quinn Yachtworks and was working as a consultant rather than a business partner.

Dermot had been back in Seattle since early October and Rachel Howe, his partner, had arrived shortly after, leaving her life in Wisconsin behind for a new life with Dermot. Dermot's twin, Kieran had found love with a feisty country singer and songwriter who had been playing small venues around the Seattle area as she took a new direction in her career.

And Ronan, the grandson who'd suffered the most at the loss of his parents, had found a brand new life away from Seattle and the memories that had darkened his life for so long. He'd brought Charlotte along on his trip back to see his brothers, introducing her as his wife.

Martin had always dreamed about the day he would turn the business over to his grandsons, but he'd known that forcing them to buy into his dream had been wrong. Their grief at the loss of their parents was something he'd been unprepared to deal with. So he'd done the best he could.

And now, with their happiness assured, he'd been able to undo at least some of the damage he might have caused. Martin cleared his throat and reached for his champagne flute. "I'm sure you boys would like to get on with your celebrations, so I'm going to make this very quick."

"Cameron and Ronan. You've chosen to make a life for yourselves outside of Seattle." Martin's executive assistant, Miriam, handed them each an envelope. "This is a down payment on each of your twenty-percent shares in Quinn Yachtworks. For the next five years, you'll receive monthly payments until Kieran and Dermot have bought out your interests."

Miriam handed two larger envelopes to the twins. "You'll want to have lawyers look those over," Martin suggested. "But those papers turn control of the yachtworks over to you two. I have officially cashed in my share and will be taking half of it out in merchandise."

Cameron frowned. "Merchandise?"

"Hull number 854," Martin said. "It's being fitted right now and as soon as it's launched, your grandfather is going to sail around the world."

Dermot gasped and he turned to his brothers with a worried look on his face. "Alone? Hull 854 is a fourty-six footer. You can't take a boat that size out alone."

"I have a friend I'll be taking with me."

"Who?" Ronan asked.

"Miriam."

This time they didn't look at each other. They just stared at him in disbelief. "Miriam? Our Miriam?"

"My Miriam," Martin said, holding out his arm. Miriam smiled and stepped to his side.

"Miriam," Kieran repeated.

"Yes. We've been sailing together for many years now and we thought it was time to retire and see a little bit of the world."

"Miriam," Ronan said. "My gosh. Congratulations. And welcome to the family." He looked at his grandfather. "You are planning to marry her, aren't you?"

"We've discussed it," Miriam said.

Martin nodded. "I've already made the offer and she's thinking about it." He picked up his glass. "So, here we are. I look at you four and your lovely ladies and I think about the trip I made all those years ago. Almost fifty years now. It seems like just yesterday that I stepped off that plane carrying your father. He and your mother would be so proud to see this. So I'd like to make a toast to my favorite boys and their favorite girls. To Cam and Sofie, to Kieran and Maddie, to Dermot and Rachel, and to Ronan and Charlotte."

Rachel held up her glass. "And to Martin and Miriam."

"To Martin and Miriam," they all said.

"May you always walk in sunshine. May you never want for more. May Irish angels rest their wings right beside your door." He touched his glass to Miriam's. "Sláinte chuig na fir, agus go mairfidh na mná go deo."

"Are you going to tell us what that means?" Dermot asked.

"Health to the men and may the women live forever."

For the next half hour, the champagne flowed and laughter filled the conference room. Martin couldn't help but remember the dark days that they'd weathered after the disappearance of his son and daughter-in-law.

But he felt their presence here now, for the first time since they'd been lost. Gathered around the table, he saw Jamie's smile and Suzanne's sparkling eyes. He saw her thick dark hair and his strong profile. And someday soon, he'd look into the faces of his great-grandchildren and know that Jamie and Suzanne weren't really lost at all.

They lived on in the children of their children.

* * * * *

THE MIGHTY QUINNS: MARCUS

Prologue

THE LATE AFTERNOON sun slanted through the grimy windows of the old stone stable. The stalls stood empty, their iron bars tangled with cobwebs and their old wooden doors battered and scarred. From the roof rafters, doves cooed softly, fluttering their wings and sending up motes of dust to dance in the sunlight.

Marcus Quinn huddled in the quiet shadows of the haymow, his arms wrapped tightly around his knees. At his feet, a small pile of wood shavings lay scattered in the musty hay. This had become his secret spot, the place he retreated to when his world got too difficult to bear. Today was his eighth birthday and nothing had changed.

He reached into his jacket and pulled out the Swiss Army knife his father had sent him last year for his birthday. The blade was sharp, honed by his grandmother's cook with the old whetstone she kept in the kitchen.

Marcus stared at the line of tiny figurines he'd set on a beam against the stable wall, counting them silently—birds, dogs, horses, fish, even an alligator he'd carved from a photo in a book. His very first carving, an owl, had been fashioned from a scrap of sapwood he'd found in the rubbish bin. Though it was crude and a bit uneven, Marcus liked the way its wide eyes watched him.

Over the past year his carvings had become much more detailed, aided by the old tools he'd found in a box in a dark corner of the stable. Marcus pulled the box from its hiding spot beneath a musty canvas and carefully inventoried the tools, touching each as he counted them. The handles were all worn smooth with age, but the edges were still as sharp as razors and free of rust.

Marcus reached down and ran his fingers over the initials carved into the front of the rough-hewn box. E.H.P. He'd wanted to ask his grandmother who the tools belonged to, but he was afraid she'd take them away from him, fearful that he'd hurt himself. Everyone treated him like a baby, always hovering over him, always concerned for his feelings. But Marcus was much stronger than they gave him credit for.

The stable door creaked and Marcus quickly shoved the toolbox back beneath the canvas, then shimmied against the wall. Holding his breath, he waited, praying that the shadows would hide him.

"Marcus! Jaysus, Marcus, come on. Nana is waiting in the car and she's pissed."

Marcus scowled. He and his two older brothers, Ian and Declan, had lived with their Grandmother Callahan for two years now, but Marcus still couldn't bear to call this place home. It was half a world away from his mother and father and the rest of his siblings, this big fancy house in a strange land where everyone talked in a funny voice and they played cricket and soccer instead of baseball and football.

Ian cursed. "Don't be such a baby. Just come on out. Nana said we can go to the cinema for your birthday. And then we'll have ice cream. She says it'll be a grand time."

Cinema? The movies. That's what it was called—*the movies.* Already his brothers had started talking like their mates at school, lacing everything they said with colorful curses and strange slang. Marcus shifted, sinking farther back into the dark. A strand of hay tickled at his nose and he fought against a sneeze, covering his face with his hands. The last of his tears still clung to his cheeks, and Marcus wiped his runny nose with his wrist, willing himself to remain silent.

His grandmother had ordered a wonderful birthday celebration with gifts and a cowboy cake and an afternoon outing in nearby Dublin. Though everyone had worked so hard to lift his spirits, it wasn't enough. After two birthdays away from home, he thought maybe this time he'd get to enjoy a celebration with his family, his ma and his da and all six of his older siblings.

He remembered the day he'd turned five, waking up in the morning and going downstairs to find the kitchen table covered with presents, all wrapped in the Sunday comics. He couldn't remember what gifts he'd received, but he remembered his mother sitting at the end of the table and watching him with tear-filled eyes.

She'd cried a lot that month and Marcus hadn't understood why. And then, one terrible night, his father had gathered them all around the kitchen table to tell them that their mother was very ill. Marcus remembered his confusion over the word: *cancer.* He'd never heard it before, but it was his father's somber expression and watery eyes that told him how serious it was.

Marcus wondered if she were crying now. There would be a phone call later that day from Da and Ma, as there had been for his sixth and seventh birthdays, and Marcus felt a sick knot growing in his stomach. It was always difficult to talk to his mother, to ignore the tears in her voice and pretend everything was all right, to lie to her and insist that he was happy living in Ireland.

Everything wasn't all right! His ma was sick—so sick, she could no longer care for her three youngest sons. So sick, his father had to go back to fishing with his uncle Seamus to make enough to pay the hospital bills. So sick that he and Ian and Declan had been sent away to Ireland so they wouldn't have to watch their mother die.

A fresh round of tears threatened and Marcus swallowed them back. She couldn't die, she wouldn't, if they'd only let him go home and take care of her. Marcus had always been able to make her laugh. He'd been her sweet baby, her silly clown, her wee boy. If anyone could make her well, he could.

"Come on, Marky!" Ian shouted. "We know you're in here. Nana's gonna take us to see *Top Gun*. It's supposed to be really neat, with jets and bombs and stuff."

"Maybe he's not here," Dec muttered. "We didn't search the attics. The little sissy could be hiding there."

"I'm not a sissy!" Marcus shouted. As soon as the words slipped out, he knew he'd made a foolish mistake.

"See?" Ian said. "I told you."

Marcus scrambled to the edge of the mow and peered down at his brothers. "I don't wanna go to the movies," he said defiantly. "You can go without me."

"It's *your* birthday," Ian said. "If you don't go, then Nana won't let us go. Grady is waiting to drive us."

"Maybe we can talk him into taking us to *Aliens*," Dec said excitedly. "Davey says it's really cool. There's this monster that comes out of this guy's chest and it's all gooey with big fangs and—"

Ian gave Dec a shove. "Yeah, right. Can you see Grady sittin' through that? He'd piss his pants." Ian looked up at Marcus. "What's the problem? Why are you actin' like a baby?"

"I'm not a baby. I just wanna go home. It's my birthday and I wanna see Ma and Da."

"We can't go home," Ian explained. "Not until Da says it's okay."

Ian always acted as if he knew everything, Marcus mused. He was only eleven, but he acted like the boss. And Dec wasn't any better even though he was just a couple years older than Marcus. They were always bullying him around. "You act like you don't even miss them," Marcus murmured, a hot tear trailing down his cheek.

Ian's expression softened. "I do. I miss them a lot. I miss Ma's cooking and I miss Da's singing."

"I miss 'em, too," Dec admitted. "I miss the way Ma

would read to us before she tucked us into bed. Haven't slept right since we came here."

Ian crawled up the ladder to the top of the mow and plopped down next to Marcus. A few seconds later, Dec joined them. They sat on the wide plank floor, their legs dangling over the edge.

"It's pretty cool up here," Dec commented.

"Nice animals," Ian added, pointing to the menagerie lined up against the wall. "Is that what you do up here? Carve those little animals?"

Marcus nodded. Though he'd always considered this spot his private retreat, it was nice to have his brothers paying attention to him for once. They usually didn't want anything to do with him. "I miss her smile," Marcus murmured.

Dec and Ian nodded, and they all sat silently, staring down into the barn. "I know a secret," Marcus ventured.

Dec turned to look at him. "You do not."

"I do, I do," Marcus insisted. "I found a treasure map."

"You're full of shite!" Ian declared. "Where?"

Marcus hesitated. He'd hoped to find the treasure himself. He'd been studying the map for months and couldn't figure it out, so he'd already resigned himself to asking for help. Between the three of them, they could figure it out.

"If we find the treasure, we split it three ways," Marcus said. He spit on his palm and held it out. "Swear."

Dec quickly shook his brother's hand. "I swear on my mother's—" He stopped suddenly. "I swear," he murmured.

Ian wasn't so quick to join in the deal. Finally he shrugged and added his promise. With that, Marcus scrambled to his feet and crossed the plank floor to the far wall. Ian and Declan followed him and waited as he brushed aside a small pile of hay.

"Here," Marcus said, pointing to a cubbyhole in the stone wall. Tucked inside was a yellowed piece of paper, rolled tightly and secured with a leather string. From the string dangled a small gold medallion with an odd inscription embossed into it.

"What's that?" Dec asked.

Marcus held up the medallion. "It's very old. I think it's a charm, like for luck. Or maybe it's magic." He unwound the medallion from the paper and showed it to his brothers, then smoothed the map out on the floor so they could all read it.

The two older boys bent down to study the pencil drawing. Dec reached out and touched a mark on the map. "X marks the spot," he said, his voice filled with disbelief. "Do you think it's pirates?"

"Could be," Ian said.

"Maybe there's gold," Marcus said, "or jewels. Enough so we could buy plane tickets to go back home."

Ian studied the medallion. "Maybe this is a clue, too. It's in some kind of different language."

"Maybe it's Irish," Dec suggested.

Ian gave him a shove. "Jaysus, Dec, you are a smart lad."

"We need to keep this a secret," Dec said. "We can't tell anyone, not even Nana." Dec wrapped the medallion around the paper and tucked it back into its hiding spot. "We'll come back later to study it."

They all crawled down from the haymow. Ian slipped his arm around Marcus's shoulders as they walked to the door. Marcus leaned into him, desperate for any reassurance that he still had a family.

"You're a clever lad, Marky," Ian said.

Marcus smiled. "If I were to ask Nana real nice, I bet she'd take us to see *Aliens*."

Ian chuckled, and Dec reached out to ruffle Marcus's hair. "Now there's an idea," Ian said. "Pretty damn smart for a seven-year-old."

"Eight," Marcus corrected.

"Yeah, right," Ian replied. "I guess you're a big guy now. Just like us."

A wide grin broke across Marcus's face. They were brothers and no matter what happened along the way, that would never change. Maybe now that he was eight, they would forget that he was the baby of the family. "I'm smart enough to know a treasure map when I see one," he said.

"That you are, Marky," his brothers said. "That you are."

1

"Do you ever wonder whether they're worth it? Women, I mean."

Marcus Quinn glanced up from the bucket of varnish he was stirring to see a gloomy expression cloud his brother Ian's face. "I don't know," he replied with a slight shrug.

"I guess I can't imagine what it would be like without them," Ian said. "They're nice to look at and they smell good. And sex...well, scx wouldn't be the same without them." He sank back into the battered couch, staring at his beer bottle as he scraped at the label with his thumbnail. "It just seems like it never gets anywhere. I remember the first girl I kissed like it was yesterday. And since then my life has gone straight to hell. You can't do with 'em and you can't do without 'em."

A chuckle echoed in the stillness of the boathouse, and they both looked over at Declan, who sat amidst the awls and chisels on Marcus's workbench, his legs dangling. "I remember that day. You looked like you were about to lose your lunch all over her shoes."

"You weren't even there," Ian challenged.

"I was," Dec replied. "Me and my mates used to watch you guys all the time. We were trying to pick up tips. The older lads were so smooth with the ladies. Except you, of course."

"Hell, you get French kissed when you're twelve years old and see if you can handle the shock," Ian snapped back.

Dec jumped down from the workbench and tossed his empty beer bottle in the rubbish, then strolled to the small refrigerator in the corner to fetch another. "She was a flah little scrubber all right," he said, thickening the Irish accent that still colored the Quinn brothers' voices. "By the time Alicia Dooley got around to you, she'd already kissed half the boys in your form at school. She even let a boy feel her up for a bag of crisps and a candy bar."

Ian's eyes narrowed. "You didn't."

Dec twisted the cap from the beer and took a long swig. "I was supposed to refuse? She was thirteen. And she had the nicest knobs at St. Clement's. I'd have been off my nut not to take advantage of a deal like that. Besides, I wanted to see what all the fuss was about."

Ian turned to Marcus, sending him an inquiring look, but Marcus shook his head. "Don't look at me."

"By the time Marky was old enough to have those thoughts, Alicia had got herself knocked up by Jimmy Farley and closed up her little schoolyard enterprise," Dec explained.

A comfortable silence descended over the boathouse. The Friday-night ritual between Marcus and Ian and

Declan had begun. Usually they'd meet for a few beers, sometimes at a pub, sometimes at Ian's place in town and sometimes in the old boathouse at their father's boatyard. They'd catch up with the week's events, the talk centering on work or sports. But occasionally they talked about women.

Marcus grabbed the bucket of varnish and climbed the ladder he'd propped up against his newest project, a twenty-one-foot wooden-hulled sloop that had been commissioned by a Newport billionaire for his son's sixteenth birthday. He'd been designing and building boats for three years now, working out of the old boathouse and living upstairs in a loft that was half studio and half apartment.

"Considering the number of women we've collectively been with, I wouldn't be surprised if we'd shared a few others," Declan murmured.

"There's a code among brothers," Ian countered. "You just don't mess with your brothers' girls, current or ex."

"You're right," Dec said. He crossed the room and held out his hand to Ian. "Sorry, bro. Won't happen again. You've got my word."

Marcus smiled to himself. The three Quinn brothers had formed an unshakable bond at an early age. After their mother's illness had been diagnosed and they'd been shipped off to Ireland to live with their grandmother, they'd learned to depend upon each other. From the moment they'd arrived in Dublin, they'd been outsiders, wary Americans forced to live in a culture whose rules they didn't understand.

And after they'd returned from Ireland, they'd become known as "those" Quinn boys, with their odd Irish accents and their independent ways, young men who could string curse words together like seasoned sailors and beat the stuffing out of men twice their size in a fistfight.

Ian had been eighteen when they'd returned and had immediately enrolled in college, anxious to get a start on his adult life. When he was accepted into the Providence Police Academy, he'd continued his education at night, graduating with a degree in criminal justice. Two years ago, he'd left the Providence PD and taken the job as police chief of their hometown, Bonnett Harbor, a picturesque Rhode Island village on the western shore of Narragansett Bay.

A year younger than Ian, Declan returned in time for his senior year in high school, bringing his grades up so he could apply to MIT. Four years of college, a knack for electronics and a stint with naval intelligence had paved the way for a job in corporate security. Declan's security consulting firm was the favorite among corporate bigwigs and multimillionaires along the East Coast.

Marcus had made the most difficult transition. He'd spent the majority of his childhood on Irish soil, away from his parents from age five to fourteen. He'd come back to a country that was as foreign to him as Ireland had been nine years before. School had been hell, and he'd avoided it whenever possible, retreating into solitude and avoiding close friendships. His brothers had been his only friends.

But his talent in art, especially carving and sculpture, had set him on an odd career path—first art school and then a few years working as a wood-carver with a boat-design firm in Boston. He'd been recruited as an instructor at a small school for boat restoration in Massachusetts. Now he ran his own show, doing commissioned wood carvings and building pretty wooden sloops based on vintage designs.

"Maybe we should take a break," Dec suggested, flopping down next to Ian on the sofa and kicking his heels up on the battered crate that served as a coffee table.

Marcus glanced up from the cockpit combing he'd been varnishing. "I'm the only one doing any work here, unless you call drinking my beer and eating my food 'work.'"

Dec grabbed the can of peanuts from Ian. "I was talking about women. We should take a break from women. You know, step back and try to gain a little perspective. We can't see the feckin' forest for the trees."

"What are you saying?" Ian asked.

"He's saying, in order to understand women, we should give up women," Marcus translated.

Giving up women would be impossible for Ian. He lived on his charm, able to navigate the most difficult situations with ease. While Marcus had few friends, Ian knew everyone and they loved him. Dec, on the other hand, was more focused. He was the thinker in the family, the one guy who was driven by the need to succeed. Any challenge, whether it was in his professional or personal life, was met with unrelenting resolve.

"We should study them," Declan suggested. "We're

three relatively clever guys. If we put our heads together, we should be able to figure women out. But you can't figure them out while you're sleeping with them, I know that. I've been sleeping with them for years and I'm no better off than I was the night I first did it."

Ian nodded. "The more women I know, the less I understand them."

Marcus rested his arms across the top of the ladder. "Maybe they're not the problem. Maybe we are."

"Speak for yourself," Dec said. "I know what the hell I'm doing in the sack. No one's ever complained."

Marcus shook his head. "I mean with…relationships. Isn't that what you're talking about?"

"And what the hell would I do with a relationship?" Dec asked. "I don't have time for that."

Marcus chuckled. "I rest my case."

"He's right," Ian said. "We want what everyone else wants. To get married. Start a life. Have a family. Look at our cousins, Uncle Seamus's boys. There are six of them and they're all married now."

"So we've got issues," Dec said defensively.

Ian straightened, as if offended by the comment. "What issues? If I had issues, I'd know about it."

"Not necessarily," Dec continued. "I once dated this psychology grad student, and after she heard about our childhood, she said it wasn't any surprise that I had an attachment disorder. She was right, because after I listened to a few more hours of her psychobabble, I detached her from my life."

"You have this disorder?" Ian said.

Marcus climbed down the ladder as he spoke. "We

all probably do. You gotta admit, after we were separated from the family, the only people we really trusted were each other."

"What about our cousins?" Ian asked. "They had the same start in life as we did, their da off working the Mighty Quinn and their ma disappearing on them. Did they have this disorder?"

Marcus shrugged. "Maybe. But they obviously overcame it since they're all married now."

"Where did *you* hear about this disorder?" Ian asked Marcus.

Marcus set the bucket of varnish on the workbench and searched for the turpentine to clean the brush. He shrugged. "Sometimes I watch Dr. Phil while I'm eating lunch."

He dropped the brush into a can of paint thinner then fetched a beer for himself. After sprawling himself in a ragged easy chair across from the sofa, he took a long drink of the cold beer.

"The way I see it, women are like peanuts," Ian declared, breaking the silence.

Dec laughed. "All right, ya daft wanker, I'll bite. How are women like peanuts?"

He held up the jar, then tipped some peanuts into his hand and popped them into his mouth. "The first handful is great," he said as he chewed. "The best thing you ever tasted. But then you keep eating them and eating them and they don't taste that special. After all, they are just peanuts, right? But then, you don't have them for a week or two and they're good again."

"And by not having them, you understand the nuts? You gain insight into their behavior?" Declan asked.

"It's not the best metaphor," Marcus said, jumping into his role as peacemaker between his two older brothers.

"How did we even get on the subject of women?" Ian asked.

Dec grabbed the peanuts and poured a measure into his hand. "Women spend most of their time together talking about men. If we spent more time talking about them, even objectively observing them, we'd be better off. And in order to do that, we need to stop sleeping with them. And stop socializing with them. Everything, full stop."

"No women? For how long?" The scowl on Ian's face was enough to tell that he wasn't in favor of the plan.

"As long as it takes," Dec said.

"My social life is crap anyway," Ian finally replied. "Since I moved back to Bonnett Harbor, I can't sneeze without half the town knitting me a bleedin' afghan. If I started dating, there'd be all sorts of gossip."

Dec looked over at Marcus. "What about you?"

"He barely dates as it is," Ian said. "This shouldn't be any problem for Marky."

"I date," Marcus said. "I just don't talk about it with you tossers."

"It shouldn't be a problem for him," Dec said. "He's stuck out in Newport on a boat for the rest of the summer."

"Just you and your tools?" Ian asked.

Marcus nodded. "Dec got me a job with Trevor Ross."

Dec held up his hands. "I got you in the door. You got the job."

Dec had provided security at a number of Ross's corporate events and parties and also advised his corporate office on a variety of matters. A passing conversation about Ross's sailing yacht and Marcus's talents had landed Marcus a new commission and a potential business partner with limitless capital.

"After I showed him my work, we got to talking, and he's interested in bankrolling the expansion of my business. I've got to find a bigger place, where I can build bigger boats. Maybe hire some new workers. Ross could throw a lot of business my way."

"What's his boat like?" Ian asked.

A grin curled the corners of Marcus's mouth. "You should see her. She's a beauty. Built in 1923. Eighty-foot wood ketch. It's all set up so you can sail it with a crew of two. He had the cabin completely refurbished but he wants more detailing, so I'm adding some vintage carvings and I'm replicating the original figure-head. I plan to live on the boat while I work. He's got it anchored off his place on Price's Neck. I start the day after I put this one in the water," Marcus said, nodding toward the wooden sloop sitting in the timber cradle.

Ian chuckled, shaking his head. "Now the man has something to say. Sometimes, Marky, I think you prefer boats to women."

"Back to the deal, then," Dec said.

"This has become a deal?" Ian asked.

Dec nodded. "We stay away from women. No flirting, no fondling, no nothing. Every week we get together to discuss our observations. After three months, we see where we are."

"No sex for three months," Ian stated.

"No women for three months," Declan said. "Complete celibacy."

"What about…you know…?" Ian raised his eyebrow and shook his closed fist up and down.

"Masturbation?" Dec asked. "Are you askin' about self-gratification, Ian Quinn? Well, you know what the church says about that. It's a sin. And besides that, it'll give you warts, pimples and, if you do it too much, your willy will dry up and fall off and you'll be turned into a wee girl."

"I'm not going completely cold turkey," Ian said.

Dec glanced over at Marcus, then back to Ian. "Well, I suppose we can make one exception to the rule."

Ian gave his brothers a satisfied nod. "And if I'm going to do this, there better be something worthwhile at the end."

"A naked woman in your bed isn't enough?" Dec asked.

"I'm talking money. Let's put a bet down. We all toss in a thousand bucks. The person who lasts longest after the three months takes the pot."

"And if you don't last three months?" Marcus asked.

"Then you throw another thousand in before you're allowed to break the pact," Ian said.

Marcus weighed the odds. Hell, he had the best chance of the three of them. And he could use the money. He'd gotten only a small advance from Ross to tide him over until the job was done. And he'd already spent the money he'd gotten for the sloop. "I'm in," he said. "I can't afford to lose, so that's incentive enough."

"I'm in," Ian said. "And I intend on winning this bet. I can easily do without women for three months."

"Game's on," Declan said.

He glanced at Marcus, and Marcus reached into his pocket and pulled out his key chain. Dangling from it was the old medallion they'd found in the stable on their grandmother's estate. It had become like a sacred relic to the three of them. Whenever one of the brothers needed good luck or a charm to swear upon, Marcus brought out the medallion.

"The minute one of us breaks the pact, we call the other two and confess," Dec said. "The money goes in the pot and the game continues until there's just one guy left."

Marcus spit in his hand, then clutched the medallion tight. Ian did the same, then clasped his brother's hand. Dec followed suit and slapped his hand on top of theirs.

"We meet once a week and we discuss what we've learned from our observations," Ian suggested. "Here's topic number one just to get us started. Why do women like shoes so much? And given the choice, would a woman prefer a new pair of shoes over a night in bed with either one of you?"

Marcus pondered the question for a long moment. Ian was right—he hadn't a clue. But he'd have plenty of time to think about his answer once he got on board

Trevor Ross's yacht. He'd also have time to figure out just how he'd spend his brothers' money.

A SHAFT OF SUNLIGHT filtered through the porthole and warmed Marcus Quinn's face. He slowly opened his eyes, and for a few seconds he was transported back to his childhood, to those days spent playing in the stable at Porter Hall.

He rolled over in the narrow berth and grabbed his wristwatch from the small shelf above his head. Wiping at his bleary eyes, Marcus tried to focus on the time, ignoring the dull ache in his head. "Eight-thirty," he murmured, sinking back into the pillows.

He'd been out with Ian and Dec last night, playing darts and pool at their favorite pub. For some strange reason, the pub had been filled with beautiful girls, an odd occurrence for a Sunday night and a place that usually didn't attract much of a female crowd. Unable to handle temptation, they'd ended up back at Ian's place, playing poker until well past two and discussing their observations on women.

The ketch rocked gently in the water as the waves slapped against the hull. Stretching his naked body beneath the sheets, Marcus closed his eyes and let his thoughts drift, the movement of the boat lulling him back toward sleep. He'd been living on board for over a week now and the boat was beginning to feel like home.

He raked his hands through his rumpled hair. But it wasn't home, it was work. And there was plenty to do today. Marcus swung his legs over the edge of the berth and glanced down at his morning erection, just another reminder that proper relief would be limited to his own devices. He had thought the bet would be easy for him. Marcus had never been a Casanova. But now that he wasn't allowed to have sex, that's all he could think about.

He dug through his clothes scattered over the opposite berth in the crew cabin, searching for something clean to wear, then gave up. It was about time to check out the small laundry room aft of the engine room—right after he started a pot of coffee. Marcus wandered sleepily down the narrow companionway, past the two spacious guest cabins.

From the time he could stand on a deck Marcus had loved being on the water. His earliest memories were of his father standing in the wheelhouse of the *Mighty Quinn,* the family swordfishing boat. Padriag Quinn had sold his interest in the boat to Marcus's uncle Seamus to help pay for his wife's medical bills. After bouncing around from boat to boat, grabbing whatever berth he could during the summer season, Paddy had been forced to accompany Seamus south for the winter to bring in more money.

The three-month summer visit became nine years as Emma Quinn valiantly battled cancer and her husband took any job he could find. Marcus's older brothers, Rory and Eddie, had worked part-time jobs, scraping together enough to contribute to food and rent. His sisters, Mary Grace and Jane, had taken care of the house and their mother.

Even with everyone contributing, things had gotten so bad while the younger boys had been gone, Paddy had sold the family home in Boston and moved them to a tiny cottage in Bonnett Harbor, Rhode Island. There, he'd worked for a boat-repair business on the western shore of Narragansett Bay when he wasn't fishing, a business he later took over from the elderly owner.

On the very day he and Dec and Ian had returned from Ireland, Marcus had wandered around the boatyard, searching for a solitary spot to regroup. He'd found the old boathouse in the farthest corner of the property and, inside, a small wooden sloop that had been left to ruin. Over the next year, he'd slowly restored the boat, and from that moment on he'd known he was destined to work with his hands—to carve beautiful brightwork and to design sleek wooden sailboats that looked pretty both in and out of the water.

A few years at Rhode Island School of Design were followed by another two years working at IYRS, a school for yacht restoration, setting him on the path to opening his own business. He'd built his first boat while still at IYRS. The twenty-three-foot wooden day-sailer took three months, and by the time he'd finished, Marcus had had three more commissions and enough money to hire two employees. Now, with the possible investment from Trevor Ross, things would start to look up.

Marcus glanced around the spacious lounge of *Victorious* as he passed through, his feet brushing against the cool teak sole of the boat. The ketch was a designer's dream, an inspiration for Marcus's future projects. He enjoyed discovering all the interesting nooks and crannies of the vintage yacht, examining the expensive restoration work. Just the maintenance costs of keeping a wooden boat afloat were ridiculous, but then Ross had money to burn.

As he turned the corner into the galley, Marcus stopped short, the breath leaving his chest. A woman, dressed only in lacy black panties, was bent in front of the icebox, that brief scrap of fabric riding up the curves of her backside. She was dripping wet, water puddling around her feet, her long hair plastered to her back.

Marcus glanced over his shoulder, deciding if he ought to step out and throw on some clothes or stand his ground. He didn't want to give the stowaway a chance to escape. Brushing aside his modesty and ignoring his slowly fading erection, Marcus braced his hands on either side of the door, then cleared his throat. She straightened, then turned and faced him, her face registering mild surprise. Her gaze slowly raked the length of his body, resting a long moment in the area of his crotch. "Good morning," she murmured, a smile twitching at her lips.

She didn't seem to be concerned about his lack of clothing—or hers, for that matter. He tried to avoid looking at her breasts, but he couldn't help himself. Her body was perfect, long-limbed and slender, with a tiny waist that flared out to lovely hips. His eyes drifted back to her breasts, lingering there for just a moment, and he wondered how it might feel to touch her, to cup each sweet breast in the palms of his hands. Damn, he really didn't need this now, not when he was doing his best to avoid thinking about perky breasts and curvy backsides.

"Are you finished?" she asked. "Or would you like

to take a closer look?" She held up her arms and slowly turned in front of him, offering him yet another glimpse of her backside.

Marcus's gaze darted back to her face, taking in the wide green eyes, high cheekbones and lush mouth now curved in a wry smile. Hell, this was every man's dream, the stuff of fantasies, stumbling on a nearly naked woman. Marcus swallowed hard. If he didn't find something to cover his crotch, she was going to see exactly what kind of effect she was having on him.

"Excuse me," he murmured. "I'll be right back." He turned and hurried toward his cabin.

"Is there coffee?" she shouted, poking her head out of the galley.

Marcus cursed softly as he dug through his clothes, looking for a clean pair of boxers. In the end, he tugged on baggy surfer shorts and made a quick stop at the head to brush his teeth. When he returned to the galley, she was still rummaging through the cabinets in the same state of undress. He groaned inwardly, wondering why she hadn't taken the chance to put on some clothes.

"May I ask what you're doing?"

"Coffee," she muttered impatiently. "Is it too much to ask that you start a pot of coffee in the morning?"

He stepped inside, moving past her. Her body brushed his, her breasts soft against his chest. He focused on the coffee, determined not to let her rattle him. The bag of beans was tucked behind a canister of sugar. Marcus pulled it out and dumped a healthy measure of the beans into the grinder. As the grinder whined, he glanced over his shoulder to find her perched on the counter, her hands braced at her sides, her long legs crossed at the ankles. He fought back an impulse to reach out and touch her just to make sure this wasn't all just a very vivid wet dream.

He dumped the ground coffee into a filter, then popped it into the coffeemaker, grateful for any distraction. After grabbing the pot, Marcus passed it over to her, and she filled it with water from the tap. They both watched until a stream of coffee began to drip into the pot. Then she reached behind her back and found two coffee mugs.

"I can't wait," she murmured, nudging his shoulder with the cups.

He filled her mug and handed it back to her, keeping his attention firmly fixed on the coffee. "How did you get on board?" he asked.

"I swam," she said. "I left my clothes and my bags on the dock. Maybe you could take the dinghy over later and get them for me?"

"Yeah," Marcus muttered. "Right." She had some nerve. He should be throwing her back in the drink. But it wasn't every day he got to enjoy the company of a naked woman, especially a woman who seemed more comfortable out of her clothes than in them.

"You're new," she said. "You're a bit older than the boys Daddy usually hires. Are you here to take over for that old barnacle Captain Davis? Please tell me he's finally retired to the Crusty Old Sailors' Home. Or was he swallowed by some accommodating white whale on his last cruise?"

Marcus bit back a curse as he poured himself a cup.

Daddy? Aw, bloody hell. The only person she could be talking about was Trevor Ross, which meant that the naked woman sitting behind him—the one he'd been drooling over—was his future business partner's daughter, Eden Ross.

Pictures of her as a little girl hung in the master cabin. But the rest of the world knew her from her tabloid exploits. She looked different in person, without the clothes and makeup and celebrity hair. Her skin was smooth and flawless, with a tiny sprinkling of freckles across her upturned nose, and her hair was a much darker blonde when it was wet. She looked almost wholesome. No, this was not the same girl who jetted around Europe, dated princes and attended Paris fashion shows.

"You're Eden," he said flatly.

"And you are?"

He turned and faced her, leaning back against the edge of the counter. "The new barnacle."

She giggled at the answer, and to Marcus's surprise, the sound sent a rush of heat through his bloodstream. "So I should call you Barney?" she asked, holding out her hand.

He wanted to touch her. At that moment it seemed like the most important thing in the world. He took the offered greeting, grasping her fingers in his, and Marcus instantly wondered how those delicate fingers would feel wrapped around him, stroking him.

He swallowed hard. "Marcus. Marcus Quinn. I'm…" He scrambled for the words. *Fighting off a serious case of lust…fantasizing about dragging you to my bed…*

wanting to know if you taste as good as you look. "Working for your dad," he finished, quickly dropping her hand.

He took a quick sip of his coffee, watching her over the rim of his cup. Was he expected to carry on a conversation with her? She didn't seem to be at all interested in getting dressed. The polite thing to do was to keep his gaze fixed on her face. He risked another glance at her breasts. Easier said than done.

"Doing what?" she asked.

"Your father hired me to do some wood carvings for the boat. I'm working on a new figurehead for the bowsprit and a piece for the wall in the dining area. And I'm carving some corbels for the lounge area and adding some ornamentation over the bed in the master suite."

"Well, well," she said, jumping down from the counter, "sounds like you're going to be a very busy man." She stepped toward him and lightly skimmed her palm down his chest, stopping when she reached his belly. Marcus held his breath and she sent him a provocative grin. "I'll try to stay out of your way. It'll be nice to have some company on board. Don't work too hard, Barney."

"It's Marcus. And you can't stay," he protested. How the hell was he supposed to concentrate on work with Eden Ross prancing around the deck naked? There was just so much a guy could take, and in ten short minutes he'd already reached his limit. All he could think about was finding a way to ease his sexual frustration. "Your father said I'd have the boat to myself. I can't work if you're here."

"Why is that?"

Was she that dense or was she simply toying with him? He'd already managed to lapse into a few brief and inappropriate fantasies. Given more time, Marcus knew what his imagination would provide—full-blown erotic daydreams that would only be erased by prolonged physical contact with a beautiful woman, like Eden Ross. From the moment he'd stumbled upon her, all he'd been able to think about was how long he'd have to wait to touch her. No, there was no way she could stay! "You just can't," he murmured.

"I'm sorry, but I don't care what you want. This is my father's boat and I'll stay as long as I like. If you have a problem with that, you can take it up with your boss." With that, she turned on her heel and disappeared down the companionway to the master suite in the aft section of the boat.

Marcus stuck his head out of the galley just in time to see her slam the door. "Oh, hell." This was trouble just waiting to happen. Eden Ross had a reputation that was known worldwide—she was a man-eater, a woman who took what she wanted from a guy then left him a quivering mass of disappointment and regret. And if she started nibbling on him, he wasn't sure he'd be able to defend himself.

A month didn't go by without a scandalous photo or article in the tabloids or a report on one of those Hollywood news shows. Eden went through men as if they were trendy fashion accessories, something pretty to keep on her arm and enjoy for the moment, then to toss aside once she found another boy who pleased her more.

Marcus shook his head and headed back to his cabin.

So she'd hang around for the weekend. A woman like Eden would grow bored with the solitude and be off to more exciting places before she could even unpack. "Two days," he said. "I'll give her two days and then she's got to go. If she doesn't, I'll just toss her overboard."

Marcus chuckled softly. He wouldn't get a whole lot of work done in the next forty-eight hours, but that really didn't matter. If entertaining the boss's pain-in-the-ass daughter was part of the job, then he'd do his best—short of sleeping with her and breaking the deal he'd made with his brothers.

But in such close quarters, there was no telling what might transpire. If his desire did eventually overwhelm his common sense, at least he'd have a decent tale to tell his brothers about the sexy little socialite he'd reeled in, then tossed back. And considering Eden Ross's reputation, she might be worth a two-thousand-dollar roll in the hay.

"Hey, Barney."

Eden stretched out on her towel, craning her neck around the mast and trying to catch a glimpse of Marcus Quinn. He'd been working on the bowsprit nearly all morning, dangling over the rail on a bosun's chair, dressed only in a pair of faded surfer shorts and boat shoes.

He'd been up early, leaving her a fresh pot of coffee and glazed donuts from the local Krispy Kreme. Eden wanted to believe he'd made a thoughtful gesture, but after a surly exchange with him over her preferences for lunch, she knew he'd merely been following orders.

Frustrated, she'd gobbled up three of the donuts and washed them down with a mug of black coffee. Why was she allowing him to bother her so? He didn't care for her, and that was fine. After all, he wasn't *that* attractive, and she'd sworn off men for at least the next month or two. But that didn't seem to stop her from wanting him. He was like…like the Mount Everest of men. She had to climb him simply because he was there—and because if his naked body and considerable assets were any indication, he'd be one incredible mountain to climb.

She watched him as he crawled back over the rail and retrieved one of the tools spread on the deck.

"Hey, Barney!"

A tiny sliver of satisfaction shot through her as he dropped the tool he was holding and strolled along the rail to the spot where she was sunbathing. "The name's not Barney. Unless you'd like me to call you—what?— how about Princess?"

"I like that," Eden teased, sending him her sexiest smile. "Your Highness would be even better, though." She picked up her bottle of suntan lotion and held it out. "Do my back?"

Marcus shook his head. "No. I'll make you coffee, I'll fetch your damn baggage, but I'm not going to be your personal slave."

"Please?" She watched his face flush and found the notion of his embarrassment completely charming. Most of the men she knew wouldn't think twice about agreeing to her request. "Are you shy?"

"No," he said.

"It's just lotion," she said. "And I won't bite."

He hesitated, cursing softly, then snatched the bottle from her fingers. Eden rolled over on her stomach and stretched out on the towel, resting her chin on her hand. She closed her eyes and waited for his touch, the anticipation making her heart beat a little faster.

A moment later his palms smoothed across her back. Eden bit back a contented sigh. She had enjoyed her share of men, though she'd slept with far fewer than the press had reported. But Marcus was different. He'd made it clear he didn't want her on board and done his best to ignore her. And even though she sensed an attraction between them, he'd done absolutely nothing to act upon it. She'd never known a man to be able to maintain such restraint. "You aren't gay, are you?" she asked.

His hands stilled. "What?"

Eden looked over her shoulder. "Gay. Usually I can tell, but—"

"You think because I haven't tried to seduce you that I prefer men?"

"Do you?" she asked. "Because there's nothing wrong with that. Or maybe you go both ways? You can be completely honest with me."

He cleared his throat, then continued to rub the lotion onto her back. "No, I prefer women. I'm just not sure I'd be able to handle a woman like you."

"Like me?"

"I'm afraid I might suffer by comparison," Marcus said.

His words cut her to the quick. In an instant, Eden knew exactly what he thought of her, how he'd already pegged her as a silly socialite with a penchant for ill-advised sexual escapades. Maybe he was right. In fact, before long, the whole world would be thinking that very same thing and have the proof of it to boot.

But her real life, the one that she lived for most of the hours of the day, was nothing like the life portrayed in the press. She wasn't a raging nymphomaniac and she didn't engage in wild orgies and she'd only danced top-less once at a nightclub, and only because she'd drunk too much champagne. "I haven't really been with that many men," she admitted.

Marcus chuckled. "Why do I find that so hard to believe?"

She felt her temper rise. "Because, like the rest of the idiots in this world, you think everything you read in the tabloids is true. They use me to sell papers, to make money. They don't care if what they write is a big lie as long as people want to read it."

"And you give them plenty of excuses to write about you," he said.

"You sound like my father," she muttered, her voice cold and dismissive.

"Funny, I don't think your father would approve of what I'm doing right now. Or how you're enjoying it." He reached up and ran his hands along her shoulders, then came back to the center of her back. He paused to put more lotion on his hands, then began to move lower.

Eden's anger slowly dissolved and she held her breath, losing herself in his touch. Marcus Quinn had very strong and sensuous hands, inflaming her desire. He also had the strange talent of provoking her ire at the very same time.

His fingers slipped beneath the strap of her thong as he began to massage lotion onto her backside. When his hand slipped between her legs, she fought the temptation to turn over and pull him down on top of her. Why couldn't he just kiss her and be done with it? Why did he insist on taunting her like this?

"That's fine," she murmured.

"You don't want me to do your other—"

"No. Thanks. You—you can go now."

"Great," he said, his voice laced with sarcasm. "Is there anything else I can get for you, Princess?"

"Now that you mention it, I don't think I can survive on donuts and coffee. Unless we tie up at the dock, the market in town won't deliver. If you could pick up some fresh fruit for me—some melon, kiwi, papaya, some really good grapes—I'd appreciate it. Make sure it's all organic, though. And there's a really good fish market in town. I don't care what you get as long as you cook it properly. The housekeeper has accounts at all the shops in town. Just charge whatever you buy."

He stood up beside her, casting a shadow over her body. For a long time he didn't move, and she wondered what he was thinking. In truth, he was probably thinking about turning her into shark bait. But if he persisted in provoking her, then she had no choice but to stand up for herself. "That's all," Eden said. "You can go now. I'll call you if I need you again, Barney."

A few seconds later she heard his footsteps on the deck. Eden couldn't help but watch his retreat, curious to see whether he bothered to look back. All of this wouldn't be half as frustrating if Marcus Quinn wasn't so damn gorgeous.

Was it the dark hair or the deep blue eyes that she liked so much? Or was it the crooked smile that he so rarely used? He couldn't be called charming or even friendly. But he possessed an undeniable masculinity, a way of commanding her attention that made him irresistible.

Perhaps she shouldn't test him so, but sooner or later, he'd have to waver. Eden sighed. She was accustomed to getting what she wanted. But this time she didn't really know what that was. Did she simply need Marcus to acknowledge the attraction, to make her feel better about herself? Or was she looking for something to distract her from the troubles looming just over the horizon?

Eden had often tried to understand her warped view of relationships. She suspected it had to do with her parents' divorce when she was seven. It had been called the divorce of the decade, acrimonious at best, downright vicious at its worst. She'd been used as a pawn in a settlement and custody fight between her grasping mother and her controlling father. When the courts had finally put an end to the fight, Eden had realized neither one of her parents really wanted her. All they had cared about was winning.

So she'd spent the school year in Malibu with her

mother and summers in Newport with her father. She rarely saw Trevor Ross, but he made up for his absences by indulging her every whim. At first, she cared nothing for his gifts, preferring his company instead. But after a time, Eden realized that the only thing she would ever have of her father was what he bought for her.

Her problems with her father extended to other men. After five or six years of dating, she knew her chances at ever making a normal relationship work were slim at best. She'd never been able to trust a man enough to let him inside her life…or inside her heart. For a long time, that hadn't made a difference. But lately she'd wanted to believe she could have a grand romance, an affair that would last longer than a few months.

There had to be something more to life than what she'd experienced so far. Something deeper, something real. And though hiding out on her father's yacht might provide the solitude she needed to sort out her life, playing games with Marcus Quinn wasn't the best use of her time.

"Just let the man do his job," she murmured. "And stay out of his way." She repeated the words again, but she still couldn't convince herself. Every time he was near, she felt compelled to look, to say something that might provoke him into conversation. And if she thought the suntan-lotion ploy would satisfy her desire for his touch, Eden was fooling herself.

Maybe he was right. Maybe it would be best for both of them if she just packed her bags and left. Eden took a deep breath and shook her head. No, she'd stay. But she'd try her best to get along with Marcus, to make him see that, at heart, she really was a good girl.

2

MARCUS sat in the cockpit of the boat, the canvas sunshade stretched across the boom providing a welcome relief from the midafternoon heat. He stared down at a sketch he'd been working on for the past hour, then tossed the sketchbook aside. It was no use. Since Eden Ross had come on board two days ago, his thoughts had been occupied with everything but work.

Every time he tried to concentrate, he'd find his mind drifting, conjuring up crazy scenarios that always seemed to end with the two of them naked and in each other's arms. It was obvious she wouldn't object to his advances. He wasn't always an expert at reading women, but Eden was like an open book—a book with really big print for those with bad eyesight. She wanted him—probably a helluva lot more than he wanted her. So why not take advantage?

With any other woman, he might not think twice. But Eden Ross was seriously out of his league. With her, it would be all about sex and nothing more. For him, it would be about badly needed relief. And though Marcus had always been a believer in no-strings sex, he was nearly twenty-seven, too damn old to feel good about it anymore. There had to be more to life than just finding physical gratification in a stranger's bed.

There were also two other huge impediments to a sexual liaison with Eden Ross. Her father—a potential business investor he couldn't afford to lose—and his brothers. Two thousand dollars was a lot of cash. But it wasn't just the money that kept Marcus from following his instincts. His pride was at stake. As the youngest, he'd always been on the losing end of most of the challenges between the three. This was one he could actually win.

"I'm going for a swim," Eden said.

He glanced up, shading his eyes against the sun. She stood on the deck above the cockpit, a towel draped around her neck, her hair tucked up beneath her wide-brimmed sun hat. He watched as she walked past him, the towel slipping from its place as she moved, offering a tempting view of her breasts.

They'd managed to avoid each other for nearly an entire day, and Marcus considered that a small victory. Eden had graciously stayed out of his way and spent her time sunning on the opposite end of the boat from where he was working. Last night she'd turned in early and this morning she had slept late. They'd managed a polite "hello" at lunchtime and nothing more.

"Would you like to join me?" she asked, turning back to face him. She tossed her hat aside, and her pale hair tumbled down around her shoulders.

Hell, he'd love nothing more than to strip off his

clothes and jump into the water with her. His mind quickly summoned an image of him swimming up behind her and pulling her naked body against his, their limbs tangling together as they played in the clear water. "I think I'll pass," he muttered.

"Suit yourself."

A few seconds later he heard a splash and then a tiny scream. Marcus scrambled out of the cockpit to the stern and stared down into the water. She broke the surface and then frowned when she saw him watching her. "Are you all right?"

Eden nodded, droplets of water glittering on the tips of her eyelashes. "It was just colder than I expected."

Marcus leaned over the rail and watched her swim away from the boat and back again. She'd discarded the thong she'd been wearing earlier, preferring complete nudity while in the water. He was almost growing accustomed to seeing her naked, although he would never become immune to the effect it had on his body. Even now, he felt himself growing hard as he imagined their naked bodies pressed against each other.

"Come in," she said. "The water is wonderful."

"I should be working," Marcus replied.

"It's almost five. My father can't expect you to work twenty-four hours a day."

"It's two-thirty," Marcus countered. "That's not almost five."

"You need a new watch," Eden said with a grin. She flipped over on her back and kicked away from him. "Besides, I'm not a very strong swimmer and I'd feel better if you were in the water with me. For safety's sake."

Marcus laughed out loud at the absurdity of her request. Yes, Eden Ross was spoiled and manipulative. But she didn't try to hide it. In fact, she seemed to delight in her flaws. Maybe he ought to answer her playful challenge—just once.

"Cover your eyes," he said.

"What?"

"You heard me. I'm not getting in the water unless you cover your eyes."

"Aren't you a prude?" Eden teased. "I've seen it all before and it wasn't that impressive."

True, Marcus mused, there were no secrets between them. But from the moment she'd jumped in, he'd fought the warm rush of desire that had raced through his bloodstream and pooled in his lap. Now the result of that desire was pressing hard against the front of his shorts. Did he really want Eden to know the power she held over him? "Turn around and cover your eyes or I don't come in the water."

Eden groaned, then did as she was told.

But Marcus didn't bother to strip off his shorts. He jumped off the side of the boat, slipping into the water with barely a sound. He swam beneath the surface, his eyes open, searching for Eden. When he came up, he was right behind her. "You can open your eyes now," he said.

She spun around and splashed water in his face. Marcus grabbed her waist and pulled her under, dragging her down beneath the surface before letting her go. When she came up for air, she spit a mouthful of water in his face, then easily swam away from him.

"I don't think you're in any danger of drowning," he said.

"I just ate a donut. I could get a cramp. Or a shark could attack me. Or I could accidentally swallow water and begin to sink." With that, she twirled around in the water, slowly sinking until she disappeared. A few moments later she popped up a few yards away.

"That was a pretty slick move," he said.

"Synchronized swimming. My mother made me take lessons. I took all sorts of lessons. Ballet, gymnastics, piano, painting, violin, ballroom dancing, horseback riding. There are more—I just can't remember them all."

"You must be quite accomplished."

She shrugged, brushing the damp hair out of her eyes. "I was never really good at any of them. The lessons were just an excuse so my mother didn't have to spend time with me. She had other things to do and I just got in the way."

It didn't take much to see beneath the bravado. For all her father's money and the comforts it provided, it seemed that Eden hadn't had a very happy childhood. Even now, the confident facade had cracks that revealed a very vulnerable girl inside. "You're a good swimmer," Marcus said.

A tiny smile curled the corners of her mouth. "Thanks." She swam up to him and placed her hands on his shoulders, allowing him to tread water while he kept her afloat. "For a while there, I thought you'd never speak to me again," she said, watching him intently.

"You do have a talent for getting on my last nerve," he said.

"I do?" Her smile grew wider. "And I never took lessons for that. Maybe I do have a true talent after all."

"Do you enjoy bothering me?"

"You're entirely too serious, Marcus Quinn. You need to lighten up." She wrapped her arms around his neck, pressing her body against his. He held on to her waist and stared down into her pretty eyes. "You can kiss me now," she murmured, her voice breathless.

"I don't think so," Marcus said. He fought the urge to touch her more intimately, to cup her breast in his palm, to nuzzle his face into the curve of her neck, to slip his hands around her backside. The battle was almost painful, raging in his head and in his groin.

"Don't you want to kiss me?"

"I do," he admitted, allowing his hands to slide down to her hips. "But not right now."

Her gaze fixed on his mouth and she moved closer, her mouth just inches from his. "When?"

"I'll get back to you on that," Marcus replied.

But Eden wasn't one to take no for an answer. In a heartbeat, she leaned closer and brushed her lips across his, running her warm tongue along the crease of his mouth. She slowly pulled back, her eyebrow arched. "There, that wasn't so bad, was it?"

He'd tried to resist, but at that moment, he wasn't sure why. With a low groan, Marcus captured her mouth with his, pulling her into a deep kiss, his hand furrowing in her wet hair. Their tongues touched, and he felt himself losing control, his fingers desperate to explore her soft flesh. His lips traced a path to her shoulder and then lower, to the tops of her perfect breasts. Her nipples peaked in the cool water and he drew one into his mouth, teasing at it with his tongue.

In his life, he'd never wanted a woman more than he wanted Eden. It had always been so easy to control his desires, but this had gotten way out of hand. He knew he could have her. And he knew he wanted her. His reason and resolve had vanished the moment her lips had touched his. This wasn't some girl he'd picked up in a bar. This was Eden Ross, his boss's daughter, the woman who was about to put a quick end to his feeble attempt at celibacy.

For a moment, they both forgot to tread water and slowly began to sink, but then Marcus pulled them back up, returning to taste her mouth. Her mouth was sweet and warm, her body clinging to his, his erection pulsing against her belly, aching for release.

She reached down to touch him, and Marcus sucked in a sharp breath, teetering on the edge of total surrender. Why did he always seem just one step behind her? Every time he gained control, she found a way to yank it from his grasp. Abruptly he pulled away, ending the caress as quickly as it had begun. "I think I've had enough…swimming for today."

He turned and swam back to the stern of *Victorious,* then slowly climbed the ladder. Their little encounter had done nothing to diminish his desire, but he was past hiding it from her. Though his body might want to take pleasure in Eden's, he was smart enough and strong enough to resist the temptation—at least for now.

"HEY!"

Eden slowly opened her eyes, then stretched her arms above her head, her cotton T-shirt riding up on her belly. She'd curled up on the berth in the lounge after her swim and had dozed off. The stress of the past week, combined with two days of jet lag and two nights filled with strange fantasies about Marcus Quinn, had exhausted her.

With a soft sigh, she sat up and rubbed her eyes. Marcus stood in the hatchway, his lean body outlined by the sun, his arms braced on either side of him. Her mind returned to their swim, to the delicious moment when he'd pulled her into his arms and kissed her.

Even now, a thrill raced through her body at the thought of his touch and the feel of his lips on her breast, the heat of his desire in her hand. He might pretend to ignore her, but now Eden knew exactly how defenseless he was in this little game she was playing. One kiss, one caress, and he'd tumbled over the edge of reason and into her arms.

"Come up top. I need your help," he said. A moment later he disappeared, his silhouette replaced by the soft light of the late-afternoon sun.

Marcus Quinn was definitely different from any man she'd ever met. Real, she thought to herself. Solid and self-assured. There was a steadiness in him that she found oddly intriguing. It didn't come from well-honed charm or extravagant wealth or even an overblown ego.

He knew exactly who he was and, by that, had quickly figured out who she was—inside and out.

Though he found her sexually attractive, Eden wasn't sure that he even liked her. When she wasn't in the process of trying to seduce him, he barely spoke to her. And though she spent hours watching him, he rarely gave her a second glance. It shouldn't have mattered to her. But for some reason, she wanted that from him, an admission that it wasn't just the prospect of sex that attracted them.

She glanced around the cabin for her sunglasses and slipped them on as she walked up the steps to the deck. She'd give anything if Marcus could see past the woman he thought she was—even just for a few hours. To the world, Eden Ross was a party girl, an heiress, a trust-fund baby. She'd become fabulously famous for being…famous. She hadn't discovered or invented or contributed anything worthwhile in her life, yet the entire world seemed to be interested in what she wore and who she dated and where she traveled. It was all so silly and superficial.

And it was entirely her own fault. She'd taken control of her trust fund at age twenty-one and promptly allowed her life to career out of control. She'd let the press invade her privacy and now she couldn't get rid of them. Once her latest and most salacious scandal hit the tabloids Stateside, her father would be through with her. He'd threatened to disown her more times than she could count, and this would definitely push him over the edge.

A sick feeling twisted in her stomach, and she wondered if it was regret or the seawater she'd swallowed during her swim. Eden rubbed her stomach and winced as she walked through the cabin to the hatch. She found Marcus on the bow of the boat, bent over his toolbox.

"Give me a hand, will ya?" he said, passing her a tool without looking at her.

She stared down at the broad expanse of his back, bronzed by the sun and shifting with sinewy muscle. Her gaze drifted across his wide shoulders. His long hair, still damp from their swim, brushed his nape. Eden's fingers tensed and she reached out to toy with a curl that rested against his neck. But when he turned suddenly, she drew back her hand.

"Are you all right?"

"I'm fine," she murmured, a hint of defensiveness in her voice. "What do you need me to do?"

Marcus pointed to a line dangling over the rail. "I need you to crawl out onto the bosun's chair. You're going to fit that wrench over a bolt and then hold on to it while I loosen a nut on the other side. Whatever you do, don't drop the wrench in the water."

"I'm not an idiot," Eden said. "How hard could it possibly be to hold on to your damn…tool." She stifled a smile, amused by the flicker of desire she saw in his eyes.

He stood up in front of her, sending her a dismissive glare. Eden's gaze drifted down, following a line of hair that began just above his belly button and ended somewhere beneath the waistband of his shorts. He'd found a way to deal with his desire, the bulge now gone from the front of his shorts.

Eden had always harbored an intense fascination with the male body. There were so many different types of men, so many facets to male beauty. Long limbs, hard muscle, sharp angles and smooth surfaces. She longed to touch Marcus again, to test his responses and gently stir his passions. Just how good would it be between them? Would he be the best she'd ever had?

All men have their breaking point, Eden mused. What was Marcus's? Did he prefer to be seduced slowly or was it better to catch him off guard? Just the thought of finding the answers to her questions was exciting.

"Are you just going to stand there?" he asked. "Or are you going to make yourself useful?"

Her gaze met his and grudgingly she did as she was told, swinging her leg over the rail and slipping into the bosun's chair. "Happy?" she asked.

"Deliriously," he shot back. He followed her over the rail and shimmied out onto the bowsprit, his legs wrapped around the carved figure of a mermaid that decorated the prow of the boat. "Now reach out and slip the socket wrench over the bolt head. And then hold on to it really tightly and don't let it move."

She stared at weathered wood in front of her, gnawing at her lower lip. She really ought to know what he was talking about, but she wasn't quite sure what a socket wrench did and what a bolt looked like. "So what are we doing here?" she asked, stalling for time.

"I'm removing this old carving so I can either restore it or reproduce it."

"You must be pretty good if my father hired you to work on his precious boat."

"I do all right," he said. His lips curled in a slight smile and Eden took it as a small victory. Strange how something as simple as a compliment could please him. She'd become so intent on seducing him, she'd hadn't taken any time to get to know who he was and what he liked.

"How long have you been carving wood?"

"Since I was a kid. My da gave me a Swiss Army knife for my seventh birthday and I used to carve little animals. As I got older, the carvings got bigger and more elaborate."

"You're an artist, then," she said.

"Okay, are you ready?"

Eden reached out to brace her hand on the bowsprit, but as she did, she lost her grip on the wrench and it slipped from her fingers, plopped into the water and quickly sank. "Oops."

"Aw, hell," he muttered.

Eden wriggled in the boson's chair. "Don't worry. I can find it. I'll just go get a mask and—"

"No, there's an adjustable crescent wrench in my toolbox. Find it and see if that will work."

Eden crawled back on board and stared down into the toolbox. Was she supposed to know what a crescent wrench was? Did most women know what a crescent wrench was? She glanced over at Marcus, then back down again at the jumble of tools. For the first time in her life she felt completely useless.

She opened her mouth to question him but then snapped it shut again. All of the fears and frustrations that had been building over the past week suddenly surged up inside her. She swallowed back the tears and pasted a smile on her face.

"I—I don't...I can't—"

"It's the silver thing that looks like a *C*," he said impatiently. "It's got a little screw barrel that makes it smaller and bigger."

Eden bent down and rummaged through the tools, but she couldn't find anything that looked like what he described. A tear dribbled from the corner of her eye, and with a vivid curse she brushed it away. "I can't," she said, shaking her head. She hurried along the rail to the cockpit, then quickly descended into the cabin.

With a shaky sigh, she sat down on the couch and pulled her knees up to her chin, pressing her face against her legs. Unwanted tears dampened her cheeks and she fought against them. She couldn't recall the last time she'd cried. It had been years, a lifetime ago. But since she'd returned home, her emotions had been bubbling just beneath the surface, threatening to spill over at the slightest provocation.

"A crescent wrench," she murmured, a fresh round of tears flooding her eyes. "I'm crying over a damn wrench."

But it wasn't just the wrench. It was the video and the pictures and the betrayal and the shame. The video had been nothing more than a silly game of seduction meant to add a bit more excitement to a night together nearly three years ago. But now it was out there, threatening to make her the object of public ridicule and lascivious speculation.

She should have known better than to trust Ricardo—to trust any man, for that matter. But she'd had a bit too much champagne, and Eden had never been one to be afraid to try something new. And Ricardo had promised to erase the tape after they watched it. She'd thought he cared about her, at least enough not to ruin her life.

But then, the blame could be put entirely on her. He'd kept the video a secret for three years, until she'd made an offhand remark to a reporter about Ricardo's sexual prowess and been misquoted. Suddenly the tape had resurfaced in the hands of an Internet entrepreneur, who'd released a few blurry stills to the European tabloid press.

When the photos had hit the papers, she'd been shocked. Confronting Ricardo had proved useless. He had simply claimed he had nothing to do with it, but she'd heard the lie in his voice. He'd taken the tape and given it to a friend, and that friend was now trying to sell it to the highest bidder.

It had been a lifetime ago and she'd been a stupid girl who had thought she was in love. And now the tape threatened to ruin her life. She didn't have the money to buy it back and Eden couldn't ask her father for help. She had found herself with no way out, so she'd run. The story would hit the tabloids in the U.S. any day now.

Eden felt a hand on her shoulder and she jerked her head up. "Are you all right?" Marcus asked.

"Fine," she said, quickly wiping the tears from her cheeks. "I—I'm sorry about the wrench. It was a wrench, right? I'll buy you a new one. I'll buy you a hundred of them."

He smiled and nodded. "The water's clear. I'll be able to find it. No big deal." He reached out and tenderly brushed the hair from her face. "I'm sorry I snapped at you."

He studied her face, his gaze skimming over her features as if trying to understand her tears. And then he leaned forward and kissed her. It was a perfect kiss, full of sweetness and warmth. The breath slipped from Eden's lips along with the frustration and confusion she felt. It hadn't come as a result of seduction or some game she'd played. It had come from simple kindness.

Strange how Marcus, a man she barely knew, could make her feel safe with just one kiss. She'd always managed to throw herself into the paths of completely inappropriate men. She didn't know anything about Marcus Quinn, beyond the fact that he knew how to kiss and he had some kind of accent. For all she knew, he could be yet another in a long line of self-absorbed jerks. But for now, his touch, his kiss, made her feel better about herself.

"I don't think we should do any more work today," he murmured, his lips warm against her temple. "I'm going to go into town and get us something really good for dinner and we'll celebrate."

"Celebrate what?" Eden asked, glancing up into his deep blue eyes.

He shrugged. "I don't know. I'm sure we'll come up with something. We've got all night."

Eden nodded, a tiny sliver of apprehension shooting

through her. One of two things would happen tonight, she mused. Either they'd become friends or they'd become lovers. The trouble was Eden wasn't sure which she wanted more.

LIGHTS LINED THE DOCK of the Ross estate, reflecting in the glassy water. The sprawling white clapboard house sat on a rise overlooking Price's Neck, the last of the sunset fading behind it. Though the house was huge, it wasn't nearly as ostentatious as some of the neighboring mansions. Marcus smiled to himself. He could have fit Porter Hall inside Trevor Ross's house at least twice, and the guesthouse alone was bigger than the Quinn family house in Bonnett Harbor.

Marcus shifted the grocery bags in his arms as he walked down to the water. He'd given Eden a few hours to calm herself and he hoped that her dismal mood had dissipated. He really wasn't adept at dealing with tears, and they came as such a surprise from Eden. She seemed to maintain such tight control of her emotions.

It didn't look as though she'd be leaving anytime soon. If they were going to live together on the boat, they had to come to some sort of understanding, and tonight would be the perfect time to work out the terms. He'd bought a ready-made meal of cold salmon, grilled vegetables and Caesar salad, along with cherry pie for dessert. Champagne was also on the menu, although Marcus wasn't too sure about the effect it would have on his self-control.

As Marcus stepped onto the dock, he saw a figure at the end, rising from a bench that overlooked the water.

Though the light was low, he immediately recognized his brother Declan. "Hey," he called.

Dec waved and waited for Marcus to reach the end of the dock. "Hey, little brother."

"What are you doing here?" Marcus asked, an uneasy feeling twisting at his gut. "Is everything all right? Is Ma okay?"

"I'm here on business."

"How the hell did you get past the gate?"

"I'm doing another job for Ross," Declan explained. "I have the security codes to the house and the gate. I thought you'd be out on the boat, but the housekeeper said your truck was gone."

"I was just getting some dinner from town," Marcus said. He set the bags on the bench. "What kind of job?"

"I'll tell you all about it over dinner," Dec said. "I assume you have cold beer on that boat and something good to eat in those bags." He peeked inside, then withdrew the bottle of champagne. "I thought you preferred Guinness."

Marcus grabbed the bottle and shoved it back into the bag. "I'm just resupplying the boat. Replacing a bottle I drank one night when I ran out of beer."

Declan pulled out a plastic bag and dangled it in front of Marcus's face. "And what are these?"

"Organic mangoes," Marcus explained.

"Since when do you eat mangoes?"

Marcus shrugged. "I like mangoes. Kiwi, too." He grabbed the bag and searched for a quick change of subject. "You said you're doing a job for Ross?"

Dec nodded. "I'm looking for his daughter," he said, giving him an odd look. "She's gone missing."

"Missing? Like kidnapped?"

Dec held out a copy of a tabloid newspaper he had tucked under his arm. Marcus took it and turned it toward the light at the end of the dock. *The National Inquisitor.*

"'Eden's Sexcapade Caught on Tape,'" Dec read.

"What exactly is a 'sexcapade'?" Marcus asked.

"Miss Ross and one of her Eurotrash boyfriends decided to make a little home movie a few years back. Somehow it got out there, and now the guy who has it is threatening to sell it over the Internet. He's released a few still photos from it to amp up the interest. The story broke in Europe last week and the tabloids picked it up here. In a few days it will be all over the news. Trevor Ross is furious and he has his lawyers working on a lawsuit against the magazine. Meanwhile, nobody seems to know where Eden is. Ross isn't even sure this is his daughter in the video, and until he talks to her, he can't confirm it."

"Don't these magazines usually make stories up?"

"Yeah, but look at the photo," Dec said.

Marcus squinted to try to make out Eden's face, but it was too blurry to see. "And you're looking for her?"

"We know she landed at JFK last Sunday, but after a cabbie dropped her off at the Plaza in Manhattan, she just vanished. Ross thought she might come here, but I didn't think so. The housekeeper hasn't seen her. She's probably hiding out with friends in New York City."

"Hiding out?" Marcus asked.

"Hell, she had to know this would hit the fan sooner or later. I don't think she's too anxious to see her father right now. It's going to cost him a lot of money to get her out of this."

"Maybe he shouldn't," Marcus said with a shrug.

"Her problems are his problems," Dec said. "If he can't control his daughter, people are going to start to think he doesn't have control over his business interests either."

"She's a big girl," Marcus replied. "She lives her own life."

"She's a silly girl with far too much money and free time on her hands. But if she does come here, I want you to call me."

Marcus nodded, then rolled up the tabloid. "I think I'll keep this. I'm not sure I'd recognize her if I saw her."

In truth, Marcus knew nearly every inch of Eden's body, from the gentle slope of her shoulder, to the soft spot behind her knee, to the sweet curves of her breasts. He'd recognize her stark naked and fully clothed, in broad daylight and in the deepest night. He could probably recognize her by the feel of her skin or the taste of her mouth or the smell of her hair. In just a few short days he had come to know Eden Ross quite intimately.

"So are you going to show me this boat you're working on?" Declan asked.

"Another time. It's a mess right now. I've got wood and tools all over the place. Wait until I'm done. Then I'll really have something to show you."

Dec reluctantly nodded. "All right. You sure you don't want to come out for a beer?"

"Nah, I'm beat. I've been working all day. I just want to eat something and then turn in."

"We're still on for dinner Friday night at Ian's place, right?" Dec asked. "I've got another job I'm working on for Ross. But that shouldn't interfere."

"Yeah, we're still on."

Dec clapped his hand on Marcus's shoulder. "Enjoy your mangoes, baby brother."

"I will," Marcus said. He breathed a silent sigh of relief, then wondered why he felt relief at all. Since Eden had come aboard he'd been looking for a way to get rid of her, and now he'd just blown his chance. Instead of revealing her presence, he'd suddenly felt a need to protect her, to preserve her privacy—or was it *their* privacy now?

He needed more time, just a day or two to figure out this illogical attraction he had to her. Every time he drew a line in the sand, they seemed to step across it, yet Marcus wasn't sure he wanted to go back. Not just yet.

He carefully loaded the groceries into the dinghy, then stepped down off the dock. The outboard sputtered to life and he steered the small boat toward *Victorious*. By the time he'd tied up, Eden had come out of the cabin and was standing on the stern, waiting for him.

She wore a gauzy white dress, the fabric so thin that light showed through it. It clung to her curves, fluttering in the evening breeze, and he imagined that she wore nothing beneath. It would be so simple to draw the dress up over her head and touch her at will.

God, she was beautiful, he mused as she smiled down at him from the deck. He handed her the groceries, and as her hand brushed against his, he realized that he'd missed her during the short time he'd been gone. The moment he'd stepped on shore, he'd wondered what she was doing and he was almost grateful to return to her presence. But had he missed her company or just the sexual electricity that constantly sparked between them?

"You look nice," he said as he climbed on board.

"Thank you," Eden replied. "Who was that on the dock?"

"No one important," he murmured.

The sound of music drifted out of the cabin, and when Marcus stepped into the cockpit, he saw a table she'd set for dinner. Candles burned through colored glass, and crystal and silver glittered in the low light. "Wow," he said. "Fancy."

Marcus followed her into the cabin and Eden began to unpack the grocery bags. But he couldn't wait any longer to touch her. He reached out and drew her into his arms, eager to taste her again. He cupped her cheek in his palm as his mouth lingered over hers, teasing at first and then delving deeper.

Eden responded immediately, her arms wrapping around his neck, her breasts soft against his chest. Her body fit perfectly against his. Marcus ran his hand along her hip and drew her leg up, pressing his hard shaft against the juncture of her thighs. He'd grown hard the moment he'd stepped on board, the moment he'd seen her in that sheer dress.

This was crazy. His attraction to her was out of control. Every touch, every kiss, had become another piece of the puzzle that he was trying desperately to solve. Why did he want her? What did it mean?

She melted against him as he kissed her, offering a silent invitation to take more. Marcus wanted to make love to her right now and get it over with, spend all his passion on one incredible coupling. But somehow he knew that once would never be enough. Her body fascinated him, every inch of silken skin, every tempting curve.

Eden's fingers furrowed through his hair, pulling him more deeply into the kiss, and a moan slipped from his throat. Though he wanted to drag her into his cabin, Marcus was loath to move, afraid that he'd break the seductive spell that had enveloped them. He reached down for the hem of her dress and pulled it up, exposing her naked legs.

"Are you hungry?" she asked, her breath warm against his lips.

It wasn't enough, his mind repeated over and over again. He wanted more. "Starved," Marcus murmured.

Eden took his hand and slowly dragged it beneath her dress, along her torso, across her stomach and up to her breast. "Is this what you want?" she asked.

He ran his thumb across her nipple, drawing it to a hard peak. Eden tipped her head back and sighed as his mouth took the place of his thumb. The fabric from her dress was so thin it crumpled between his fingers, then fell back down, hiding her from his eyes, tantalizing him with glimpses of her naked body.

Marcus tried to recall a time when he'd felt so desperate to possess a woman. But his mind refused to focus. His senses were operating on overload, the scent of her perfume making him dizzy, the feel of her skin driving him mad, and the sound of her voice urging him on.

Eden trailed her fingertips along his chest to his belly and then dipped below the waistband of his shorts. The moment her hand brushed against his erection, Marcus's breath caught in his throat. He reached for her wrist to stop her, certain that now was not the time to test his control. He was so close to the edge that it would be over in a heartbeat.

When she wrapped her fingers around him, cool and firm against his heat, Marcus knew it wasn't over. The pleasure was about to begin. Slowly she began to stroke him, gently and softly at first. Each caress was a revelation, waves of pleasure racing through his body until every nerve was alive with need.

Marcus wanted to share the feeling with her, to have her experience all that he was enjoying. He slipped his hand between her legs and touched her, the damp of her desire coating his fingertips. She leaned back against the bulkhead for support, and he moved with her, bracing one hand next to her head, the other hand teasing at her clitoris.

The world spun around them, sucking them into a vortex of need. He couldn't think, he could only feel, drowning in wave after wave of intense sensation. And as if she could read his body, Eden increased her pace. Marcus felt his knees go weak, and it took all his strength to remain upright.

He slipped a finger inside her, matching her movements, then drew away, teasing at the center of her desire. It was so simple, this encounter, pleasuring each other with their hands. It was a perfect antidote to the tension that had bubbled between them for the past few days.

Drawing her toward the sofa in the main salon, Marcus fought to maintain his self-control. He wanted to pull her down, trap her beneath his body and sink into her until she surrounded every inch of him. But instead he continued the seduction with his fingers.

In the end, they lasted as long as they could, and when Eden finally allowed herself to climax, Marcus wasn't far behind. He felt her convulse around his fingers and then collapse against his body. A moment later he exploded in her hand.

Tangled in each other's arms, Marcus pulled her close and pressed his face into the curve of her neck, letting the spasms that coursed through his body subside. There wasn't any need to speak. There was no regret, no confusion over what they'd just shared. It seemed perfectly natural and right, and when those feelings arose again, Marcus knew that they would simply act upon them.

His promise to his brothers drifted through his mind, bringing with it a wave of guilt. But Marcus brushed it aside. This wasn't just any woman he'd made love to. How could he possibly deny such a powerful physical attraction? He was just a man.

Eden sighed softly and pressed her lips against his temple. It was such a simple act, but Marcus felt a strange rush of emotion well up inside him. Everything was different between him and Eden now that they'd surrendered. They didn't have to hide their desire for each other—they could act upon it.

For now, Eden's body belonged to him and his belonged to her. As long as it lasted, they would enjoy this powerful and intense attraction. And for now, he wouldn't think about how it would end. Or if it ever would.

He lay next to her for a long time, considering all that had happened between them in such a short time. When he knew Eden was asleep, Marcus slipped off the sofa and retrieved a blanket from a nearby cabinet, then gently covered her.

He grabbed a beer from the icebox in the galley and crawled out on deck. The stars had come out, twinkling brightly in the inky blue sky. He sat down on the foredeck and stretched his legs out over the side of the boat, listening to the soft lap of the water against the hull of the boat.

He wasn't sure how long he sat staring up at the sky. When he felt a soft caress on his shoulder, he looked up to see Eden standing above him. She'd wrapped herself in the blanket and had an uneasy expression on her beautiful face. "I woke up and you weren't there," Eden murmured.

Marcus reached out and captured her hand, then gently pulled her down beside him. He took the blanket and wrapped it around his shoulders, then tucked her beneath his arm until her body molded to his.

"Are you hungry?" he asked.

She shook her head. "I didn't want to do that."

Marcus pulled back and looked down into her eyes. "You didn't?"

"Well, I did," she explained. "But I didn't. It was… wonderful. I—I don't want you to think that I…that I—"

Marcus pressed his finger to her lips. "I'm not sure your father would approve, but we couldn't have avoided it for much longer, Eden."

"I want you to know that it's never been like that for me before. I—I know you think that I'm…well, that I have—"

"I don't," Marcus interrupted. "It doesn't matter. All that doesn't make a difference to me. It's just you and me, here, on this boat. That's all we need to worry about."

"You make it sound so simple," Eden murmured. "I seem to make life very complicated for anyone I get involved with."

"Then we'll just keep things simple," Marcus said. Somehow, under the starry night sky, with Eden sitting beside him, the notion seemed almost possible. But in his heart Marcus suspected that sooner or later Eden would leave. After all, what could he possibly offer a woman who could have anything…or anyone?

3

THE SCENT OF FRESHLY brewed coffee wafted through Eden's stateroom, teasing her awake. She smiled and sighed, then opened her eyes, hoping to find Marcus in bed beside her. But the opposite side of the bed was cold and empty.

Her smile faded to a frown and Eden sat up, brushing the hair from her eyes. She still wore the gauzy cotton sundress she'd put on the previous afternoon, but she didn't need a reminder that she and Marcus hadn't completed the seduction begun yesterday evening.

A tiny shiver skittered down her spine as she recalled the sensations his touch had sent spiraling through her body. All the sexual experiences she'd had in her life seemed to blur together behind that single moment with Marcus. Her desire had been undeniable, so strong that it had obliterated the past. And their shared release had been so strangely intimate that it teased constantly at her thoughts.

Eden sighed as she toyed with the hem of her dress. He had no right to be so good at it, she mused. After all, Marcus Quinn was just a regular guy. A man with such a great talent for seduction ought to be famous—or at least have a publicist.

She giggled and flopped back into the pillows. For the first time in weeks she felt happy…relaxed…and safe. The outside world didn't exist when she was on this boat. And with Marcus occupying her thoughts, she had no time for reflection on her past indiscretions.

"Today is a new day," Eden murmured. Her confidence bolstered, she climbed out of bed and shimmied out of her sundress. A quick search of her cabin turned up a pale blue bikini, one of her more conservative choices in swimwear. She stepped into the bottoms and pulled them up, then slipped into the top. She could go topless, but it would be much more fun to let Marcus fantasize about what was beneath the tiny scraps of fabric—and then let him undress her later.

She wandered through the cabin, listening for Marcus, but the boat was quiet, the clanging of the rigging the only sound. A quick check of the deck turned up nothing. She saw the note on the chalkboard when she stopped in the galley for coffee. "Went to town," she read. "Be back before lunch. Call me if you need something." He'd written his cell phone number on the bottom of the note, signing it with an *M.*

She stared down at his handwriting, running her fingers across the casual scrawl. A fleeting sense of loneliness settled in her heart and Eden brushed it aside. So she'd grown used to having him around. He wasn't unpleasant to look at and he had a certain masculine charm that she found appealing. But it wouldn't do to get too attached to him. After all, they moved in different circles and lived in different worlds.

Eden sat down on the sofa, impatient for her day to begin. She didn't like being alone. When she was alone, her mind wandered to all her troubles, to the horrible stories that were probably being told in the media, to the anger and frustration that her father was no doubt feeling right now. But then, maybe the story hadn't reached the States.

With a soft curse, Eden stood up and strode to the crew cabin at the bow of the boat, standing outside Marcus's berth for a long moment before opening the door. She couldn't help but be curious. He wasn't much for conversation, so there would probably be very little forthcoming from him. Maybe there were a few clues to the man hidden amongst his belongings. Hesitantly Eden stepped inside and shut the door behind her.

The cabin was small, about a quarter the size of the stateroom she'd taken in the aft section of the yacht. His clothes were scattered all over, draped from the upper bunk and tossed into half-open drawers. Eden grabbed a shirt she recognized and pressed it to her nose. She breathed in a scent of his soap mixed with the fresh smell of salt air.

Twisting the shirt in her hands, she moved to the small cabinet next to the berth and picked through his selection of bedtime reading: a dog-eared paperback by Tom Clancy, two Horatio Hornblower books that she recognized from the ship's library and a book on antique tools. Beneath the books, Eden found a stack of magazines and flipped through them. *"Wooden Boat, Science*

Digest, The New Yorker," she read, happy to see there were no girlie magazines. But when she reached the bottom of the pile, Eden froze. *"The National Inquisitor."*

Her heart twisted in her chest, making it difficult to breathe. The headline was splashed across the top half of the cover. "Eden's Sexcapade Caught on Tape." Below the headline was the horribly grainy photo of her and Ricardo locked in a steamy embrace, the same photo that had appeared in the European magazines. She knew it was her. The Cartier watch was a dead giveaway.

Strange how she'd reached the level of celebrity where she'd become known by her first name only. There was no mistaking who they were talking about. There was only one Eden stupid enough to get herself mixed up in such a mess.

She slowly sat down on the edge of the bunk. What was Marcus doing with this? Had he picked it up at the grocery store yesterday? If he had, then that meant her father probably knew all about it by now. Tears of humiliation pressed at the corners of her eyes.

She'd come looking for clues about him and instead found everything he needed to pass judgment on her, all the sordid little details of her past, regurgitated once again for the public to savor. A sob welled up in her throat and she hurried out of the cabin, his shirt and the tabloid still clutched in her hands.

"Why the hell did he have to be here?" she muttered as she strode back to her stateroom. She'd wanted to spend some time alone, to figure out how to deal with the mess she'd made of her life. And now, because Marcus Quinn was here, she'd be forced to explain it all to him—a complete stranger!

Well, she certainly didn't owe him any explanations. And if he came looking for them, then she just wouldn't be here to make them. Eden grabbed her bags from beneath the berth and tossed them onto the bed. She didn't bother to fold her clothes. The sooner she got off the boat, the better.

But as she stuffed her underwear into the suitcase, Eden realized that she couldn't get off the boat with her belongings unless she threw her suitcases overboard and floated them back to the dock. Marcus had taken the dinghy.

She wasn't about to ruin a custom-made set of Goyard. She loved her luggage. Over the past few years, it had been the only constant in her life, and balanced against the humiliation of seeing Marcus again, she'd definitely choose to save the luggage rather than save face.

Eden grabbed a pair of faded jeans and a T-shirt and tugged them on. It was always best to dress down when she traveled. With sunglasses, a hat and a wrinkled linen jacket, she had about a twenty-percent chance of going unnoticed. She would head back to Manhattan, get a suite at the Belleville and hide out for a few days until she figured out her next move.

It wasn't the Ritz or the Four Seasons or the Peninsula, but she'd be safe there. The staff at the trendy Hotel Belleville were perfectly discreet, and she loved the Frette bathrobes and the French breakfasts and the handsome Italian concierge who always did his best to make her laugh. And the hotel was usually off the tabloid radar.

Once she was dressed and packed, Eden dragged her luggage up to the cockpit. She was nearly finished when she heard the dinghy approach. Marcus waved at her, but Eden didn't respond, watching him from behind the dark lenses of her sunglasses. He tied the dinghy behind the boat and crawled up the swim ladder, swinging a gallon of varnish up onto the deck.

He saw her luggage and stopped, a frown creasing his brow. "Are you going somewhere?" he asked, stepping into the cockpit.

Eden avoided his gaze. In fact, she avoided looking at him at all, avoided his broad shoulders and his narrow hips, his thick hair curled at the nape of his neck and his deep blue eyes. Even now, in the midst of her hurt and humiliation, she ached to touch him.

"I'm leaving," she murmured. "I was just waiting for you to get back with the dinghy."

"Life on board gotten a little too boring for you?" he asked.

She heard the sarcasm in his voice and it cut deep. Of course that's what he'd think. He'd assume she was ready to jet back to Europe and throw herself into the middle of another scandal. "It's just time to leave," she said.

"Does this have anything to do with what happened last night?" Marcus asked. "Because I realize it didn't mean anything to you. And that's all right. We were just…scratching an itch."

"It's nice to know that you think of me as an itch," she said. "It's better than a slut or a whore."

He blinked, taken aback by her candor. "What are you talking about? I never—"

"Oh, be honest, Barney. You can tell me what you really think of me. Everyone else seems to have an opinion. I bet the clerk at the grocery store thinks she knows me well enough to comment. And the guy at the gas station, I'm sure he has a few choice words." Eden reached down and grabbed the copy of the *Inquisitor* from the front pocket of her tote, then tossed it at him. "I found that in your cabin. I'm sure it was much more entertaining than the Tom Clancy novel." She shook her head. "I can't believe you spent money on that. I would have told you the truth for free had you asked."

"I didn't buy that," he said.

"Oh, are they giving them away on every street corner? I shouldn't be surprised. Hometown girl gone bad. Makes an interesting story." Eden grabbed her bags and hauled them to the stern of the boat, then struggled to crawl down the swim ladder to the dinghy. But the weight of her suitcase set her off balance and she nearly lost her grip on the ladder. An instant later, Marcus grabbed the bag and pulled it back on board.

"Give me my suitcase," she said. "I want to leave."

"You don't have to leave," he said.

Eden stared up at him for a long moment. In truth, she didn't want to go for so many reasons. The prospect of facing the public was terrifying to her. The photographers would hound her twenty-four hours a day. People would stare and point and laugh—and then they'd have the nerve to ask her for an autograph or a photo. Eden wasn't sure she possessed the energy to get through it without falling apart at the seams.

But the prospect of staying with Marcus was even more difficult to bear. He'd look at her differently now. He'd wonder whether what they shared was something she'd shared with other men. He'd question her motives every time she touched him. And in the end, distrust and jealousy would set in and everything good would be ruined.

"Give me my luggage," she said.

Marcus shook his head. "I can't do that."

"Fine. Then I'll leave without it. Once I get settled, I'll send for it." She jumped off the bottom of the ladder into the dinghy, then sat down in the back of the little fiberglass boat and stared at the outboard. She'd ridden in the dinghy in the past, but someone else had always ferried her back and forth to the ketch.

She reached for the starter cord and gave it a yank, but it snapped back and nearly pulled her shoulder out of joint in the process. She pulled again, but the same thing happened. Tears threatened and Eden swallowed them back. She stood up, prepared to swim back to shore, but his voice stopped her.

"It doesn't make any difference," he said.

Eden drew a shaky breath and looked up at him. "What?"

"What I read in that tabloid. I know that's not you, Eden. At least not all of it. And maybe the rest is what *was* you, last week or last month or last year."

"Three years ago," she said.

He nodded. "That's a long time ago."

"You don't know me," she said.

"I realize that. But that could change…if you stayed."

"Are you asking me to stay because you want to sleep with me?"

Marcus chuckled and shook his head. "Are you under the impression that all men want to sleep with you?"

"No," she said, a reluctant smile twitching at the corners of her mouth. "The gay ones don't. And probably most of the guys over seventy don't. But the rest do. They may not admit it, but they would if presented with the opportunity."

"You have a very high opinion of yourself, don't you, Princess?" Marcus said, holding out his hand.

Reluctantly she placed her fingers in his outstretched palm. He smiled at her and suddenly her anger and humiliation dissolved. "I prefer to think of it as a good grasp of the reality that is my life." She stepped back onto the ladder and he helped her into the cockpit.

Eden stood in front of him, her hand still tucked in his, his eyes locked on hers. She felt her knees tremble as he leaned toward her and she knew she was about to be kissed. But all her emotions had been rubbed raw, and if he kissed her, Eden knew it wouldn't stop there. She wanted more, something to soothe the pain and make her forget. But she and Marcus had formed a friendship of sorts, a trust that went beyond their physical attraction. That's what she needed to sustain her right now.

She stepped back, tugging her hand from his. "If I'm going to stay, maybe we shouldn't…you know…"

"What? We shouldn't swim after eating? Shouldn't eat mangoes unless they're ripe? Shouldn't watch television in the dark?" he prompted teasingly.

"I usually rush into things without thinking," she said. "And look where it's gotten me. Maybe we should…take a breath? Slow down a bit?"

He considered her request for a long moment. Eden couldn't tell if he was disappointed or indifferent. "Well, if that's the deal, then you'd better start wearing clothes while you're on board. No more skinny-dipping, no more topless sunbathing, no more transparent little dresses without underwear. And no more morning coffee in the nude."

"Then you're all right with slowing things down?" Eden asked.

"It's not my decision," he said. "It's yours."

She considered his answer for a long moment. Suddenly she didn't want to slow down. If anything, she wanted him more than she had before he'd gotten all noble and heroic on her. "If I want to sunbathe topless, I certainly can," Eden said.

"Then don't expect me to keep my hands to myself," Marcus warned.

Eden stared at him, trying to keep from smiling. She felt so alive inside when they were at odds, the anticipation of surrender enhanced by antagonism. "You forget that you only work here, Barney. This is my father's boat and I can do whatever I please. If I want to take off all my clothes right now, I could. And there wouldn't be anything you could do about it."

"First, you're usually wearing next to nothing anyway, so it wouldn't come as much of a shock. Second, I've seen it all before. And finally, if you choose to do this, then be prepared to suffer the consequences." Marcus grabbed the gallon of varnish he'd brought on board and turned toward the foredeck.

Eden stared after him. The consequences? Somehow she couldn't quite believe that the consequences would cause any sort of suffering at all. In truth, the consequences of tempting Marcus Quinn would probably be sheer, unadultcratcd pleasure.

With a sigh, Eden picked up a suitcase and dragged it to the aft companionway. It was only a matter of time. And any thoughts that either one of them had about keeping their relationship platonic were simply the fantasies of two very deluded people.

MARCUS SAT CROSS-LEGGED on the foredeck, his back braced against the side of the cabin, a small slab of teak jammed up against a stanchion. He'd been working on a series of carvings for the cabinetry above the double berth in the master suite—fish and crustaceans and other underwater life. He'd been working on the crab for the past few days and was nearly finished.

A shadow blocked his light, and he glanced up to see Eden standing over him. "That's nice, Barney," she said.

"Thanks." Marcus squinted against the setting sun. "You're in my light."

"I thought you might like some dinner. I made a salad and some sandwiches."

He levered to his feet and brushed the wood shavings from his lap. "Yeah, I could eat."

Their fight earlier that day had been forgotten and Eden seemed to be much more relaxed. He couldn't say the same for himself. He found himself aching to touch her again, but then he remembered the agreement.

Hell, it wasn't an agreement at all. Instead, it had become some sick brand of sadomasochistic torture.

It was as if they'd silently agreed it wouldn't happen and now they were just prolonging the agony to make it more pleasurable for the both of them when it did. Marcus had spent every hour since she'd come on board thinking about stripping off her clothes and yanking her down on the bed and slowly burying himself inside her. If they didn't consummate this relationship soon, Marcus was going to be left with no choice but to take matters into his own hands—or hand.

Marcus followed Eden back to the cockpit as he pondered their relationship. It was a word he'd avoided for so long, but there was no other way to describe what they'd been sharing. They did seem to get along—they talked and laughed all the time. And there was an undeniable sexual chemistry between them. He wanted her more than he could ever remember wanting a woman. Didn't that pretty much define what a relationship was? Sure, it was primarily based on uncontrolled lust, but that wasn't all bad, was it?

When he stepped into the cockpit, Marcus noticed the table she'd set, this one much less elaborate than the one last night. Candles flickered from little glass cups, and a bottle of wine had been uncorked. Eden pointed to a spot beside her at the table. He sat down and poured himself a glass of wine, then filled her glass, as well.

"Should we make a toast?" he asked.

"And what would we toast?" she asked, sliding into place next to him.

He held up his glass. "To…friendship," Marcus said.

Eden raised her eyebrow, then shrugged. "All right. To friendship."

Marcus took a quick taste of the wine, then dug into the salad she'd prepared. He'd never been much for lettuce, but it tasted pretty good, kind of tangy and sweet at the same time. She'd made a ham-and-cheese sandwich with the Italian bread he'd bought, but she'd sliced little dill pickles onto the sandwich, adding a taste that wasn't all that bad.

She watched him as he ate, slowly sipping her wine and picking at her salad. "It's good," he said.

"Contrary to popular belief, I'm not a useless bimbo who only knows how to shop and party."

"That's not what I think of you," he said.

"I'm an expert at grilled cheese and hot dogs and that's about it. My mother was gone a lot, so I usually ate supper with Maria, our housekeeper in Malibu. She used to make the best Mexican food."

"I love Mexican food," Marcus said.

"Well, I ate it, but I never learned to cook it. Another thing I'm completely mediocre at."

Marcus grabbed his glass and sat back in his chair. "Why do you do that?"

"What?"

"Talk about yourself in such a negative way. I know you're not useless or a bimbo. And I know there are a lot of things you probably do very well."

"Do you? I don't think you really know me at all."

"Then tell me," Marcus said, setting his fork down. "I'd like to know more about you."

She regarded him with a suspicious look. "You want to know about the videotape, don't you?"

"If that's where you want to start, then go for it," Marcus said.

"If I'm going to tell you about the video, then you need to tell me something about yourself first."

"Ask me anything," Marcus said.

"Why do you have an Irish accent?"

"I don't," Marcus said.

"You do. I noticed it the moment I met you. It's there, but it's very faint."

"I grew up in Ireland," Marcus explained. "My ma got sick when I was about five years old, and my da sent me and my two brothers to live with my grandmother. We were there for eight years. I had a really thick accent when I got back, but I learned to hide it. Hiding it helped me survive at school."

After he finished, Marcus drew a deep breath, the detail of his reply surprising him. He'd always been so guarded when talking to women, especially about his childhood. His answers usually consisted of three- or four-word replies. But suddenly, he felt compelled to reveal his life story to Eden. Was it because he wanted her to do the same? Or was it because he'd come to trust her? After all, neither one of them had lived a fairy-tale life as a child. She would understand better than anyone.

"But you are an American," she said.

"I felt Irish," Marcus said. "It was all I knew for a long time." He took another sip of his wine, the alcohol relaxing him. "Now your turn."

Eden drew a deep breath. "All right. I thought I loved him and I wanted to keep everything between us exciting because there were so many women who wanted him. So I let him turn on the camera. And we watched the tape later and it was exciting and fun. He promised to erase it, but he kept it. A few months ago, after I said some rather unflattering things about him in the press, the tape suddenly reappeared. I think he gave it to a friend who gave it to a guy to put on the Internet."

"It doesn't make me think any less of you," he said, his jaw tight. "But it sure as hell makes me think a lot less of this guy. He deserves a proper smackdown."

Eden laughed. "And you would do that for me? Defend my honor?"

"Yeah, I would. And I'm good with my fists."

She reached out and took his hand, weaving her fingers through his. "My hero," she murmured, pressing her lips to the spot below his wrist.

It was such a simple gesture, unplanned and uncomplicated by any thoughts of seduction. But his reaction was instant and intense. The heat of her lips on his skin felt like a brand, lingering long after she'd drawn away. Marcus swallowed hard and flexed his fingers, wondering why they'd gone numb. But Eden didn't seem to notice.

"Maybe I should have you negotiate this problem with my father," she said.

"He's going to be angry with you." It wasn't a question, more a statement of fact.

Eden nodded soberly, then set his hand down on the table. She placed it flat and distractedly began to trace an outline of his splayed fingers. "More than angry. He's threatened to disown me before, and this will probably push him over the edge. A few years ago, I wouldn't have cared, but lately my father and I have actually started to get along."

"How long do you plan to hide out here?"

"A few years maybe," she said, sending him a smile. "It's not like I committed murder. I had sex and we videotaped it. People have sex all the time. It's a very natural thing."

The desire between the two of them had seemed perfectly natural, Marcus mused. But for some reason he didn't like thinking about Eden in bed with other men, especially smarmy Eurotrash playboys intent on betraying her. "Right," he said.

"You don't agree?"

"I thought we weren't going to go there," Marcus said.

"Talking about sex isn't having sex," Eden said.

"It is for me," Marcus replied. "You've already cost me a thousand dollars. Maybe two thousand, depending on how my brothers are interpreting the rules."

Eden picked up her wineglass and slowly ran her finger around the rim. "Explain, please."

"We made a bet, Ian and Dec and me. To be completely celibate for three months. I lasted just over two weeks."

Eden's eyes went wide and she laughed. "But we didn't…have sex. We had foreplay. That doesn't count."

"It all counts," Marcus replied. "I've already lost the original thousand I put in just by touching you. And I may have to put up another thousand if my brothers don't go easy on me." Marcus sighed. "I'm thinking maybe I just won't tell my brothers. They'd never need to know."

"It's not like there's a videotape," Eden teased.

Marcus chuckled softly. At least she had a sense of humor about it. "No, thank God for that."

Eden slowly set her wineglass down and got to her feet. His gaze skimmed over her slender body, the thin cotton of her tank top clinging to the curves of her breasts, the flowing fabric of her skirt revealing long, tanned legs. Her skin had a rosy glow from the sun, and as she stepped closer he felt the heat from her body.

"So the only thing standing between us and a fabulous night in bed is a couple thousand dollars?"

Marcus stared up at her, his fingers twitching with the need to touch her. "I don't have that kind of money right now."

She tipped her head to the side and gave him a naughty smile. "Do you take American Express or would you prefer a check?"

"I thought we weren't going to do this," Marcus murmured.

"I find the idea of buying your body intriguing." Eden reached out and slipped her fingers through his hair, smoothing the strands away from his temples. Gently she turned him in his chair, then straddled him, her hair falling in soft waves around his face.

"You think you can have your way with me?" Marcus whispered, pulling her close enough to kiss.

"Maybe we shouldn't ignore our desires. Maybe it's best to just act on them."

Marcus groaned inwardly. She had no idea what it was costing him to resist. The past few days had been sheer torture, and a night in bed alone would be enough to turn him into a sex-starved maniac. But there was still something holding him back, some instinct that told him that sex with Eden would not be simple.

Though Eden played the uninhibited temptress, Marcus had come to know the girl she really was—scared, lost, vulnerable and distrustful of men. If he crawled into her bed now, she'd probably find some excuse to discard him within the week.

"Princess, how long are we going to play this game?"

She frowned. "What game?"

He reached up and cupped her cheek in his palm, forcing her gaze to meet his. "Dragging me off to bed isn't going to solve any of your problems. You should call your father and tell him you're here," he said.

He felt her stiffen in his arms and she quickly twisted out of his grasp. Marcus watched her walk to the stern and climb up on the top of the aft cabin, her attention focused on the sunset. "He's probably already written me off," she shouted, her voice breaking.

Marcus's heart softened as he watched her facade crumble before his eyes. "I'm sure that's not true."

"You don't know my father," she said, spinning around to face him, tears swimming in her eyes. Marcus had never really understood women, not deep down. But, oddly, he seemed to understand Eden. Right now, all she really wanted was a warm body, a distraction from her troubles. If he weren't here, there'd be someone else willing to provide comfort and a little affection.

Marcus stood and crossed the cockpit. When he reached the aft cabin, he held out his hand. "Come on," he said. "Let's finish dinner. After that, I'll take you for a ride in the dinghy. There's a cove just over there I want to explore."

She gnawed on her lower lip, then finally nodded her head. Eden bent down, and Marcus grabbed her around the waist and lowered her back into the cockpit. Her body brushed against his, and when she stood toe to toe with him, she wrapped her arms around his neck and kissed him softly.

"I like you, Marcus Quinn," she said, smiling sweetly. "You're a nice guy. I haven't known many truly nice guys."

God, she was beautiful, Marcus mused as he smoothed his hand over her cheek. He couldn't take his eyes off her face. He leaned forward and brushed another kiss across her lips, his only intent to keep her in his arms a bit longer.

Her lips parted and his gazed fixed on her mouth. The craving was acute. Just one more taste and he'd be satisfied. Marcus kissed her again, this time allowing himself to linger a bit longer.

Eden moaned softly, a silent invitation for him to

take more. He furrowed his fingers through her sun-kissed hair and molded her mouth to his, enjoying the sweet taste of her tongue as he deepened the kiss.

His heart slammed in his chest and desire snaked through his veins. Marcus wanted to strip the clothes from her body, to possess her with his hands, to make her cry out as he had last night. This dance they were doing, advance and retreat and advance again, was more than he was prepared to handle.

Their kiss grew more intense with every heartbeat, Marcus pulling her tight against his body. She fit perfectly, and when he pulled her leg up against his thigh, her skirt fell away and he found her naked beneath. It would be so simple to drag her down beside him, to slide his shorts down and bury himself inside her.

He was already hard and ready, and every time she wriggled against him, he felt himself flirting with a complete loss of control. She reached down and stroked his erection through the fabric of his shorts, but Marcus gently grabbed her hand and placed it on his chest.

He brushed the hair from her eyes, his gaze meeting hers. "Why don't you put on some warmer clothes?" he whispered. "It's going to get chilly once the sun goes down." It wasn't what he'd wanted to say, but for now it was the right thing to do. Eden needed time and space, not another guy looking to drag her off to bed.

When he made love to her, it wasn't going to be an impulse. It would be slow and deliberate and as close to perfect as Marcus could make it. And no matter what happened in the future, she wouldn't need a videotape to remember her night in bed with him.

THE DRIFTWOOD CRACKLED and popped in the fire, sending sparks whirling into the night air. Marcus bent down and tossed another piece of wood into the flames, then returned to sit on the blanket with Eden. She glanced over at him, watching the play of light on his handsome face.

When she'd jumped a flight back to the States, she'd made a silent promise to herself: no more whirlwind love affairs. She'd learn to control her penchant for instant infatuation and take her time. Yet, even though she'd broken her vow just days after she made it, Eden couldn't make herself believe an affair with Marcus would be wrong.

"I always thought that in order to have fun, I had to be entertained," she said. "I'd go out to clubs and parties, and most nights I'd leave bored to tears. And all we have here is the stars and a fire and it's wonderful."

"That's too bad," Marcus said with a boyish grin. "Because I can provide entertainment."

"This sounds intriguing," Eden said. "Does it involve taking your clothes off?"

He reached into his jacket pocket and withdrew a quarter, then held it out in front of her. "Magic," he said. He waved his hand over the quarter, then closed his fist over the coin. He held out both fists to her. "Which one?"

She tapped his left hand, and when he opened it, it was empty. "I'm impressed," she said as she tapped his right hand. But that was empty, as well. Eden giggled, delighted with his little show. "We have something in common. We can both make money disappear. You limited yourself to a quarter. I've managed to make my nearly three-million-dollar trust fund disappear."

Marcus's jaw dropped. "Three million? That's a lot of money."

Eden nodded. "I know." She ran her hands through her hair, angry that she'd even told him that. But she'd become so accustomed to being open with him that it had just slipped out. A long silence grew between them and Eden knew what he was thinking. Three million would have bought Marcus Quinn a lot of crescent wrenches.

"That's not all I can do," Marcus said. He stood and brushed the sand off his jeans. "When I was kid, I wanted to join the circus." A moment later he was standing on his hands. He bent his elbows and lowered himself to the ground, then pushed back up again.

Eden clapped, her mood restored. "Bravo, bravo."

Then he walked over to her on his hands and, after a few more push-ups, leaped back to his feet. Marcus bowed, then dropped down next to her. "I'm a man of many talents."

"Yes, you are."

He leaned forward and grabbed a small piece of driftwood from the pile near the fire. "This is my real talent," he said, reaching into his pocket. He withdrew a red pocketknife and opened the blade, then held it up to the light of the fire. "It's been sharpened so much there's not much blade left." He glanced over at Eden. "What's your favorite animal?"

She shrugged. "I don't know. When I was younger, I always wanted a bunny."

Marcus began to carve, taking little bits away until a rabbit magically emerged from the weathered piece of driftwood. It took no more than two or three minutes before he placed it in her hand. Eden held it up on her palm and examined the detail. "It's lovely," she said.

"It's yours," he said. "But you have to show me a trick in return."

Eden thought for a long moment. "There is one thing I can do," she said.

"Show me," Marcus urged.

She stood in front of him and slipped out of her jacket, letting it drop to the sand. Eden paused, watching the expectation fade on his face.

"That's it?" he asked.

She shook her head, then slowly shimmied out of her T-shirt, leaving her naked from the waist up.

Marcus's gaze slowly scanned the length of her body, lingering at her breasts for a long moment. He leaned back, bracing himself on his elbows. "This is getting pretty good."

Taking her time, Eden unbuttoned her skirt, then slid the zipper down. She hooked her thumbs in the waistband and skimmed it over her hips. Just for fun, she turned as she pushed the skirt to her ankles and stepped out of it. Tipping her head back, she ran her fingers through her hair. When she was certain her striptease had had the proper reaction, she faced Marcus and smiled. She smoothed her hands over her belly and then let them drift up to her breasts.

Marcus drew in a ragged breath. "Nice," he said, his voice cracking slightly.

Her gaze dropped to his lap, to the erection pressing against the confines of his jeans. "I haven't been practicing for very long, but I think it's entertaining, don't you?"

With a playful growl, Marcus scrambled to his feet. Eden turned and ran toward the water, her laugh echoing in the quiet night. He caught up with her before she was able to dive in, wrapping his arms around her waist and swinging her off her feet. When he set her down, he slowly turned her in his arms and kissed her. "If I knew we were allowed to take off our clothes, I would have showed you a trick I know really well."

"Show me," Eden challenged, wriggling in his arms.

Marcus picked her up and carried her to the blanket, then gently set her down. "I'm not impressed," she said, running her hand down his chest to toy with the top button on his sodden jeans.

Marcus grabbed her hand and pinned it above her head. "You will be."

His voice was soft and enthralling, and a shiver ran through her body as the night breeze sent goosebumps skittering over her skin. "For this to work, you have to stay absolutely still," he warned. "If you don't, one of us might get hurt." He grinned. "And kids, don't try this at home."

"What kind of trick is this?"

"Promise you won't move?"

Eden nodded her head. They'd played little games like this before, but tonight Marcus's playfulness had an edge to it, a hint of danger that Eden found strangely exciting. "Promise," she replied.

He dropped a kiss on her mouth, then moved to a spot beneath her ear. "Remember, stay very, very still."

Eden closed her eyes and sighed, focusing on the feel of his mouth on her skin. It became a lazy seduction, Marcus taking his time as he seduced her with his lips and his teeth and his tongue. When he finally reached her breasts, her nerves were on fire, and when his tongue circled her left nipple, Eden bit her bottom lip to keep from crying out. Every inch of her body tingled in anticipation, but her impatience got the better of her. When she reached out to guide his lips lower, he stopped, his breath hot on her skin.

"Be careful," he warned. "I can't do this if you move."

Surrendering to his rules, Eden clasped her hands above her head and waited for him to begin again. And when he did, she found herself even more aroused, the sensations of his touch racing through her body like electric currents. Her toes and fingertips tingled and she felt her pulse pounding in her head.

His lips drifted lower, to her belly and then beyond. Marcus slipped his hand between her legs, and Eden was almost afraid to move, afraid she might shatter the very instant he touched her there. His tongue slipped between the soft folds, teasing at her clitoris. Eden held her breath, aching for release yet wanting his seduction to last.

It was as if he knew her body, stringing her along until her desire was more than she could bear, then drawing away for a moment so she could relax. It became exquisite torture, so acute that Eden begged him to let her come. But Marcus was in control and he seemed to take great delight in testing the limits of her body and her mind.

Tears welled up her eyes; tears of frustration and confusion. Why did it feel so different with Marcus? It was so easy to surrender to him, to allow herself to experience complete pleasure. He stripped away all of her doubts and insecurities about men, crumbling the control she was trying so hard to maintain.

Unfamiliar emotions swirled around in her head, mixing with the waves of pleasure until she could no longer think. He touched her once more with his tongue, and an instant later her body convulsed in an explosive orgasm. He continued to lick at her until the last spasm left her body, then he pressed a kiss to the inside of her thigh.

"Like that trick?" he asked softly, his lips soft and damp on her skin. Marcus lay down beside her, drawing the blanket around her body until she was nestled into his warmth.

Eden closed her eyes, exhaustion overwhelming her. "I could stay here all night."

"We can if you'd like."

She gave him a dubious look. "Sleep outside?"

He nodded. "It's a perfect place. We have blankets and it doesn't look like rain. We're out of the reach of the tide. If we keep the fire going, we'll be warm enough."

"I've never slept outside," Eden said. "Aren't there animals? Spiders and snakes?"

"I'll protect you," Marcus said.

Eden unbuttoned his shirt and pressed a kiss to his

chest. "I had a really nice time tonight," she said. "I can't remember the last time I enjoyed myself so much."

Marcus drew back and looked down into her face. "You certainly did enjoy yourself."

"Not just that," Eden replied. "Everything was perfect. The fire, the meal, you. I don't need anything more than this. Not right now."

He furrowed his fingers through her hair and held her close. Eden felt his heart beating in his chest, the rhythm slow and steady. When she'd left Europe, she'd expected her life to become much more complicated. But everything seemed so simple now. How long could it possibly stay that way? Eden mused. And what would eventually destroy this happiness that she'd found with Marcus Quinn?

4

MARCUS STARED DOWN AT the carving of the lobster, running his fingers over the raw teak. He was rarely satisfied with his work, always coming up with something else he might have done better once all the wood was carved away. But this time he'd gotten it right. It was perfect the way it was.

He glanced over at Eden, who was lounging in the cockpit beneath the sunshade, surrounded by canvas pillows. She wore one of his T-shirts and nothing else and was intently reading a volume of Robert Frost's poetry she'd found in the ship's library.

His gaze slowly drifted up her legs to the tiny patch of hair at the apex of her thighs. He'd touched her in the most intimate way last night, tasted her desire and brought her to a powerful climax. Every moment they spent together seemed to lead to another more electric encounter.

Marcus couldn't help but wonder what it would be like to move inside her. He'd wanted to do that last night, to toss aside his clothes and slide up along her naked body and lose himself between her legs. The thought of being inside her when she'd come was almost too much to bear. To feel her heat and dampness and then the spasms that had rocked her entire body.

She might not have refused him, but he sensed they were both biding their time, unwilling to take the next step yet unable to stop the growing intimacy between them. This unquenchable need he had for her now bordered on obsession. He thought about her a million times a day, with every breath and every heartbeat.

He'd had other relationships based on sex alone and they had always left him cold. But with Eden there was an unexpected connection, a willingness to discard all inhibitions between the two of them and enjoy each other's bodies without hesitation.

In the past, women had described him as indifferent and aloof. He'd become a different man when he was with Eden. But by dropping his guard, he'd also left himself wide open to getting coldcocked by a woman he didn't really know. He knew that her skin was incredibly soft and her hair smelled like pears. He knew that when he kissed her she liked to run her palms beneath his shirt and that right before she climaxed, she held her breath.

He also knew she was fickle and capricious, unwilling or unable to stay with a man more than a few months. How long would it be before she grew bored with him? And what excuse would she use to cast him aside? Marcus wasn't sure how he'd feel once that possibility became a reality, but he wouldn't delude himself into believing their relationship would last forever.

And what had he risked by being with her? His heart was at the top of the list. Even though he'd worked hard to keep his feelings in check, Marcus knew that he'd grown fond of Eden Ross. If she suddenly disappeared from his life, he would miss her.

He was also lying to his brothers, which brought a whole different kind of guilt. If they'd had anything as adults, it was complete and utter honesty among them. And he was also risking his chance with Trevor Ross, a man who wouldn't feel too kindly about lending money to a guy intent on seducing his daughter.

"Is it finished?"

Marcus looked up from the carving to find Eden watching him. He nodded. "I think it is." He held it up to show her and she smiled.

"It really is beautiful," she said.

He looked down at the carving again. Was it really? Or did he simply believe it was because Eden said so? He rubbed his hand along his chest, brushing away the flecks of wood. It didn't really matter.

The sound of Marcus's cell phone broke the silence. Eden set down her book and stretched her arms over her head, his T-shirt riding up her belly. "If that's your wife, tell her you'll be home next month. I haven't finished with you yet."

Marcus grinned as he reached for the phone. "I'll be sure to tell her that."

She returned his smile. "And tell her that I especially appreciated your efforts on the beach last night. On a scale of one to ten, I'd give you eight hundred and seventy-four."

He flipped open the phone and glanced at the caller ID. He didn't recognize the number, but he knew the exchange was local. "Hello?"

"Quinn? Trevor Ross here. I'm up at the house and I wanted to check on the progress out there. I'm coming down."

"Mr. Ross," Marcus said, "how are you?"

Eden's smile froze. Slowly she shook her head. "Don't tell him I'm here," she whispered.

"Things are kind of a mess," Marcus continued. "Everything is a work in progress right now. I'd really rather you—"

"I'll take that into account. Bring the dinghy up to the dock."

The other end of the line went dead and Marcus shut his phone. "I'm supposed to go get him from the dock. He wants to see how the work is coming along."

"You can't!" Eden cried. "He can't know I'm here."

"How am I supposed to stop him?" Marcus countered. "He owns the bleedin' boat. I can't keep him off his own boat."

"Don't get him from the dock."

"I have to, Eden," Marcus said. "Maybe it's time you talked to him. Now is as good a time as any."

She shook her head. "No. I'm not ready. Please, Marcus, don't tell him I'm here. I can't face him."

Marcus saw the desperation in her eyes. He reached out and grabbed her hand, dragging her toward the aft cabin. "Clean up your mess down there, hide your clothes and make up the berth, then go forward and hide in the crew cabin. He won't go up there."

Eden threw her arms around his neck and hugged him tight. "Thank you."

Marcus wrapped her hands around her waist and turned her toward the aft hatch. "And put on some clothes. If he does catch you here, it would be nice if you weren't half-naked."

He hurried to the main salon and picked up every last trace of Eden's presence. What the hell was he doing? If Ross discovered Eden on board, he'd be furious. And if he discovered Marcus had been messing around with his daughter, then Marcus would be out of a job. This commission promised to finance his business for the next six months. He had bills to pay and new projects lined up. But he couldn't do any of it without the pay-check from Trevor Ross.

He climbed back out to the cockpit, nearly colliding with Eden in the process. She'd stuffed everything she owned into her bags and was dragging them along behind her. By the time she disappeared through the companionway, Trevor Ross was striding across the lawn. Marcus jumped into the dinghy and started the small outboard, then headed for shore, running over in his mind the explanation he'd make if Eden was discovered.

When he pulled up alongside the dock, he looped a line around a cleat and steadied the small skiff as Ross stepped on board. "Good morning," Marcus said.

Ross nodded. He was a man of few words. Marcus had learned that upon first meeting him. In truth, he understood why Eden feared him. Trevor Ross could be quite intimidating. But he and Marcus had gotten on well from the start, and though the man owned half of Rhode Island, Marcus wasn't cowed. "I think you'll be pleased with the work so far," he said.

"I'm sure I will." He stared out at the horizon as the boat skimmed across the water. "The truth is, I didn't drive all the way out here just to see how the project was going. I came out to see if my daughter was here."

"My brother, Dec, mentioned that she might come here," Marcus said.

"Then you know about her...situation?"

"Not entirely," Marcus said, dancing on the edge of a lie. "He said you're worried about her and wanted to find her."

"You don't have children, do you, Quinn?"

Marcus shook his head. "I'm not married."

"Think long and hard before you get married. And then think twice as long about having children. Eden has been nothing but trouble from the day she became a teenager. Her mother let her run wild, and the older she got, the more impulsive she became. Sometimes I think she purposely causes trouble just for the attention it gets her." He shook his head. "She's been engaged four times. Four times. And I spent nearly a half million on the first wedding before she decided to call it off. If I could find the right man for the job, I'd pay him a half million to take her off my hands. What do they call that? A dowry?" He chuckled drily. "Maybe I ought to make that a part of our deal."

They rode the rest of the way to *Victorious* in silence, Marcus observing Eden's father as he navigated the dinghy. Ross was in his late fifties, his dark hair graying at the temples. He appeared fit and in good health, but there were permanent lines etched in his brow, as if he spent a good portion of the day scowling.

When they reached the boat, Marcus tied it up to the ladder and Ross climbed on board. He joined him in the cockpit and pointed to the carving he'd finished that morning. "This will go above the bed in the master suite," he said. "If you remember, it's going to be framed with carvings of seashells."

Ross nodded. "Very nice." He stared at it for a long time, then drew in a quick breath. "I don't know why she doesn't come home," he said. "She must know I've been trying to reach her."

"Maybe she's afraid you'll be angry with her," Marcus suggested.

"You're damn right I will," Ross snapped. "She's gone way too far this time. She's embarrassed me, but worse, she's made a fool of herself, as well." He calmed himself, then forced a smile. "Well, let's move along. What else can you show me?"

"I should be able to restore the figurehead." They walked to the bow of the boat and Ross examined the pieces that Marcus had spread out. "I've removed the damaged pieces and I'll replace them. The new teak will weather to the same shade over time."

Ross paced along the edge of the deck. "Maybe I should just buy the damn tape," he muttered. "It'll probably cost me a couple million, but she's my daughter. But then I think maybe it's better to just wash my hands of her. She's made her bed, so let her lie in it." He glanced over at Marcus. "What else?"

"I've finished the corbels for the main salon and I've got part of the wall carving done down there."

When they got into the main salon, Marcus risked a look down the companionway to the door of his cabin. Though it was a big boat, he knew Eden could hear every word of their conversation. The anger and disgust in Trevor Ross's voice was evident. He talked about Eden as if she were nothing more than a nuisance—a very expensive nuisance, but one that could be easily disposed of. "This one will take the longest to carve," Marcus said. "It's very detailed and there's much more relief than on the other two."

"Nice work," Ross said. "I'm impressed. I think with your talent and my money, this deal would be good for both of us."

"I'm always looking for opportunities," Marcus said.

"When you're finished here, we'll talk. I'm definitely interested in investing. And I'm sure I could steer some more business your way."

"That would be great," Marcus said, reaching out to shake his hand.

"And if Eden shows up here, I want you to call. You'll do that for me, won't you?"

"Do you really think she'd come here?"

Trevor Ross shook his head. "She always loved sailing. That was one thing we shared. Before I bought this boat, we had a thirty-five-footer. Eden and I used to sail out to Block Island and back." He shook his head. "She cried the day she found out I sold that boat. Like I'd stolen a little piece of her heart."

"Maybe things will work out," Marcus said. "Maybe this situation will give you a chance to talk."

Ross shook his head. "I doubt it. She'll probably go back to her old ways as soon as the scandal dies down. Eden isn't happy unless she's in the middle of a mess. She has the attention span of a two-year-old." He rubbed his palms together. "That's that, then. Good work. I've got my driver waiting to take me back to the office."

Marcus followed Ross on deck, then ferried him back to shore. He waited until the older man had disappeared inside the house before he stepped back into the dinghy and headed out to the boat. When he arrived, he found Eden waiting for him in the cockpit. He could tell she'd been crying, her eyes red-rimmed and watery. But she'd dried her tears before he'd returned.

"What a pleasant visit," she muttered. "You two seemed awfully chummy."

"He's my employer," Marcus said.

"So are you going to turn me in? You could probably squeeze a half million out of the old man as a reward. Did you see how smooth he is? He'll do you a favor if you do one for him. Don't even think of letting him invest in your business."

"I can't do it on my own. I'd never get the money from a bank, not to do what I want to do."

"Fine. Go ahead then. But don't come crying to me when he takes it over and chops it into tiny little pieces to sell."

"He's not going to do that. The business isn't worth anything without me."

"So now I know where your loyalties lie," she murmured. "After all, what am I to you? Just some girl you've been messing around with for the past few days."

"Don't say that." Marcus cursed softly. This was about to turn into a nasty fight, and he wasn't sure he was prepared to do battle with her. Yes, if he revealed Eden's presence, there'd probably be a nice chunk of money waiting for him. But how the hell was he going to explain what he'd been doing with her? "I'm not going to tell him you're here. But that doesn't mean I'm going to stop trying to convince you to talk to him."

"You heard him," Eden said. "He barely tolerates me. He thinks I'm a silly, stupid girl."

"Are you?" Marcus asked.

She fixed her gaze on his, doubt flickering across her expression. "No," she said in a barely audible voice.

"Then maybe it's time to prove that to him. You can't change the past, Eden. Stop whining about it and change the future."

"Why didn't you just tell him I was here?"

Marcus shrugged. "You asked me not to."

"You mean, the longer you hold out, the more he'll pay," she accused.

Marcus shook his head. She was obviously spoiling for a fight and wouldn't be satisfied until she got one. But he knew it was her father, not him, she had an issue with. "Jaysus, Eden," he muttered, "not everyone in the world is motivated by greed. I'm through fighting with you. This is your problem with your father and I'm not going to get in the middle of it." He climbed out of the cockpit and walked to the foredeck, anxious to put some space between them.

Even angry with her, he still wanted to yank her into his arms and kiss her senseless. What would it take to prove that he cared, that he wouldn't betray her as other men in her life had? He wanted their relationship to be open and uncomplicated, but as time went on, he seemed to get more tangled in the mess that was her past.

"If you tell him I'm here," Eden shouted, "then I'll tell him exactly what we've been doing."

Marcus spun around and strode back to her, crawling back into the cockpit. Hell, he'd had enough. If she wanted a fight, then he'd give it to her. "Go ahead, Princess," he said, standing toe-to-toe with her. "I don't give a shit. Tell him how you felt the first time I made you come. Tell him how you murmured my name when I went down on you last night. Tell him how much you want me to fuck you. Because I know you do, Eden."

He saw her hand coming and blocked the slap before it could make contact, his fingers clamping around her wrist. They stood frozen, both of them breathing hard.

"I don't want you," she murmured.

"You do," he said. "Just as much as I want you."

She shook her head, tears spilling out of her eyes. Marcus loosened his grip, suddenly angry with himself for pushing her so far. But he wanted her to see the truth. There was something happening between them, something that neither one of them wanted to define, and the hell if she was going to blame him for it.

"I've been protecting you from the minute you arrived," he said, "and I'm going to continue to do that for as long as you want me to. You can believe whatever you want about my motives, Eden—I don't care. But don't you dare try to sell the story that this wasn't mutual between us."

She flexed her fingers and Marcus finally let her go. "Stay away from me," she murmured. "Just leave me alone."

"No problem," he replied.

"And don't tell me how to run my life."

"Somebody should," he replied. "Because you're doing a damn pitiful job of it on your own."

"And you think you have the magic key to happiness?"

"At least I know where I'm going, Eden. I've got a plan."

"One of us needs to get off this boat," Eden warned. "And I'm not leaving."

"Not to worry, I will," he said. He stalked to the rear of the boat and climbed back down the ladder to the dinghy. With a flick of his wrist, he started the motor and steered out into the water, trying to calm his temper.

Though he hadn't known Eden long, this afternoon's conversation with her father had been a revelation. She was a grown woman, beautiful and desirable, yet she was still a child, trapped in the past. She wasn't angry at him—he was simply a convenient target. Marcus fought the temptation to glance back at the boat. Now that he'd walked away, all he could think about was going back, pulling her into his arms and kissing away all her fears.

His thoughts wandered back to the previous night on the beach. How had they managed to go from un-mitigated passion to uncontrolled anger in less than a day? If this was how it was going to be between them, life on board together would be intolerable.

Marcus took a deep breath. He'd finished most of the crucial work. He could take the rest back to the shop and do it there, leaving Eden to her own devices. But they'd shared far too much for it to end so quickly.

"How the hell did you think it would end?" Marcus muttered to himself. Would they just shake hands politely and then go their separate ways? Would she make up some silly reason for having to leave, then try to convince him that it was for the best? No, this was the way it was bound to happen, with anger and accusations.

He glanced back at the boat and saw her standing in the cockpit, her arms braced on the boom, watching him. He'd give her time to cool off and then he'd go back and get his things. It was better this way, to end it quickly, to get out without too many scars. Before long, she'd be a distant memory—a very vivid but distant memory.

EDEN PUNCHED IN THE code for the garage and waited for the doors to open. She glanced over her shoulder, watching for any sign of the caretaker. Thank God her father hadn't changed the code for the security system on the house. She'd managed to get inside and grab some fresh clothes and the keys to several of her father's cars without being detected.

Sarah, the housekeeper, usually finished by early afternoon and, when the family wasn't in residence, spent her evenings with her grandkids in Middleton. The caretaker for the estate normally worked on the grounds in the morning, but today he was mowing the west lawn, out of view of the driveway and the garages.

She stepped inside and perused her choices for transportation—the vintage Thunderbird was far too flashy and the Ferrari had a stick shift that she didn't know how to operate. Then there was the black Mercedes convertible. She wouldn't seem entirely out of place in Newport in that car.

She unlocked the door and tossed her bag into the passenger seat, then slipped behind the wheel. As she reached for the ignition, she glanced up at the rearview mirror, catching sight of her red-rimmed eyes.

Drawing a deep breath, she gathered her resolve, trying to ignore the ache in her heart. She'd been wrong to get angry at Marcus. But he'd had no right to speak to her in that way. They had no claims on each other. They were barely friends—friends with benefits, nothing more.

She didn't need him—for protection or sex. In truth, she didn't need anyone, not her parents, not her friends. From now on, the only person she would depend upon was herself. A ragged sob tore from her throat, and Eden forced back the tears that threatened to return.

Why was she so upset? The man drove her crazy. And he was starting to interfere in her life, trying to make decisions for her, telling her what she should and shouldn't do. What did he care if her life was messed up? It was *her* life, not his. Eden had always lived in the moment, and there was absolutely nothing wrong with that. People who planned their lives were…boring and unimaginative.

But some of Marcus's accusations had rung true. Eden was forced to confront the fact that she really had never set any goals for her life. She'd just expected that happiness would find her. But that hadn't happened yet, and over the past several years she'd begun to wonder if it ever would.

She'd been happy with Marcus, though. The short time they'd spent together on the boat had proved to her that happiness could be found. She just had to look a little harder for it.

Odd how she hadn't found it where she'd thought she would, with some handsome heir to a European fortune, a man who could take care of her and her money in the style to which she'd become accustomed. She'd found it with an ordinary guy from a regular family.

Eden had never been one to dwell on the past or to regret her mistakes. But since she'd met Marcus, she'd begun to feel the first deep pangs of remorse. Maybe she hadn't lived a life she could be proud of. She'd blown through most of her trust fund and would soon be forced to marry for money or ask her father to support her. But there were other choices.

She reached up to find her face damp with tears and impatiently brushed them away. "And you can begin right now," she said. It wasn't too late to make something more of herself. The problem was, she wasn't sure that she was qualified to be anything more than Eden Ross, international party girl.

Eden backed the car out of the garage, then pushed the remote for the garage door. She slowly navigated the curving driveway and when she reached the main gate she punched in the code. A minute later she was on Ocean Avenue, heading into Newport.

As Eden steered toward the Newport Bridge, she noticed a sign for the local discount store. Though she'd never shopped there, she understood that the store had everything a regular person could possibly need to live comfortably. Sarah, their housekeeper, had been quite excited when the store opened seven years before. And it was supposed to be cheap. Since Eden had arrived in the States, she'd lived off the cash in her wallet because she didn't want her credit cards traced.

The parking lot was packed, and Eden pulled the Mercedes into a distant row, then covered her hair with a baseball cap and slipped on her sunglasses. "You can do this," she said. "Just act like a regular person."

She slipped out of the car and locked the door behind her, then strolled up to the front entrance. Grabbing a shopping cart, she figured it would serve as a good weapon in case she was recognized. But to her surprise, she was able to stroll the aisles with barely a curious glance from other shoppers.

The variety of merchandise astounded her. She could buy a television, nacho chips and diamond earrings in the very same store. She grabbed some pretty pastel skirts and a few T-shirts and two pairs of sandals before discovering the beauty aisles.

Eden suddenly felt rather proud of herself. She was just a regular person wandering the aisles. If only Marcus could— She stopped the thought before she had a chance to finish it. Every experience she'd had over the past five days had involved him, and without even realizing it, she'd let him become a part of her life.

She'd been swept away by a man she hadn't even known a week ago. He had restored some order and serenity to her life and now it felt as if she couldn't exist without him. She wanted him here by her side, sharing this simple experience with her. She needed to hear his voice and hold his hand.

A lump of emotion clogged her throat and she swallowed it back. God, this was ridiculous! The pattern had become so familiar it was a wonder she couldn't recognize it. He'd shown her simple affection and undeniable passion and suddenly he'd become the focus of her life.

Eden shook her head, pushing aside all thoughts of Marcus Quinn. It was time to move on with her life, and this time she would be in control…not Marcus and not her father.

As Eden passed the hair color, she paused, then picked up a box and studied the photo on the front. If she really wanted to blend in, then it was time for a drastic course of action. She'd dye her hair. If she wasn't a blonde anymore, then no one would recognize her. And how difficult could it be if everything she needed came in the little box?

"I'm not a complete idiot," she murmured as she read the directions. "Regular people do this all the time."

A medium brown came as close to her natural color as possible, so she tossed the box into the cart and then looked for a pair of scissors. She'd cut her hair, as well, just to make sure.

Satisfied that her first experience at a discount

store had been a great success, Eden headed toward the checkout counters. But as she waited in line she noticed the racks of tabloids standing in her way. She winced as she saw her name splashed on the covers of *Gossip Weekly, The National Inquisitor* and *WOW!*

Thankfully they'd blurred out the indecent parts in the photos. And though the lighting wasn't the best, her body didn't look that bad. She'd been twenty-three when the tape was made and a bit thinner than she was now. Her hair had been cropped short back then. As she looked at the picture, she tried to recall everything that had happened that night, but her mind was blank.

She couldn't imagine forgetting any of the details of her time with Marcus. She'd always remember how smooth and warm his skin was and how she could follow a thin line of hair from just above his navel to his waistband and beyond. And how his voice sounded when he said her name, and how the dimple in his right cheek would appear when he smiled. She would remember how he'd kissed her that first time, passionately at first and then, before drawing away, giving her one short and sweet kiss for good measure.

And how he'd seduced her with his lips and his tongue, how he'd drawn out her desire until it had become an orgasm more powerful than she'd ever felt before. A dull ache settled inside her, a longing that would have to go unsatisfied.

Though she had multiple regrets about past lovers, she only had one with Marcus—they hadn't had sex. They'd done everything but. It would have been nice to experience that one last thing with him, to have that memory to tuck away with the others.

No doubt there'd be other men in her life. But Eden couldn't imagine wanting a man more than she had wanted Marcus. For the entire time she'd been on board *Victorious,* she'd found herself in a perpetual state of anticipation. He'd barely have to look at her and her mind would wander off into strange fantasies involving the two of them, naked and aroused.

"Ma'am? You'll have to remove your merchandise from the basket before I can check you out."

Eden glanced up and found the checker staring at her expectantly. "Right," she said.

She set the hair dye and the scissors on the conveyor belt, then grabbed the latest issues of *The National Inquisitor, Gossip Weekly* and *WOW!* The checker glanced at the magazines, then looked up at her. Eden held her breath, hoping the baseball cap and dark glasses were enough to hide her identity.

Eden set the clothes and shoes on the belt. "Can you believe that Eden Ross?" she said to the checker. "What was that girl thinking?"

"Girls with her kind of money don't need to think," the checker said.

"No, probably not."

"That'll be thirty-six forty-seven."

"That's all?" Eden pulled two twenties out of her wallet and handed them to the cashier. She couldn't remember the last time she'd walked out of a store for less than a thousand dollars!

The checker slipped the magazines into a plastic bag,

then counted out Eden's change. "You know, you look a lot like her."

Eden forced a smile. If she didn't play it completely cool, she'd be found out in a matter of seconds. "I know. I asked my hairdresser to do my hair just like hers. But after seeing this, I've decided to go back to my natural color. What girl would ever want to be like her?"

"I wouldn't mind the money," the checker said. "She's got it made."

"Maybe," Eden replied. "Or maybe it just seems that way." She grabbed her bags and hurried to the door. When she reached the parking lot, she breathed a long sigh of relief. Leading a regular life might not be as difficult as she thought.

It would be a way to prove to her father that she wasn't just some useless party girl. She could find a job, rent an apartment, make a life for herself away from polo players and society parties and friends she couldn't trust. Away from the tabloid press.

Eden steered the car toward the Newport Bridge and headed west toward Jamestown. She was a smart girl. Once she established herself, she would go to her father, apologize for all the trouble she'd caused and ask him to give her a second chance. After a time, he'd have to forgive her. The sun was beginning to set, and she flipped down the visor and turned on the radio.

As she drove, her thoughts returned to the last words she'd said to Marcus. It really hadn't been fair to walk away from him as she had. It wasn't his fault she'd made a mess of her life, and she hadn't meant to blame him for anything. But Marcus's opinion was the one that truly mattered to her, and when he'd turned on her, her defenses had automatically risen.

The thought of Marcus selling her out had caused a brief panic. Assuming that he'd choose the money over her hadn't been fair. But Eden had been looking for an excuse to push him away and she'd found it. It was far better than allowing herself to get swept up into fantasies about their future together. Though she and Marcus were great together sexually, there was nothing that made her believe they'd ever share any more than just uncontrollable lust.

Marcus was a bright man. Sooner or later he'd discover that even though Eden appeared exotic and exciting on the surface, the novelty of screwing a celebrity would soon wear off. He'd see her for what she really was—a woman filled with fears and regrets and carrying baggage no sane man would want to drag around for the rest of his life.

After crossing the bridge, Eden turned onto Highway 1 and headed south along Narragansett Bay. She'd drive until she found an inexpensive place to stay. Almost immediately she passed a small motel across the road from the water, then slowed the Mercedes and made a U-turn.

She pulled into the parking lot and drove up to the neon sign that indicated the office. Eden frowned. It wasn't glamorous and it probably didn't have room service or a masseuse on staff, but it was a start. She'd get a room, cut and dye her hair and make a plan. And tomorrow morning she'd begin her life all over again.

MARCUS GRABBED A BEER from the refrigerator in Ian's kitchen, then leaned out the screen door. "You guys need another?"

Ian and Dec stood next to the grill, staring at the hamburgers that Ian was cooking for their dinner. "We're good," Ian shouted.

Marcus glanced at his watch again, wondering why it was taking so damn long to cook a few lousy hamburgers. He'd stopped by Ian's simply to check in and waste an hour before heading back to Newport. But from the moment he'd arrived, he'd been preoccupied with thoughts of Eden. He wondered what Eden was doing, how she was feeling, whether she'd come to her senses and seen the truth of the situation or whether she was still angry at him.

He imagined how he'd make things right with her. There was a certain simplicity in taking her into his arms and kissing her until she surrendered. But he was also prepared to apologize for his harsh words and seduce her slowly. However it went, he was determined to get back to the place they'd been, that wonderful state of constant arousal and anticipation.

Marcus glanced over at his brothers, grateful they couldn't read his thoughts. For now, what he shared with her was a tantalizing secret, something that defied description and analysis. He'd have to find a way come clean. But there was no way he could tell his brothers the truth of his life right now.

With Eden, he didn't try to make sense of it. What had happened with her was a complete break from everything he'd known about desire. It was as if a giant wave had come and swept him out to sea, caught him in a current that was impossible to escape. He'd fought it at first, but then Marcus had realized that the only course was to surrender. To just let himself drown.

He sat down on the picnic table and bent forward, bracing his hands on his knees and staring at his beer bottle. When he touched her, it was pure pleasure. When she touched him, it was exquisite torment. When release finally came, it was a sensation that was unmatched in his lifetime.

He remembered his first experience with losing control at a girl's touch. The world had seemed to shift on its axis, and from that moment on Marcus had known that sex was something he didn't want to do without. But now, with Eden, he realized it was something he couldn't live without.

There was only one partner he wanted, one person who could provide the kind of pleasure he sought. Eden had become his drug of choice, her body so addictive that he found himself barely existing between fixes. Marcus shook his head. How was it possible that he felt this way and they still hadn't had sex yet?

"Hey! Are you planning to speak anytime soon?"

Marcus glanced up, pulled from his thoughts by Dec's voice. He blinked. "What?"

"What's wrong with you?" Dec asked.

"Nothing," Marcus replied. "I've just…got some things on my mind."

"Here's a question," Ian said. "Should a guy ever be completely honest with a woman? Or is it always better just to tell her what she wants to hear?"

"Always be honest," Marcus said at the very same time Dec said, "Tell her what she wants to hear." They glanced at each other.

"If you're not honest, it'll come back and bite you in the ass."

"Have you been watching Dr. Phil again?" Ian asked.

"So you'd tell her that her hair looks like crap and her butt does look huge in those pants and that you'd rather drink varnish than have dinner with her parents?" Dec asked. "Hell, Marcus, you'd get kicked to the curb with the rest of the garbage. No wonder you can't keep a woman."

"That's not what I'm talking about," Marcus murmured. Hell, he didn't know what he was talking about. All he knew was that he'd been honest with Eden and it had led to a relationship more intense than any he'd ever experienced. By stripping away all pretense, they'd had a chance to know each other in a very intimate way.

"I think there are very specific things you should never tell a woman," Ian ventured. "Guy secrets. You know, those universal truths that all guys know but we need to keep to ourselves to preserve the future of the male species."

"Like what?" Dec asked, clearly curious.

"Like when we look at other women, we really are looking at other women," Ian said. "And thinking about what they'd look like naked."

"And that no matter how many times a woman wants to have sex with you, it's never gonna be enough," Dec added. "And that no guy likes to cuddle after sex."

Ian nodded. "And that we really do read *Playboy* for the pictures and not the stories. Universal truths."

"Be honest. Have you ever been with a woman when you've been completely satisfied with the quality and frequency of the sex?" Ian asked.

Yes, Marcus mused. With Eden, even though they hadn't actually had sex, he'd been completely satisfied. There was a certain excitement that came from the anticipation, waiting to share that final intimacy, thinking about having sex, even avoiding sex, that made the need more acute.

"I rest my case," Ian said after weighing Marcus's silence.

Marcus took a long sip of his beer, then shrugged. "Maybe none of us has found the right woman." He glanced over at his brothers as they stared at him. "Yet."

Ian groaned, rubbing his forehead with his fingertips. "Jaysus, Marky, this is what comes from being stuck on that boat all alone. You're not making any sense. What's wrong with you? You're sounding like a bleedin' romantic."

"So that's not what you want out of life?" Marcus asked.

"First off, you can't talk to women, so how can you be honest with them? They have no capacity for logical reasoning. They're driven by emotions. Let me tell you, getting into a real conversation with a woman is like stepping on a land mine. One stupid move, one offhand comment or misplaced adjective and—boom— you're dead."

"And you can't depend upon women," Declan continued. "They may have your back now, but the minute you don't agree with them they'll cut your legs out from under you. You want someone who'll have your back? That's what brothers are for."

Marcus took another sip of his beer. In truth, he'd been thinking the same thing about Eden just a few hours ago. But that had been at the end of a brutally honest conversation, the kind of conversation that had exposed some pretty raw emotions. It may not have been a pretty argument or a fair fight, but at least it had been honest.

"Women are not the enemy," Marcus said.

Ian stared at Marcus for a long moment. "Did you break the pact?"

"No!" he lied. "I've just figured out a few things for myself."

But hadn't the pact contained a fatal flaw? He and his brothers had assumed that the only way to figure out women was to stay away from them, to make a vow of celibacy and stick with it. But Marcus had learned more about women in the week he'd spent seducing Eden Ross than he'd learned in his previous twenty-seven years. She was a complicated, perplexing pain in the ass, but he knew her better than he'd ever known any other woman in his life.

"So are you planning to share with us?" Declan asked.

Marcus shook his head. "Not at the moment."

A long silence descended on the group as Ian and Dec stood at the grill and stared into the fire. Marcus fought the urge to tell them everything, to explain it all in the hopes that they would be able to offer some explanation. To confess that he'd been the first to break their pact and succumb to the pleasures of the flesh.

But what had gone on between him and Eden defied description. Hell, he'd been trying to put words to it for days with no luck. "Any luck on finding that girl you were looking for, Dec?" he asked, anxious to shift the topic.

"Eden Ross?" Dec sat down on the picnic table next to Marcus. "Nothing yet."

"Louise Wilson over at the diner mentioned that there were a couple of guys wandering around Bonnett Harbor asking if anyone had seen her," Ian said. "They're promising a big payday for information. Ten thousand for a tip that leads to a photo of Eden Ross. I'm thinking I ought to be out looking for her."

"She must be close by then," Dec said.

"Why do you say that?" Marcus asked.

"Those tabloid photographers usually know more than the local cops. They can afford to pay for information. And when it comes to celebrities, folks are anxious to talk, especially for cold, hard cash. I'll just wait until they smoke her out and then I'll grab her up and take her home to daddy."

"What if she doesn't want to go?" Marcus asked. "She's an adult. She makes her own decisions."

"Whose side are you on?" Dec asked. "It's my job to find her. I don't get paid unless I find her. Ross is your boss, too. Watch out for his interests and he'll watch out for you."

Marcus was starting to understand how the rest of

the men in Eden's life had felt. It was difficult to resist a woman who made him feel the way she did. All she had to do was touch him or look at him in a certain way, and he felt his desire begin to burn.

Dec poured a bit of his beer onto the charcoal as the flames licked at the burgers. "Hell, if I were Ross, I'd think about putting that girl in a convent, locking the door and throwing away the key. I wouldn't mind getting a look at that tape, though. See what all the fuss is about."

Marcus fought back a surge of anger, struggling to maintain an indifferent facade. He'd never been the jealous sort, but the notion of his brother staring at images of a naked and aroused Eden cavorting with another man didn't sit well with him. Marcus jumped to his feet and set his empty beer bottle on the picnic table. "I gotta go," he said.

"You haven't had anything to eat," Ian said.

Marcus shrugged. "The wind is supposed to pick up later tonight, and I've got to set another anchor." Marcus started toward his truck parked in the driveway next to Ian's house.

"So how's the job going for you?" Dec called. "What did Ross think about the work?"

"He thought it was great," Marcus yelled, giving them both a wave. By the time he slipped the key into the ignition, his thoughts were firmly fixed on Eden. He'd been away from her for three hours, too long in his book. He needed to touch her, to inhale the scent of her hair and feel the warmth of her body against his.

Eden had become a basic need for him, like food

or water. He wasn't sure when it had happened, but as he pulled onto the street and pointed the truck toward Newport, he felt the hunger grow even more. When he touched her again, he wasn't going to stop until they were both completely sated.

5

MARCUS STARED AT HIS watch, then looked out across the water at *Victorious*. Midnight. And Eden was gone. Marcus had returned to the boat five hours before, fully expecting her to be waiting for him, ready to smooth over the rift between them. But when he'd climbed on board, he'd found the boat silent and empty.

He stood on the end of the dock, his arms braced on a piling, feeling helpless to do anything but curse himself for driving her away. Hell, Eden could be on a plane back to Europe at this very moment, ready to return to the glamorous life she'd left behind. Or she could be checking into a luxury hotel in New York City. Or she could be sitting in a coffee shop in downtown Newport. Even if he wanted to find her, it was impossible.

He sat on a nearby bench and stretched his legs out in front of him, tipping his head back to look up into the starry sky. Inhaling a deep breath of the damp night air, Marcus tried to put order to his thoughts. Where would she go? She'd been determined to avoid her father, so maybe she'd returned to California, to her mother. Or she could have called friends.

Wasn't this how he'd always expected it to end between them? One day Eden would be there, and the next she'd be gone, no explanations, no apologies. Marcus sighed. In truth, he ought to be glad it was finally over. They'd made a quick and clean break. He could go back to his work without having to worry about Eden and the drama that seemed to swirl around her.

Yet he couldn't help but worry a little. The way Declan talked, there were people out there looking for her—and not just her father. Reporters, photographers, they all wanted a piece of her. He felt as if he were the only one qualified to protect her.

Though she wanted everyone to believe she was tough and resilient, Marcus knew better. He saw something of himself in her bravado. As a kid, he'd covered up his loneliness with a false confidence, hoping that if he appeared to be sure of himself, then others wouldn't notice that he was a bundle of fears. Eden was lost like that now, trapped by her insecurities and fighting to prove that she was strong enough to survive.

Eden had handled that kind of attention in the past, but she was much more vulnerable now. Could she withstand another onslaught from the press or her father? Or would she capitulate and go back to the life she'd led before? Marcus shook his head and sighed.

He'd come to her rescue, keeping her presence on board *Victorious* a secret. But she could take care of herself if she had to. She had her father's money. That kind of money could get her out of almost any mess.

He raked his hands through his hair. So that was it. Eden was gone and Marcus would go back to life as he'd known it. But it would never be the same for him. Marcus couldn't imagine ever meeting a woman now without comparing her to Eden, without wondering if he'd ever experience such crazy, uninhibited desire again.

His cell phone rang and Marcus reached inside his pocket and pulled it out. He glanced at the caller ID—the Sandpiper Motel. Frowning, Marcus flipped open the phone and held it to his ear. "Hello?"

"It's me."

Her voice sounded shaky and strained, as though she was on the verge of tears. Marcus sat up straight. "Eden? Are you okay?"

"Can you come?"

"Are you at a motel?"

"I can't remember what it's called. I'm in room five."

"Are you all right? Tell me."

A sob tore from her throat and Marcus winced. "No," she replied.

"Are you alone?"

"Yes," she said, her voice now barely audible.

"I'll be there in twenty minutes, sweetheart. Stay right where you are. Don't go outside and don't open the door to anyone but me. And if anyone tries to get in, then you call the police or 911, all right?"

"O-okay." She hung up the phone and Marcus jumped to his feet. His mind raced with all the possibilities. Had she been hurt? Was she being threatened? Obviously something had happened to upset her, but what? Hell, maybe she'd called her father and it hadn't gone well.

As he sped along Ocean Avenue toward Newport, he felt oddly relieved. She wasn't gone yet. And when she needed help, she hadn't hesitated to call him. Marcus grabbed his phone again, ready to ask for Ian's help. But then he thought better of it. If he told Ian about Eden, then Ian would feel compelled to tell Dec, and Dec would have to tell Ross.

The fifteen-minute drive across the bay to Bonnett Harbor was accomplished in ten minutes, and by the time Marcus pulled the truck up to the front of the Sandpiper Motel he was determined to grab Eden and take her back to the safety of the boat.

He jumped out of the truck and found the door to room five. Marcus knocked softly, and a moment later the door opened a crack in front of him. Eden peered out, then stepped back as she let him enter. She closed the door and stood against it, dressed only in her panties and a bra, a towel wrapped around her head. Marcus strode into the room and glanced around, but Eden was alone.

"Thank you for coming," she murmured.

He faced her, his heart twisting at her tear-stained cheeks. Marcus held out his arms and Eden crossed the room and stepped into his embrace. "Are you all right?" he asked, his hands smoothing over her narrow shoulders to rest at the small of her back.

God, it felt good to touch her again, to feel her warm body beneath his hands. He'd grown accustomed to touching her whenever the whim struck and he didn't like doing without.

"It's stupid," she said, burying her face in his chest.

"What? Tell me. I'll make it all right," Marcus said. "I swear I will."

"You can't."

He drew back and cupped her face in his hands. "I can try. Just tell me what's wrong."

Eden wiped her nose on the back of her hand and drew a ragged breath. "It's green," she murmured.

"What's green?"

Eden reached up and brushed the towel off her head. "My hair."

A laugh slipped from his throat, and the moment it did Marcus wished he could take it back. This was one of those times when honesty was probably not the best policy.

Eden's expression crumpled into tears and she ran to the bed and threw herself face-first onto the mattress. "I know! It looks ridiculous. I wanted to dye my hair so people wouldn't notice me. I might as well have a neon sign attached to my head now."

Marcus sat down on the bed and gently turned her over to face him. "I'm sorry. I wasn't laughing at your hair. It was just a laugh of relief. I thought you were hurt or in trouble."

She plucked at her hair. "What do you think this is?"

"Jaysus, Eden. You scared me. I thought…well, you don't want to know what went through my mind. I'm just glad you're all right."

"But I'm not all right," she said. "Look at my hair."

God, even with the green hair she looked beautiful. How was that possible? "Well…it's green. How did that happen?"

"I don't know. The box said medium brown and it came out green. I should sue. This isn't even close to medium brown."

"Why did you dye your hair?"

"It's part of my plan," Eden said. She gave him a narrow-eyed glare. "This is all your fault, you know. You told me I needed a plan, and I made a plan and now look at me."

"Unless that plan includes clown college, then I'm not sure what you're going to do with green hair."

She gasped, but then a reluctant smile twitched at the corners of her mouth. Marcus reached out and tipped her chin up, forcing her to meet his gaze. "I'm sorry about what I said on the boat." He couldn't wait any longer and he covered her mouth with his, desperate to taste her again.

With a groan, she threw her arms around his neck and pulled him down on top of her. Her tongue met his, the kiss deepening until Marcus felt a pleasant warmth seep through his body. When he finally had a chance to take a breath, he gazed down into her eyes, fingering a curl at her temple. "It's not that bad," he said. "It's not like it's bright green."

"What is it then?" she asked.

"Avocado?" he ventured.

She wrapped her legs around his waist, then turned him over until she straddled him on the bed. "Tell me it's pretty," Eden demanded. "Tell me I'm beautiful."

Marcus stared up at her as he ran his hands up her rib cage and cupped her breasts. "You know you are," he whispered, slipping his fingers beneath her bra.

Eden reached back and unhooked it, letting the lacy scrap drop between them. Marcus couldn't keep from touching her. His thumbs lazily teased at her nipples.

"Say it," she ordered, closing her eyes.

"You are the most beautiful thing I've ever seen," Marcus admitted. Even with her damp hair an odd shade of green it was the truth. There was no one in the world more beautiful than Eden.

Marcus shifted beneath her, slowly growing hard with each passing second. It never took much for her to arouse him, he mused. Eden noticed his discomfort and pressed her hips against his. "Do you still want me?" she asked, rubbing against him, the answer evident to both of them.

"I always want you," Marcus murmured.

A satisfied smile curved the corners of her mouth and she stopped moving. "I believe you," she said as if his answer were some sort of test. With that, Eden rolled off him and stood beside the bed, staring at herself in the mirror above the dresser.

Marcus closed his eyes and fought back a wave of desire, willing his erection to subside. "Do you want to tell me about your plan?" he asked, grimacing as he rolled over onto his stomach.

She smiled as she continued to stare at her reflection. "I hadn't considered clown college, but that's not a bad idea."

"And I'm sorry I made light of this very serious situation. Now tell me."

"I thought it might be easier to blend in if I changed my looks. So I decided to dye and cut my hair."

She ought to have known it was an impossible task. Even with mousy brown hair and everyday clothes Eden Ross would still cause a stir wherever she went. It was all in the way she carried herself, as if she expected to be the center of everyone's universe. "And why would you want to blend in?" he asked.

Eden sat down beside him, tucked her knees up beneath her chin and wrapped her arms around her legs. "You'll think it's silly."

"Nothing would surprise me," Marcus said.

"I don't want to be Eden Ross anymore. If I don't look like me, then I can be anyone I want. Madonna reinvents herself all the time. I can be just a regular person."

"Eden, you're not a regular person. Like it or not, you're a celebrity."

"But I could be a regular person. I could get a job and a place to live and do something interesting with my life. But only if you help me." She took his hand and clutched it to her chest. "You have to help me. Besides, I can't leave Newport yet."

"You can't?"

"Because we're not done."

Marcus ran his hand along her arm, chuckling softly. Though the attraction between them had been there all along, this was the first time Eden had ever admitted that she didn't want it to end. He leaned forward and kissed her breast, his tongue tracing the outline of her nipple. "I'm not finished with you, either."

Eden jumped up from the bed and hurried to the window, peering out from behind the curtains. "We have to figure out how to get out of here," she said.

Marcus leaned back on the bed, linking his arms behind his head. "There's always the door."

She turned and shook her head, the damp green curls tumbling around her face. "There are photographers out there."

Frowning, Marcus rolled off the bed and hurried to her side. "Where?"

"The dark sedan with the tinted windows. They showed up about a half hour after I did. I thought the clerk recognized me."

"And they saw me come in?" Marcus asked.

"They probably have a nice photo of you. But it does them no good if I'm not in it, too. You're just an ordinary Joe going into a motel room. Not very interesting. So we're probably safe so far." She glanced up at him. "If they catch us, you'll be a celebrity, too. Eden Ross's new boy toy." She giggled. "I'm not sure you'd appreciate the publicity."

"So what do we do?" Marcus asked.

"Oh, that's easy." She walked over to the phone and picked it up. "First, I dial 911." She paused, then spoke into the phone. "Hello. Yes. I'm staying at the…" She looked over to Marcus.

"Sandpiper," he said.

"Sandpiper Motel. There's a dark sedan parked on the street in front of the motel, and I think the man inside is planning to steal a car. He's been looking at a Mercedes convertible in the motel lot."

Marcus frowned. "This is against the law," he whispered. "Reporting a false emergency."

Eden put her hand over the phone. "They're harassing me. That's against the law, too." She pulled her hand away. "Yes. I'm in room twelve. My name is Eugenia Montevecchio. Yes, I'll wait right here. Please hurry. I think he might have a gun."

Eden hung up the phone and grinned. "Now we just have to wait until the police arrive, and once the photographers are occupied, we sneak out. We'll have to take your car, though."

"Great plan, unless we get arrested for falsely reporting a crime." Ian would not be pleased. "And who the hell is Eugenia Montevecchio?"

"My alias. I'm also Liselotte Bunderstrassen and Carmella Ramirez della Fuego. So where should we go? We could go to New York. My hairdresser is there and he could fix the mess I made."

Marcus shook his head. "I have to work, Eden. And why waste money on a hotel when you can stay on the boat for free?"

Eden shook her head. "No. I'm done with anything that has to do with my father. If he's going to disown me, then I should begin dealing with it right now. Once I'm rid of his car, there's nothing more connecting us."

"Except the money."

She drew a deep breath. "I have just enough left in my trust fund to start all over, to find a place to live and to buy a car. I just have to find a job."

"And what will you do?" Marcus asked.

She shrugged. "I'll figure that out later. For now, we need to worry about getting out of here without being photographed or arrested. Are you going to help me with that?"

Marcus nodded. Strange how easy it was to get swept up in one of Eden's little adventures. And he wasn't even considering the consequences. If Ian ever discovered Marcus's complicity in this, he wouldn't think twice about tossing them both in jail. And once Ian was done with him, Dec would have a few things to say. "Get your things together," he said. "I know the police chief in this town, and his guys are pretty quick to respond."

"How long is it supposed to take?"

"I don't know," Marcus said. "Read the directions." He crinkled his nose. "This stuff really stinks. And I don't like these damn gloves."

"You can't use your bare hands," Eden said. "The dye would burn them."

Eden sat perched on the toilet in the glass-block bathroom of Marcus's loft, her body wrapped in a towel, her head covered with hair dye. They'd made an easy escape from the motel last night and were now comfortably settled at his place.

Eden wasn't sure what she had expected, but it wasn't this. From the outside, the two-story building looked like a ruin of peeling paint and weathered wood. The clapboard facade overlooked a boatyard cluttered with timber boat cradles and rickety ladders. Wide sliding doors on the first floor opened to a spacious workshop. Half the second floor was a loft apartment with a wall of windows on both sides, overlooking the workshop and the water.

The airy loft had a cozy feel, with timber framing and exposed beams. Marcus had carved the posts with unusual patterns that she recognized as his own art. A galley kitchen lined the wall to the right, and on the left was Marcus's bedroom with old sails draped down from the beams for privacy. The only walls in the loft were glass block and surrounded the bathroom.

She'd never really thought about Marcus's life off *Victorious*. She knew he lived somewhere, but there'd never been much cause to consider where. Now she was forced to acknowledge that there was more to Marcus Quinn than the beautiful body sunning next to her on deck or the soft kisses waking her up from an afternoon nap or the deep blue eyes watching her from across the cockpit. He had a real life, friends and family, a place that he called home.

Eden scanned the directions. "Fifteen minutes," she said. "How long has it been?"

Marcus held out his arm so she could see his watch. "Ten," he guessed. "Maybe twelve."

Eden's gaze drifted up from the light dusting of hair on his belly to his broad chest. He was barefoot and bare-chested, dressed only in faded jeans that rode low on his hips. She reached out and ran her fingertips over his stomach, and he backed away as if her touch tickled. There were a lot of things she liked about Marcus and his body was near the top of the list.

She'd been with handsome men, but they'd been handsome in a premeditated way. They spent hours on grooming to look perfect—three-hundred-dollar haircuts and weekly manicures, an expensive stylist to choose the perfect clothes. But Marcus was sexy by just being a man. He combed his hair with his hands and wore faded Levi's because they were comfortable. His smooth skin was tanned from weeks of work in the sun rather than a few days on a Mediterranean beach or a few hours at a tanning salon. There was something to be said for a man who didn't have to work at looking like a man.

A tiny smiled twitched at the corners of Eden's mouth as her gaze fixed on the top button of his jeans. She fought the temptation to reach out and unbutton it, to draw the zipper down and expose him to her touch. It wouldn't take much to make him hard, and after that she could bring him to a climax with her fingers or her lips. Marcus hadn't ever tried to resist her.

Eden drew a deep breath. Or they could take the last step in their slow journey toward the inevitable. They'd come so close over the past week, but Marcus had always stopped short, as if he were waiting for an invitation to possess her, permission to lose himself in her body.

A tiny thrill raced through her at the thought of opening herself to him, the sensation of feeling him move inside her. She wanted to make love to him, but it also frightened her at the same time. Things were already too perfect with Marcus Quinn.

Searching for a distraction, she reached out and

grabbed a bottle of cologne from the back of the toilet, then sniffed at it. "It doesn't smell like you," she murmured.

"And what do I smell like?"

Eden shrugged. "Sweat. Sawdust. Seawater. It's a very intoxicating scent."

"There are times when I want to smell nice," Marcus explained. He tossed the plastic bottle from the dye into the wastebasket, then ripped off the gloves.

"When you want to seduce a woman?"

"Maybe," Marcus admitted. "Don't you make yourself smell good when you want to be seduced?"

She unscrewed the cap and tipped a bit of the cologne onto her finger, then slowly drew it down along his naked belly, circling his belly button with her fingertip. "Sometimes," she said, pressing her nose to the spot and inhaling deeply. "How many women have you seduced with this bottle of cologne?"

"I don't kiss and tell."

Eden shrugged. "Then show me how you do it. I want to know. Give me all the details."

Marcus grinned. "You know how I do it, Eden. I've spent the last week seducing you."

"Oh, really? And I thought I was seducing you."

Marcus chuckled. "Maybe it was a joint effort."

"But it obviously hasn't worked," she said.

"It hasn't?" Marcus stepped back. "I recall some rather powerful reactions on your part. Were you faking it, Eden?"

She reached out and hooked her finger in the waistband of his jeans, drawing him closer. "I'm just saying that we haven't done everything possible." She nuzzled her nose against him, then bit at the fabric of his jeans.

He shook his head slowly. "I could live the rest of my life with you, Eden, and I don't think we'd ever get to everything possible between a man and a woman."

"True. We've merely scratched the sexual surface, so to speak." She stood up and nudged Marcus aside, then bent over the sink and began to rinse her hair. "So what are your fantasies? What do you imagine we'll do next?"

"I was thinking we'd have breakfast," he said.

Eden stood up, water dripping from her head. Without a thought, she discarded the towel, letting it fall to the floor. Then she reached out and unbuttoned his jeans, slowly drawing the zipper down.

"What are you doing?"

"I need your help," she said. "In the shower. I can't get this stuff out of my hair."

Eden turned and stepped inside the shower. She glanced over her shoulder to see him stripping his jeans off, his penis already growing hard. A moment later he joined her, standing behind her as she turned on the water and adjusted the temperature.

Eden moved beneath the water and tipped her head back while Marcus grabbed a bottle of shampoo and squeezed a measure into his hand. Slowly he worked it into her hair, massaging her scalp. Eden closed her eyes and sank back against him, his erection nestling in the small of her back.

She reached around and grabbed his hips, holding him close as she gently rocked against his body. A moment later he turned her around, his arm snaking around her waist as they both stepped beneath the shower. Warm water sluiced between their bodies, making their skin slick and sensitive.

She was here in his shower, a spot so completely familiar to him. They were no longer living a fantasy, existing on a luxurious yacht, far from the real world. This was real, and her need for him so much more intense.

Eden reached between them and slowly began to caress him, his erection hard and smooth against her palm. When she touched him, she felt the current that connected them, a desire so strong that it was like a magnetic force…undeniable…unflinching.

A soft groan rumbled in his throat and Eden looked up at him. Marcus's eyes were closed, his lower lip caught between his teeth. She pressed her mouth to his chest, kissing and biting until she found his nipple. Every time they were together there was something new to find, some unexplored spot, some surprise sensation. But it wasn't just physical pleasure that she took from his body.

When she was with him, naked and entwined in an embrace, she was no longer Eden Ross. All her life fell away and she became someone else, simpler, more satisfied with life.

Suddenly Marcus sucked in a sharp breath. His hands grasped her wrists and he pinned them behind her back, pressing her against the cool marble wall of the shower. "Slow," he murmured, his breath hot against her neck.

"Show me," Eden said, grazing her teeth along his shoulder. "Seduce me."

He stared down at her, his gaze probing hers, water

droplets clinging to his dark lashes. His lips parted and she waited for him to speak, but he didn't. Instead he gripped her wrists in one hand, gently restraining her, and his other hand skimmed over her damp skin.

Eden's breath caught as his thumb grazed over her nipple, drawing it taut before moving to her other breast. And still he looked into her eyes, watching her every reaction and responding to it with his touch.

Every nerve in her body was alive, awaiting his caress, aching for the sensations her body seemed to crave. She felt desperate for more, but Marcus took his time, bringing her along slowly. And when he finally slipped his fingers between her legs, Eden cried out, surprised by the shock that raced through her body. She closed her eyes as he played with her, so gentle yet intent on his purpose.

The water continued to fall, the sound of her breathing echoing against the walls of the shower. Marcus moved down her body, his lips hot against her skin, until he knelt in front of her. He parted her with his fingers and then tasted her. Eden hadn't been aware that he'd freed her hands, and the moment she realized it, her fingers tangled in his hair.

It was delicious torment, his tongue slipping back and forth against her, sending wave after wave of pleasure through her body. Through the haze of desire, Eden pressed her hips forward, searching for her release. And when she felt it coming, she held her breath. But Marcus had sensed that she was near and stopped before she could tumble over the edge.

He slowly stood. Eden instinctively reached out and

took him in her hand, stroking him gently. There wasn't a way to stop this now, even if she wanted to. They had to finish what they'd begun the moment they'd met. They had to feel what it was like to possess each other completely.

She rubbed his penis against her, slipping it between her legs, then drawing back, tempting him to come inside her if only for a moment. She felt him hesitate, but Eden looked up at him. "Don't stop," she whispered.

It was all the urging he needed. He stepped out of the shower for a moment and returned with a box of condoms. He fumbled to open it, and Eden grabbed it from him and tore the box, tossing all but one foil packet aside. She gently sheathed him, his tightly held breath warning her to take care.

Then, with a low moan, Marcus spanned her waist with his hands and lifted her off her feet. He wrapped her legs around his hips, and Eden felt him pressing at her entrance, waiting.

He kissed her, his mouth devouring hers. Eden caught his lower lip between her teeth and bit, holding him still as she sank down against him. Inch by inch, she took him inside of her until he was buried entirely. She released his lip and they waited, both breathless with anticipation, gazes locked.

When he began to move, Eden moaned, the ache inside her building. She smoothed the damp hair from his forehead, intent on watching his eyes as they made love. She'd never risked such an intimacy with another man, knowing there would be nothing to see beyond lust. But with Marcus there was more. A fierce possessiveness, a desire so intense that it frightened her and a vulnerability that made her feel safe.

His gentle movements soon turned more desperate, and Eden arched back against the wall of the shower as he drove into her. His gaze dropped to her lips and he kissed her again, his tongue mimicking his lovemaking.

He gasped for breath and Eden could tell he was close. She closed her eyes and surrendered herself to the tension building inside her. He filled her so completely, a sensation that was new and unfamiliar and a bit painful. But it was the pain that made it more real, and Eden focused on that, surprised at the pleasure it brought.

She danced along the edge of release, stepping closer and then drifting away. And when Marcus suddenly stopped, she was a heartbeat from completion. Eden drew a shallow breath, and then he slipped his hand between them and touched her.

Her eyes flew open to find him gazing intently at her. A moment later she felt the first spasm strike and watched as Marcus instinctively surrendered at the very same time. He tightened his grip on her hips as pleasure washed over them both, yet he still didn't close his eyes.

And when it was over completely, a tiny smile curved the corners of his mouth. He drew a shaky breath, then dropped a gentle kiss on her lips. "I'd like to carry you to the bed," he murmured, "but I'm not sure I can still walk."

Eden slowly regained her feet, Marcus wincing as he slipped out of her. She pulled him beneath the water and gently removed the condom, stroking him softly as she did. Something had changed between them, some bond had suddenly been strengthened.

A sliver of fear shot through her as Eden realized she no longer had control over her feelings for Marcus. She'd believed herself in love before but been fooled. Could this be wishful thinking or did her feelings for him run deeper? She shivered, her body trembling.

"What is it?" he asked.

Eden glanced up at him, then shook her head. "The water. It's getting cold."

He took her hand and led her from the shower. Wrapping a soft towel around her body, Marcus dried her. But the goose bumps still pricked her skin.

Eden stepped to the mirror, and Marcus stood behind her, combing the tangles from her newly colored hair. She stared at her reflection, not recognizing the person looking back at her, wondering how she'd managed to lose herself so completely.

"What have I done?" she whispered.

Marcus smiled. "At least it's not green anymore."

MARCUS AWOKE SLOWLY, his limbs twisted in the sheets and his face buried in his pillow. Without opening his eyes, he reached out for Eden. But her half of his mattress was empty. He sat up and peered through the curtains of sail that hid the bed, but the loft was empty.

With a low curse, Marcus crawled out of bed and grabbed his jeans from the floor, then tugged them on. He glanced in the bathroom as he passed, then crossed the loft to the windows that overlooked the workroom. But as he turned, he noticed Eden sitting at his desk tucked in the corner, her gaze fixed on his computer screen.

He silently came up behind her and placed his hands on her arms. She jumped in surprise, glancing over her shoulder at him. "I'm sorry. I didn't want to wake you."

"It's nearly midnight. Come back to bed."

"In a few minutes," she said.

"What are you doing?"

For a long moment she didn't speak. "Finding out where I've been and what I've been doing."

"What?"

"It's been reported that I've entered drug rehab in Arizona. There's another report that I've suffered a nervous breakdown and I'm staying at a spa in Switzerland. And then there's the story that I've been kidnapped and my father is desperately trying to arrange a ransom."

Marcus squatted down beside her and grabbed hold of her hand, twisting his fingers through hers. "But none of that is true."

"They're not going to leave me alone," Eden said. "If anything, it's going to get worse. I was stupid to think people would forget if I just disappeared for a while." She pointed to the computer screen. "But the speculation is always going to be there. It's never going away."

"But it will stop eventually," Marcus said. "Sooner or later don't you think they'll stop searching, stop speculating?"

She shrugged, then clicked on to another screen. "For nine ninety-five we can watch a clip from my video. Would you like to see it?" Her voice was cold and flat.

Marcus frowned at the sudden shift in her mood. "No, not really."

She turned on him, and he saw a flicker of anger in her eyes. "Why not? Aren't you curious? Every other man in the world is. Ah, but you got the real thing, didn't you?"

"Eden, I don't—"

"Maybe you should sell your story. I'm sure there'd be money in it for you."

"Are you deliberately trying to provoke me?" Marcus asked.

She jumped out of the chair and pushed past him, pacing along the length of windows that overlooked the workshop. Marcus watched her for a long moment, noting the tension in her shoulders. He suspected this wasn't really about the video, yet he wasn't sure what to make of it. They'd just spent the most incredible night together and she—

Marcus drew a sharp breath. Did she regret what they'd done? They'd both been so cautious in taking that final step. And now that they had, there was no going back. There was something happening between them and they couldn't deny it any longer.

He crossed to Eden and grabbed her arm, pulling her around to face him. "If you think I have anything in common with that guy on the video or any other guy you've been with, you're wrong. Don't blame me for your past, Eden. And don't be so quick to count me as part of it."

"Sooner or later *you'll* blame me for my past, won't you?"

Marcus shook his head. "Why would I do that?"

"You don't think you will, but just wait. Here, let me show you who I really am. All we need is a credit card. Do you have a credit card?"

"Stop it," Marcus muttered.

"No, we've always been honest with each other. Why not look at it? We can enjoy it together, as so many others will."

Frustrated, Marcus decided to call her bluff. If she wanted a fight, he knew that watching the video would easily put him in the mood. "All right. Why not? I'll go get a credit card." He gently set her aside, then crossed the room to his dresser. His wallet was where he'd left it earlier, and he picked it up and tossed it at her. "Go for it."

Marcus watched the emotions play across her face. He wanted to pull her into his arms and kiss the fears out of her. He wasn't sure what had caused the upset, but Marcus sensed that she was doing her best to put distance between them.

Maybe it hadn't been a good idea to make love to Eden. Though she kept her emotions under control, when she did show them, they were raw with confusion. But resisting Eden and the pleasures her body promised had become an overwhelming task, and he wasn't superhuman. There wasn't a moment in the day when he didn't want to touch her or kiss her. But falling in love with Eden would be a disaster in the making.

Marcus had never been in love, of that he was certain. There had been women in his life who'd kept him interested for a short time, but in the end he'd stepped back, unwilling to put his heart at risk.

Maybe Eden felt the same as he did. They could go so far, enjoying each other's bodies without sacrificing their hearts and souls. But Marcus already sensed that they were wandering into dangerous territory now, unfamiliar to them both.

Marcus slowly crossed the room, then took his wallet from her stiff fingers. "You're the one who wants a fresh start," he murmured. "If that's true, then forget the mistakes you made in the past. Walk away, Eden. Start your life now. Tell me what you want to do and I'll help you."

Eden drew a ragged breath and nodded. Then, her bravado crumpling, she wrapped her arms around his neck. Marcus scooped her up and carried her back to the bed. He lay down beside her and pulled her body into the curve of his, nestling her backside into his lap.

"Do you want to change your life?" he murmured, his chin resting on her shoulder.

"I'm not sure I have much choice."

"You do. You can leave here today, hop a plane, and be back where you came from by tomorrow evening."

"I can't," she said. "I want to stay here with you."

"Then stay," Marcus said, "and stop looking back."

"We can't hide out here forever," she said. "Sooner or later we both have to go out into the real world again."

Marcus nodded. "I know." He realized that by pushing her to find a new life, he might just lose her for good. Why not allow himself this chance to get close? To finally see what it would be like to let a woman inside his life? He and Eden were similar in one way—their unhappy childhoods had molded them into cynical, wary adults. But at least Eden had searched for something more. She believed she could fall in love. Marcus had never truly believed it could happen for him. And even with Eden wrapped in his arms he still couldn't make himself believe it.

"Sooner or later they'll find me," she said.

"I know," Marcus replied.

"And if you're with me, you'll get caught up in it, too. Promise me that you won't hate me."

He kissed the spot beneath her ear. "I could never hate you."

"I have to call them. My parents," she murmured. "And I will, I promise. But before I do, I just need to know that I can do this on my own. That I can start again." She laughed softly. "Where am I going to live? What kind of job will I get? What if I can't do this?"

She rolled over and faced him, her eyes filled with doubt. His fingers came up to stroke her cheek. "You can stay here with me for as long as you want. I'll help you."

Marcus kissed her, gently parting her lips with his tongue. For now, she belonged with him. He needed to keep her close, to grasp at that tenuous connection they'd found with each other.

It wasn't just desire driving him anymore. And though the physical release was intense, there was something more to it, something he wanted to hold on to. Marcus searched his mind for an explanation of what he'd found, but there were no words. It was more than satisfaction or release. Was it contentment?

Eden reached down between them and slowly unbuttoned his jeans. By the time she worked the zipper open, he was already growing hard with anticipation. And when she wrapped her fingers around him, Marcus closed his eyes and surrendered to her touch. He'd worry about all the complications later.

6

SHE SEDUCED HIM AGAIN in the middle of the night, waking him with her caress. Half-asleep, Marcus had thought he was dreaming at first, but as he'd drifted toward consciousness he'd felt the heat of real desire pounding through his veins.

The clothes they'd worn to bed had easily been discarded, and in the darkness he'd explored her body by touch. When she'd climbed on top of him and taken him inside her, Marcus had found himself instantly aware of every movement she made and the effect it had on him. Caught in a dreamy half sleep, his body had responded instantly, attuned to every sensation. She had rocked above him, slowly at first, in complete control of herself and his responses. Blind to the beauty of her body, Marcus closed his eyes and let his imagination take over.

She'd climaxed without him even touching her, her orgasm quiet but intense. And the moment he'd felt her spasm, Marcus had joined her. When he'd finished,

Eden had curled up beside him and fallen asleep as if nothing had happened.

Marcus turned his head and gazed at her in the early morning light, her face resting on the edge of his pillow, her fingertips nearly touching his face. Their encounter in the shower had been based on raw and very mutual need. But Eden's silent seduction had been different.

As if awakening from a bad dream, she'd found some sort of comfort in his body and her power over it. When he'd tried to touch her, she'd simply linked her fingers through his and pinned his hands above his shoulders, interested only in physical release and nothing more.

He reached out and took a strand of her hair between his fingers. It was darker than it had been, now a warm shade of honey. Curls surrounded her face, making her look much younger than she actually was. Marcus wondered at the contrasts—the sweet, vulnerable girl and the determined seductress.

He liked both in his bed. With others, he'd always preferred to sleep away from home, making it easier to leave when he felt the need. But he wanted to keep Eden close.

The sound of Marcus's cell phone echoed in the loft, and he carefully rolled out of bed and grabbed his jeans from the floor, finding the phone in his pocket. He flipped it open and recognized Dec's cell number on the caller ID. Marcus paused, wondering if he ought to answer it.

He finally pushed the button as he walked across the loft to the bathroom. "Hey," he murmured. "What's up?"

"I'm downstairs," Declan said. "Do you have coffee?"

Marcus stared at his reflection in the mirror, rubbing his palm over the stubble on his jaw. "No, we'll have to go out. I'll be right down."

He quickly grabbed his jeans and pulled them on, then shrugged into a T-shirt. His deck shoes were at the door, and he slipped into them before crossing back to the bed. Bending over Eden, he kissed her forehead. Her eyes fluttered open and she smiled up at him. "I have to go out for a bit. I'll bring back breakfast," he said.

"Don't leave," Eden murmured, wrapping her arms around his neck. "Stay here with me."

Marcus groaned as he tangled his fingers through Eden's tousled hair. He kissed her again. "I have to go. Dec is downstairs waiting. If I don't show, he'll come looking for me and he'll find you."

Eden's smile brightened. "Invite him up. We can all climb back into bed."

Marcus growled playfully. "I don't think that would be a good idea."

"Then take me with you. I'd like to meet your brother."

"Not today," Marcus said, pressing a kiss to her forehead. "I'll be back soon. Promise."

Eden slowly let her hand drift down his chest, then hooked her fingers in the waistband of his jeans. "Don't keep me waiting."

When Marcus got downstairs, he found Dec perched on the hood of his BMW, dressed in khakis and a starched blue oxford. He slid to his feet as Marcus approached, holding up a bakery bag. "How did you know I was here?" Marcus asked.

"I took Ma to early mass and I saw your truck," Dec said. "I brought breakfast."

"Let's go out," Marcus replied. "I need something more substantial than that."

Dec shrugged, then nodded toward his car. When they were inside, he glanced over at Marcus. "What's up with you?"

"What do you mean?" Marcus asked.

A frown furrowed Dec's forehead. "I don't know. You just look…odd."

Marcus raked his hands through his hair. "Thanks."

"I thought you were staying out on Ross's boat."

"I figured it would be easier to finish up the smaller pieces here. More room and better equipment."

Dec studied him for a long time before starting the car. He looked both ways before pulling out onto the street, then headed for their favorite diner on the main street of Bonnett Harbor, only three blocks away. "I got a call last night from Ian's dispatcher. Eden Ross was spotted over at the Sandpiper Motel. A couple of tabloid photographers got a tip from the night manager and they staked out her room."

"So what did she have to say?" Marcus asked, trying to appear as indifferent as possible.

"I didn't talk to her. She managed to slip out without anyone seeing her. But the photographers mentioned there was a man with her and he was driving a pickup. Ian has her voice on 911 calling in the photographers as car thieves. That's how she created the diversion."

Marcus nodded. "Interesting. So where do you think she is now?"

"She can't be far," Dec said. "She had her father's Mercedes and left it behind." He paused. "She must have gone home at some point to get the car, and we missed her."

We. Somehow Dec had assumed that Marcus was part of the "team." And for a fleeting instant Marcus thought about telling his brother the truth. In his opinion, Eden needed to talk to her father and ease Trevor Ross's mind regarding her whereabouts. The longer she stayed under the radar, the more difficult it would be to explain to everyone involved why she'd waited so long. Hell, Marcus had given up any hope that Trevor Ross would invest in his business now. He'd cut his losses. In truth, he much preferred to take Eden's side in the matter.

But that wouldn't square him with his brothers. In their eyes, family loyalty came first, far ahead of any passing affections he might have for a woman. Dec and Ian both had a job to do, and he'd stood in their way.

Even if he wanted to come clean, how the hell was he supposed to explain himself? Had he become so enamored that he'd lost the ability to think for himself? Marcus had to admit that Eden Ross was pretty persuasive, especially when she turned on the sex appeal. And Marcus had never been good at reading a woman's true intentions. He'd been drawn in before he realized what was happening.

"What are you going to do?" Marcus asked.

"Ross is sending a security detail over to the house

to watch for her. Ian put out an APB on her after she called in that false emergency. And I've got a new assignment from Ross."

"What is it?" Marcus asked.

Dec pulled the car into the parking lot of the diner and switched the ignition off. "Nothing you'd find interesting."

Marcus watched a subtle shift in his brother's expression and recognized the signs. Ian and Dec had always kept secrets from him when he was younger, but Marcus had devised an easy way to recognize a lie. Dec tried too hard to look indifferent, and Ian hid his lies with elaborate distractions. Considering that every emotion Declan felt could be seen in his face, Marcus could tell he was lying now.

"Would you like to tell me about her?" Marcus asked, grateful to find a way to deflect attention from his own lies.

Dec sighed. "She's nothing special, certainly not enough to tempt me."

"Be careful," Marcus warned. "You've got money riding on this."

Dec laughed sharply. "I've got money riding on Eden Ross, too. And there's no way I'm going to lose on either one of those deals."

Maybe Dec already had, he mused as he stepped out of the car. Eden was safely hidden in Marcus's loft. And if Dec's mystery lady was anything like Eden, then Dec didn't stand a chance with her either. In truth, the agreement they'd made and the money they'd put down made it all the more difficult to remain celibate. Given the choice, he'd take Eden over the money any day.

When they walked into the diner, they found Ian enjoying a cup of coffee at the counter, dressed in his uniform. He happily joined them at a booth along the front windows. Alice, their favorite waitress, dropped three menus on the table and filled their coffee cups.

Ian glanced over at Marcus and frowned. "What's wrong with you?"

"See, I asked the same thing," Dec said.

"Nothing," Marcus said. "I'm tired. I've been working late. I'm hungry. Is that enough or do you want more?" He'd been having mind-blowing sex with the most beautiful woman in the world. A guy had a right to look different.

"Any luck with Eden Ross?" Ian asked, turning to his younger brother.

"She's in the wind," Dec replied. "I checked the cab companies, the private limos, even the bus station. She just vanished. Whoever she was with must have had transportation. She could be anywhere by now. Why is it so damn hard to find this girl? Sometimes I feel like she's right under our noses."

"Did anyone besides the night manager actually see her?" Ian asked.

"Nope. But the photographers gave me a photo of the guy. Can't make out much. He's tall, over six feet, with dark hair. And she let him into the room like she knew him. There's been a rumor going around that she's been kidnapped," Dec said. "Ross hasn't gotten any ransom note, but it doesn't seem like she's being held against her will."

Ian nodded. "She checked into the motel alone and paid cash for one night. If she'd needed help, she could have asked then. And why would she steal her father's car?"

"Doesn't sound like a kidnapping to me," Marcus said. His brothers turned to him, clearly uninterested in his opinion.

"Maybe so," Dec said. "But given the rumors, Ross is about ready to call in the FBI."

Marcus shifted uneasily. This was getting out of hand. He had to talk to Eden.

Marcus took another sip of his coffee, then set his cup down. "I really need to go. I've got a lot of things to do today and I'm good with just the coffee." He grabbed his wallet and withdrew a twenty, then tossed it on the table. "Breakfast is on me. I'll talk to you guys later."

"Where are you going?" Ian asked. "First you cut out on dinner the other night and now breakfast. For a guy who runs his own business, you seem to be on a pretty tight schedule."

"I thought you were hungry," Dec said. "If I didn't know better, I'd think you have a woman stashed back at your place."

Marcus scoffed, shaking his head. "Yeah, right. If I had a woman in my bed, I wouldn't be here having coffee with you tossers."

"Good point," Ian said.

Marcus slid out of the booth, but Dec stopped him

before he could make his getaway. "When you go back out to the Ross place, let me know if you see anything."

"Or anyone?" Marcus asked.

"Just keep an eye out. She went there once—she may stop by again."

Once Marcus stepped outside, he drew a deep breath of the damp morning air. The minute he got home he was going to have a talk with Eden. The longer she dragged this out, the more consequences there would be in the end. They both needed a plan or this affair of theirs would turn into a major disaster.

EDEN ROLLED OVER IN bed and opened her sleepy eyes, squinting to see the clock on the beside table. Pans clattered in the kitchen, and she flopped back into the soft pillows and stretched. A pleasant exhaustion settled over her, and she smiled to herself as she drew the sheet up over her naked body.

Thoughts of Marcus drifted through her mind, images of his handsome face, eyes closed, passion suffusing his features. Her fingers tingled and she reached out and grabbed his pillow, inhaling his scent.

When it came to desire, nothing seemed to stand between them. When he was inside her, she felt completely vulnerable and infinitely powerful at the same time. She'd discarded the last of her inhibitions. With Marcus, sex was an adventure to be shared.

Eden crawled out of bed and drew the sail around her body. "I thought you were going to bring me breakfast in bed," she called.

A few moments later an older woman appeared, a

dish towel clutched in her hands. "I'm sure I could make you something if you wanted," she said softly, her words tinged with an accent.

Eden drew a sharp breath, then forced a smile. "I'm sorry," she murmured. "I thought you were Marcus."

She smiled warmly and nodded. "I'm not."

"Are you the maid?" Eden asked.

"I do occasionally clean up after Marcus," she said. "That much is true. Are you sure I can't get you some breakfast, dear?"

"I—I'm just going to get dressed," Eden said.

"That would be a fine idea. I'll just get back to work."

Eden scrambled to find something to wear, but the only clothes within reach belonged to Marcus. She pulled a pair of his boxers from a pile of clean laundry on the floor, then slipped into a T-shirt. By the time she got to the kitchen, the housekeeper was heating water in the teakettle.

"Can I make you a cup?" she asked.

"Yes," Eden replied. She sat down on one of the stools and observed the woman. She wasn't dressed like a cleaning lady. She wore a pair of tailored pants and a cotton sweater set in a pretty shade of blue. An uneasy realization dawned and Eden's stomach lurched. "You're Marcus's mother, aren't you?"

She glanced up and smiled. "I am." She held out her hand. "Emma Quinn."

Hesitantly Eden accepted the gesture. "Liselotte," she said. "Liselotte Bunderstrassen."

"What a lovely name," Emma said. "Lisa…?"

"Just Lisa is fine," Eden said.

Emma reached into a canister on the counter and withdrew a handful of tea bags. "Earl Grey or chamomile?"

"Chamomile," Eden said.

"How long have you and Marcus known each other, Lisa?" Emma asked as she set two mugs next to the cooktop.

"Not long," Eden said, then swallowed hard. She certainly didn't want his mother to think this was a one-night stand. "But long enough. He's very sweet."

"He always has been. He's the baby of the family and he's a sensitive soul. Always watching out for others."

"Yes," Eden said. "That's true." She paused. "He doesn't talk much about his family. I know he has brothers."

"He has four brothers and two sisters. Do you have siblings?"

Eden shook her head. "No, I'm an only child. I never thought much about having sisters or brothers. I got so little of my parents' time as it was that I didn't want to share." She drew a deep breath. "But now I wish I had a sister or even a brother. Someone I could go to when I needed help. Someone who would always be on my side."

"Husbands are good for that, too," Emma said.

She'd made no attempt to hide the inference, and Eden couldn't stop a smile. "Marcus and I—we haven't... There's no reason to believe that— I do like him an awful lot."

Emma Quinn reached out and patted her hand. "A mother can only hope," she said. "Marcus would do well to find a wife. He needs someone to shake up his life, someone bright and outgoing, like you. He keeps to himself far too much."

Eden wasn't sure how his mother would feel if she knew the truth. Would she be so eager to marry off her son to a notorious party girl who was the star of her very own sex tape? Emma Quinn might be looking for a daughter-in-law, but Eden knew she wouldn't be on the short list.

The teakettle began to squeal, and Marcus's mother hopped off the stool and fetched it, filling both mugs with water. "Do you take sugar or milk?"

"Just plain," Eden said. She wrapped her hands around the mug. "Tell me about your family."

"I married Paddy Quinn when I was twenty-four. He'd grown up in Ireland and came over here to fish on a long-liner—a swordfishing boat. He came from a family of fishermen. I grew up here. My mother was Irish. My true father died before I was born. He was killed in the war, and my mother married an American G.I. who sent her off to Boston to live with his family."

"How did you meet your husband?"

"We were introduced by friends. A blind date, you might say. We fell in love, but my mother didn't want me to marry him. She wanted me to return to Ireland with her after my stepfather died, but I refused."

"How did you know you loved him?" Eden asked.

"I didn't at first. But every day, in little ways, he showed me that my happiness was the most important thing to him, more important than his own. He made me feel…" She smiled. "Safe. I know it doesn't sound like much, but it was to me. And later on it was all I needed."

"No," Eden murmured. "It sounds wonderful. I know exactly what you mean."

"And then we had Rory and Eddie and Mary Grace and Jane. And then Ian and Declan and finally Marcus. Would you like children?"

Her question took Eden aback. She'd never thought about having a family of her own. She hadn't exactly had a good example to follow. The quick answer would have been no, but the thoughtful answer was much more surprising. "Yes," she murmured. "I'd like to believe that someday I might have a family of my very own."

Eden sipped her tea as Emma Quinn busied herself around the kitchen. They chatted about Marcus and his talents as a boatbuilder and wood-carver. And gradually Eden began to realize that the man she believed Marcus to be—quiet, solid, tenderhearted—was the man that his family knew, as well.

For the first time in her life she'd judged a man correctly. But was she the woman that Marcus believed her to be? Or had she simply been convinced she could be something more?

Suddenly Eden felt a frantic need to protect her reputation. She'd get the tape and destroy it before Emma Quinn and the rest of Marcus's family found out who she really was. Eden sipped at her tea and tried to calm her nerves.

She'd never really cared what people thought of her. Why had that suddenly changed?

MARCUS SAT ON A LOW bench and stared out at the harbor. Sailboats bobbed at their moorings, the rigging clanking as they rocked. It seemed like months since he and Eden had been on board *Victorious,* but it had only been little more than a day. In that time, so much had changed.

On the boat they'd been swept away by their physical attraction to each other. But now she was sleeping in his bed and living in his loft. He'd grown used to having her with him, and though the sex was incredible, he found himself enjoying the small, quiet moments they spent outside of their passion for each other. It was becoming more difficult to imagine a day without seeing her—or touching her.

Was it just the sex? The notion wasn't that farfetched. He'd never enjoyed such an intense relationship with a woman, nor one that required so little commitment. Eden didn't ask anything of him beyond his willing participation in their bedroom activities.

But he couldn't help but feel as if they were biding their time. To believe that they could continue on like this was foolish. Though he'd insisted that she call her parents, he'd done nothing to remind her of her promise. For now, she belonged entirely to him, dependent on him for his protection. There was a pleasant security in that. But if he let things go on as they had been, he might never be able to let her go.

He chuckled to himself. Wouldn't that be poetic justice? He'd thrown himself into a purely physical relationship only to come out on the other side wanting more. Would he become one of those daft wankers who spent years pining after a woman they could never have? He shook his head. Hell, no. When Eden finally left, he wouldn't look back.

He stood and walked toward the boatyard, his hands shoved in his pockets, his thoughts occupied with the odd turn in his feelings. When it came to women, he'd never looked beyond the next night in bed. But with Eden, he'd let himself see a future. Though it was hazy and dim, it was there, just beyond his reach.

Marcus clenched his fists. Would he grab for it or would he let it evaporate before his eyes? He stopped at the entrance to the boatyard and stared up at the sprawling building that held a retail store, the repair shop and a sail loft. How could he ever believe that he had anything to offer Eden? Sure, the sex was fantastic, but even Marcus knew that a real relationship couldn't be built on only that.

He was a regular guy. He made his living with his hands, and it wasn't much of a living at that. He'd never questioned his financial success until now. But Eden deserved more than a crudely furnished loft above a shabby boatyard. His mind flashed an image of the Ross compound on the bay, the sprawling white clapboard house and the beautiful grounds, the garages filled with fancy cars, and servants who waited on the family hand and foot.

And what did they have in common? What would they share if the passion ever wore off? They'd led completely different lives on opposite ends of the spectrum. Even if Marcus dedicated the rest of his life to making her happy, he'd be doomed to fail.

When he turned into the parking lot for Quinn's Boat Works, Marcus noticed his father in front of the service bay door, surrounded by crates, a crowbar clutched in his hand.

"Da," Marcus called. "What do you have there?"

Paddy Quinn stood staring at the job at hand. His gray hair was mussed by the breeze and his cheeks were ruddy. Though he'd celebrated his sixtieth birthday last year, he didn't show his age. His body was trim and his arms were muscled and the deep wrinkles brought on by years on the water only added character to his face. "New outboards," he said. "We had to unload them here. The forklift is busted."

Though Marcus's Irish accent had all but disappeared, his father's brogue was still thick. Paddy had lived the first twenty-two years of his life in Ireland. Marcus's mother, who'd been born in America, had adopted her accent from her own mother, Nana Callahan, the very same grandmother who had cared for the boys in Ireland.

"It's Sunday, Da. Leave it for tomorrow."

"It's a holiday weekend. The store will be busy," Paddy said. "By the way, your mam's looking for you."

"Is she in the store?"

"Nah, she walked over to the boathouse."

"When?" Marcus asked, turning toward the loft.

Paddy frowned. "Might have been twenty minutes ago. She's takin' her sweet time about it. You'll probably find her cleanin' your kitchen." He straightened and hitched his hands on his hips. "Can't ever stop makin' up for time lost, I fear. She needs to get her motherin' in now while you boys'll still have it. Give her a break, will ya?"

"I better go see what she wants," Marcus said.

Marcus strode through the yard to the boathouse. He took the stairs two steps at a time and threw open the door to the loft. He stopped short when he saw his mother and Eden seated comfortably at the counter, both enjoying a cup of tea.

They both turned when he walked in, and Eden graced him with a delighted smile. "Hi," she said. "Your mother stopped by."

Emma Quinn pushed off the stool and stood, her hands clutched together in front of her. Even after her long battle with cancer she was a lovely woman, tiny and trim, her face unlined and her eyes bright. She wore her dark hair short and tucked behind her ears in a very proper way. Marcus had always remembered her smile, had seen it in his dreams when he was a boy, and it still warmed his heart. She smiled at him now.

"Hey, Ma."

"Well, I must be going," she said to Eden. "I'm sure you two have…things to do." She held out her hand. "It was a pleasure meeting you, my dear. I hope we'll see each other again. Perhaps you can come to the house tomorrow. We're having a picnic to celebrate the Fourth, and I'd love it if you could join us."

Eden took his mother's hand, then thought better of it and wrapped her arms around Emma Quinn, giving her a fierce hug. "I'd like that," she said.

Marcus gave them both a long look before he stepped up and took his mother's elbow. "I'll walk you out, Ma," he murmured. His gaze caught Eden's and she smiled again. What the hell was she so happy about?

He walked his mother down the stairs out to the boatyard. Emma Quinn had been silent along the way, but Marcus didn't expect it to last. When they stepped outside, she turned and faced him. "She's a lovely girl, Marcus."

"She is," he agreed.

"Though I can't help but think that I've seen her before. Is she from here in town?"

"No," Marcus said.

"Hmm. Very pretty. But an odd name, that one, don't you think?"

"She introduced herself?" Marcus asked.

"Liselotte Bunderstrassen." Emma sighed and shook her head. "It's not Irish, that's for sure."

"I think it's German, Ma."

His mother stared at him. "And that's all you have to say? It's German? You have a young lady wandering around your apartment in her knickers," she said. "Would you care to explain?"

"Not right now, Ma," Marcus said. "And I'd appreciate it if you'd keep this between the two of us."

"And who would I be telling?" she asked as if insulted by the notion.

"Oh, I don't know. My sisters. My father. Your ladies down at St. Joe's."

She pushed up on her toes and gave Marcus a peck on the cheek. "I hope you're practicing that safe sex they're always talking about. If you're having relations, use a condom. Not that I want to know if you're having relations. It's not something a mother needs to know. And considering it's against the church, I'd rather not know so I don't have to confess it." She paused. "So have you been using a condom?"

"Ma, I'm not going to discuss my sex life with you."

She patted Marcus on the shoulder. "Then you talk to your da. He knows the score on those things."

"Tell Da I'll be down in a minute to help him with those crates."

His mother gave him a quick kiss on the cheek. "He'll be fine. It's Sunday and he shouldn't be working anyway. You go upstairs and tend to your guest and I'll take care of your father. And I hope to see you both tomorrow."

"We'll see, Ma. I've got a lot of work to finish." Marcus watched as she walked back through the boatyard, weaving around the timber cradles and wooden ladders. There were times when his mother still treated him like a teenager. She'd missed so much of his life and the lives of Ian and Declan that she was sometimes unable to accept they were grown men.

At least they'd managed to get beyond past hurts. When he'd returned from Ireland, his relationship with his mother had been in tatters. The anger had lasted years, and he'd kept his distance, afraid to allow her back into his life for fear that he'd lose her again. But over time Marcus had come to understand the choices she'd made.

He couldn't imagine what she'd gone through while he and his brothers had been growing up in Ireland. His older siblings refused to speak of it, as did his father, but he'd heard from a family friend that the priest had been called for last rites five separate times.

Her illness had nearly destroyed Marcus's family, and the specter still hung over them all. But his mother had taught them all that they must live each day and stop worrying about the future. She had an amazing outlook, considering what she'd been through, and she never wasted time feeling sorry for herself.

So why couldn't he apply that theory to Eden? What would be, would be, and worrying over it wouldn't change anything.

Marcus slowly climbed the stairs to the loft. Eden was waiting for him, perched on a stool, her mug of tea clutched in her hand. "I'm sorry," she said. "She came in and was cleaning up in the kitchen. I thought she was the housekeeper."

He frowned. "You thought I had a housekeeper?"

"Well, I didn't know," Eden replied. "Your place is pretty clean for a guy."

Marcus crossed to the refrigerator and pulled out a carton of orange juice, then poured himself a glass. "So what did you talk about?"

"Nothing, really. You, mostly. Did she say anything about me?"

"You mean about Liselotte Bunderstrassen?"

"She asked my name. It's the first thing that came to mind. You didn't think I was going to admit to being Eden Ross, did you? I wanted your mother to like me."

Marcus sat down beside Eden. "She thought you were pretty. And she reminded me that we need to practice safe sex."

"You told her we were having sex?" Eden cried.

"You're in my bed at ten o'clock on a Sunday morning." He looked down and frowned. "And wearing my underwear. My mother's not an idiot."

"I'd never tell my father we were having sex."

"He knows you're not a virgin."

Eden took a sip of her tea. "But he doesn't know the details. He's a very powerful man. If he wanted to make you disappear, he could. Like Benny, my summer boyfriend when I was sixteen. He caught us swimming naked off the pier one night."

"And he had Benny killed?"

"No," Eden replied. "He's not a mobster, he's just a businessman. He called in a favor and had Benny's father transferred to Alaska. They moved two weeks later and I never saw him again."

"Well, your father isn't going to find out about us because you're going to call him today and you're going tell him you're all right."

She stared at him, her lips slightly parted. "No. I'm not ready to talk to him."

"Then I will," Marcus said. "I'll call him and tell him you showed up on the boat, that you're sorry for everything that's going on and that you'll be coming to see him soon."

"Don't try to run my life," Eden snapped.

"Someone has to. You're not doing it for yourself. Eden, he's your father and he has a right to know you're okay. At least give him that much." A stubborn pout settled onto her pretty face, and Marcus knew he had pushed her about as far as he could. "The sooner you face your problems, the sooner they'll go away," he added.

"And what am I supposed say?" she asked. "'Hi, Daddy, I just wanted to let you know that you'll probably be getting a call from my former lover, who will probably try to extort a few million dollars from you. So you wanna have lunch?'" She shook her head. "See, it's not so easy."

Marcus reached out and smoothed the hair out of her eyes. He could understand her problem. It had taken him nearly a year to confess to Nana Callahan that he'd broken her favorite crystal vase. A sex tape and extortion were a bit dodgier than that. "Maybe you should write him a letter. Or send him an e-mail."

"I will," she said. "Sooner or later I have to. Don't worry, Marcus, I don't expect you to take care of me forever."

That was it, Marcus mused. The perfect admission of where they stood. She was biding her time with him until she worked up the courage to face her real life. And when she did, they'd be finished and she'd leave.

"Can we go back to bed now?" she asked.

"Are you still tired?"

"Not at all," Eden said. She grabbed his hand and dragged him along behind her. "In fact, I'm wide-awake."

Marcus resisted but only for a moment. Eden might be able to divert his attention for an hour or two, but all the desire in the world wasn't going to dissolve the cloud that hung over them.

He crawled into bed beside her and pulled her up

against his body, kissing her forehead. She seemed to fit perfectly against him, her legs tangled in his, her arms wrapped around his neck. Marcus slowly smoothed his hand over her back, then slipped his palm beneath the T-shirt she wore.

As he caressed her soft skin, he closed his eyes and tried to memorize the feel of her. There would come a night when she no longer slept in his bed, a night when he'd want to remember every perfect detail about her. A dull ache settled inside him. Though Marcus didn't want to admit it, he'd miss her. Even though Eden could be a pain in the ass, she'd become his pain in the ass, at least for a while.

"Your mother invited me for a picnic tomorrow," she murmured.

"I made our excuses," he said.

Eden pushed up on her elbow and met his gaze. "But I want to go."

"You can't," Marcus replied.

"Why not? She invited me. I don't want to be rude to your mother." She paused. "Why don't you want me to go?"

"Isn't it obvious?"

"No, it's not. Are you embarrassed to be with me?"

Marcus groaned and threw his arm over his eyes. He'd already decided that he could handle her leaving, but he didn't want to dissect his feelings before she did. "You're the one who's trying to hide out here. If you go to a family dinner, then your presence is not going to be a secret anymore. My brother Declan will be there, and he's spent the last week looking for you."

"Looking for me?"

Marcus pulled his arm away. "He works for your father. That's how I got the job on the boat, Eden."

"What does he do for my father?" Eden asked.

"Security, private investigations, background checks. Anything your father asks. And right now, among other things, he's looking for you. So is my brother Ian. He's the chief of police in this town. And I'm supposed to be looking for you, too, for that matter."

"Your brothers are looking for me and you're hiding me?"

Marcus nodded. "So can you see why a family picnic might be a wee bit awkward? Hell, Ian would probably arrest you on the spot for that little 911 call."

"And that's all? That's the only reason you don't want me to go?"

"Isn't that enough?"

"I thought maybe you were ashamed to be seen with me." She drew a deep breath. "Let's not pretend that I'm every mother's dream. I have a reputation. My life is splashed all over the media. I guess I'd be a little hesitant to introduce me to your family."

"That's not it," Marcus said.

"But there is something else, isn't there? If I went to this picnic, then this would be all over, wouldn't it? You and I would be over."

She was right. As long as she was hiding from her troubles, she was his. The moment she faced her problems, she'd be gone, out of his life without a second glance. It may be selfish, but Marcus wasn't going to feel guilty. Why shouldn't they take as much pleasure as they could from each other? A sexual connection like theirs didn't come along every day.

"Everything is perfect right now," Marcus said. "It's just you and me. Uncomplicated."

She stared at him, her eyes shadowed with indecision. "So you just want to stay like this forever?"

"I don't think that's possible, Eden," Marcus said.

Eden smiled ruefully. "You're right. I know you are. But it could be for a little longer, couldn't it?" She picked up her pillow and smoothed her hands over it. "I'm just not ready."

He watched Eden crawl out of bed and disappear behind the canvas curtains. She wasn't ready for what? To go out into the world again or to leave him? He could see it happening in his head. If they both believed it would end, then it would. Gradually they'd pull away from each other. Promises made would be broken. Instead of spending time together, they'd make excuses to be apart, creating a distance that would protect them both when their affair finally came to end.

Marcus fought the temptation to go to her and draw them closer again, to reassure himself that she still cared. He could do it easily, with sweet words or a passionate kiss. But in his gut he knew this was for the best. He'd had her for a week, a lot longer than he'd ever expected for her to stay. He would have to let her go soon and it was about time for both of them to face that truth.

7

EDEN STOOD IN THE DOORWAY of the coin laundry and gazed at her surroundings through dark sunglasses. "This is nice," she said. "But why are we here?"

"I have to do laundry," Marcus replied, flicking the brim of her baseball cap. "In the real world, so will you. Clothes get dirty and you have to wash them."

"I don't have to wash them," she said. "I send them to the cleaners and they wash them."

"This isn't the Ritz. Most people wash their own clothes."

"I know that," Eden said. There were times with Marcus when she felt like a complete idiot. Yesterday she'd tried to operate his dishwasher and managed to flood his kitchen with suds. Then she'd tried to make toast and set off the smoke alarm. And last night she'd cleaned up cookie crumbs with furniture polish only to have Marcus slip and fall on the hardwood floor.

The past twenty-four hours had been a lesson in how little she knew about day-to-day life. Though she thought she could at least cook something simple, macaroni and cheese from a box had been a disaster. After her fiasco with the furniture polish, Eden had been forced to scratch cleaning off the list of things she could do well. And though grocery shopping seemed like an easy task, the store layout confounded her. If she was a failure at the coin laundry, then she might as well give up her dream of starting a life of her own.

"I know how to do the wash," she said. "I used to watch Sarah do it. She used to let me push the buttons and turn the dials."

"Good," Marcus said. "Then this should go quickly."

He dragged the duffel bag inside the door and dumped the contents into a wire basket on wheels. Eden smiled as she watched him pick through the laundry. Their clothes were all jumbled together, and anyone walking by might think they were a couple, perhaps even husband and wife.

A tiny thrill raced through her at the thought. What would it be like to make a life with Marcus? She'd been so careful not to allow herself such thoughts, but the longer she spent with him, the more she enjoyed the silly fantasy playing out in her head.

They shared an incredible physical attraction, so their life in bed would never be dull. But was there something beyond that between them? And if there was, how would they go about discovering it?

Eden boosted herself up on a nearby washing machine, kicking off her flip-flops and tucking her bare feet beneath her. "I know why you wanted to do the laundry," she said. "So you could play with my underwear and I wouldn't think you were pervy."

He picked up one of her bras and fingered the lace and satin. "I'd rather play with what's underneath your underwear," Marcus said in a matter-of-fact voice.

Eden giggled, removing her sunglasses and glancing around the empty Laundromat. She grabbed the front of Marcus's T-shirt and pulled him toward her. "We're all alone here," she said, straightening her legs on either side of his hips. She wrapped one leg around his thigh and drew him closer.

He gave her a skeptical look. "Eden, behave yourself."

Unfazed, Eden took his hand and slid it beneath her skirt, pressing his palm to her inner thigh. "Haven't you ever done it in a public place?"

"Have you?"

She grinned and slid his hand higher. "Believe it or not, I haven't. Contrary to the stories the press puts out, my sex life has not been terribly adventurous. What about you? Where's the most exciting place you've ever done it?"

He gave her a wary glance. "I think my shower ranks right up there."

"You haven't been a very adventurous boy either," she teased, her hand sliding down to his crotch.

"You asked for the most exciting place, not the most public," he said, leaning into her until her palm pressed fully against him. "Are you doing this just to get out of helping me with the laundry?"

Eden leaned forward and took his lower lip between her teeth, tugging at it. "I'm really excited about doing the laundry. Can't you tell?" She moved his hand up a bit higher, enjoying the game and wondering what Marcus's limits were. How far would he go to possess her? Would his desire be so overwhelming that he'd risk making love to her right here? Or did he have secret boundaries? His hand slid up until it rested at the juncture of her thighs.

Marcus gasped, his gaze meeting hers. "You're not wearing underwear," he said.

"All my panties are in the wash. What about you?" She slipped her hand down the front of his jeans. "Oh, I guess yours must be in the wash, too."

He nodded, holding his breath as her fingers danced along the length of his penis. Almost instantly he began to grow hard, and Eden left her hand where it was, enjoying his discomfort.

"Don't mess with me," Marcus warned, sliding his thumb between the soft folds of her sex. He found her clitoris and rubbed it gently.

"Then don't mess with me," she countered.

She waited for him to stop, but he'd obviously decided to accept her challenge. Eden smiled as he continued to caress her, surprised at how easy it was to become aroused even in a public place.

Her fingers closed around him and she leaned forward, whispering into his ear. "I know you want me," she murmured. "I can feel it."

"I do," he replied. "But not as much as you want me."

She playfully bit his earlobe. "We'll see about that. I think you want me badly enough to imagine me naked. Imagine me lying on your bed, ready for you. Think of it," she whispered. "You could touch me wherever you wanted. You like to touch me, Marcus, don't you?"

He groaned as she began to stroke him. A desperate "yes" was all Marcus could manage. He slipped his finger inside her again, then withdrew it in a rhythm that was all too familiar to Eden. Maybe he'd been right. Maybe she did want him more.

The door rattled, and they both turned and watched as an elderly woman walked inside, a wicker basket tucked beneath one arm. Eden waited for him to stop, but he didn't. Instead his caress became more intense. Her breath caught in her throat as she realized he intended to win the game at all costs. To a casual observer, it wasn't clear what they were doing. Marcus's hand was hidden beneath her skirt and Eden's was protected by the shadow of his opposite arm.

She caught his gaze and smiled. "You want to be inside me, don't you? Do you remember how that feels?"

He nodded. "Do you?"

"Hard and thick," she said.

"Tight," he countered. "And warm."

Eden felt herself grow faint. For a moment, the power shifted as a wave of pleasure raced through her. A moan slipped from her lips and she fought the temptation to surrender.

"Go ahead," Marcus urged. "There's no reason to stop yourself."

Eden bit her bottom lip hard, the pain making her focus. "You go first."

"You can't make me," he said.

"I can." Eden leaned forward. "Just imagine my

mouth on you. Soft…and warm…my tongue teasing until you can't think of anything else but how good it would feel to come. If we were alone, I'd do that for you. You'd lie back and close your eyes and I'd—"

Marcus's free hand found her nape, and he pulled her into a kiss, his moan lost between them. An instant later he came in her hand, her caress suddenly damp and sticky with his orgasm. She enjoyed a short moment of triumph, a satisfied smile on her lips.

The first spasm caught her by surprise, and after that she had no choice but to capitulate. He watched as she came, knowing that he hadn't lost by much.

"You're a bad girl, Eden Ross."

"I can't seem to help myself," she said as she withdrew her hand from his jeans.

He arched his eyebrow, his hand sliding along her thigh. "And I was planning to take you to the hardware store after we were finished here."

"Hardware?" Eden sighed. "That sounds very intriguing, Marcus. There are tools and all kinds of hard things at the hardware store, aren't there? When can we leave?"

Marcus glanced around. "I think we'd better finish the laundry." He winced as he reached out and began to toss clothes into the machine next to her, a damp spot seeping through the front of his jeans.

"You could take those off," Eden suggested, "and toss them in the wash."

"Don't you think we've gone far enough for your first visit to the Laundromat?"

"You're right. I'm completely satisfied with the experience," she said. "How about you?"

He chuckled softly. "The evidence of that is all over your fingers." He grabbed a towel from the pile and took her hand to wipe it dry. When he was finished, he held up the towel. "Warm water. Towels and sheets go in warm water. Unless they're white—then they go in hot."

"Interesting," Eden said. "Why?"

Marcus opened his mouth, then paused. "I'm not sure. Because it says so on the detergent bottle." He picked up her bra. "I think this is what they refer to as a delicate. I don't have any delicates of my own, but they go in cold."

"Good to know," Eden said. She watched him fill three washers with clothes, add detergent, then select the proper temperature for each. As far as Eden could tell, she could have learned how to do laundry by reading the detergent bottle. There wasn't much to it. But the sex was great.

"Now you just put the quarters into the slots and the machines will start." He shoved his hand in his jeans pocket and winced again.

"Need some help?" Eden teased.

"I think you've done enough in there already," he said.

Eden giggled, then picked up the copy of *In Style* that she'd brought along to read. Casually she flipped through it, glancing at the photos and finding nothing of interest. But one photo made her pause, and she stared at it for a long time, her breath frozen in her throat.

"What's wrong?" Marcus asked.

"Nothing," she said.

Marcus slowly pulled the magazine from her hand and looked at the picture. "It's you," he said, "with some guy."

Eden nodded. "His name is Andreas. He's—"

"He's got his hand on your ass," Marcus said.

"He's my boyfriend," she finished.

Marcus glanced back down at the photo, scowling. "You have a boyfriend?"

"I did," Eden said. "Up until the time I took off. I didn't want to face him once everything hit the press. His family is very...well, they're old European money. His father is a baron and his mother is a Greek princess. They weren't fond of me, but Andreas loved me."

"Maybe he still does," Marcus said.

"I can't see how." Eden took the magazine from his hands and studied the photo. "That was such a great party," she said. "That was Cannes. The film festival. We drank so much champagne, and then a bunch of us went down to the beach and ripped off all our clothes and jumped into the sea."

"Sounds like fun," Marcus said, his voice flat.

"I'm having more fun doing the laundry," she offered. But her words didn't seem to pacify him. "I don't miss him." She drew a deep breath. "I don't. He was my boyfriend, but it wasn't like it is with you."

"You weren't sleeping with him?" Marcus asked.

"No, I was. But we didn't...we weren't—" She cursed softly. "It just wasn't the same as it is with you."

He nodded, distractedly rummaging through the pile

of laundry. Frowning, he straightened. "I forgot fabric softener," he said. "I'm just going to run and get some."

Without another word, he turned and strode to the door. Eden watched through the plate-glass window of the Laundromat as he disappeared down the sidewalk. He'd never seemed squeamish about her past before. Why was he so touchy now?

Eden put her sunglasses back on and picked up the magazine, turning to the photo. She tried to recall the details of that night. It had been fun, but nothing about it had been memorable. In contrast, she remembered all the little details of her time with Marcus: what he'd worn that night on the beach, the sound of his voice when he'd first said her name, the color of his eyes when he'd looked out at the water. Every sensation of every caress was burned into her brain so deeply that it had become a part of her.

No, she wasn't falling in love with him. From the very start she'd decided that their relationship would be just about sex and nothing more. And until now it had been. She glanced down at the photo again, then closed her eyes, imagining Marcus standing beside her, smiling for the cameras.

Eden's eyes snapped open and she shook her head. Of all the fantasies that she'd imagined with Marcus, that one was the least likely to come true.

THE NOONDAY SUN WAS high overhead, beating down on Marcus's back. He wiped the sweat from his brow with his forearm, then grabbed the crowbar from his father's hand.

"Your ma says you've found yourself a new lady," Paddy said, watching him over the top of the crate.

Marcus worked the nails that held the crate closed. They'd returned from the Laundromat a few hours before. He'd left Eden upstairs with the employment section of the Providence newspaper, determined to help his father. "What else does she say?"

"That she has a name that ties the tongue in knots and that she's quite fetching." Paddy raised his eyebrow.

Marcus chuckled. "Fetching?"

"Pretty," Paddy amended.

"She is," Marcus agreed. He levered the crowbar against the corner of the crate and popped the top off. "Is that all you have to say?"

"Do you want to hear more?" Paddy asked.

He turned and faced his father, bracing his hands on the edge of the crate. "Not really."

Paddy shrugged. "There it is. Enough said."

They continued to work in silence for a few more minutes, Marcus's mind swirling with a question he'd been anxious to ask. He took a deep breath. "How did you know with Ma? What was it that made you realize you were in love?"

Paddy seemed as surprised by the question as Marcus was that he'd asked it. It was no wonder. Marcus and his father had rarely talked of personal matters. The three youngest Quinn boys had run their lives on their own for so long that Paddy had been left on the sidelines. And Marcus had always taken his questions and concerns to Ian and Dec. But they were in no position to offer advice on this subject. And he was in no position to ask them.

"I—I knew the minute I met her," Paddy said.

"Come on." Marcus shook his head. "How is that possible?"

"She walked in the room and I gave my mate a nudge and said, 'There's the girl I'm to marry.' And that's what came to pass."

"But how did you know? You must have had some doubts. Weren't you afraid you were just caught up in the moment?"

"No," Paddy replied. "I felt it in my gut." He patted his stomach. "Whenever she wasn't around, I had this ache, like I'd eaten too many turnips."

"Did you tell her?" Marcus asked.

"I may have been in love, boyo, but I wasn't a bleedin' eedjit. Of course I didn't tell her. Not straight off, anyway. I would have sent her runnin' for the hills. She had no interest in me. At least that's what I thought. I come to learn later that wasn't the case. She shouldn't have loved me, but she did."

"Why shouldn't she have loved you?" Marcus asked.

"Her ma, your Nana Callahan, didn't approve. She'd just learned that your mother had inherited that big house in Ireland and a fair bit of money, as well. She was determined to take your mother back there and marry her off to some rich Irishman, not a scrappy fisherman."

"How did you get her to stay?"

"One night I screwed up my courage and I told her how I felt. I knew she might laugh at me, but I had one chance to convince her, so I tried. And she didn't laugh." He grinned. "She cried. Buckets of tears. Scared the shite out of me. She turned over that house and all the money to your grandmother and stayed with me. Even though it caused a terrible row between them, she chose me. Later on, when we could have used that money to pay for her hospital bills, she was too proud to ask. She'd made her choice and she wasn't about to admit that she might have made a mistake."

"But she didn't make a mistake," Marcus said.

Paddy shook his head. "I don't believe so. And neither does your ma."

"You've never me told that story before."

"You've never asked." He took the crowbar from Marcus's hands and began to pry open another crate. "What's the use of offerin' advice if you're not ready to hear it? Maybe you're ready now?"

"I guess I am," Marcus admitted.

"Then what the hell are you doing opening crates with yer da? Why don't you go tell this girl how you feel? Seize the moment, boyo. It won't get any easier as time passes."

"But I don't know how I feel about her," Marcus said.

"Sure you do." His father patted him on the shoulder. "You're just afraid to admit it. Don't try to fool yourself. You might lose the best thing to come along."

Marcus yanked off his gloves and shoved them into the back pocket of his jeans. "You'll be all right with the rest of these?" he asked.

Paddy nodded. "I can manage."

As he walked toward the boathouse, Marcus thought about what he might say. But no matter how he tried to parse it, the words just wouldn't come. Maybe he didn't love her. Maybe this was all about desire and lust and physical release. There were no words for that and he was just imagining himself in love.

How the hell was he supposed to know, short of— Marcus stopped in his tracks, groaning softly. The only way to gauge his true feelings for Eden would have been to avoid sex.

Wasn't that just crap? he mused. Had he simply abided by the deal he'd made with his brothers, maybe he'd have been able to figure out how he truly felt. But now he was forced to look at everything through a haze of desire.

Marcus strode toward the boathouse, and when he reached the stairs he took them two at a time. He walked inside the loft and found Eden staring at a box of brownie mix, intently reading the directions.

"I'm making brownies," she murmured, ignoring his entrance.

Baking, Marcus mused. Another step on her journey through real life. No matter how badly she failed, Eden seemed to meet each new challenge with optimism. "That shouldn't be too difficult."

"It shouldn't be." She looked up at him and smiled. Once again Marcus was struck by how pretty she was. Her face was scrubbed clean and her mussed hair fell in careless waves. Even from across the room Marcus knew how she'd smell, all fresh and fruity.

He walked over to her and slipped his arms around her waist, resting his chin on her shoulder. He'd become so accustomed to her presence in his apartment that he was almost taking it for granted. But Marcus knew better. He reminded himself that she could be gone in the blink of an eye. He'd do well to enjoy himself while she was here.

"I did it," she murmured as though making a confession.

Marcus kissed her neck, wondering what household disaster she might have perpetrated this time. "Will it cost a lot to fix?" he asked.

Eden turned around in his arms. "I wrote to my father. Just like you asked." She reached across the counter and snatched up a sheet of paper and waved it in front of him. "I e-mailed it to his office. Now maybe you'll quit bugging me?"

Marcus felt his breath freeze in his throat. He'd been pushing her toward this, but he'd never fully considered the consequences if she fulfilled his request. Eden was getting past her mistakes and making amends. Soon she wouldn't need his protection. She'd go back to the world she knew and forget all about him. "Good," he said. "I'm sure you're going to ease his worries."

"I said I was sorry for the embarrassment I've caused him, but I've put my problems in the past and I'm getting on with my life." She smiled wistfully. "And I actually meant it."

"I would hope so," Marcus said.

"No, it's true. Usually when I speak to my father I'm always promising him whatever he wants to hear, just so he won't get upset. But this time I really do believe I'm going to change. And I called my mother," she added almost as an afterthought.

"How did that go?"

"She wants me to come home. She's getting a divorce from her fourth husband and she needs someone to be there to tell her how young and beautiful she looks."

"Are you going to go?"

Eden nodded. "I really should. Now that I've settled things with my father, I should try to make things better with her. After seeing you with your mother, I realized that my relationships with my parents are really messed up. And part of that is my fault."

Marcus nodded, knowing that it would be foolish to disagree. He couldn't keep her here forever, like some pretty bird in a cage. They both had to face reality. "When are you leaving?"

She shrugged. "Friday afternoon." Eden wrapped her arms around his neck. "Are you going to be sad to see me go?"

Marcus shook his head. "Not at all. I've got six or seven women who've been dying to crawl into my bed. I'll just ring one of them up and they'll be over in a flash."

She opened her mouth in mock surprise, then slapped his chest. "And not one of them could make you feel the way I make you feel."

"I'm not sure of that," Marcus said, spanning her waist with his hands. Before she could protest, he captured her mouth, kissing her deeply. She sank into him, her hips pressed against his. His passion surged and suddenly he needed to have her, right then and there.

The clock was ticking, and every minute that passed was one less that they'd spend together. He didn't want to bother with seduction or foreplay. His brain screamed with the need to bury himself deep inside of her and forget all the confusion she'd caused him.

Reaching down, Marcus grabbed the hem of her T-shirt and yanked it over her head, breaking the kiss for just a heartbeat before resuming his assault on her mouth. His hand smoothed over her body as he tried to memorize every detail, the sweet hollow at the base of her spine, the gentle curve of her neck and the soft swell of her breasts.

Frantic to possess her, Marcus ripped off his own shirt and tossed it aside, then unbuttoned his jeans. With a wicked laugh, Eden reached down to touch him, but he grabbed her hand and pulled it away.

"Don't," he warned.

She seemed stunned by the ferocity in his voice but then nodded her assent. He skimmed the skirt over her hips, and a moment later she was completely naked. No matter how much he touched her, he couldn't seem to get close enough. There was only one way.

Grabbing her waist, he wrapped her legs around his hips and carried her over to the old oak table. Marcus set her down on the edge, then gently pushed her back. His hands slid beneath her thighs, drawing them up, and he stood between her legs and stared down at her body.

There would be a last time for this, for them. The thought banged inside his brain like an alarm bell. How was he supposed to live without this? He unzipped his jeans and tugged his boxers down. His erection brushed against her belly.

He didn't want to bother with a condom and he didn't

care about the consequences. Every other barrier had fallen between them and he wanted to rid himself of this one, as well. Marcus needed to feel every inch of her surrounding him, but he knew it wasn't his choice. With a soft groan, he bent over to kiss her. "I have to go get—"

"No," she murmured. Eden reached down and guided him to her damp entrance. "It's all right. I want it this way."

He held his breath, then pressed against her. She was hot and tight, and the sensation of entering her was nearly enough to push him over the edge. Eden arched back on the table, moaning softly as he began to move. Marcus let his gaze drop and he watched himself disappear inside her again and again. The sight added to the pleasure, like an erotic movie winding out before him. He rubbed his thumb against her clitoris, and Eden cried out, her hands gripping the edge of the oak table, her eyes closed.

He knew he wouldn't last long, but it didn't matter. He wanted to be buried inside her and let his orgasm consume him. The tension began to build, a wonderful discomfort that promised an explosive release. He gave himself over to the feelings, and when Eden tightened around him, Marcus knew it was time.

Her spasms closed in on him and he drove into her once more, burying himself to the hilt. And then it was there, washing over him like a warm rain, soothing nerves that were on fire. It seemed to last forever, surge after surge of pleasure.

His knees went weak and he braced his hands on

the table, leaning against it as he caught his breath. It had happened so quickly, yet the satisfaction was just as intense.

Eden stretched her arms above her head and groaned lazily, a contented smile on her face. When she opened her eyes, they were still glazed, as if she hadn't quite returned to reality. Marcus didn't move, anxious to stay connected as long as he could.

She smiled at him and pushed up on her elbows. "What was that about?" she murmured.

He shrugged. "I don't know." In truth, he wasn't sure how to explain himself—he had merely followed his instincts. "You're so beautiful. Sometimes I just have to have you."

Eden reached out, and he wove his fingers through hers, drawing her up into his embrace. "How am I ever going to do without this?" she asked, her lips pressed against his chest.

"Don't leave." The instant he said the words Marcus wanted to take them back. But they were easier to say than the other words rattling around in his head. *I love you.* That's what he'd wanted to say because that's what he felt. For the first time in his life he was sure, and yet he couldn't bring himself to tell her.

"I thought you wanted me to go. You kept—"

"I know what I said, Eden."

"And now you don't want me to—"

"No," he said. "You're right. You need to go. This is starting to get a little too comfortable for me."

"And that's not a good thing?"

He shook his head. "No, that's definitely not a good thing."

She nuzzled his chest, her breath warm against his skin. "This was supposed to be fun. If we get all serious, it will just be ruined."

Marcus ran his fingers through her hair, brushing it back from her face. Though he'd like to believe in love at first sight, he knew that the chances of making that kind of relationship last—hell, any kind of relationship—were fifty-fifty at best. And though it would be difficult to say goodbye to Eden, it would be far more difficult to let himself love her only to lose her later.

This was for the best, her leaving. He'd just have to keep telling himself that until he believed it.

EDEN DIPPED THE BRUSH into the bottle of pink nail polish and carefully painted her big toe. She glanced up at Marcus, who was comfortably stretched out on the other end of the sofa, a sketch pad resting in his lap.

He had one more design to complete for her father's commission and had been worrying over it all day long. But she sensed his preoccupation was more about her leaving tomorrow than about his work.

They'd made an agreement when they'd first met that they would enjoy each other and then move on—and they certainly had enjoyed each other. Eden had never been one to stay too long at the party. Things were always so ugly when they turned the lights on.

She sighed softly and went back to her pedicure. Over the past few days, they'd settled into an odd type of domestic bliss. Eden imagined that newly married couples spent their evenings in much the same sort of mundane pursuits—watching a game show on television, cooking spaghetti, making love on the kitchen floor.

But the more she'd come to enjoy playing house with Marcus, the more restless she'd become. It was simple to ignore what was going on in the outside world when she was wrapped up in his life. Though they spent fabulous nights, and sometimes entire afternoons, in bed, outside of their sexual attraction, she felt…confused.

Marcus had a life—he did his work, he ran errands, he talked to his family. But Eden was trapped in a strange limbo between two worlds—a past that she was determined to leave behind and a future she couldn't quite see.

She dipped the brush into the nail polish and started on her other foot. There were things to do, places to go to find work, but she'd hesitated to make a decision. Was Marcus the cause of her procrastination? Was she hoping that he'd suddenly profess his love for her and all her problems would be magically solved?

Life with Marcus was exciting and interesting. They talked about important matters and joked about silly things. He respected her opinion and listened to her advice when it came to his work. And Eden admired everything that he'd made of his life so far.

But Eden had no illusions that it would be that way in the real world. If they stayed together, then he'd take on her past, as well—the celebrity, the press, the constant speculation and innuendo that seemed to follow her everywhere she went. Even if she moved to a mountaintop tomorrow, they'd chase after her for at least another year or two, trying to eke out one more salacious story.

She couldn't ask him to be a part of all that. Even the most devoted lover would tire of the constant intrusions, as her past lovers had. Eden didn't want to see what they'd shared turn nasty and awful. For the first time in her life she'd walk away while the memories were still worth remembering.

She studied Marcus as she fanned her toes to dry the first coat. Emotion surged up inside of her and she fought it back, gathering her resolve. Her thoughts wandered back to the encounter that they'd had earlier that week.

He'd been almost frantic to possess her, and she'd felt the same. They'd dropped the pretense that they were casual lovers and now made love without protection. Eden had always covered her own birth control, yet still insisted that her lovers use condoms. But it was different with Marcus. Deep down she knew she could trust Marcus. And he obviously knew that he could trust her. She'd wanted to share that one last thing before she left.

They could do this and they could do it right. Leaving didn't have to be full of anger and recriminations. Goodbyes could be bittersweet. Maybe once life became simple for her again she could come back. And maybe if Marcus hadn't found someone else, he might fall in love with her.

Marcus tossed the sketchbook aside and crawled across the sofa to sit next to her. Gently he took the bottle of polish from her fingers and started on her second coat.

"First you color my hair and now you do my toes," Eden said. "You're a handy guy to have around."

He looked up and smiled. "I studied art in college. This can't be any harder than Oil Painting 101."

"Beauty college for you, clown college for me. I think we have a very promising future ahead of us, don't you?" Her breath caught the moment she said the words, and Eden sent him a teasing smile, hoping that he'd take her comment as a joke.

"I think we'll be very happy together," he murmured. "I could dye your purple wigs and you could entertain my customers at the beauty shop." Marcus twisted the cap back onto the bottle and handed it to her.

"I could do your toes," she offered.

"No, thanks. Pink really isn't my color." He leaned back into the sofa and stretched his arm out, casually toying with her hair. "What time is your plane tomorrow?"

Eden closed her eyes. "Two," she said. "I have a stop in Washington, D.C., but I'll land in L.A. at about eight-thirty. My mother is sending a car to pick me up at the airport."

"Did you get a reply from your father?"

She shook her head. "I wasn't really expecting one." Eden drew a deep breath. "Once I get back, I'm going to have to deal with the video, and it's probably not going to be pleasant. My mother's already called her lawyer, and I have just enough left in my trust fund to pay for him. If he can't get the tape back, then I'm going to have to suffer the consequences." She reached out and grabbed his hand, then squeezed it tight. "There's going to be a lot written about me, but I want you to know that what's on that tape was nothing close to what we had."

"I know," Marcus murmured.

Eden groaned. "I don't want to talk about this. Not now." She got up from the sofa and walked over to the kitchen, then walked back to Marcus. "Let's go out. There must be a club around here somewhere. We'll get dressed up and drink champagne and go dancing. It'll be fun. A celebration of our last night together."

Marcus shook his head. "You know what will happen, don't you?"

"So what? Let's risk it. I need some excitement. Don't you ever get bored sitting around here?"

"Not with you around," Marcus said.

Eden smiled. "Is that a yes?"

He sighed. "All right. But if things get crazy, we're going to leave."

"You do dance, don't you?"

"Badly," he said. "Although I can do the chicken dance. My niece taught me. And the Hokey Pokey. Does that count as a dance or is that technically a game?"

Giggling, Eden grabbed his hands and pulled him to his feet. "I'll give you a quick lesson. We need music." She ran over to the cabinet that held his stereo equipment and flipped on the radio, scanning through the stations until she found suitable music. Then, with a sexy smile, she wiggled her way back to him, swaying her hips provocatively and turning in circles to the music.

Marcus watched her, desire flickering in his eyes. She held up her arms as she approached, then pressed her hips against his and moved with the music. He tried to mimic her movements but he was off beat.

Eden grabbed his hips. "Just listen to the music. It's like sex."

"I can see that," Marcus murmured, staring down at his groin. "And what if I have the same reaction on the dance floor as I'm having now?"

"Oh, that happens all the time," Eden said.

He stopped. "Really?"

She nodded and pulled him back into the dance. "That's why you're only allowed to dance with me." She turned around and moved her backside against his crotch, knowing full well the effect it was having on him. She placed his hands on her hips and bent over, rocking back against him with the beat of the music. Slowly he began to get the hang of it and Eden smiled. "You're doing well," she said. "See, it's not so hard. I mean, the dancing. The other is impressively hard."

"I've always been good at sex. And you can't convince me that this is anything more than foreplay to music." He grabbed her waist and spun her around, then pulled her into his arms and began to slow dance with her.

But Eden wasn't about to be deterred. She hitched her right leg up along his hip and tucked his hand beneath her thigh, then began to move against him again.

"If you don't stop that, we're never going to get out of here." Marcus bent her back at the waist and pressed his mouth to her neck.

Eden turned around and rubbed her backside against his crotch again. "I knew you'd like it," she said.

But Marcus liked it a bit too much. With a playful growl, he grabbed her around the waist, picked her up off her feet and carried her toward the bed. They both tumbled onto the mattress, and he stretched out on top of her, pinning her arms above her head. His mouth came down on hers, and Eden lost herself in his kiss, the familiar taste of him like an addictive drug.

"Don't you think it's strange?" he murmured, nipping at her lower lip.

"What?"

"I teach you how to do your laundry and you teach me how to dance and each time we manage to make it about sex." He nuzzled her neck. "Sometimes I wonder if I'll ever get enough of you."

Eden swallowed hard. This would have to be enough. She was leaving tomorrow. They had one night left together. If they stayed in this apartment, she knew she'd begin to question her decision. "Good. I want to leave you wanting more. I'm going to haunt your dreams at night and inhabit your fantasies during the day. I plan to make your life miserable once I'm gone."

Marcus stared down at her, the smile fading from his face. "You will. I know you will."

Eden wriggled out from beneath him, uneasy with his shift in mood. "Good. Now get dressed. We're going out and we are going to dance."

Marcus rolled over on the bed and covered his face with his hands. "All right," he said. "But I'm going to have to take a cold shower before we go. And if you do that to me again at the club, I'm going to be forced to drag you into a dark corner and deal with the situation in the proper way."

"I'm counting on that," Eden teased.

8

THE DANCE FLOOR WAS crowded, lights flashing in time with the music and the noise deafening. Marcus held Eden around her waist as they moved. He felt people's eyes on them, but he took his cue from Eden and pretended he didn't care.

It was an odd feeling, being the center of attention. Thankfully no one had come up to bother them or ask for Eden's autograph. The club catered to the wealthy summer crowd in Newport, and the manager had been more than happy to usher Marcus and Eden inside ahead of the rest of the line and provide them with a table in a quiet corner.

A waitress had appeared just moments after they'd sat down with a bottle of Cristal and two champagne flutes. Marcus had reached for his wallet, but the waitress had assured him that the bottle was on the house.

Once he got used to the fact that he was drinking two-hundred-dollar champagne as if it was water, Marcus began to enjoy himself. There was an infectious energy in the club that wasn't present in the establishments he usually visited. Pool and darts were the main activities at his local pub, and that usually involved drunk men and not scores of beautiful gyrating females.

The music began to wind down, and Marcus bent his head and gave Eden a slow kiss. She smiled up at him, slightly tipsy from the champagne they'd drunk. "Isn't this fun?"

"It is," Marcus admitted. "Are you getting tired?"

She nodded. "Take me home. I want to tear off your clothes and make crazy love to you for the rest of the night."

He glanced around. "Let's go then." Marcus laced his fingers through hers and led the way to the door, Eden walking behind him as he pushed through the crowd. When they reached the bar, he flagged down their waitress and gave her a generous tip, then continued toward the exit.

Outside, the air was cool, a breeze coming off the ocean. Marcus wove through the small group still waiting to get inside, and Eden held on to his arm, leaning into him. Everyone stared, but Marcus pasted a smile on his face and nodded at people as he passed.

"Hey, Eden Ross! It's Eden Ross!"

The guy came out of nowhere, his video camera clutched in his hand. At first, Marcus didn't understand what he was saying. But then Eden's fingers tightened on his arm, digging into his biceps. She stepped behind him again, hiding from the curious looks of the crowd.

Marcus held out his hand to warn the guy off, but he continued to approach, staggering as though he'd had too much to drink.

The video camera focused on Marcus now, and Marcus quickly moved his hand in front of the lens. "Hey, buddy, just turn that thing off. We don't want our picture taken, all right?"

"Jus' lemme get a picture of her. Who gives a rat's ass about you?"

Marcus cursed as the man tried to muscle his way past him. He grabbed his arm and gave it a yank, but the guy turned on him, swinging with his free hand. Eden screamed and scampered back, but Marcus had no intention of running from this fight.

"Hey, Eden, is this your new man?" the drunk asked. "Why don't you both just do it right here on the sidewalk and I'll tape it? We can all make a million."

Marcus wasn't sure what happened next, only that it involved pure instinct and no reasoning at all. His fist came up and connected with the drunk's nose, and the guy staggered, then fell backward onto the pavement. Marcus bent down and grabbed the video camera, searching for a way to extract the tape.

The drunk's wife started screaming for someone to call an ambulance and the police, and an instant later the bouncer stepped into the fight, grabbing Marcus from behind. The bouncer had at least fifty pounds on him, but Marcus had been schooled in street fighting from an early age. He brought his heel down on the bouncer's instep, and the moment his grip loosened Marcus spun on him.

In one sure movement, he tossed the video camera to Eden, then gave the bouncer a swift uppercut to the chin. The punch had little effect beyond a momentary stun, and the bouncer returned with a cross that grazed Marcus's eye.

Marcus noticed the drunk stumbling to his feet and decided that retreat was in order. He wasn't about to fight them both. He held up his hands as if to surrender, and when the bouncer lowered his fists, Marcus took off. He grabbed Eden's hand and pulled her across the street. "We have to get out of here," he shouted. "Right now."

The crowd surged toward them as if to get a better look at Eden. But Marcus knew the streets of Newport well enough to make a quick escape. They ducked down a side street, then cut back through an alley. Eden was slowed by the sexy shoes she'd decided to wear, but they managed to reach Marcus's truck in less than a minute. Marcus helped Eden inside, then grabbed a baseball cap from behind the seat and put it on his head. He hopped in the driver's side and placed his hand on Eden's shoulder. "Get down," he ordered.

Eden did as she was told and they wound through the back streets until they were well away from downtown. "That was a mess," Marcus muttered, steering the car toward the Newport Bridge.

Eden sat up and stared out the rear window. "I'm sorry."

He glanced in the rearview mirror. "I don't think they're following us."

"Who?"

"The photographers," he said. "The guy with the video camera."

"He wasn't a photographer," she said. "I think he was

just a tourist. Usually the tabloid photographers wear credentials. That way, they don't get beat up."

Marcus cursed beneath his breath. "Great. I just assaulted some poor git from upstate New Hampshire just to protect your honor."

"You really hit him hard," she said. Eden held up the video camera he'd tossed to her during the fight. "And you stole his camera."

"Me? You stole it. I just wanted you to get the tape out. This is why I didn't want to go to that club. I warned you."

"Why are you so upset? I go through this all the time. Everywhere I go there are people taking my picture and shouting questions at me. You just have to ignore them."

"I don't need my picture taken," he said.

"Why? Are you ashamed to be seen with me?" Eden asked.

Marcus stared out the windshield at the late-night traffic over the bridge. "Don't be ridiculous. We went out, didn't we?"

"Then what's the problem? I thought we were having fun. Don't let some tourist with a camera ruin our whole night."

"I just can't stand by while some idiot insults you. Did you hear what he said?"

Eden sank back down in the seat, her arms crossed over her chest. "Of course I did. But I didn't let it get to me. He was drunk, and a lot of people think celebrities are fair game. I've just learned to let it roll off my back, Marcus. He doesn't make a difference to me."

"Then who does?"

"You do," Eden snapped. "My mother and father do, to some extent, although that can be hit-and-miss at times. Some of my friends—but not many. And Sarah, my father's housekeeper, and Maria. And that's about it. Oh, and your mother. I hope that she has a good opinion of me."

Marcus glanced over his shoulder as they turned onto the bridge. "I don't want to provide amusement for some lady waiting on line at the grocery store."

They drove the rest of the way to Marcus's place in silence. He wasn't angry, just frustrated. He and Eden were like a runaway train, heading for the end of their relationship at top speed, and there was nothing he could do about it. At this rate, there was destined to be a huge crash with at least one casualty—him.

In the past, he'd never given a second thought to breakups. In most cases, he was glad to be free of the responsibility for some woman's happiness. But with Eden, he was loath to face the inevitable.

He craved the feel of her naked body against his, the sensation of sinking into her moist heat and the act of bringing them both to a mindless ecstasy. It wasn't just the sex. He loved spending time with her. He loved falling asleep with her in his arms and waking up to her sweet smile. He loved her.

He glanced over at her and fought the urge to reach out and touch her. Maybe it was better this way. This incident just proved that he couldn't live in her world, and she wasn't willing to give up her world to live in his.

"You're all right?" he asked.

Eden nodded. "I'm fine." She glanced over at him

and forced a smile. "Thanks for standing up for me. Nobody's ever done that before."

"No problem."

EDEN STOOD IN FRONT of the kitchen sink and filled a glass with water. Marcus watched her from his spot on the sofa. Since they'd returned home, she'd been curiously silent.

He shouldn't have reacted the way he had, blaming her for what had happened. But how could she expect him to understand or to tolerate behavior that she'd grown immune to? From the start Marcus had protected her, and he wasn't about to stop now.

She had no more control over the situation than he had. Well, maybe a little control. If she hadn't made that video, then the drunk with the camera probably would have had to find some other insult to hurl at her. And perhaps Marcus could have tolerated a different one.

Eden sat down at the end of the counter and picked up the camera, fiddling with the buttons until she'd managed to rewind the tape. She walked out of the kitchen, her gaze on the view screen, filming her surroundings as she went.

When she reached the sofa, she turned the camera on Marcus. "Smile," she said.

He held his hand up in front of the lens. "Stop."

"Why?"

"You got in enough trouble the last time you appeared on video. And I've had enough of cameras for one night."

"Come on, don't be so depressing," Eden said with a

pout. "I don't want to spend our last night together all gloomy and doomy. Smile."

Marcus shook his head and covered his face with his hands. "Go away, Eden."

"I've got an idea. We'll just make a little video of our last night together and then you'll have something to remember me by."

"I'm not going to play this game with you."

She pried his hands away from his eyes and trained the camera at his face, standing above him. "Tell me. What did you think the first time you saw Eden Ross?"

"Nice ass," he muttered. "Naked girl. Big trouble."

"And what about later?" she continued. "Did you want to touch me?"

The answer was obvious. From the moment he'd met her he'd thought of nothing else. "No," he lied.

"I don't believe you," Eden said, peeking out from behind the camera. "Take your shirt off."

Marcus refused, but Eden wasn't about to be deterred. "Then you hold it," she said, handing him the camera, "and I'll take my clothes off." She pointed to the miniature screen on the back. "Just watch me through that and try not to jiggle the camera."

Marcus grudgingly pointed the camera at Eden. She reached down for the hem of her dress and slowly drew it up over her head. She wasn't wearing a bra and had chosen a sexy black thong as her only underwear. She let her hands drift up her torso and over her breasts, then brushed her hair away from her face, playing to the camera and to the man behind it. She was deliberately tempting him, and Marcus was loath to admit that it was working.

Eden slowly walked up to him and took the camera, then pulled him to his feet. "Your turn," she said, dragging him toward the bed.

"Why are we doing this?" Marcus asked as he unbuttoned his shirt.

"Have you ever seen yourself make love to a woman?" Eden asked. "Aren't you curious? Come on, it's liberating. It's like having someone else in the room…but not really."

He'd never refused Eden anything before, at least not sexually. And he was intrigued. She was right—they should spend their last night together doing something more interesting than arguing. But this was just a reminder of a big mistake she'd made in the past. He grabbed the camera and turned it off.

She stared at him, her mouth pressed into a tight line. "It doesn't have to be awful like the last one," she murmured. "It can be sexy and wonderful and real. I want you to remember that it was real."

"Eden, I'm not going to forget you."

She nodded. "I know. But I want to share this with you. I trust you, Marcus. I know you would never use this to hurt me."

He drew a deep breath, then handed the camera back to her. "Just promise me we're going to burn this tape after we watch it," Marcus said, letting his shirt drop to the floor.

Eden smiled. "No, I'm going to leave it with you as

a memento of our time together. Every now and then you can watch it and it will be like I'm here."

Marcus kicked off his boat shoes, standing in his bare feet. "I don't think so," he said. He undid his belt and Eden let the camera drift lower. "It would be a sad substitute for the real thing."

"Slower," Eden ordered, kneeling in the center of the bed and tucking her feet beneath her. "Take your time."

"Are you the director?" he asked.

"For tonight," she replied.

As he lowered the zipper of his khakis, Marcus was forced to admit that Eden's little game was a huge turn-on. Undressing had always been a necessary step, but now it was entertainment. His sexual liberation at Eden's hands had had no limits, and he didn't want to stop now. "Is that slow enough?"

"Run your hand over your chest," she said.

Marcus watched her, but Eden wasn't looking at him. She was looking intently at the screen. If he wanted to seduce her, then he'd be forced to do it through the lens of the video camera. Smiling, he did as she ordered, smoothing his palm over his chest and belly.

When he reached his pants, he slipped his fingertips beneath the waistband of his boxers. He heard Eden take a sharp breath and her eyes went wide. A tiny smile quirked at the corners of her mouth. "That's very nice," she said.

Marcus slid his hand downward and was surprised to find that he was already hard. Though he was famil-iar with the art of pleasuring himself, he'd never done it in front of anyone. But he wasn't embarrassed to do it for Eden as long as she found it…arousing.

"Touch yourself," she murmured. "The way that I touch you."

He pushed his boxers down, freeing himself from the confines of his clothing. Marcus slowly began to stroke himself, tipping his head back and imagining that it was Eden's touch on his body. He grew harder with each movement, the sensations coursing through his body more intense because of her presence.

Marcus kept his pace slow, knowing that he wouldn't finish on his own. He opened his eyes and looked at Eden. She ran her tongue along her lower lip, and he smiled, imagining her tongue running along the length of his shaft.

As if she could read his mind, Eden crawled off the bed and handed him the camera. She knelt down in front of him and tugged his boxers and khakis to the floor. Marcus kicked them aside, and a heartbeat later she took him into her mouth, her tongue caressing the tip of his penis with every stroke.

Marcus held up the camera and watched her through the view screen, his attention completely focused on Eden's lips and his cock. He'd watched the occasional porno, but this was something much more tantalizing. It was happening to him.

Eden glanced up and smiled. "Tell me what you want," she said. She ran her tongue along the length of his shaft. "You're the director now."

"Take your underwear off and lie down on the bed," Marcus ordered. He walked over to the dresser and set the camera on top, focusing the lens on the bed. When he returned, Eden was lying across the sheets, her hands skimming over her body.

Marcus watched her for a long time as she touched herself, his fingers clenching with the urge to take over. But she was still performing for him, bringing his desire to a fever pitch. He'd never wanted a woman this badly, and when he finally spread her legs and pushed inside of her, Marcus was almost mindless with need.

The camera recorded every sigh, every stroke, but Marcus wasn't aware of any of it. The moment he entered her, he was lost in a whirlwind of pleasure, Eden's body responding to his every movement. He was rough and then gentle. She came twice without his touch, and it was only then that Marcus allowed himself to join her.

His orgasm sent uncontrollable tremors through his body, as if every nerve and muscle had been waiting for release. When he was spent, Marcus lay down beside her, his leg thrown across her hips, his fingers tangled in her hair. Though his mind was void of rational thought, one thing broke through the haze.

How was he supposed to live without this? Without her?

THEY HADN'T SLEPT AT all. They'd spent the night making love and then talking and then making love all over again, caught in an intimate cocoon. Eden curled into Marcus's body and closed her eyes against the early dawn's light at the windows.

"Promise me something," she said.

He turned and pressed a kiss to her temple. "What?"

"Don't bring another woman into this bed for a while. I don't want to have to imagine that. If you promise me, then I won't."

"I promise."

Eden knew he'd keep his word, at least for a little while. She trusted him completely. She pressed her lips against his chest and smiled. They'd watched their home movie, giggling over it at first but then allowing themselves to enjoy what they'd done.

Eden wasn't sure what had possessed her to do it, but in the end she was glad that she had. Now this night would come to memory when she thought about a sex tape. This night full of unbridled passion and complete satisfaction with a man she loved.

She didn't know how long it would be before they saw each other again—or even if they would—but perhaps when he needed her he might watch the tape again and remember how good it had been between them.

Eden pushed up on her elbow and looked down into his eyes. "Do you ever wonder what it would have been like? If I hadn't been Eden Ross and...you know. How do you think it would have ended? Would we have been different together?"

Marcus picked up her hand from his chest and studied her fingertips, twisting her fingers between his. "I don't know. You are Eden Ross and things are exactly as they are. We can't change that."

"When we began, it was all about sex. It was very uncomplicated and I thought that's what I wanted."

"But?" Marcus asked.

Eden sighed. "Do you ever think it might have been

better if we'd believed there could be more between us?"
She reached out and slowly ran her hand along the ridge
of his collarbone, then traced a line down the center of
his chest. Pressing her palm to his warm skin, Eden felt
the slow, steady beat of his heart. What would it take to
possess Marcus's heart? Did she have it already or had
he just lent it to her for the time they'd been together?

Marcus kissed the top of her head. "I don't know."

He grew silent and Eden cursed herself for bringing up the subject. He didn't answer because he didn't
want to hurt her. It was obvious he had resigned himself to her leaving.

He slowly pulled his arm out from beneath her
head, then sat up. "I'm going to get us some breakfast.
There's a bakery in town that opens in a little while.
If I get there when they open, the cinnamon rolls are
still warm."

Eden drew the sheet up to her chin. "All right," she
said. "Do you want me to come with you?"

Marcus ran his hand along her arm, his gaze following his fingers. He shook his head. "I won't be long.
You could make some coffee."

Eden smiled sleepily. "I know how to do that," she
said with a trace of pride. Of all the things she'd attempted so far, coffee had been a success.

She watched him get dressed, admiring the masculine beauty of his body, the long legs and well-formed
arms, the wide back and flat belly. She'd touched him
so many times, in so many places, that she'd lost sight
of how the pieces fit together. Eden took a mental pic-

ture of him, then closed her eyes and tried to imprint it on her memory.

When he was dressed, he bent over the bed and kissed her forehead. "I'll be back in a bit." A few seconds later the door latched shut, and Eden rolled over, burying her face in the pillow.

Saying goodbye to him at the airport would be impossible. The moment he touched her, she'd lose herself in his embrace. And then it would be awkward and frustrating. He'd feel compelled to kiss her and make some promise that they'd see each other again. And she'd be forced to do the same. And then she'd cry and the tears wouldn't stop.

Eden crawled out of bed and walked to the kitchen. She grabbed the coffee from the cupboard next to the sink and poured the ground beans into the filter. Then she added water and flipped the switch. Her eyes fixed on the stream of hot liquid as she tried to rid her mind of the worry.

But it was no use. Eden turned and grabbed the phone, then rummaged through the drawer for the directory. There had to be an airport shuttle. She flipped to the back and found a service listed under 'Limousines,' then dialed the number, hoping there would be someone in the office but content to listen to a schedule. To her surprise, someone answered.

"Good morning, Newport Shuttle."

She cleared her throat. "Hello. I'm interested in getting a ride to the Providence airport today. I'm in Bonnett Harbor. When does your shuttle run?"

"We have a shuttle that leaves Newport in about ten

minutes," the woman said. "And then we have one every hour on the hour. And we do have a pickup in Bonnett Harbor this morning for our 5:00 a.m. shuttle. Are you interested in leaving right away?"

Eden hesitated for a moment, glancing around the loft. It would be better this way, she mused. No good-byes, no promises and no regrets. "Yes, that would be fine."

"And where will the pickup be?"

"There's a diner right on the main street. It's called the Harborview. I'll be waiting there."

"The shuttle will be there in about fifteen minutes. I'll radio the driver and let him know."

"Fine," Eden said. "I'll be ready." She gave the dispatcher her name and Marcus's number, and after she'd noted a confirmation number, Eden hung up the phone. She hurried over to the bed and began to gather her clothes from the floor. Most of her luggage was still on *Victorious,* along with some of the things she'd brought from Europe. But she had her tote and stuffed what she could inside it. What didn't fit, she tossed into a shopping bag, and five minutes later she was dressed and ready to go.

Eden stood at the door for a long moment, gazing around Marcus's loft. It was a cowardly way to leave and she knew he'd be hurt. But this way she wouldn't have to face the very last instant before they parted. The moment when she'd hold her breath and wait for him to ask her to stay, and then he wouldn't. It was better to believe that it could have happened than to know that it hadn't.

She hurried down the stairs and out into the boat-yard. The sun was already up and the town had begun to stir. Eden ran to the street, then glanced around to make sure Marcus wasn't on his way home. The diner was five minutes away, and when she got there, the first customers were already seated at the counter.

Eden sat down on a bench outside, and a few minutes later a van pulled up with *Airport Shuttle* emblazoned on the door. Eden handed her bag to the driver and he opened the door for her. But she hesitated, knowing this was her last chance to change her mind.

Her thoughts wandered back to the previous evening, to the fight on the sidewalk. Marcus's eye was black. She'd watched the bruise grow over the course of the night. It had been a reminder of the problems she still needed to face. And for now, Eden wanted to face them alone.

She smiled at the driver, then crawled inside the van and took a seat next to an elderly woman. As the van wound through the streets of Bonnett Harbor, Eden smiled. She'd come a long way from the silly party girl who had hidden out on board *Victorious*. The changes had come so quickly that she wasn't sure who she was right now. But she knew she was ready to make something out of her life, to become the kind of woman who might deserve a life with a man like Marcus Quinn.

MARCUS TURNED OFF THE ignition to the truck and leaned back in the seat. He'd made the drive to the Providence airport in less than a half hour on empty highways not yet clogged with rush-hour traffic. But now that he was here, he wasn't sure what he was going to do.

He'd come home to find Eden gone, a note left on his pillow scrawled in big letters. *No regrets.* Nothing more, except an *E* at the bottom with a little heart beneath it. At first, he'd been angry. Why would she sneak out? Had she planned this all along?

But then he realized that she had been dreading their goodbye as much as he had. It was so much easier just to avoid it. Yet Marcus couldn't let it end there. He needed to see her one last time, just to look into her eyes.

He didn't know what he was going to say or if he'd say anything at all. But he wanted to kiss her and let that be the last thing between them, not some letter on his pillow. He glanced at his watch. Her plane didn't leave for hours, but there was always a chance that she planned to catch an earlier flight. Hell, he wasn't even sure she was at the airport.

Marcus clutched the steering wheel and drew a deep breath. This was it. If he had any intention of asking her to stay, now was the time to make that known. Every ounce of his being told him that it was the right thing to do. No matter what she was going through, she was better off with him. And she had to see there was more to what they shared than just sex. There was trust and affection and honesty and a friendship that had been growing since the first day they'd met. And though they'd spent less than two weeks together, it had been enough for Marcus to see that he was in love with Eden Ross.

These feelings were so strange and confusing, how

could they be anything else? Marcus glanced at his watch, then closed his eyes. He'd wait ten minutes, and if he still felt the same way, then he'd walk into the airport and find her and ask her to stay.

He stared at the clock on the dash, watching as it ticked through the time. Each minute seemed to drag by, yet it only confirmed that asking her to stay was the right thing to do. They needed time to talk about a future, to consider all the pitfalls and the possibilities.

When the ten minutes were up, Marcus drew another deep breath, then smiled. There was no doubt in his mind. He needed Eden in his life. He didn't want to think about what he'd do if she refused him. That wasn't a possibility, for he'd thought of every argument to convince her not to go.

He jumped out of the truck, then ran across the parking ramp to the stairwell. When he reached the ground floor, he headed to the terminal, watching the signs for the airline he was looking for. He got on line behind several people, and when he reached the ticket clerk, Marcus gave her a charming smile. "I'd like to know if a passenger has checked in yet. Her name is Eden Ross."

"I'm sorry, sir, we're not allowed to give out information on our passengers."

"I just need to know if she's here in the airport."

"You could have her paged."

Marcus shook his head. "No, I don't want to do that. Then the whole airport will know she's here. She has a flight out at two to Los Angeles. How do I know this? Because I know her and I know when she's traveling. Did she check in yet?"

"Are you a friend of hers? Or a reporter?" the woman asked, sending him a suspicious look.

"A friend, I swear," Marcus said. "Actually, more than a friend."

She studied him shrewdly. "Well, I suppose it wouldn't do any harm. She did check in, but she's already gone. She switched her ticket to an earlier flight, and it left about ten minutes ago."

Marcus shook his head. "You're sure?"

The ticket agent nodded. "I exchanged the ticket myself. She was anxious to get back home. And to avoid spending any time waiting in the airport."

"Thanks."

"Sorry," she said.

"So am I."

As Marcus walked back out of the airport, he wondered if maybe this was what was meant to be. If he was supposed to have stopped her, then he wouldn't have wasted ten minutes screwing up his courage to stop her. He would have left earlier and driven faster and parked in the tow-away zone and run into the airport and gotten to her on time. But instead he'd dragged his feet the entire way.

It would be a long drive back to Bonnett Harbor if he planned to beat himself up about this. Eden was gone and there was nothing he could do about it now. If these feelings continued, then he'd have to deal with them. But for now, he'd try to get back to his life as it had been before he'd met Eden.

As he walked out to the car, Marcus's cell phone rang. He yanked it out of his pocket, saying a silent prayer that Eden had decided to say goodbye after all. He frowned as he saw his home number on the caller ID. Marcus flipped open the phone. "Hello?"

"Marcus. It's Ian. I'm at your place and I just wanted to let you know that I'm going to borrow your video camera."

"No problem," Marcus said. "It's in the—"

"I've got it," Ian interrupted. "Hey, I didn't realize you bought a new one."

"A new—" Marcus's words died in his throat. "No, you can't use that one."

"Why not? It looks much nicer than your old one. Hey, thanks, bro. I've got to go. I have to tape a meeting for the town board. I'll talk to you later."

"No," Marcus said. He heard the phone click on the other end. With a curse, he punched his home number. The phone rang ten times before he hung up. "Bloody hell," he muttered. "I knew we shouldn't have made that video."

Either Ian or the town board was about to get an eyeful. Marcus crossed back to the parking ramp. On the way home, he'd stop at the police department and talk his brother into giving him the tape. If he was lucky, there wouldn't be any questions. Otherwise, he'd have an awful lot of explaining to do.

9

EDEN STOOD ON THE DECK of her mother's Malibu beach house staring out at the Pacific, her coffee cup clutched in her hand. She'd been back in California for a week, and as the days had passed, she'd begun to grow restless. This wasn't her home anymore, this sun-washed house with the fussy decor and the celebrity neighbors. Though she'd spent most of her youth holed up in the pretty lavender bedroom, nothing here felt right.

She closed her eyes and breathed deeply of the salt air, trying to recall the only place in the world where she did feel right. Marcus's loft. Now when she thought of her favorite place to be, it was there, above the boatyard in Bonnett Harbor, in the bed draped with old sails.

It seemed a lifetime ago, but it had only been seven days since she'd left. She'd picked up the phone hundreds of times, prepared to call him and just see how he was. But Eden had promised herself that she'd sort out her life before she contacted him again. He'd already suffered enough because of the mistakes she'd made, and she wasn't going to add to his troubles by making more.

She reached up and touched her bottom lip, running her finger along it and recalling the sensation of his kiss. Time after time, she'd caught herself lost in a daydream about him, the memories so vivid that she could almost feel him. And then the ache would begin, the longing for the weight of his body on hers, for the hard heat of his shaft buried deep inside her.

As she remembered each perfect moment, she couldn't help but wonder if she'd ever experience such pleasure again. The prospect of living the rest of her life comparing every man to Marcus Quinn was enough to make her a bit crazy.

"Darling! You aren't dressed yet?"

Eden turned to see her mother walking toward her, dressed in ultrafashionable workout wear. Pamela Ross was nearly fifty, but daily workouts and a Beverly Hills plastic surgeon had made it possible to shave off at least ten of those years.

Her latest husband—and soon-to-be ex—was a financial consultant for the Hollywood movie studios. He had been tossed out a few weeks before Eden's arrival, and already Pamela had been in constant meetings with her lawyers. After her fourth failed marriage, it was clear that Pamela Kitteridge Ross Wilsing Antonini Frasier had turned marrying well into an art and divorcing well into a financial windfall.

Once the divorce was final, she would come away with at least five or six million, enough to keep her in

Prada and Gucci until she found another man willing to take her on.

"You should have come to Pilates with me," Pamela said. She lifted her warm-up, revealing her stomach. "There are twenty-one-year-old girls in class that don't have abs like mine. I've got a yoga class this afternoon. It would do you good, darling. You seem so tense."

"I can't go out," Eden said. "There are photographers everywhere."

"They're parked right outside on the road," Pamela said, studying her French manicure. "But what harm can they do? Just fix yourself up, put on something pretty and let them take a few pictures. After that, they'll go away."

"No," Eden said. "I won't give them the satisfaction. They're like vultures, always hovering, just waiting for me to step into the road and get flattened by an oncoming truck so they can pick my carcass clean."

"How long are you going to continue to pout?"

"I don't know, Mother. But when I'm finished, I'll be sure to let you know."

"Life can't possibly be that bad." She sighed. "Your father called last night and he's decided to buy that silly tape for you. In a few days everything will be forgotten and you can get on with your life."

Stunned, Eden stared at her mother. "You're kidding. He's going to buy the tape?"

Pamela nodded. "He was adamant. Was mumbling on and on about some letter you sent him. I think you ought to call him and thank him for his generosity. And make sure you tell him you're calling at my suggestion. It always pays to keep that piece of bread buttered on both sides."

Eden closed her eyes and drew a deep breath. She'd been prepared to fight this battle on her own, to go to court with expensive lawyers and plead her case.

"All your friends have been asking about you."

"What friends?" Eden murmured. "I don't have any friends. Once they find out I don't have any money left, I'm sure they won't be asking."

"Well, then you'll have to find a way to make some money," her mother said. "And I think I have an idea. A job opportunity for you."

"A job?" Eden's interest was instantly piqued. She'd already come to the conclusion that she wasn't really qualified to do anything. She'd attended college for only three semesters before leaving to pursue her life as a party girl. "What kind of job?"

"You'll see. A friend of mine is coming over for coffee and she'll tell you all about it." Pamela wrapped her arms around Eden's neck and hugged her tight. "I'm so glad you're home, darling. Just think, we can go out to the clubs and have some fun now that I've given Harold the heave-ho. Good Lord, he was a stick-in-the-mud."

"I'm not going clubbing with you, Mother."

"Why not? I need to be around exciting people again. I'm thinking my next man will need to be younger, ten, maybe twenty years. Can you imagine me with a boy toy?"

Eden fought back a shudder. "Are you interested in spending time with me or spending time with the people I seem to attract? If it's with me, then why don't we just sit here and talk?"

"About what, darling? You and I have nothing in common—except maybe your father. And I don't want to talk about him."

Eden felt tears of frustration pushing at the corners of her eyes. She'd hoped that she and her mother might be able to forge some type of relationship now that she was back. But the longer she stayed in Malibu, the more she realized it wasn't possible. Pamela craved the celebrity that Eden had, and Eden couldn't wait to rid herself of it.

She thought back to the conversation she'd had with Marcus's mother. Had she been born to Emma Quinn, perhaps Eden might have become a different person. But she couldn't blame her troubles entirely on her parents. By the time she'd turned eighteen, she'd known that the choices she made were entirely her own. "I'm sorry I've made such a mess of my life, Mother. I never wanted to embarrass you and I'm going to do my best to make some positive changes."

Her mother blinked, taken aback by Eden's apology. "Are you seeing a therapist, darling?"

"No," Eden replied. "I've just had some time to think. You and Daddy gave me everything I could possibly want. But you never gave me what I needed."

"What could you possibly have needed? Your father and I gave you everything."

"I needed parents who cared about me. You gave me things, possessions."

"And what's wrong with having nice things?" Pamela asked.

Eden sighed softly. Her mother would never understand. "I think I'm going to go lie down. I didn't sleep well last night."

She turned and walked toward the French doors, but her mother reached out and grabbed her hand as she passed. "You're a beautiful young woman," Pamela said. "Isn't that enough?"

Eden shook her head. "No, Mother, it's not. Not nearly." She wandered back into the beach house, unable to continue the conversation. As she passed the phone, she again fought the urge to pick it up and call Marcus. He would understand how she was feeling. She could tell him anything and he always listened.

"You can't take a nap," Pamela cried, following Eden inside. "Sally Petzell will be here in a few minutes and she wants to talk to you about that job."

"What kind of job is it?" Eden asked.

"Oh, I don't know. Something in television." Pamela ran her fingers through Eden's hair. "Why don't you go put on something pretty? And comb your hair." She wrinkled her nose. "This color really does nothing for you, darling. I'll take you to Nando and he'll fix this for you."

"No!" Eden said, pulling away. "I like my hair the way it is."

Pamela hitched her hands on her waist. "Get dressed, Eden. If you meet Sally looking like that, you will be an embarrassment to me."

Sighing, Eden walked back to her bedroom and rummaged through her closet for something decent to wear. Her wardrobe was scattered around the world, some on the boat, some at Andreas's apartment in Paris, some at her favorite hotel in Monaco. Once she found a new place to live, she could finally put a life together and gather all her belongings in one place.

She found a taupe silk blouse and a little navy skirt that looked simple and conservative. A pair of embroidered mules completed the look. Eden was just combing through her hair when she heard the doorbell ring.

When she returned to the living room, her mother was already deep in conversation with their visitor, a tall bleached blonde with a husky voice. She was dressed exactly like Pamela; in truth, they looked like sisters.

Eden held out her hand. "Hello," she said. "I'm—"

"Eden Ross," the woman said dramatically, rushing toward her. "Who doesn't recognize you? Sally Petzell. I'm a producer over at the Entertainment Network. I understand you're looking for a job."

"I—I am."

"You've never done television before," Sally said.

Eden shook her head. "I've been on television but never on purpose."

"So what do you think you could do for the Entertainment Network? How would we use your…talents?"

Eden considered the question for a long moment. "Maybe I could do something with fashion. I've been to all the runway shows in Paris and Milan and New York and I have a very good eye for what's going to be big. I'm known for my fashion sense."

"Interesting," Sally said, pursing her lips. "Go with me on this. Fashion is…boring. Everyone thinks they know about fashion, but who really cares?" She grabbed

Eden's hands and gave them a squeeze. "You have something special. You're much more."

"More than what?" Eden asked.

"Just more. You're parties and champagne and handsome men with expensive European sports cars. Here's what I have in mind for you. It's a quirky take on a dating show. Reality television is so big now that we'd have no problem selling the concept. We'd call it Eden's Adventures in Paradise. You'd travel the world to romantic locations looking for that perfect man. Every week you'd go out on a fabulous date with some heir to a European fortune or maybe even a prince or a Venezuelan polo player. You know, the kind of guys you've always dated. I hear the king of Spain has a son who's available." She pulled out her BlackBerry and typed a quick note to herself. "I'm going to have Katie give him a call."

"You want me to date on television?" Eden asked.

"Not just date. We want you to party. We want you to get crazy and wild, all those things that you do so well. We want you to show these men the best time they've ever had."

Pamela clapped her hands giddily. "Doesn't that sound like fun, darling? You'll travel, you'll stay in wonderful hotels and be catered to morning, noon and night. And you'll get paid for being yourself. What more could you ask for?"

"No," Eden said flatly.

"No?" Sally frowned. "No to what? The prince of Spain? That was just an example. How about the prince of Wales? Now there's a man you could loosen up."

Eden shook her head, backing away. "No. I'm not going to do this. I'm not going to make a fool of myself anymore, especially not for the public's enjoyment."

"Eden, darling, consider this carefully," Pamela said. "You don't have much left in your trust fund, and I certainly can't support you. Your father has cut you off."

Eden shook her head. "I—I have to go. It was nice meeting you." She nodded at Sally Petzell, then hurried back to her bedroom. Eden rummaged through her closet until she found her old luggage, then threw it onto the bed.

"What are you doing?"

She glanced up to see her mother standing in the door. "I'm getting out of here."

"Where are you going?"

"I don't know. But I can't stay here. Call a cab for me and have them park up by the Fergusons' house. I'll walk up the beach. The photographers won't know I've left."

"What has gotten into you, Eden?"

"Not what," Eden replied. "Who."

"Who?"

She turned and faced her mother. "His name is Marcus. Marcus Quinn. And I'm pretty sure that I'm in love with him."

It was a perfect summer day on Rhode Island Sound, the sky blue, the water calm. Marcus dangled from the bosun's chair over the bow of the boat, the restored figurehead clamped into place. He braced his hands on the bowsprit and stared up at the mainstay, watching as a small pennant fluttered in the gentle breeze.

He'd been living on board *Victorious* again, finding the solitude preferable to the emptiness of his loft. Eden had been gone for a week now, and in all that time he'd been unable to convince himself it was for the best.

Every day he woke up hoping that she'd return and every night he'd lain in bed convincing himself that she wouldn't. Their time together had been a lovely holiday that was never meant to go beyond a couple weeks. Their lives had moved in completely different directions from the start, and though the roads had intersected in one spot, they now veered off again.

He closed his eyes and swallowed back the lump of emotion stuck in his throat. Missing her had become a physical pain, nagging and chronic. His mind constantly replayed their time together, and he lost himself in elaborate plans on how he might convince her to come back.

But always in the end he was left with the realization that what they had shared had been a fantasy come to life and not real life at all.

"Is this what you were looking for?"

Marcus glanced over at his brother Ian and nodded. He held his hand out for the wrench, then fitted it over the bolt.

"It looks really good, Marky," he said. "You do some amazing work. Hard to believe you started out with those little animals in Nana's barn." He shook his head. "Dec and I always used to think you were a queer one, spending all your time up in the haymow. You didn't talk much back then."

"I didn't have a lot to say," Marcus replied.

"Still don't," Ian countered.

"Shimmy out there and put that socket wrench over the bolt. I need to tighten this a little more."

Ian did as he was told, lying on his stomach and reaching over the bow. Marcus carefully tightened the last bolt, then swung the bosun's chair back to the rail of the boat. He crawled back on board and dropped the wrench into his toolbox.

"I'm almost done here," Marcus said. "Maybe a week and that's it."

"What's up after this?"

Marcus shrugged. He felt as if he was at loose ends. In truth, he wanted to go find Eden and make things right between them. Their relationship hadn't had a proper ending. There were so many things left unsaid that Marcus couldn't seem to move forward.

"Did you bring my video camera back?" Marcus asked. He'd been waiting for the moment to pose the question casually.

Ian cursed. "Yeah. We didn't use it after all," Ian said. "One of the guys brought his camera and it had a tripod. But I lost the tape. I pulled it out of the camera and set it down somewhere and—"

"You lost the tape?" Marcus asked, his stomach twisting into a knot. God, this was all he needed. The furor over Eden's first sex tape was beginning to cool. All she needed was another home movie to hit the market. Hell, she'd trusted him with this one and now it was out there.

According to Dec, Trevor Ross had purchased the

other tape for a tidy sum. Due to that unexplained expense, he'd decided to hold off on further investments, including Marcus's business. But with the check for the commission and a generous bonus, Marcus had enough to get by for a while.

"I'm sorry, I—"

"I need that tape," Marcus insisted. "Come on. We'll go over to the station right now and get it."

"What is so damn important that it can't wait a day or two? I have the tape. It's in my office somewhere, I'm sure of it. Jeez, Marcus, what has gotten into you lately? You've been acting really weird," Ian said.

Marcus shrugged, then grabbed the beer he had wedged against the rail. He stared out at the horizon, his gaze fixed on the white sails of a boat nearly a mile out into the sound. "I was talking to Da the other day. Doing a bit of research on our…project. He told me he fell in love with Ma the moment he first saw her. Do you think that's possible?"

Ian frowned. "There is something wrong with you."

Marcus cursed. "Just answer the question. Is it possible to fall in love in a day or a week? I always thought it took a long time."

"No," Ian said after some consideration. "I think it's definitely possible. Yeah, it could happen. Kind of like lightning striking. It doesn't happen often, but when it does, it knocks you on your arse."

"What are the odds?" Marcus asked.

"You want a number?"

Marcus leaned back and closed his eyes, turning his

face up to the sun. "Yeah. A hundred to one? A thousand to one?"

"I don't think it makes a difference," Ian said. "When it happens, it happens. It's not a science, Marky."

"I know." He paused and glanced over at his brother. "I mean, I figured that's the way it was."

"So how are you doing with the pact?" Ian asked.

"Fine. Women don't come swimming out here every day, so I'm safe."

Ian lowered his voice. "Between you and me, I think Dec might be breaking the vow of celibacy."

Marcus scoffed at the notion. "He's got a girl?"

"You know he's been playing bodyguard to some radio-talk-show lady named Dr. Devine. He says she's an uptight egghead, but I'll bet she's gorgeous. There's no way he'll survive guarding a beautiful body without indulging in it at the same time."

"Dec is pretty tough when he wants to be," Marcus said.

"Not that tough. No guy is that tough. We all have our weak spots."

"Maybe we should call off the deal."

"No way!" Ian cried. "Dec is going to cough up two thousand, and I intend to make him pay. Hell, he's the one who suggested this—I think we should hold him to it."

"I thought you were the one who came up with this brilliant idea."

"Nope, it was Dec." Ian pushed to his feet. "Let's go get some lunch. All this hard work has made me hungry. Afterward, we'll go look for your tape."

Marcus got up and gathered his tools, then carried them down to the cockpit. He braced his arms on the boom, his gaze coming to rest on the dock. How many times had he caught himself looking for her, hoping that the next time he looked she'd be standing there waiting for him?

"Get a grip," he muttered to himself. It was over. And if he wanted to fancy himself in love with Eden Ross, then this torture would go on forever. As soon as he and his brothers called an end to this ridiculous pact, he'd go out and find another woman to occupy his mind—and his body.

Ian climbed down into the cockpit and stood next to Marcus, staring over the water to the Ross mansion. "This is the life, huh?"

"It looks like it from the outside, doesn't it? But it's not that much different from ours when you strip away all the pretty stuff."

Ian gave him an odd look, a frown wrinkling his brow. "You're turning into a bleedin' philosopher, Marky. I don't know the cause, but I'm gonna figure it out."

"There's nothing wrong with me," Marcus murmured. "I swear."

It was easy to say but not so easy to believe. He was determined to forget her and he vowed to do just that. Starting right now.

EDEN STARED OUT THE tinted window of the limousine, watching the familiar scenery of Ocean Avenue pass by. She'd hopped the red-eye last night at LAX and had arrived on schedule in Providence just shortly after noon. The limo had been waiting and whisked her away on the fifty-minute drive home.

"Home," she murmured. How many homes had she had over the years? Malibu, Newport, her father's house in Providence, her favorite hotels scattered across the world, even *Victorious* had been a home. But home was no longer a place, it had become a person. Marcus Quinn was home to her now.

The limo turned off Ocean Avenue and continued along the winding road toward the water. The gates of her father's house loomed in the distance, and Eden's nerves began to fray as they approached. She smoothed the skirt of her tidy Armani suit and ran her fingers through her hair.

She'd called her father yesterday afternoon, requesting a meeting with him. To her surprise, he'd agreed and asked her to meet him at the house for a late lunch.

The limo pulled into the circular drive and her father's chauffeur jumped out and ran to open her door. Eden thanked him and asked him to leave her bag in the foyer.

With a steely resolve, she walked up to the house and rang the bell. A moment later the door flew open. Sarah Corrigan stood on the other side, a smile coloring her cheeks rosy. The housekeeper threw out her arms and gathered Eden into a fierce embrace. "You're home." She kissed both of Eden's cheeks.

"I am," Eden said. "I've missed you." Tears flooded Eden's eyes. She'd avoided seeing Sarah during her last visit, knowing that she couldn't test the housekeeper's loyalty to her father. In truth, she'd been so ashamed of her behavior she hadn't been able to face the woman who was like a second mother to her.

But that didn't seem to matter to Sarah now. "I've made all your favorites. The minute your father told me you'd be coming, I started cooking. And your room is made up."

She took Eden's hand and led her through the house. "He's in the study. I took him coffee a few minutes ago and I think he's a little nervous. He's pacing."

Eden stopped in the hallway and grabbed Sarah's other hand. "Thank you," she murmured. "And not just for today but for every day that you watched over me and fed me and read me to sleep. I know I've never said this, but you were one of the only people that made my childhood tolerable. And I'm sorry if I've disappointed you in any way." Eden sniffled, brushing an errant tear from her cheek. "I just wanted to say that."

Sarah kissed her again, then pressed her palm to Eden's cheek. "Go see your father. When you're finished, you and I will spend some time catching up."

"I'd like that," Eden said. She turned to the door of the study and took a deep breath. The rest of her life started today, at this moment. And though she wasn't sure what the future held, she was finally ready to face it.

Eden knocked softly on the study door, then opened it. Her father looked up from his desk, his reading glasses perched on the end of his nose.

"Hi, Daddy," she said.

"Come in," he said. He pointed to one of the leather

wing chairs, silently ordering Eden to sit. "Your mother says you've run through most of your trust fund. I suppose you're here to ask for money. Well, I'm not going to give you any more."

"I realize that," Eden said. "And that's not why I came."

"You went through nearly three million in four years, Eden. I put that money in trust for you so that you would get a good start in life, maybe go to school, find yourself a husband, settle down. I'd be a fool to give you more."

"I know that, too," Eden said. "And I'm not here to ask for more. I'm here to tell you that I've made some decisions about my life."

"That's it?"

"From now on, I think it's best that you hear these things directly from me. You won't have to read about them in the tabloids."

He leaned back in his chair and studied her intently. "That will be a change."

Eden took another deep breath, attempting to calm her pounding pulse. "First, I should tell you that I've fallen in love. You may not approve, but that really doesn't matter to me. I plan to spend the rest of my life with this man."

Her father threw his hands up and shook his head. "Who is it this time? I hope he has money so he can finance your lifestyle."

"Actually, he doesn't. He works for a living. In fact, he works for you. Marcus Quinn."

Her father gasped. "How is it possible that you even know Marcus Quinn?"

"It's possible," Eden replied. "I've come back here to be with him, if he'll have me. I don't want to live without him, Daddy. I can't."

"You're going to propose to him?" her father asked.

Eden shrugged. "I don't know. Maybe. I just want to make sure that he and I have a future together and we're never apart again."

"Eden, you're still very young and—"

"Daddy, this is what I want. I know I've said that before and you have no reason to believe me this time. But so much has changed for me. I want to have a life with him and I'm willing to do whatever it takes to make that happen."

"What do you see in this man that you didn't see in the others?"

Eden smiled. "Oh, Daddy, there's so much. He's kind and he's steady and he watches over me. And when I make mistakes, he helps me to understand what I've done wrong, but he doesn't judge me. He lets me be myself but a better Eden Ross than I've ever known."

"How will you live?"

"That's why I asked for this meeting," she said.

"Well, now we get down to business."

"I don't want money. I want a job."

Trevor Ross chuckled. "You've never had a job in your life."

"I know, but it's time I did something productive. And I was hoping you could find a place for me in your company. It doesn't have to be anything important. I could work in the mail room or I could do filing. I'd be willing to go back to school to learn what I needed."

"You're not serious," Ross said.

"I am," Eden replied. "But I'll understand if you don't want me working for you. I can't offer much in the way of references or previous experience. But I promise I'll work hard."

He considered her offer for a long time, his face caught in a deep scowl. "All right," he finally said. "But the first time you screw up, I'll—"

"I understand," she said. "And I won't."

He stood and held out his hand, then realized what he was doing and pulled it back. He circled his desk and gave her a perfunctory hug. "Report to the Providence office on Monday morning at 9:00 a.m. I'll have you meet with Human Resources and see what we can find."

Eden smiled, emotions overwhelming her. The first piece of her plan had fallen so easily into place. "Thank you, Daddy." She wrapped her arms around his neck and gave him a long hug. "I promise I won't disappoint you."

He drew back, and for the first time in a long time Trevor Ross smiled at his daughter. "I suppose I have Marcus Quinn to thank for this?"

"Maybe," Eden said with a smile. "A little bit."

"Well, why don't you invite him to lunch with us? He's down on the boat, finishing up the job I gave him." Her father paused. "He's good at what he does, Eden. I like his work. And I like him. You could do a lot worse than Marcus Quinn."

"But I couldn't do better," Eden said. She drew a deep breath and steadied herself. "Wish me luck."

He reached up and cupped her cheek in his hand. "How could he refuse such a beautiful woman?"

Eden pushed up on her toes and kissed her father's cheek. "Thank you, Daddy." She hurried to the door, but her father's voice stopped her.

"There is one other thing." He opened the drawer of his desk and pulled out a videocassette, then held it out to her. "I just received this by messenger. I thought you might like to dispose of it yourself."

"I'll leave that up to you," she said with a grateful smile. "And I promise, I'll do my best to pay you back, Daddy. I'll make you proud of me."

He nodded, and Eden hurried out of the study through the main hall. She threw open the wide doors to the terrace and kicked off her shoes. The grass was cool on her feet as she ran down the lawn toward the water. When she reached the dock, Eden shaded her eyes and stared out at *Victorious,* rocking at anchor.

Her heart began to beat faster again and she couldn't help but smile. Though it had been only a week, the days had seemed like years since she'd seen Marcus. She felt like a silly schoolgirl, all flushed and nervous.

It was a first date of sorts. From now on, things would be much simpler. She wouldn't have to always be watching her back, waiting for her past to catch up with her. She had a chance to begin again.

The dinghy was tied up to the swim ladder, and she couldn't see Marcus anywhere on board. Eden shrugged out of her jacket. She'd made the swim once before, the day they'd met. Making it again would give her time to calm her nerves and prepare her for her proposal.

She finished stripping down to her underwear, then dived neatly off the end of the pier. The water was warm and clear, and as she swam she felt a curious serenity overcome her. For the first time in her life she knew exactly what she wanted, who she wanted, and he was waiting on that boat. She ought to have been afraid or at least a little nervous, but Eden realized that she had nothing to lose. She'd already lost it all and was determined to get back what she couldn't live without.

Even if he didn't accept her proposal, she wasn't about to give up. Now that she'd be living in the area, she'd find a way to convince him that what they had was worth saving. No man had ever touched her the way Marcus had, and in her heart Eden knew they were meant to be together.

By the time she reached the boat, she was breathless, not from the swim but from anticipation. She'd thought about Marcus so many times over the past week, imagined them together, lost in an endless kiss. As Eden climbed the swim ladder, she shivered, the breeze causing goose bumps to rise on her skin. She brushed the wet hair from her eyes, then walked to the hatch for the master suite.

He was there, sitting in the center of the berth, his back to her, tools spread out around him. A tiny smile twitched at Eden's lips as her gaze slowly took in the broad shoulders and narrow waist. Her fingers clenched and Eden realized that she knew exactly how his skin would feel, how his mouth would taste.

The man had burned himself into her being, and everything about him, from the tiniest detail, now fascinated her. She stood in the hatchway, her arms braced on either side of her, her body still dripping water.

Eden watched as he shifted, then slowly straightened, his back still to her. She held her breath, wondering if he'd sensed her presence. "Hi, Barney," she said softly.

He tipped his head back and took a deep breath, as if he'd merely imagined her voice. But then he slowly turned. His gaze met hers and Eden felt her limbs go weak.

His blue eyes scanned her body, and Eden shifted, the attraction between them intensifying by degrees. "I missed you," she said.

He crawled off the bed and crossed the cabin to stand below her. Eden took a step down, and a moment later he grabbed her waist and swung her into the cabin. Without speaking, Marcus cupped her face in his hands and kissed her, frantically, deeply, starved for the taste of her. His hands moved over her body, touching every inch as if he needed to prove that she was real.

When he finally drew back, his fingers skimmed over her face, tracing every feature. "You're here," he said.

"I am."

"I've been having these dreams and sometimes I was so sure you were with me. And then, I'd wake up and you wouldn't be."

Eden ran her finger along his lower lip, and he kissed her fingertip, holding her hand to his mouth. "I got all the way to California only to realize that we weren't finished," Eden said.

"No," he murmured, kissing her palm. "We aren't. I'm not sure we'll ever finish with each other."

Eden smiled, her gaze searching his. "I'm counting on that. I'm back to stay. I've asked my father to give me a job."

"You're here for good?" Marcus asked. "Here with me?"

"If you'll have me."

Marcus took a deep breath and then shook his head, a smile playing about his mouth. "I don't know, Princess. You can be a real pain in the ass."

"I'm working on that," Eden said solemnly, wanting him to know she meant it. "You have to give me time."

"I guess I could do that," Marcus conceded with a twinkle in his eye. He pushed her back toward the bed and then tumbled them both onto it. "But you may have to convince me."

Eden stared into his handsome face, her fingers smoothing his hair out of his eyes. This was the man she loved, and though she hadn't said the words yet, she knew it in her heart. "We'll have to leave that for later. My father wants you to join us for lunch up at the house. I think he wants to talk to the man who has finally tamed his daughter."

"Oh, I don't think I want to tame you, sweetheart," Marcus said. "I like you just the way you are."

"Well, I suppose I can't rid myself of all my wild inclinations," Eden admitted.

"Are you sure I don't have time to tear your clothes off and make love to you before we eat?"

Eden thought about his offer, then shrugged. "Only if you're very, very quick about it."

"Sweetheart, when it comes to making you moan, I'll do it any way you want."

Eden giggled and rolled on top of him, tossing aside her bra and shaking out her wet hair. "I bet you won't last five minutes," she challenged.

Marcus grinned. "I'll take that bet."

Epilogue

MARCUS PULLED THE TRUCK up in front of his parents' house on a quiet street in Bonnett Harbor. He switched off the ignition and then leaned back in the seat. "Are you worried?" He glanced over at Eden to see her fidgeting in the passenger seat, a plate of brownies on her lap.

It had been two weeks since she'd come back from California and they'd spent nearly every free moment together. She'd started work the Monday before last, and while she was away, Marcus had finished the project on *Victorious.* At night they'd slept on board, preferring to keep to themselves.

After Eden's father had bought the video back, there'd been no more speculation about what was on the tape. And though she'd been hounded by the press, with each day that passed, their interest in her dimmed. A former party girl who now worked as a file clerk for her father's business didn't hold much interest for the general public. Ian still hadn't found the other video, and Marcus was beginning to worry about what had become of it.

"Before we go in, there's something I need to tell you," he said.

"What? Is my hair all right?" She reached up and smoothed her hand over her head. "Do I have something in my teeth?" Eden grabbed the rearview mirror and twisted it so she could see her reflection.

"No, you look beautiful," Marcus said. "Perfect."

"Then what?"

He drew a deep breath. "You know that tape we made?"

Eden nodded.

"Well, it kinda got lost. I mean, I think I know where it is. Or Ian does."

She gasped. "You gave the tape to Ian?"

"No, no. He took it. By mistake. It was in the camera, and he borrowed the camera without my permission and—" Marcus paused. "I'm sorry. This is a mess, but I really don't think it's going to turn up on the Internet. I just think it's temporarily misplaced."

Eden stared at him for a long moment, then smiled. "I was wondering when you were planning to tell me." She grabbed her purse and reached inside, then handed him a camcorder tape. "It was sitting in front of the door when I stopped by your loft to pick up the mail last week."

"Oh, jeez," Marcus said, relief flooding through him. "I'm sorry. This is getting shredded the minute we get home."

Eden snatched the tape back. "No! I think we should

make a sequel." She popped the tape back into her purse. "But from now on, we'll make sure to keep it in a safe place, all right?"

Marcus leaned across the seat and kissed her, his mouth lingering over hers for a long time before he drew away. Life couldn't get more perfect. He and Eden were together and there wasn't any doubt in his mind that it would be forever. And it was finally time to let his brothers in on their secret affair. He'd chosen Sunday dinner with the Quinns to be her coming out party. He hoped his family would accept her, but even that didn't really matter.

"Are you ready to go in?"

Eden stared straight ahead, worrying at her lower lip with her teeth. "In a minute," she said.

"Are you nervous?" Marcus asked.

"No," she said, her voice tight. "Yes. Am I supposed to be? I feel a little sick. Maybe we could do this in phases? One family member at a time?"

"You've already met my mother and she likes you, so that means everyone else will, too."

"But how's she going to feel when she figures out I lied to her about who I was? She thinks I'm Liselotte Bunderstrassen."

"Well, that's what the brownies are for," Marcus said.

Eden frowned. "That's going to make it all better?" She stared down at the plate, a skeptical expression on her face. "They're just brownies from a box. Maybe I should have bought a cheesecake or a pie or something a little fancier."

"They'll love you," Marcus said, reaching over to

smooth her hair from her face. "Because I love you." He'd waited a long time to admit his feelings to Eden, but there was no use denying them any longer. He had fallen hard and there was no going back, not that he'd ever want to.

A slow smile curled the corners of Eden's mouth. "You do?"

Marcus nodded, pulling her across the seat into another kiss, this one much deeper and filled with desire. "I do."

"I love you, too," she said softly, smoothing her hand over his face.

He kissed her again, savoring the taste of her mouth. "Now are you ready to go in?"

Eden shook her head. "I don't think I'll ever be ready."

Marcus pressed his forehead to hers and looked intently into her eyes. "I can tell you exactly what will happen. Rory and Eddie are going to be amused that I've managed to find a woman at all. Mary Grace will give you a big hug and tell you that you're prettier than your pictures. Jane will be completely starstruck. Ian will probably want to arrest you and Dec will be pissed off big-time. Da won't know who Eden Ross is, nor will he care, but he'll love you. Ma will be happy to see you. And I will be by your side no matter what happens, okay?"

Eden reached into her pocket and withdrew a wad of cash, then handed it to him.

"What's this?" Marcus asked.

"To settle the deal with your brothers. Two thousand dollars. Daddy gave me an advance on my paycheck. I figured I should pay since I'm the one who seduced you."

Marcus shook his head. "Oh, no, I'm the one who seduced you, so I should pay."

"You're remembering all wrong!" Eden cried.

Marcus grabbed the plate of brownies from her lap and set them on the dashboard, then picked her up and pulled her into his lap. His lips captured hers, and as he kissed her he ran his hand over her body, lingering on her belly. He slid his palm beneath the cotton peasant top she wore and found warm skin and then the soft flesh of her breast. "I don't think you're remembering it correctly," he murmured, biting at her lower lip. "Would you like me to remind you of exactly what happened?"

Eden moaned softly as his thumb teased at her nipple, bringing it to a stiff peak. "Yes, please," she said.

He kissed her again, this time seducing her mouth slowly and thoroughly. Eden wrapped her arms around his neck and sighed, a contented sound that made his blood warm. She was finally home and happy, and as long as she slept in Marcus's arms, he wouldn't need anything more.

* * * * *

REQUEST YOUR FREE BOOKS!
2 FREE NOVELS PLUS 2 FREE GIFTS!

✦ Harlequin®

Blaze

red-hot reads!

YES! Please send me 2 FREE Harlequin® Blaze™ novels and my 2 FREE gifts (gifts are worth about $10). After receiving them, if I don't wish to receive any more books, I can return the shipping statement marked "cancel." If I don't cancel, I will receive 6 brand-new novels every month and be billed just $4.49 per book in the U.S. or $4.96 per book in Canada. That's a saving of at least 14% off the cover price. It's quite a bargain. Shipping and handling is just 50¢ per book in the U.S. and 75¢ per book in Canada.* I understand that accepting the 2 free books and gifts places me under no obligation to buy anything. I can always return a shipment and cancel at any time. Even if I never buy another book, the two free books and gifts are mine to keep forever.

151/351 HDN FEQE

Name   (PLEASE PRINT)

Address   Apt. #

City   State/Prov.   Zip/Postal Code

Signature (if under 18, a parent or guardian must sign)

Mail to the **Reader Service:**
IN U.S.A.: P.O. Box 1867, Buffalo, NY 14240-1867
IN CANADA: P.O. Box 609, Fort Erie, Ontario L2A 5X3

Not valid for current subscribers to Harlequin Blaze books.

Want to try two free books from another line?
Call 1-800-873-8635 or visit www.ReaderService.com.

* Terms and prices subject to change without notice. Prices do not include applicable taxes. Sales tax applicable in N.Y. Canadian residents will be charged applicable taxes. Offer not valid in Quebec. This offer is limited to one order per household. All orders subject to credit approval. Credit or debit balances in a customer's account(s) may be offset by any other outstanding balance owed by or to the customer. Please allow 4 to 6 weeks for delivery. Offer available while quantities last.

Your Privacy—The Reader Service is committed to protecting your privacy. Our Privacy Policy is available online at www.ReaderService.com or upon request from the Reader Service.

We make a portion of our mailing list available to reputable third parties that offer products we believe may interest you. If you prefer that we not exchange your name with third parties, or if you wish to clarify or modify your communication preferences, please visit us at www.ReaderService.com/consumerschoice or write to us at Reader Service Preference Service, P.O. Box 9062, Buffalo, NY 14269. Include your complete name and address.

HB11B

SPECIAL EDITION

Life, Love and Family

NEW YORK TIMES BESTSELLING AUTHOR

DIANA PALMER

brings you a brand-new Western romance
featuring characters that readers have come to
love—the Brannt family from Harlequin HQN's
bestselling book *WYOMING TOUGH*.

Cort Brannt, Texas rancher through and through,
is about to unexpectedly get lassoed by love!

THE RANCHER

Available November 13 wherever books are sold!

Also available as a 2-in-1
THE RANCHER & HEART OF STONE

www.Harlequin.com

HSE65709DP

Harlequin® Desire is proud to present

ONE WINTER'S NIGHT

by New York Times *bestselling author*

Brenda Jackson

Alpha Blake tightened her coat around her. Not only would she be late for her appointment with Riley Westmoreland, but because of her flat tire they would have to change the location of the meeting and Mr. Westmoreland would be the one driving her there. This was totally embarrassing, when she had been trying to make a good impression.

She turned up the heat in her car. Even with a steady stream of hot air coming in through the car vents, she still felt cold, too cold, and wondered if she would ever get used to the Denver weather. Of course, it was too late to think about that now. It was her first winter here, and she didn't have any choice but to grin and bear it. When she'd moved, she'd felt that getting as far away from Daytona Beach as she could was essential to her peace of mind. But who in her right mind would prefer blistering-cold Denver to sunny Daytona Beach? Only a person wanting to start a new life and put a painful past behind her.

Her attention was snagged by an SUV that pulled off the road and parked in front of her. The door swung open and long denim-clad, boot-wearing legs appeared before a man stepped out of the truck. She met his gaze through the windshield and forgot to breathe. Walking toward her car was a man who was so dangerously masculine, so heart-stoppingly virile, that her brain went momentarily numb.

He was tall, and the Stetson on his head made him appear taller. But his height was secondary to the sharp handsomeness of his features.

Her gaze slid all over him as he moved his long limbs toward her vehicle in a walk that was so agile and self-assured, she envied the confidence he exuded with every step. Her breasts suddenly peaked, and she could actually feel blood rushing through her veins.

She didn't have to guess who this man was.

He was Riley Westmoreland.

Find out if Riley and Alpha mix business with pleasure in

ONE WINTER'S NIGHT

by Brenda Jackson

Available December 2012

Only from Harlequin® Desire

HDEXP1212